STALEMATE

Vol. 3 of the Three Worlds Saga

Carol A. Strickland

Other books by Carol A. Strickland

Touch of Danger– vol. 1 of the Three Worlds Saga

Lost in the Stars– vol. 2 of the Three Worlds Saga

Worlds Apart– vol. 4 of the Three Worlds Saga

Applesauce and Moonbeams– wacky soft sci fi

Nothing Personal– ditto but wackier

Burgundy and Lies– sweet historical romance

Infinite thanks to the awesome editor of the first version of this novel, Anselm Audley, and to award-winning Colleen Doran for her art.

Humble thanks to Kristine Cayne for her advice on Québécois. Her comments indicate that some advice from another person I used in previous novels was wrong (or sometimes– horrors– correct French instead of Montreal-ish patois), and I apologize for that. Any mistakes in this area now are entirely my fault. (Hint: I could use a Québécois-speaking, Montreal-based beta reader.)

Many, many thanks to (English-speaking) beta reader Gretchen Hodges! Beta readers are gold.

Thank you, Karen Younts, for insisting that Lina work at Midnight Delivery. The company it was based on has changed an awful lot from when this was first written, but I hope MD's general ambiance gets the main points across. It's a wild 'n wacky world!

I finally started availing myself of the massive research and knowledge that gravitates to the Rhine Research Center, which is just down the road in Durham, NC. What took me so long? I apologize to them for embellishing psi phenomena (though there is some jaw-dropping real-world stuff in the scientific record), and will try to incorporate more realistic aspects as I learn more. Jeannette B. and everyone else there: so many thanks, not only for help with the books' concepts, but with my own psychic growth.

Thanks on the other side of the psi coin to Sue B., who taught a school for psychics (okay, it was supposedly for holistic healing) in Durham many years ago. I split this colorful lady in two for this series, and morphed each part to fit the role they had to fill. (Sorry about what happens in vol. 5.)

1

Londo Rand paused before entering his apartment here in Affiliated Systems Mega-Force Legion Headquarters. Behind him Yullowei and Mix conspired in the dimmed corridor. Sparks flickered within Yullowei's colorful uniform, reflected in Mix's metallic one, and strobed the walls of the hallway enough to reveal a faint patterning that hid its myriad of electronic sensors.

"Gooood NIGHT, Londo," they chorused to their team leader. It had been days since anyone had laughed, but they did so now.

As Londo walked in, he raised his chin. "Puter," he instructed the air for their benefit though he didn't glance at them, "lock my quarters behind me. No access, no interruptions." The door sealed with a satisfying hiss, shutting out the raucous laughter.

Lights were on. His apartment felt different, though everything looked the same. It was more than spacious, furnished in neat, masculine lines to accommodate his duties in both the Mega-Legion and society. But it didn't seem as empty as before. "Lina?" he called softly.

Londo's sharp hearing targeted the sound of even breaths, so he rose into the air and darted to the center couch of the living room. Below him, his bride lay asleep, surrounded by study tablets and a note padd. A cloud of auburn curls cushioned her head. The smooth, inviting line of her leg peeked out from under the gauzy skirt of a white nightgown that offered little contrast to her pale skin.

He knelt next to her. "Lina…" he said, but her green eyes were already opening. "Hi, honey. I'm home."

She threw her arms around him. There was nothing now but her, but him. The world stilled elsewhere to accommodate their reunion.

Somehow their embrace ended up in the neighboring chair, Lina in Londo's lap, hugging him tightly. "Don't you ever do that to me again!" she demanded between kisses.

"Do what?"

"Go off and leave me for days like that."

Carolina O'Kelly held him at arm's length so she could take in his face again. Those melting-chocolate eyes drew her in as she ran her fingertips over the line of his bronzed jaw and through his straight, dark hair. "Oh, Lon, I missed you so much. I was so lonely! You've been messing with my mind," she accused him. "Making me fall in love with the most wonderful man in the universe, talking me into a wedding, of all things. And then you ran out on me!"

"I dreamed of you, *chérie*," Londo whispered to her. "Every time I went to sleep. You're more beautiful than I remembered, sweet Lina…"

Their kisses turned harder, demanding, and his tongue tangled with hers the way he wanted their bodies to echo.

He tried to push her dress down, but it wouldn't go. Puzzled, Lon examined the situation. The gown was a sleeveless satin leotard with an attached sheer skirt. Its neckline scooped very low, Lina's delectable breasts straining against a line of lacing that went all the way down. The slit skirt let one long, bare leg free for his hand to slide up, to find the soft warmth of her ass to squeeze. But he couldn't even get his fingers under the material, much less push it aside. He frowned at it.

"I had a little accident with some glue." Lina's eyes were merry.

"Very funny." He looked for another opening, but the complicated lacing on the front prevented it. At least the skirt peeled off easily.

Londo pretended a pout. "You're making me work for this, aren't you?"

"You went out with the boys tonight. You must be punished."

So he began the happy task of unlacing her. "Did not. The meeting just lasted for a long time. Afterward we had a press conference, and then they wanted me for individual interviews, dozens of 'em. You gave up on me." He huffed at the lacing. Even though he had it undone a few inches, the material still wouldn't budge. "What the hell is this?"

"It doesn't come off until it's all unlaced. I was wondering why a woman would want to wear something like this, but about an hour and a half ago I figured it out: to teach her husband a lesson."

All he had to say was "I'm sorry," in any of three languages and the sound-activated material would slip off like water, but Lina was not going to tell him that. Not yet.

"I've had a few days to think about this marriage," she said instead. "You must admit we stumbled into all this a little quickly."

He grunted.

"I don't know about you, but I've started to make plans. Besides the sex, that is. Though I have thought about that a lot."

He licked where he'd just unlaced and then blew on the spot.

"Ooh. Legion Protocol certainly has its own rules of just what we can or cannot do, so we have to take them into account, I suppose. They don't approve of me at all. Terran, you know." She made a sour-milk face at him, hoping that she'd caught Ms. Yency of Protocol's expression to best effect.

Lon leaned so his mouth was right next to her ear. "Damn everyone in Protocol and let me in, *chérie*." He licked the back of her ear and squeezed her next to her lacing. "C'mon, Lina. C'mon, baby."

"Um." She pushed him away from herself. "And I didn't give up on you. I just fell asleep." She brushed her hair back with her fingers. "Here I'd spent an hour trying to look just right for you. Now I'm all rumpled. Lon, let me brush my hair at least."

"*Non, non, non.*" He gave her a lascivious grin. "I have plans to rumple you up some more tonight. You're going to be very, very rumpled." Without a trace of effort he stood up with her in his arms as she caught her breath. "You can straighten up in… oh, two or three days, when we come up for air."

Flying quickly– very quickly– into the bedroom, he laid her down on the mattress and crawled over her.

"Only two days?" She wrapped her arms around his shoulders.

"Tell me the easy way in," he whispered as they came out of the kiss. "There is one, isn't there?"

"Well…" She pretended to consider as he covered her neck with kisses. She rose in his arms. "Let's get you out of these smelly old clothes and see how it goes, okay?"

"Smelly?" Londo realized that it had been a long, hard day. He sniffed his faux leather vest and pulled it off. "Tell you what, Kitten. Let's have one quick round on the bed and then adjourn to the bathtub. Champagne and chocolate. Real champagne– they call it bubblywine here. The chocolate… and other things… should keep you awake." Despite their short acquaintance he was quite aware that alcohol put her to sleep.

"Mm hm. And then?"

"And then the couch, and then the rug, and then the dining table, and then back in the bed for a few times."

"And this is what," she counted on her fingers. "Two hours?"

He let loose a laugh and rolled with her across the bed until he was on top again. Straddling her, he pulled his pinstriped gray shirt out of his pants. "The quick way in, *chérie,*" he ordered.

"A clue." She smiled craftily, running her hands down the long length of him. "Think–"

"No. The solution. Now."

"Uh oh, he's gone team leader on me again. Well… Boots off. No boots on the bed."

While he hurried to obey her, Lina knelt behind him and opened his shirt to pull it off his arms. Then an undershirt came off over his head, interrupting him with his boots and socks. She nuzzled up against him, kissing his honey-dark skin as it was revealed, trailing her hands along the line of hard muscles on his shoulders and chest, rubbing her cheek against the back of his neck.

Lon smelled of hot sweat and wonderful tropical nights, not clean and cool and otherworldly like… Yes, this was right, this was the one for Lina. She'd made the correct choice. There was no other choice to make. There was no other, not any more. Ignore even the memory of him. Londo was here. He was her life, her future, her joy. He held a love for her the likes of which she'd never even imagined before. She cherished it and she cherished him.

And oh, he smelled so… Londo. She closed her eyes to hold the sensation in her heart forever and then came out of it, kissing her way across the back of his shoulders.

He shook his head at her and laughed, but this time the laugh was inside him.

She turned him around to look at him curiously. "What?"

He went back to unlacing. "I thought… I thought you might have had second thoughts about the marriage while I was away."

"I sense some abandonment issues we haven't dealt with yet. I said 'even unto eternity,' Mr. Londo Rand, and I keep my word. I'm still here, and I'll be here until you're sick of me."

"That will never happen, not in a million lifetimes together." He stopped unlacing and decided to pull off his belt. Then he took her into his arms again, just to have the pleasure of holding her, of truly touching another.

Suddenly she became very serious, her eyes welling up. "Oh Londo, I never thought I could miss anyone as much as I did you. How often does this happen? And for how long? If I just had an estimate, I could take it a lot–"

"*Bon ben*, I can just about guarantee that it won't–"

A buzzer went off from his Legion ring. "Damn!" Lon gestured with an open hand that squeezed into a fist. "What?!"

It was Legion Commander Magnos– Stoan Kinrol's– voice that came out of a speaker hidden somewhere. "Valiant, we need you for communications duty."

Londo paused a second in incredulity. "You're joking; refused. Not tonight. You can find someone to take my place."

"Can't do that. Everyone's in official mourning, Legionnaire. Still we follow procedure."

"There are exceptions to everything, Commander. I have tonight off. Period. Rand out."

He stared at his fist for a second. "Damn."

"What?" Lina gazed at him, trying to rememorize every detail.

He grimaced an apology. "It's Stoan. He has doubts about us. About you. It's–"

"Mind control," Lina said. "Some strange telepathic woman comes out of nowhere and marries the great and powerful Valiant. Well, who Out Here wouldn't think that? He'll get over it. I hope."

"*Mais,* in the meantime he's being a royal pain in the ass. He spent the entire mission harping about it. The thing is, he's a really great guy, someone you could trust your life to. He's the commander of the Mega-Legion for a reason. Now he's running this campaign against you– and he has followers. You heard about… about Aiko…"

"We've known for days. *They* told me when it actually happened. Oh, Lon, I'm so sorry. So sorry!"

He nodded, not looking at her, licking his lips. Lina had spirit guides that told her *things.* "Maybe it's Aiko's death that's making Stoan so edgy. She's… She *was* a good friend of his, too. And as commander he has a responsibility to his people, so he holds himself at fault."

Lina sat up on the pillows and smoothed Londo's hair. "If you want, I can take us home tonight. I've been practicing teleporting. Biofilter in place." She tapped her head. "No quarantine needed in either direction any more. I've been going home to feed the cats every day, call in to work and come back, but there's no reason we can't go home now that you're back. Let's get away from this for a while."

He heaved a sigh as he pulled her to him. "No. If we run I'll just give those people more ammunition against you. We'll stay here tonight. The funeral will be in five days. Can you stand staying here until then?"

"As long as you're here. I know you must be taking this very hard, love. How are you doing through all of this?"

He closed his eyes with the pain and admitted what he'd tell no one else. "Not well at all."

Lina clasped him to her. He laid his head on her shoulder, hugging her hard. She stroked his hair and rubbed his back.

They were silent for long minutes. "God," he whispered, wiping his eyes. "I thought I'd gotten it all out on the trip back."

"Tell me about her," Lina said. "Tell me about the good times."

"This is our wedding night," Londo groaned. "I'm not supposed to be thinking about old lovers."

"You can't help it," Lina assured him. "Lon, why don't you just take a while and tell me about her. Let's see how you feel then."

"I thought… I thought the two of you would hit it right off. She was so… nice. A serious girl, but she could tell stories that would have you rolling on the floor, you'd be laughing so hard."

"She said she knew some really embarrassing stories about you," Lina smiled as she cradled her husband.

"*Oui.* She knows a whole lot. Knew a whole lot."

"So what's an embarrassing story about her?"

"Her? Oh, *crisse*… She'd have a fit if she knew I told. She could jump into trouble and make it deliberately worse before she cleaned up everything again, just so she'd have a good yarn to tell me. She knew I liked stories."

He paused, thinking. "There was one time when we were going to bust up this weaponry cobble shop in the middle of the night, and we knew we had to shock everyone so they'd be too stupefied to… These types don't think under pressure. They might blow up the entire neighborhood accidentally. So what does she do but take off her boots and–"

The door buzzer cut through his next word and then sounded once more. "Intercom on," Lon directed to the air, and Stoan's voice again came to them. "Londo, open up!"

"God. Stoan," Lon said. "Leave us in peace. Go away."

A creak from far down the hall told Lina that something odd was happening. The apartment door let out a protesting shriek as she heard it open.

"*Skurn* him!" Lon muttered. Giving his damp eyes a final swipe, he scrambled forward on the bed to position himself protectively in front of Lina. She teleported the skirt back around herself as he reached back to take her hand.

Stoan entered the room, his face a little bluer with anger than usual, followed by the woman Lina recognized as Nurunori, aka Andri something– parastrength for a power, she remembered, like Forte back home. She was subcommander of the Legion. Very tall, taller than Londo, like most of the people Out Here, and lithe; hair in a startlingly short pink bob.

But Stoan was even taller. His parapower had to do with electromagnetism, with the emphasis on magnets. He was in full costume tonight: dark blues and blacks with what seemed to be scientific symbols scrolling back and forth on the material on his chest, like he was plugged into the old game of Pong.

The two interlopers regarded the two in bed: Londo with his powerful chest and arms bared as well as his feet, Lina behind him in her nightgown. Lon's clothing scattered on the bed and rug.

"My door better be fixed by morning, Stoan," Londo warned.

The tall man stared him down. "You've refused comm duty–" Stoan started.

"Comm duty is not the most pressing duty a team leader pulls," Lon growled. "I was called away after my wedding for an important mission, knowing it would last for days, and I went. So now I'm back and I'd like to have at least a few hours alone with my wife. My *wife*," he repeated. "I think that rules can bend for that. I've seen them bend for much less before. For people who didn't want to miss a rocketball tournament, or who had distant cousins visiting. Stoan, this is my wedding night."

"We've been too slack in the past. It's time we got back on track. Communications duty, Valiant."

"If… if Lon goes on duty," Lina thought hard, trying to spare Lon from getting in trouble, "could I go with him? That way we could at least talk."

"A prisoner sharing Mega-Legion comm duty?" Stoan's eyes on her were hard. He could see that the laces on her gown were half-undone. Lon had always liked well-endowed women, and apparently he'd been about to enjoy himself. "I don't think so," he drawled.

"Prisoner?" Lon asked. "Since when?"

"Jae told me that was over," Lina told Stoan.

"Jae was wrong. He and I will be having a conversation about how he handled this situation." If anything, Stoan's complexion darkened.

Lon bounded to his feet. "What's this about Lina being a prisoner?" He turned to her. "How long? What happened?"

Stoan spoke before Lina could. "Carolina O'Kelly… Rand has been under arrest for the past five days. I assigned Jae to oversee the process."

Lon couldn't speak for a few seconds. His face flushed red. "And you didn't bother to *tell* me this little detail?!"

"You never informed him?" Andri gasped at Stoan.

"We needed Lon's full attention on the matter at hand," Stoan growled back.

"I've been keeping people company on communications duty all along," Lina declared. "And two… no, three times I caught something that never showed up on the monitors."

Lon tried to catch his breath. What was that she'd said? "Three times?"

She nodded to him. "So it's not like being with you at the monitors would mean I was totally useless."

"No," Londo said. "Don't worry about it, Lina. I'm not taking comm duty tonight." He turned to Stoan, his eyes narrowing, brows coming together to form his famous frown. "There's no reason. There's no precedent."

"Londo, be reasonable," Andri began. She had a remarkably soft voice for such a powerful woman. "This could mean a huge strike against your record."

"For not pulling an easily-substitutable duty on my wedding night? No. I think it might backfire against whoever tried to smear that record."

Stoan raised splayed hands toward the Legion's most powerful member. "Work with us. I'm doing this for you. There are too many questions about this so-called marriage that need to be cleared up. Who knows if there will be an annulment or something similar before an investigation concludes?"

"Wait a minute." In spite of her resolution to be calm, cold fury bubbled up from Lina's core. From the very start, before she'd done the first thing here on this world of Sarastor, Stoan had accused her of being a mind controller, something they seemed to have big problems with Out Here. The only evidence he'd had was that his friend, Valiant, had fallen in love with another Terran, and apparently to Stoan Terrans were the waxy yellow buildup of the universe. Except for Londo.

Lon raised an eyebrow as he realized that his wife was speaking Panlingua without the translator. That would explain the study tablets.

Lina stood to take her husband's side. "Who do you think you are, to threaten annulment?"

"I am commander of the Legion." Stoan glared at her. "And I'm calling for an official investigation."

Lon took a step forward. Andri quickly placed herself between Lon and Stoan. "You can call for an investigation," Lon declared, "but there is absolutely no chance in hell of an annulment. Get that through your head. Let's step outside for a few minutes," he warned, but Lina put her hand on his shoulder to stop him.

She looked directly into Stoan's eyes, daring him to try something. "I don't think that will be necessary, Londo. Tell me, Stoan, have you ever been to Earth?"

He braced himself, his gaze shifting to study her face. "No, I haven't."

"It's a beautiful planet. How far is it by hyperspace travel, Lon?"

Londo could read her; he knew what she had in mind. "A little under a day, third-level hyperspace. Three days at first-level." He half-grinned a threat at Stoan.

"A day or three. That's a long time," Lina mused. "But Stoan, I'm willing to let you visit the place a lot faster than that. I can teleport you there right now. You can even stay at my house. Feed my cats while you're there, if you would. Just make sure you don't rile them or they may bite or claw you." She made a sour face as if considering. "Terran medicine isn't up to Sarastoran standards. I'd treat them well if I were you."

She didn't think that Stoan knew what a cat was, much less how big one might be. He was going to say something, but she held up her hand to stop him. "Of course, it might take you a while to contact someone who has access to hyperspace travel in order for you to get back. You seem fairly resourceful; I figure it might take a day or two. There aren't many people there who speak Panlingua. Not many who have access to hyperspace, is that right, Lon?"

"I can count them on the fingers of one hand."

"Or you could let Londo and me have a few hours together. We'd still be here. You'd still be here."

"Two choices," Lon said, looking sideways at his wife, his grin still there. He caught one of the ribbons from her gown and started to twine it in his fingers. "Which one would you prefer?"

"She can't teleport me, Londo."

"Just because I wouldn't before doesn't mean that I can't now," Lina replied. "I didn't want to mess up your rather intricate magnetic field. But Stoan, I've been practicing while you all have been away. I really think I could do it, and you'd never notice the difference."

"Are you threatening me?"

"I'm giving you an example." She held up her hand and a credit card appeared in it. "Check it out." She flipped it to the commander, who caught it and stared at it intently. "The chip in it contains–"

"Coded magnetic information bits," he finished for her. He was a master of electro-magnetism, after all.

"You can recognize them?"

"Of course." He blinked as the card disappeared from his hand.

It appeared simultaneously in hers. "Port here. Port back."

The card appeared in his hand. "And the information is still there, bit for bit." His raised eyebrow confirmed it.

"I can do that for a person now. Try me if you wish. But make your decision."

She could see the struggle on his face. Finally he said, "I'll reassign your comm duty tonight, Londo. Only tonight. You owe me."

"Thank you, Stoan," Lon said gently, not wanting to damage their friendship further. "I'll check in sometime tomorrow morning. Late."

"Six-fifty hours." Stoan pivoted on his heel and left the room. Andri gave them both a measuring look and silent shaking-head shrug before she followed.

Londo turned to Lina and made a face. "Threatening the Legion commander," he *tsk*ed.

She wobbled with relief. "Sorry. It was the only thing I could think of, next to punching him out. Or having you do it." One nudge from mega-strong Valiant could turn most people into globs of jelly. "I didn't get you in trouble, did I?"

Lon laughed and smoothed her hair. He pulled on the ribbon to bring her closer to him. "*At last,*" he sang softly, "*my love has come along.*"

"*My lonely days are over,*" she sang in response.

They finished it together: "*And life is like a song.*"

They heard the front door close.

He watched her as she slept next to him, their heads sharing the same pillow, and he stroked her hair lightly. It was so wonderfully strange to be able to touch someone like this without fear of injuring them. Hair was soft and so was skin, but in a different way. Only with Lina could he do this. Only she had soothed his cells not to respond to her as they did the rest of the universe, with a wall of sheer power that set him forever apart.

Her face was so innocent, almost childlike, those sweet lips slightly parted. Gently rising and falling, her breasts moved against his chest so he could feel her heart beat. Ah. He felt her mind rising through the waters of sleep into consciousness. Londo wondered at his own new ability to sense that even as her eyelashes fluttered and those magical green eyes opened, gazing into his.

She flushed beautiful rose. "How long have you been awake, Lon?"

"Just a little while." He gave her a kiss. "I just wanted to admire my lovely bride, *ma belle.*"

"It's really true," she breathed. "You're back. And we're going to be together– forever." She touched his cheek and ran her hand down the line of his neck to his shoulder where she paused. He was still wearing her necklace, her favor, the simple gold chain from their wedding. She pulled his arm out from under the sheet. "C'mon, c'mon," she said. "Let's see it."

Lon chuckled as he slid his right arm under her. "It hasn't disappeared, Kitten," he told her as she compared their wedding rings. "Were you expecting it to?"

"I don't know," she admitted. "The flowers– they did. Almost right away."

"And the wedding clothes?"

She shook her head. "Still around, as far as I know. Wiley's researching the symbols on them. They're different from these." On each ring a large diamond– white for Londo, green for her– sat in the center of a crest made up of a starburst enclosing a circle enclosing a triangle.

"You know that it comes apart."

She nodded, pleased that he'd been playing with his ring too. "Two pieces. Wiley says he can't figure out the metal. It's like a piece of faerie."

"If they disappear, we'll get regular rings," Lon reassured her. "It's the vows that make a marriage, not the hardware." Still, he wondered at both mysterious rings.

It had been a miracle, a series of miracles. Voices and lights that had appeared when Lina had accepted his proposal. They'd suddenly been clothed for a wedding. Their minds had been opened. Their souls had met and mingled, reuniting as only true soulmates could. He knew that Lina and he would be together for all eternity, but best of all, they would be together in this lifetime as well. It was hard to believe that Terry could have orchestrated all this…

"This is bigger than Terry Whatsherface," Lina told him.

Lon laughed. "I'm going to see if I can have her name officially changed to that," he said and became serious again. "But you're right."

Terry Rhodes had been out to kill him. She'd come after a sperm sample, some blood, and who knew what else. Lina had suspected that it had something to do with a baby Terry wanted from him. He had different ideas about that.

And Dr. Menlo– Menlo had only wanted to study him. He'd stripped Londo of his powers and then used innocent Lina as bait, or perhaps a catalyst, to seduce him when in fact he'd seduced her. They'd lost their virginity together. And when his powers had come back, she had been the one to figure out how the two of them could still be together like they were now without the remotest possibility of him accidentally harming her during the process.

"Other people don't get all this fuss." Lina turned to gaze anxiously into Londo's face. "Day before yesterday, Londo, there was this planet, another world, Aldierra–"

His fingers intertwined with hers. "Don't worry about it, love," he told her. "We're married and that's that. Apparently the universe wants us married, too."

She settled back on his chest. "So do I."

He squeezed her hand and kissed the top of her head. "I told you," he said. He'd told her that she'd want him, told her that she loved him, told her that she'd marry him.

"So tell me, Mr. Honeybear Rand," Lina asked dreamily as she turned her face to his, "Are you ever unsure about anything?"

"Never." He kissed her again. "Ever." Kiss. "Ever." Kiss. "I want you to understand that from the start."

"You may always be sure of yourself, but I'm always right. Remember that." She wrinkled her nose at him.

He touched that nose with his. "We'll have time to test that hypothesis. Later," he said. "Wife, let's make love."

They lips met, slow and warm, and then Lina pulled away. "How much time do we have?" she asked. "Your meeting with Stoan…" She couldn't see the clock for Lon's shoulder.

"Did I say, 'Let's make love unless we don't have enough time?' I did not." Londo made himself sound hurt. "Making love requires no schedules."

"Funny," Lina said, "that's not what I remember. Every fifteen minutes or so: wham. Wham. Wham. What'll Stoan say when you're not there?"

"'I bet they're having a very good time.'" Londo murmured against her neck, his hands traveling on her. "No schedules. Not today."

"Mm. Yes, Londo. Whatever you say." She could feel the silent laughter deep within him.

2

Jaeson Rallene paused at his communications terminal between calls. Most of the others had wobbled off to sleep shift upon their return, or had found some loving arms to cry into. He'd volunteered for this duty tonight. The loving arms he wanted were busy elsewhere. His mind reached out to the other mind he knew, but that one brushed him away, closing off, without even realizing she was doing it.

But there was another mind he could now sense, almost at the same vibration as hers, one who was thinking only of her tonight; another mind whose edge he skirted, hovering just beyond perception. Londo was making love to his bride, enjoying her to the fullest and striving to please her, to show her how he felt about her. His mind was entwined with hers.

Jae dared to look closer, to see through Lon's eyes, feel with his skin. His heart pulsed with the same strong beat and heat flushed through him. A soft groan and he snapped out of it, looking around quickly at Kinesis and Sratscratch. Only Scratch looked up.

"Neutrino?" she asked.

He faked the end of a yawn, stretching in his chair. "It's been a rough time here, too."

She nodded and went back to work.

It was still the middle of Sarastor's long night. Lina had stolen a peek at the clock and Lon pretended that he didn't see her do it. Now he held her hand as she stepped daintily into the foaming, softly-churning bath with him. Such a woman. His now.

He placed the bottle of alcohol-free bubblywine on the shelf above the hot tub, righted the wineglasses from where they'd been held between his fingers, and set them there, too. Then he drew her down with him into the warm water, the heady scent of *lammas* rising from the froth.

She'd pinned her hair up but tendrils fell around her face, just as the women in his dreams always had. Smooth shoulders and a slender neck, that beautiful pink mouth, those lustrous dark-fringed green eyes that saw all the way into his soul. Oval face and skin so smooth you couldn't help but touch it. The bubbles framed those full, round breasts. Below the bubbles were even more delights. His bride forever.

He told her how beautiful she was and talked of their future together as they sipped the wine, but for some reason she seemed troubled.

"Lon," she finally said but paused. "Lon, there's… Something happened while you were gone. I don't know…" She didn't look at him.

He took her chin in his fingers and turned her face to him. "We both have a lot to tell each other," he said softly. "But there is a time and a place, love. Not now. Not tonight. It's still our wedding night."

"Lon, this is important."

He shook his head at her. "Nothing's as important as us. Nothing." He touched her nose with his. "Love, honor and *obey*.

"I don't recall that last part."

"It was in the fine print, love of my life."

She was about to say more but he kissed her quiet.

"Twenty minute break for me," Jae announced, and pushed himself away from his station, hardly noting Scratch's nod and lingering glance. He was used to the looks: there's Jaeson Rallene, Neutrino, the Last Feithi, of that advanced and beautiful race the likes of which there'd never be again. He made sure that his features set into the perfect mask that hid his true emotions from others.

Jae brushed shoulder-length blond hair back from his eyes, his fingers glancing over the tips of his ears. With an easy panther's stroll, he emerged into the empty corridor and then rose up to fly quickly to a small, darkened lounge that he knew would be deserted.

He turned on a window screen and stared down onto the city with all its lights, as if night didn't lie on the land, as if it could be successfully repulsed by the hand of man.

Lon had had one of his nightmares. Jae could see some of the afterimages: the frozen pictures of Aiko's face, twisted in agony as she died in Londo's arms. Jae had started in his chair, a cold sweat breaking out over him even as Lina had shaken Londo awake.

But now they were wrapped around each other, whispering words of reassurance and comfort. The death visions were receding from Londo's mind as he relaxed into the security of Lina's embrace. Jae sank into it as far as he could before he thought one or the other would notice.

Suddenly he stood straight and shook them out of his head. A vase of narsaws sat on a table. He grabbed and hurled it against the wall where it shattered satisfyingly loud.

Damn him anyway! Damn Londo Rand– he'd promised, he'd promised! Damn Londo and changed circumstances!

Jae balled his hands into fists and pounded them against the window screen, its surface cool against his cheek. Londo lied sometimes. To others, often; to him– just sometimes. Rare occasions. Londo liked to keep his secrets and there was always that sliver of his soul that didn't even trust his best friend.

But this. Lon had promised him. They'd made plans.

"Jae-Jae," Lon had told him years ago, "someday I'm going to fall hard for some girl."

"You're too crazy about women," Jae'd joked.

"Girls are great. You should try them some more."

"Takes too long to warm 'em up. Not worth the trouble."

Lon had laughed at that. "I like the warming process," he said. Foreplay was all he could do. Any further would be death for the girl. "And someday… I keep thinking that someday someone's going to come along…"

Jae hadn't said anything. Londo liked his fantasies. Let him believe them if he wanted.

"And this is what we're going to do. You want children, Jae."

"Oh, so suddenly I'm in this plan?"

"*Mais oui.* I'm going to marry this girl and you'll have sex with her in my bed for me."

"I will?"

"Yes." Lon had held his head at that slight angle he took whenever he made a Team Decision that wasn't strict protocol. "And I will watch. I'll set her up for you, if you want. That way you can be in and out."

"Efficient."

"*Oui.*" Londo watched Jae closely. "Could you consider… doing it with the same woman over years? For me?"

"What, make it a three-way?" Jae's mouth quirked into a smile despite his desperation. "You know me, Londo. I can do it with anyone."

"And be happy?"

"So I have to be happy when I do it? Lon, if it gets me you, I'll be ecstatic."

Londo nodded. "You'll be rewarded for your good deeds. I'll arrange artificial insemination so she can have my babies, and then she'll have your children, too, so you won't have to be the last Feithi anymore. I'll be Papa Londo to your kids, Jae. She can live with me days and then we two will have her nights."

"Right. And this girl will go along with all this."

"Of course. She'll have two Legionnaires this way. She won't refuse." Lon had sat back with a satisfied smile on his face, proud to have figured it all out so neatly.

But now Londo could have sex with the woman he'd chosen. Where would Jae fit in? He'd thought often of Lon's plan, of how he would be inside this woman, whoever she'd be, and he'd still be able to reach out and touch his beloved Londo and imagine himself having him instead of the girl. That would be worth it, but the promise of children from such an arrangement– Jae had hung his hopes on this. An almost-marriage with Londo, an arrangement Lon could live with.

Jae had watched the women Londo had associated with through the years, and lately with dread he'd thought that perhaps he'd settled on Aiko. Aiko was a friend, a valued comrade, but she was too tight-assed for Jae's tastes, too proper to consider taking to bed more than once. Londo and Aiko: Jae had held his breath, hoping that Lon would find someone else soon.

And then Lina showed up.

Again Jae slammed the heel of his fist against the screen. Lina. What the hell did he feel about her? She was a woman, a hard-headed woman who, even if she ever did truly fall in love with Jae, would never betray Londo. She'd be forever forbidden to Jae, but for some reason he wanted her more than he'd ever wanted a woman before.

He could look into her eyes and see his own soul, that was it. Some kind of narcissistic something was going on. He should mention this to his therapist. Saichan might be able to suggest something. Of course, Saichan would yell at him for what he'd done the other night with her.

Londo might do worse if he ever found out. No, *when*. Lina would tell Londo, Lina who didn't know when to keep her mouth shut. After all, she'd been innocent of wrongdoing.

They'd just stopped a planetary invasion– someone trying to invade Sarastor, for orb's sake!– and Lina had been hopped up on stims to accomplish her part in the mission. When she'd started to come down he hadn't realized it, that she'd be hallucinating from them, but she'd been dressed in wispy Feithi robes that had clung to her body, naked underneath, and her eyes had sparkled at him, and she had laughed with that musical laugh of hers and he had held her in his arms… And suddenly before even he realized it they were naked and wrapped around each other.

It had taken so long before Jae realized that she thought that he was Lon, finally come home. He'd stopped as soon as he knew, but they'd been so close, so close… His body ached to remember, ached for release. She was ripe perfection for a woman, and now it was Londo and not Jae who was feasting on the fruits of her.

He slid to the floor next to the screen, covering his eyes with his hands. Shards, he wanted her. He wanted Londo and now he wanted her, too.

Would Londo let him sit on the bed and watch?

The sound of movement made him look up. Kinesis stood in the doorway, silhouetted by the lights beyond. "Neutrino," he called softly, concern written on his features. "Fifteen minutes."

"I'm coming," Jae replied, getting up slowly. "Sorry."

"It's okay. We're all taking it hard. Orenya– Aiko– was closer to you than most of us."

"Yeah," Jae said, and returned to his station.

Londo ran into Lina's clothes as he went through his own dresser. There was an instant of irritation, quickly squelched, that she should invade his space. She was his wife and here she'd just commandeered one deep drawer. Women's underwear. He smiled at the concept of there being women's underwear in his dresser. Jeans. Tee shirts. He flipped through them. Starfleet this and *Star Trek* that.

He scowled at the tee shirt that said "I'm an Official Legion Prisoner" in a mock-tourist style. It was making light of something that should never have happened. She was his wife, not a criminal!

There were more tee shirts under this one. *Non non non,* this wasn't what he pictured her in at all. She should be in tight little knit dresses, reds and blues and greens, with shiny four- and five-inch heels, not the ragged running shoes that were lying here.

Time enough for that once they got things straightened out.

Once Lina woke, the kol-vanasche would clean up and put away his discarded clothing from last night but not hers. He'd have to program it to recognize her clothes and put them… where? Lon looked around the bedroom. It was empty in here. He had a wife now. They'd go shopping for some more furniture, a dresser for her at the very least. He could put in another closet over there. What could they do with that space there so everything wouldn't look thrown together?

Scratching his head, he went to the kitchenette to order a breakfast for her that would be fresh when she was ready for it. Two bottles of Coke stood in one of the cooling drawers. She'd probably teleported those in from Earth for him. Maybe he should tell her his favorite brands of beer. That could be handy.

A large narsaw arrangement sat on the table with a congratulatory card attached, addressed to Valiant and Starfleet. Starfleet? Apparently someone else had seen those tee shirts.

The card was signed with almost a hundred names, people he'd never heard of. Lina'd been busy making friends, despite being under arrest. Jae would have seen to her. He needed to have a talk with Jae later on today anyway. He'd find out what had gone on without upsetting Lina. Lon made a mental note.

Next he checked to see if he had any messages. Of course there were dozens, but he left them to handle later. He'd been looking for one from Hal. No luck; his father must be on a lengthy mission, not to have checked in. But he paused when he saw he had a message from Maria, the White Puma. What was she doing calling him from Earth here in care of the Legion?

He played it: A female Terran native imprisoned on Sarastor in Legion HQ, some kind of megapara, had told Maria that Lon was going to bail her out of trouble when he got back. Wilder Mem-Bazer had given Maria a lot of grief as she tried to sort things out. Lon laughed. He could picture Wiley having to deal with Maria when she was mad.

His chuckle died on his tongue. How did Lina get to speak to outsiders if she'd been a prisoner? How had she met the people who'd signed the card on the narsaws? Mind controllers were imprisoned in force field cells.

Londo taped a quick message telling Maria that yes, he was aware of the problem, and that he was on his way to straighten out things right now. Thanks very much for her concern and yes, he'd introduce the megapara to the ParaNet when he got back to Earth. Yes again, she could be very helpful to them. And Dr. Mem-Bazer must have just been having a bad day. He was usually quite a nice guy. Have Hal give Londo a call if she saw him before Lon did.

Lon sent the message back to Earth and hoped that the White Puma wouldn't try to brain him when she finally figured out what was what and who the Terran national was. Maria didn't have mega-parastrength, but she knew how to use what parastrength she had. Plus she knew how to make Lon's life miserable if she wanted to. She and Mama Ruth were too tight!

Lon had left Lina sleeping. He congratulated himself on wearing her out in ways that left her smiling in her dreams, like he would be tonight. Best she was there and not here. He could tell her the outcome when she awoke. He hoped it would be good news.

Odds were it wouldn't.

Stoan's human receptionist nodded Lon in and, after taking a deep breath, he entered the commander's office. It of course was much larger than others since a commander had to deal with a wide spectrum of situations– including possible mind control of its members. One long wall was covered with a gridded display of stilled video depicting the almost two hundred fifty-year glory of the Mega-Legion. Plaques, trophies, awards, and medals formed the basis of another wall.

Londo knew he could have this office. He could easily win election to the rank of commander if not for his duties on Earth, which kept him from full-time status.

Stoan's desktop was an ordered collection of padds and screens. Behind it, the commander himself started to open his mouth.

Londo took first strike. "She's not a mind controller."

Stoan had begun to get up out of his chair to meet the Alpha Team leader, but sank back at the words. "That's the question. I haven't had time to contact anyone about this. We have the funeral and all accompanying business to take care of first. This is now second priority."

Lon took the seat on this side of Stoan's desk. "It'd be easiest just to drop this idea."

"The Legion doesn't accept easy answers." Stoan slid one padd out of its position and gestured. A 3-D video appeared above it. Londo watched reports from the preceding days: Despite being taught about Legion security, Lina had made several attempts to get a non-Legion-affiliated lawyer.

"I'd have done the same," Londo declared.

Lina had tried to bribe Brügz Sikrichat, a former commander himself. In the report, Brügz shrugged his shoulders. "It came across as her first time bribing someone. She wasn't very good; it was half-hearted. And she didn't offer money." She'd told him that some artwork he was interested in would provide him more pleasure than "mere" money. Besides, Brügz didn't think she could afford a sizable bribe.

Lon snorted.

She'd run from security once, which had made Jae throw her in a force field cell. "Not sure how he caught her or why he released her," Stoan muttered. "Jae's busy and I haven't had time to question him about this, much less the invasion."

"Invasion?!"

Stoan's expression startled. "She didn't tell you about it?"

"Ah, no, sir."

"A world called Aldierra sent a fleet to hit Sarastor and then the rest of the Affiliated Systems while we were away. We think they may have been responsible for luring most of us to the *Travern* disaster so they'd have a quick time of it." Bombs had been set off on the hyperspace ship, stranding five thousand people in the void and requiring all available Legion personnel to respond with aid. Aiko had been killed by malfunctioning munition.

Grinding his teeth, Londo shut down the memory of Aiko dying to concentrate on the present. "Aldierra? That sounds familiar."

Stoan raised his eyebrows at him.

"Lina may have said something about it last night. Mentioned the name."

"Yes?"

"I guess I wasn't listening at the time."

Now it was Stoan's turn to snort.

"I'll find a lawyer to handle this, if that's what it will take. Someone not associated with the Legion, Level Five."

"Legion lawyers are good enough."

"Legion lawyers want to please the Legion commander. I want someone impartial. I want this investigation shut down now. There's no need to waste our time on it."

Stoan leaned back in his chair and took a moment to study Londo's face. "I hate wasting time," he said, "but this isn't. I've scheduled the trial for tomorrow when we should have it today. Wish we could take more time for research, but mind control needs to be quashed as soon as it's detected."

"She's not a mind controller."

"As of now, you're her arresting officer. I'm keeping the scope of possible contamination limited. Make sure she arrives at the trial on time. No funny stuff between now and then. I want her on a tight leash, every moment accounted for. If it's not, she won't be the only one under the gun. I'm watching your actions as well."

Instead of confirming with a "Yes, sir," Lon merely snapped a nod at his commander. But he couldn't resist saying, "This is one battle you'll lose," as he left.

Londo returned to his apartment to find Lina cleaning up from the breakfast he'd ordered. She was dressed in the dark robe he'd originally bought for Aiko, but he brushed that thought out of his mind. This was Lina's robe now. It wasn't right to think of Aiko when he was with her.

"I take it charges aren't dropped?" Lina asked after greeting him in a way that warmed him from head to boots.

"I'm your arresting officer." Lon understood the twang of alarm he felt within her. "Our hearing's scheduled for tomorrow morning. Don't worry. I have feelers out to non-Legion-affiliated defense attorneys. I just need to make sure we're always recorded, so people can see you're not sneaking off to report to Emperor Yanist-Glory for your evil plotting." He nodded at the tiny recording camera that hovered nearby.

"Okay, I won't do that today. But I do need to feed the cats. You've never met them. As long as we're there, can I quit my job?"

"What, port to Earth?" Londo's brows knit. He was used to the trip taking about ten hours in hyperspace. But Lina was faster. Apparently she'd been to Earth several times in the past few days. "You've got this trick down pat?"

"It's safe enough," she told him. "Most people get nervous their first or fifth time. There's a bit of empty in the ride."

"Bit of empty?"

"You'll see."

Londo screwed up his courage. He'd made the trip once already, but he'd been dead at the time. "*D'accord*, we'll go to Earzth." Having her being in the porn biz would play havoc on PR, though not as much with Legion PR. Porn wasn't a sin Out Here, but still, anything that smoothed the path…

"Can I go like this?" He spread his arms to indicate his famous, black faux-leather Valiant uniform.

Lina laughed. "You'd give everyone a heart attack. The civil suits from that alone would put you in the poor house."

"As long as we were there together."

Delight filled Lina as they walked hand in hand to the master bedroom. Their bedroom, together. This marriage thing was going to be wonderful, especially since Lon was the other half of the deal. As soon as she figured out how being married to him was supposed to work, she could get on with her life. *Their* lives. She loved happy endings.

Lon poked through dresser drawers. "How long is this going to take? I've never quit a job before. Or formally met cats."

"You just tell me when you need to leave," Lina told him as she gathered her own clothes. "I know you have…" *the funeral preparations* "business to attend to."

"That's not an answer," Lon said.

"I dunno. An hour for the job? Terran. Oh, it might take longer. Not more than three for the whole trip, is that okay? We need to play with the cats, poor things."

The vast closet muffled him. "Good enough."

Fifteen minutes later Lina returned to the bedroom from the quick shower she'd taken in the guest bathroom. Now that they were married, they'd probably be using the same bathroom, wouldn't they? She chewed the inside of her cheek about that. All the women at work said separate bathrooms made for good marriages. She'd have to consider it, maybe try it both ways to see what worked best.

She could sense that Lon was doing something to his hair in the ensuite, but she didn't want to pry. Lord knew he had enough hair product in the cabinets. Instead she fretted about what to say when she turned in her notice. Should she be gracious, or should she let loose with the truth about some people and how she felt about them?

What do you think? her spirit guides asked her. She frowned at the ceiling.

"All right, I'll be good," she muttered darkly. The door to the master bath swooshed open and she did a double-take. "You're kidding, right?"

Lon clutched his chest and pointed at her. "Absolutely not. No way!"

He stood in a gray suit, striped tie at his neck. His two-button jacket fit him like something out of a magazine ad. Narrow pants were cuffed over shoes that had been polished to mirrors.

She wore a beige tee shirt under a baggy pink overall. The knees on it had frayed almost to holes. Her tennies had worn and stained spots, with sad ties that had lost their plastic tips.

"What are you supposed to be, a lawyer?" she accused him.

"You're not going out in public in *that*," he declared. "You're not even wearing that in private. Take it off. Let me burn it."

Lina threw her arms around herself. "It's my favorite!" she cried.

"Say it ain't so. Please, baby."

"Well, hell, Lon, we aren't going to the Oscars. You'll scare people. They'll think you're a fed. All you need is a briefcase or a badge to go along with it."

He looked down at himself and frowned. "Am I supposed to take the lady in the farmer's sack's word for this?" he asked. "Where's your 'crappy suit'? You said you had one. Better crappy than that."

"I don't wear the suit to the office, for pete's sake," she huffed. "They'd think I was going on a job interview. Which is where I wear the thing. Wear jeans."

"To work?"

"It's what normal people wear."

"Not the places I go to."

"Then you don't go to normal places."

Lon rubbed his nose as Lina held out the top of her overalls to examine them herself.

"Are they really that bad?" she asked.

"Baby," he said, "*anything* else is going to be better than that." He whirled his index finger at her. "Get back in what you were wearing the other night down in the corridor, when I came home. We'll use that as a starting point."

"Who wears dresses to work? I'm not in upper management." Now she returned his finger whirl. "We'll both start with jeans. And tee shirts."

She had to push him to the jeans section of his closet. He emerged with tee shirt and sport coat accompanying them, nothing in his usual black.

"Are you sure?" he asked her reflection in the mirror. "I look like a bum."

"You look like a Research Triangle neo-yuppie. Guess that's the best we can do right now."

"Yuppie." He made a face at himself and turned to check the jacket's fit in the back. With a shrug he gave her his attention.

"*You* look like a bum. Light of my life," he quickly amended.

She wore her jeans, the sad shoes, and a tee with a UNC logo so faded it was almost illegible. "Standard work apparel," she informed him. "You're still too fancy."

"This is as informal as I get for business strangers," he insisted.

"But–"

He shook his finger at her. "First impressions are essential for great leadership. If you don't really have it, you can fake it as long as you look sharp." He scowled at her the way he did when he wanted to make a point. "Rands always look sharp, Mrs. Rand."

He saw the pained expression on her face and corrected himself. "I mean, *Ms. Ra*–"

"Don't say it and you won't get used to it," Lina warned.

"Not Rand?"

"My name's O'Kelly. Maybe you could change your name?"

Cocking his head at her, he offered, "Londo O'Kelly. Too many 'o's,' Lie. Besides," he faked a falsetto, "Ah doan belawng ta you."

"I do not sound like Gomer Pyle."

"Gomer Pyle on hormones." He huffed out a sigh, his lower lip protruding in a defeated pout, but at least that pout turned up at the ends.

Lina breathed a little easier. She didn't want to do anything that might jeopardize Londo's love for her. "Honestly, Lon, I've never remotely understood why a woman would give away her identity just because she got married, when her husband doesn't have to. It's not a rejection of you or your name. I think you have a fine name. So do I."

He tapped his chin with a knuckle. "I thought about it while I was away. Somehow I didn't think you would change to 'Rand.' But I really think we should have the same last name, *d'accord?*"

"You'd really do that?" But this was Londo *Rand!*

"Yeah. Yeah, I would. So what are we going to do? Hyphenate? O'Kelly-Rand? Rand-O'Kelly?"

She made a face. "Too long. And hyphenations sound so snobby. How about O'Rand? O'Randly?" They both made faces at each other. "Maybe something new. I have friends who did that, just came up with something."

After a moment's thought, he gave a quick nod. "Let's walk. I owe you a behind-the-scenes tour of HQ anyway. We can figure this out before we head for Earth."

"That quick?" She ported a sweater to her. Around here, people didn't like bare arms.

"Why not? We can come up with a temporary name, see how it wears, and have the option of changing it later before we make it official."

"Hunh. I see why you're a team leader."

He laughed as he put his arm around her to guide her through the apartment. "That and many other reasons."

After a moment's hesitation, she let herself be led. But the dark hallway outside blinked red as soon as she stepped into it. It was a subtle warning, a dashed line that appeared at the top of either side of the wall to follow her. "That wasn't there before," Lina whispered to Lon.

Lon rubbed his Legion ring and made gestures in the air. In answer, a screen appeared, scrolling quickly through writing Lina couldn't follow. "The puter doesn't know what to make of you," Lon surmised. "As a prisoner, you have a zero security level. With a high-security guard– that's me– you should be allowed wherever I escort you."

"Legion spouses are level two," Lina knew.

"That's absolute minimum. The youngest Legion kids are level two," Lon said. "So the puter thinks you're illegally in a level two area, but it's not quite sure. If it really objected, you'd know."

They made their way from the residence levels of HQ downstairs to the public areas of the ground floor. "I guess I can't offer you that tour until we get all this straightened out," Londo told her as they settled with soft drinks behind thick greenery that defined a corner of one of the main lobbies. "Let's start with the basics. Name."

Lina's face glowed as she realized this really was his first priority. He was committed to the marriage– and her. *My gosh, Valiant's going to change his name!* It wasn't just the sex; it was love. Never before in her life had she been loved, and now here he was, lavishing her with it. She wasn't ever going to give him up!

The scowl he gave was a gentle one of deep thought. "Let's make it a good one. Memorable. Where do we start?"

"I make lousy capital F's and J's," she offered. "So no names beginning with those."

"That certainly narrows the field." Londo swirled his glass in his hand. "To tell you the truth, I'd like something flashy. This is my chance. I've been stuck with Rand most of my life, and to me it's just sat there. Bland and Rand."

"Even though it's Maximus' name, too?" Lina asked. "Rand's always meant Maximus to me."

His left eyebrow raised meaningfully. "Another reason not to keep it."

Londo did have his issues. He loved his adoptive father, but wanted to make his own name in the world. Literally, it seemed. "Okay. How about something like Picard? Uhura? Kira? 'Kira Carolina' would be so cool. I love Colonel Kira."

"Last name first?" Lon pretended to seriously consider. "Efficient. Just think: 'Kira Lina.' I take it these are *Star Trek* names?" Lina nodded with a sly grin and Lon shook his head. "Why not just Lina and Londo Startrek?"

"I like it." Lina gave a laugh of delight. "Or we could shorten it to Star. No, Starr, with two r's, as in Ringo. The Starrs of Starhaven." Starhaven was Londo's house in the Rockies, where they were going to live.

"Actually," Londo said slowly, "I think you may be on to something. Give me some more star names."

"There's Betelgeuse, Rigel, Delta Orion…"

"C'mon, be serious. Starhawk…"

"Starfalcon," she said with a smile at Londo Falcon Rand.

"I don't think so. Starstorm, Starlight, Starbright, Starkers, Starkey…"

"Starhaven, Starhart, Starsky, Starry Starry Night…"

"Um, Starheart. You said that already. Starlight. Said that. I like both of them. Starwars. Have to get Lucasfilm's okay on that. Or Disney's, which would be harder."

"Lonestar. Blackstar. Whitestar. Brightstar. *Étoile...*"

"Let's keep it in English," Lon said. "*D'accord.* Starwind– that's nice. And I liked Starlight and Starheart, too. Let's make a list."

Lina ported in her note padd from upstairs. She straightened from snuggling against Londo and wrote "Starlight, Starhart, Starwind." They contrived as many possibles as they could, but when they narrowed down the list, these three remained.

"Let's see what we have." Londo scrutinized the list. "Lina Starlight. Londo Starlight."

"The L's seem to collide. But other than that, I like it."

"*Mets-en*, we'll give that a B rating."

"Lina Starwind. Londo Starwind."

"It just occurred to me. Can anyone make any jokes about breaking wind with that?" Lon asked.

"Not to your face and expect to leave alive. Now it sounds like a horse to me for some reason."

"A horse?"

"Starwind, the Magic Horse. I don't know, it just sounds horsey."

He chuckled at that. "Wina Stawwind," he said gratingly in an Elmer Fudd voice, and she giggled. "It's beginning to sound a little wimpy to me."

"Wimpy. Okay, that gets it a C or C-minus at least. Mustn't have Valiant being wimpy."

"Lina Starhart. Londo Starheart." Each tasted the sound.

"Carolina Angelina O'Kelly Starhart. Londo Falcon Rand Starhart." Lina cocked her head, considering. "It's got possibilities."

"The Starhearts of Starhaven," Londo mused. "Every marriage should have a heart in it."

"I was thinking it should be spelled h-a-r-t. As in a wild hart."

"I was thinking h-e-a-r-t. As in a wild heart." Londo bent to kiss her. "Like I'm wild about you."

She rifled his hair. "I can live with it. It's cool."

"We'll try it out. Give it a couple days and revisit. Maybe we'll have other ideas."

Lina stared at the tiny list on her padd. "Is it this simple? Will we have to register it somewhere? Hang a sign?"

"*Aucune idée.* No idea."

"Why don't we see how we wind up spelling it? We'll spell it spontaneously and see what comes up consistently. I'm open to either way."

"So am I. *Bon,* we have the basic name figured out, Ms. Starheart…"

"That's the hard part, Mr. Starhart," Lina said. She had a zazzy new name, how about that? Of course she was more interested in her new husband. She drank in the sight of him, just loving him– and then her thoughts paused. "Oh god, Londo. What if they're right?"

"What?"

"What if– somehow, subconsciously, I don't know– what if I'm controlling you? Doing whatever it is that's considered mind control?"

Immediately he gestured to bring up a privacy field before turning to her. "What in the world would make you think that?"

"Lon… You're Valiant, and I'm just some nobody from the wrong side of the tracks. Admit it, that's what everyone's been saying. We got together through… well, through somebody's machinations, and that's the only way we'd ever have met. I can't imagine a more unlikely pairing."

"Are you happy with it?"

She matched her gaze with his. "Lord yes. But I keep thinking that might be the problem."

"As in…"

"I want you so bad. Maybe somewhere in the back of my mind… maybe I wanted to lock you in," she whispered.

Remember we're being recorded, he told her telepathically and she nodded at the tiny camera ball that floated in the air above them. **Lina, think back to that time when you were in fourth grade, with the bully who beat you up.**

And?

And what would you have done with him? How would you have taken over his mind?

She thought about it for a moment, then showed Londo.

Ah, so that's how it's done.

Well I couldn't say for sure, but it seems to me that that would work. Psychic hooks.

D'accord. *Are you doing any of that with me?*

She smiled and laid her head on his shoulder. "No, Londo. Not a bit."

"Well, good. I don't feel you doing it. And I'm not doing any of that to you."

"What?" she raised up to stare at him.

"I mean, I don't think I have you under my mental control either. I want you so bad, Lina." He gripped her hand fiercely. "You are the most important thing in my life. I'm not losing you for anything."

Behind their privacy field no one could watch them.

"You register here." Lon touched the wall in the dark security corridor that led to the outside of HQ.

Instead of a screen lighting up in response, a large, uniformed man actually stepped out of the wall. He gave a half bow to Londo. "What service do you require?" the man asked, and a crease appeared between his brows. "We don't usually provide services for you, sir."

Lon acknowledged the statement with a lesser nod of his own. "You will be providing them in the future. This is my wife, Carolina Starheart."

The man's eyes opened wider, considering Lina, though his face revealed nothing else. "Yessir."

"She'll be requiring escort on occasion."

"Of course, sir. But fair warning: with the funeral, Legion Security is running thin."

"Understood. I'll be escorting her these next few days. I just want to show her how things work."

"I teleport," Lina blurted.

Lon rubbed his nose. "Right. That might cause Security problems."

The guard looked from Londo to Lina to the floating camera, and then back again to Lon. "I think we might have a protocol for teleporters," he finally said. The edges of his mouth stretched as if he were concealing a grimace.

"I'm sure there is one, somewhere in the records. If not, we'll work out something in the coming days."

"Yessir, Valiant." The man hesitated before saying, "Ah, the puter doesn't know what to make of Mrs. Valiant's security rating."

"We're working on that. This is all very new on a number of levels."

The guard gave another bow and stepped back into the wall.

"How did he do that?" Lina asked. She flattened her cheek against the wall so she could more closely check it for a hidden door. "Was he real or a hologram?"

"Real. If I'm not here to escort you outside, you call for a guard. You don't go out alone."

Outdoors beckoned her from the end of the hallway. "For how long? Until this mind control thing is over?"

"For always." Lon turned her around to return to the main lounge. "You're the wife of Valiant. I have enemies. You noticed the other day?"

"I might have." As a small army was doing its best to blow the two of them to smithereens.

"We will keep you safe. *I* will keep you safe. This means you call for a Security escort every time you leave HQ, unless I'm with you."

Lina gave a noncommittal sound at that.

"No arguments about this."

Outside they passed a couple dressed in the pleated parachutes that were such a popular fashion, and Lon nodded pleasantly like he knew them. They bowed back. When they were out of listening distance, Lon said, "So tell me about this invasion attempt. The fleet from… Aldierra? Never heard of that planet. It's not in this sector."

He gestured and some kind of buzzy something happened around them. "Don't want anyone to overhear," he told her.

She tried to joke about the invasion and how they'd dealt with it, keeping Jae's name out of it as much as she could without denying him his major role in stopping what could easily have turned into a planet-wide massacre. Jae. She didn't want to leak any thoughts about *that* to Londo until the right time. When would be that be? Maybe today. Tomorrow latest. For sure. Yes.

Lon's jaw dropped when she told him how the world essence of Aldierra herself had possessed Lina, using her as a focus to send a death threat message to every last citizen of that distant world: *Stop misusing me, stop being such beasts, or I will kill you at the end of three seasons!* Well, that part couldn't be joked about. It was scary. Lina watched to see how Londo would take it all.

"Twenty billion people?"

"Actually, a bit more."

"So you're now the Speaker for Aldierra."

"I guess it only entails checking in with the planet on the appointed day and relaying what she's decided. In the meantime I'd like to see what they come up with to pacify her, if I could. Maybe we can help."

"*Bon,* no problem, as long as it doesn't take too much time. Speaking of time, I think if we're going to Earth…"

"Sure," Lina said. "Brace yourself."

3

They ported in to the front corner outside a corporate building.

"Is it over? Are we here? *Crisse,* that was quick!" Londo exclaimed. "Eighty parsecs? That fast?"

Lina beamed at him, clearly basking in his approval.

"Manoman, Lina, holy shit *ostie,* that's amazing. And you say it's permanent?"

"Yep."

He put his arm around her waist. "That's past efficient, more into the realm of miraculous."

"I like it."

"That's my wife who did that." Lon noticed the recording camera had come along, and gave her a nod of approval for that as well.

Then he looked over her workplace: a four-story brick-faced building attached to an even larger if lower concrete block warehouse. A contrasting color pattern in the brick that framed the lines of windows could have been better designed at little extra cost for much more pleasing impact. Then again, maybe this pornography distributor didn't want to stand out in the neighborhood.

Porn. And Lina. If she hadn't told him, he'd never have guessed. He had so much to learn about this wife of his.

Lina shivered slightly under his hand but didn't seem uncomfortable. With her touching him, he could sense the world on a more human level. This was a cool day. He noted the sensation curiously and shivered to see what difference that made. The wind was brisk but there was no snow in shadow pockets around the building. Trees were just beginning to show signs of life after the winter. A few in the parking lot were even trying to bloom. What a change from Montreal.

As they walked toward the entrance, he said, "I was expecting a dark basement somewhere down a back alley. I mean, *pornography*. In the Bible Belt, no less."

"If this gets out, it's going to be a scandal, Lon."

"Meh. Why do you work here if it's so scandalous?"

Lina shrugged. "I never thought very much about other people's opinions."

"A non-conformist bohemian arteest." He grinned at her. "That's what I like about you. Well, one of many things. So why worry about what others say now?"

She nudged him. "Gee, I don't know, Valiant."

He raised his arm to wrap it around her shoulder and squeeze. "Ahh, it's no problem, Kitten. Don't worry about it."

A sign on the lawn showed the place to be "MidD," as in Midnight Delivery, but otherwise the building stood in bland anonymity within the industrial park. Lina slid her identification card through a wall's electronic slot and Lon made an impolite noise at the primitive security system. He was used to retinal scans, voiceprints and more.

The doors opened for her badge. "Well, what do you know? They haven't cut me off yet."

The receptionist looked up and let out a shout. "Lina! Hell, girl, we all thought you'd gotten some kind of tropical disease and died. Welcome back!"

"Thanks, Kaya." Lina leaned over the counter to hug the hugely-pregnant black woman. "Haven't you had that baby yet?"

"She was waiting for you to tell her when to be born."

"Uh huh." Lina considered Kaya's belly. "It won't be long. Maybe a week, no longer. This one wants to be a Pisces. She's a little sweetie, she is."

"Friday's my last day."

"Good timing. Here, I've brought along a guest. Let me sign him in."

"Sure, hon," Kaya said, giving Londo a very approving once-over.

Lon was always amazed at how much stock people took in his uniform. Unless he was pointed out in some fashion when he was in civilian clothing, they often didn't recognize him.

Kaya winked at Lina. "It seems you did pick up something down there, hm? Where were you?"

"Tiawa, French Polynesia," Lina explained. She scribbled in the check-in book as Kaya handed Londo a guest badge.

He wrote on it and stuck it to his jacket: "L. Starheart." He'd kept the "e" in "heart" without an inner debate, because it was enough to remember that he had a new name. He'd get used to it eventually; it sounded so much better. Lon Rand, shadow of Hal Rand– no longer!

A phone call required Kaya's attention so Lina took Londo's hand and led him to the elevator. "We're going to play this as normally as possible," Lina informed him. "No need to alarm the natives, okay?"

Londo grinned. "*D'accord.*" He kept looking around. At the employee pictures board. "Lousy picture of you." At the federal regulations postings, the Employee Excellence notes. "That's a better picture," he said, spotting her 2x3 face on the board from a good thirty feet away.

"I'm sure they'll rip that one down as soon as they hear what I have to say," Lina muttered as the elevator opened for them.

When they once again had their privacy, Lina sidled up to Londo, her hands deep in his back jeans pockets. Nice. They stood nose to nose and belly to belly. "Now you're in my territory," she told him with a swagger to her chin. "I'm team leader here. These are all my people, not yours. *Comprends-tu?* You follow my orders here, no questions allowed, pet."

"Arf. All hail Empress Carolina." He enjoyed turning her "I'm not your pet" routine back on her.

They disengaged from each other at the third floor. It amused Lon to hear their presence announced from the far side of the building as he listened past the walls. He heard "Lina's back!" repeated again and again from one area in particular. An unexpected shriek of "LinaLinaLina!" behind him made him jump.

"Hey, Heather." Lina turned.

The woman was no kid to shriek like that. "When did you get back?"

"We just got in."

"We…?" Heather finally looked at Londo, recognizing his presence. She cocked her head suspiciously at Lina and leaned down to grab her left hand. There was a ring. "Ahh! You did! You are!"

"Heather, this is Lon," Lina said, and Lon shook Heather's hand.

But she only looked at Lina. "Shit. You're finally going to do it, aren't you?"

"Eeyup." Lina smirked at her.

"Oh shit. I'll run and take cover while you deliver the bad news. Come and see me afterward!"

"I'll try. We're on a tight schedule."

Lina laughed. "*Freedom,*" she sang softly as Heather ran down the hall in the other direction to tell her coworkers. "Honey, if you only knew how good this feels. To finally leave this place. I was always too afraid."

"I'm beginning to understand. Come on, let's get this over with, eh? Give it a quick killing blow."

"This might take a little time. I'll bet anything that things haven't run according to my instructions while I was away."

"You're a bossy bitch. A regular dictator."

She elbowed him for that, and he let go one of his full-bodied laughs. It was good to rattle someone else's cage about that, especially his timid little Lina. It was fun to tease her.

"I can't help it if I like to run things. And the word is bitch, not *beetch.*"

"Secret identities are a pain," Londo groaned, covering his accent as he had since they'd arrived.

"It'll only be for an hour. I'll keep it to that, I promise."

"And then you'll go back to be-eenk mah leetle poosy *chat*?"

"I'll be anything you want me to be, honeybear."

"*Bon.*"

They pushed through fire doors into a new section of building. Here sprawled Marketing. Offices framed an open area where a dozen people milled around expectantly. As soon as Lina's face appeared around the corner, they all surged forward. "Lina! Lina!"

People clamored but didn't hug her, Lon noticed. These might have been close enough to know about her fear of being touched. Of course, they couldn't know that he'd cured her of that. Heh.

Sure enough, most were dressed along the same lines as Lina. Some were worse. Only one of the women wore a skirt, and that looked like it had been bought third-hand. Two men wore baggy shorts, layered sweaters, socks and sandals. Lina would need instruction in proper fashion, as he had endured so many years before.

She introduced him to the group, but they weren't interested in him once the surprise of Lina being married had worn off. Odd not to be the focus of attention.

So Londo hung back, letting them babble and catch up as he looked around. The surroundings all seemed very businesslike, sedate and usual. Wall-to-wall commercial carpet, gray walls, sales charts and team charts and credit union notices. A bulletin board posted current ads from magazines along with web banners: lots of bare-breasted women– well, that he wouldn't have found anywhere else. A poster-sized catalog cover of a woman in rather unrevealing lingerie provided a focal point for one otherwise boring wall.

But as he ambled around on his own, peeking into people's cubicles, he saw the real nature of the business. Printouts of catalog and webpages in progress lay everywhere with skimpy lingerie modeled on mostly white, silicon-breasted women. They advertised vibrators, dongs and more, with explicit diagrams for toy usage. Abundant action shots from pornos served as backdrops.

A computer screen displayed a digital contact sheet of porno photos. Whew! It seemed that only the tamer ones actually made it into the catalog. He glanced back at his bride through the cubicle walls and snorted to himself. Lina working here!

Then he rubbed his nose. Yeah, Lina working here. He'd really rushed them into marriage. He had no doubt that they should be together, but there was so much to learn about each other. In some ways he felt like he'd known her forever, but in too many ways they were strangers.

This was going to be hardest on her. He'd turned her entire life upside down. Unfortunately, they were in for a pound now and she'd have to adapt or drown.

She'd survive. If he were any judge of character– and he was the best at that–
she would prevail with bonus points.

Still, he'd have to take this porn stuff and the cats– *maudite marde*, she said
she had a herd!– with as good grace as possible. This was part of that "compromise" stuff she'd mentioned just before the wedding. He'd make up all the
trouble to her. He'd give her everything she ever wanted.

She'd never want to leave him.

Londo wandered from cubicle to cubicle, wondering which one was hers.
When he saw it he knew. It held a ficus tree, carefully mulched, and pots of green
plants that were starting to turn sad and brown in her absence. An Olympia doll
sat sentry on top of her monitor, and a bulletin board full of official company
notices also held pictures of costumed people who could only have been from
Star Trek.

He stopped. There was a picture of him, too, cut out from some glossy magazine. He smiled in surprise. He was up there with *Star Trek*. And cats, and a
picture of an angel holding the earth.

A huge stack of work waited in her in-box. The message light on her phone
blinked. He checked out her top-of-the-line Macintosh setup with interest. A
couple of glossy printer's proofs lay on the desk beside it. Londo peered at them
and swallowed hard. Hot stuff. How could anyone–?

"It takes about two weeks before you get immune to it," Lina said behind
him. "I see you found the place."

"Uh huh," he said, and pointed to his picture on her bulletin board. He struck
the same pose and publicity smile as it held.

She laughed and blushed. "I'd forgotten about that."

"Right next to *Star Trek* and the cats. I'm honored."

"You should be," she said and gave him a quick kiss. "Sharon's on her way
so I can talk to her in her office. Leigh and Ed will show you around after they
get out of a meeting. What else? Ah…"

She looked around to see if anyone was looking and then ported a pile of
green computer printout in front of him on her desk. "Employee price list," she
explained. She drew out some catalogs from a drawer, then ported in what was
labeled an employee order form.

"I figure we might as well take advantage of the discount while I still have a job."

He grinned at her. "More order forms, please." There were only six ordering lines on it.

"You aren't going to embarrass me, are you?"

"Well…"

"Oh god." A half-inch stack of order forms appeared. "Good enough?"

"It's a start."

"Ask around if you think you're ordering junk. Some of it is. Do you want some coffee? A Coke? This may take a while. Or it may take five minutes. They may want me to get the hell out of here."

"I'll be fine."

"You tell me if you need to take off sooner. Oh, here are Leigh and Ed."

She made the introductions. Leigh was a large woman, perfectly coiffed but wearing a scrawny pink and purple boa wrapped around her neck, above the requisite tee shirt and jeans. Ed was balding and more than slender, with a tendency to hunch. His face was prematurely grained, though the lines that couldn't be attributed to smoking seemed to be the result of smiling. Leigh squealed as she found out that Lon Starhart had married their Lina. She admired Lina's ring.

"An emerald!" Neither of them corrected Leigh. "This design is just way too cool. It's like a signet ring a lord in the Middle Ages would wear."

"Isn't it beautiful? Look, you guys have time to take Lon on a quick tour, don't you? He's been curious about the place. Show him the bodies."

"Sure," Ed said, looking hard at Londo. "Has anyone ever told you you look like someone famous? I can't quite place it…"

"Oh, I run into that all the time," Lon said casually. "Guess I just have one of those faces." He cracked his knuckles leisurely and slouched. "You betcha, a long list of faces," he said in a cunning imitation of King Browne, the host of *The Browne Blast* on late-nite. "Name a face and I can do him, you betcha, you betcha."

Lina giggled at him while the others smiled at the cleverness of the gag.

"Can you do… Jack Nicholson?"

It was a familiar imitation. Londo's eyebrows actually arched like triangles, his eyelids narrowing as he made his ghastly grin. "Just get a load of me," he snarled *à la Nicholson*. "Can I get a cheese sandwich around here?"

"You've got to do Nixon…"

Lon shook his non-existent jowls in reply, growling a few sentences and flashing the V sign.

"Maximus. Can you do Maximus?"

One of his favorites. He stretched himself up to his full height, looking down at them from above, and lowered his voice a tone or two. "Freedom can never be bought and sold," he intoned gravely. "It is not a commodity like corn flakes sitting soggy in… my… bowl." The rephrasing always brought a good laugh, and it didn't fail now. Hal frowned at him whenever he pulled this. Hal was uncommonly proud of that particular speech.

"You looked just like him!" Leigh clapped. Ed joined in: "That's perfect! Wo-oww!"

"Just throw money." Lon grinned at them.

Lina put her arms around him proudly. "I found him in a traveling carnival."

"A carnival."

She returned his sour stare. "Next to the dog-boy. They paid me to take him away."

"Patti is here today," Leigh mentioned.

"Patti!" Lina exclaimed. "Keep him away from– Oh, I can say it. After all, I'm quitting. That bitch. Bitch, bitch, bitch." The three of them snickered at Lina's blasphemy. She turned to Lon and poked her finger at him. "If you see Malibu Barbie approaching, run for the hills. You'll thank me later."

He grinned. "Malibu Barbie. I'll be watching for her."

"Lina?" A voice said from down the hall.

"There's Sharon. See you in a while, Lon."

He took her hand and squeezed it. "Good luck, *chér*– honey."

"Thanks." She left and he was alone with Leigh and Ed.

"Where do we start?" Ed asked.

Lon said, "How about the bodies? That sounded interesting."

"Well, the bodies are mostly in pictures here in Marketing," Ed said. "Everything that's printed or goes online gets put together here…"

They wandered through the area and demonstrated the way they assembled print catalogs, amazing Londo at their nonchalance at the subject matter. As they ventured into other areas of the building, the two filled him in on office gossip.

For being in the South, Londo heard a variety of accents as they proceeded through departments. Thick southern drawls seemed rare while a softer, subtle lilt predominated. Yet there were also many people working here who had definitely been born and raised in New Jersey, New York, the Mid-West, and Mexico.

He strolled through a new products room with samples of vibrators, lotions and vibes, another few rooms filled with nothing but videos. Accounting, information systems, order processing… This was nuts and bolts business that Lon was unfamiliar with, but Lina was.

The next stop was the warehouse. Lon used his paravision to peek into the myriad boxes stacked two stories high. He'd never seen so many sex toys or dirty videos! According to daily goals posted on a bulletin board, they were sending out 15,000-plus orders a day.

Quality Control held another sample room, this one walled by fencing and stacked boxes. Its deflated love dolls caught Lon's eye. He fought down a giggle. Lina working around love dolls. Else would get a kick out of that, wouldn't she? *Euh*, maybe not. It was difficult to tell which way Else's sense of humor ran. Or if she had one. She could be a very odd step-mother. What would Lina make of her?

"This one's our most popular," Ed told him, handing him a soggy piece of peach-colored plastic with painted features.

"Who's in there?"

Blocking the doorway with their backs to Lon, Ed and Leigh assured the employee that they were giving a tour. Londo regarded the doll with her shocked, open-mouthed face and on impulse blew her up in two breaths: one to test the strength of the material, and the other to finish the job. Careful; don't make her explode. That final breath got her full-size in a moment. She bulged perhaps a trifle more than she should, and he noted a leak in a seam that hadn't been sealed well.

Leigh and Ed turned around as he snapped the air nozzle closed. They boggled at the suddenness of the love doll's inflation. Shit, he'd blown his disguise!

"*Sank heaven,*" he began to sing with his best Chevalier swagger, "*for leetle gulls, for leetle gulls get beeger ev'ry day...*" He tossed the doll into the air and bounced it around like a volleyball for more diversion.

They laughed at it then, laughing at the impression and forgetting about the unnaturalness.

The three of them moved on, hanging over the railing of the mezzanine into the warehouse. "Valiant," Leigh suddenly said.

"What?"

"Can you do Valiant? You look like him, a little."

"You think so? Hm, Valiant." Lon made a show of squinting his eyes, pretending to come up with the impression. "What would he say here? Ah, I know: 'Zis is a raid!'"

They howled as he stood straight up, over-scowling his Valiant scowl, the one he'd always worked on to be different from Hal's. He pointed his index finger toward heaven. "'In zhe name of liberty, in zhe name of decency, I arrest you all! You can srow all zhe vibrators you want, but zhey weel just bonzz off mi!'" He opened his jacket wide, stuck out his tee-shirted chest and pretended to deflect a barrage of rubber goods with it.

They clapped at that and he bowed grandly for them. "As good as the Maximus?" he asked.

"Oh no, that was very good but Maximus was even better," Leigh assured him. "You've got him down flat."

Leigh and Ed gave him sample paks of sex lube and a couple strings of novelty condoms as souvenirs. He stuffed them in his jean pockets. Then they came to the rooms lined with file cabinets filled with therapist approvals on their videos and age verifications for actors, guarded under lock and key.

"When we're really raided," Ed said, "This is what they come for. The company pays therapists big bucks just to keep them on retainer so they'll be able to testify that anything we sell has scientific value."

"Do they ever turn anything down?"

That was the next room on the tour, filled with boxes labeled BURN.

"We've got in-house reviewers, like me and Lina. We screen stuff before it ever gets to the therapists, to save them time and us money. Anything we reject, they don't bother to send the therapists. It gets destroyed. Anything the therapists reject gets destroyed, too, unless it can be salvaged by editing."

"So what kind of stuff gets rejected?"

"Kids." Leigh said. "Violence. Bad attitude towards women."

"Animals. Rape," Ed added. "People pretending to be kids. Incest."

Leigh nodded. "Unwilling sex partners who become willing during the course of events. If it's doubtful, we reject it."

The tension that Londo hadn't realized had been building in his shoulders slid away. Now he could see how Lina could work here. Nothing wrong with healthy sex. This seemed to be an honest business, even if it was going to be a royal pain for his Terran PR people to spin.

They took a shortcut back through the call center.

"F–ing obscene callers!" one operator muttered loud enough for only Lon to hear.

The operator next to her was on the phone, reading from her computer screen in a very blasé manner, "Secure around the scrotum and at the onset of ejaculation, unfasten the– Ejaculation, sir. You tie it around your balls and when you start to come, you tear the strip off for extra power. Yessir. Sorry I wasn't being clear. What color would you like that in? We have red, black, brown, and glow-in-the-dark green."

Londo jounced in place as he peered about. He had to bring Jae here. And Hal. Hal would get a big kick out of this. Maybe he could bug the place and play back the recording after the next ParaNet general meeting. As it was, the spy camera was traveling with Lina. He should have brought a second one. He didn't even have a spare cell he could photograph with.

"Yes ma'am?" They were passing a new "pod," as they called it, of operators. "The beads were part of your free gift. No, they weren't supposed to have a clasp. They're not a bracelet; they're anal beads. They–" Pause. "Yes, ma'am, that's what you do with them. You're welcome."

One pod was separated from the next by a glass display wall in which dozens and dozens of sex toys preened their naughtiness. Lon couldn't quite grasp the extent of it all at once and had to gape. Dildos and dongs– Ed explained that dongs were realistic dildos, which meant that dozens of stiffies stood at attention, produced not only in Caucasian and black flesh tones but in neon colors, glow-in-the-dark models, and decorative glass. Some were hollow strap-ons for use by either gender.

Tunnel masturbators of elastomer and jelly materials ran the same colorful gamut, with labia and sometimes even anal openings available for use. Other models were molded from lower human torsos, made from materials so realistic you wanted to reach in and give them a teasing spank. Bullet vibes, cock rings and ben wa balls, flimsy whips and velvet handcuffs, a bevy of folded love dolls, their amazed faces all gazing at him…

Lon felt like a tourist seeing the Grand Canyon for the first time. It was almost a giant adult arcade game, exhibited for his amusement. Londo needed controls and grabber claws to reach inside…

Beside him, Leigh let out a gasp and then whispered, "Bitch at nine o'clock."

Ed tried to hide them behind double doors, but Londo caught a glimpse of Malibu Barbie dressed in a leopardskin miniskirt and spike heels striding toward them. She had given Ed a dismissing glance when she spotted Londo.

She swerved to intercept. Now she was swinging her hips, poking out her breasts, tossing her very long, very bleached hair back and forth. She had a professional smile, but the professional Londo was reminded of usually plied her wares on night streets.

As Barbie sidled up to Londo, Leigh said, "Lon, this is Patti. She manages audio ads for us. It's a separate office from Marketing."

Londo shook her hand. "Pleased to meet you."

"Lon just married Lina," Ed mentioned.

"Our Lina? How very sweet," Patti purred in a plastic kind of way, taking Lon's arm as they walked down the hallway. She pressed her body against his. Londo backed away as he could. "Tell me, what do you do?"

"I'm in security," he said. "Ed and Leigh were showing me around. If you'll excuse us–"

"Oh, no problem. I'll come along. Security must be sooo interesting. Do you use a gun?"

Ed and Leigh exchanged grimaces Patti couldn't see. "Don't let us interrupt what you were doing," Leigh said.

Ed slipped behind them.

"But it's my pleasure," Patti said, bumping up against Londo again. She chatted gaily about nothing and smiled up at Londo. "Ooh, such muscles," she said when she tried to press against his arm and the skin didn't yield to her.

"Patti Whitehurst, call the operator. Patti Whitehurst," Kaya's slightly nasal voice on the intercom rang through the hallways.

"Damn," she said under her breath. "I'll be right back. You don't go anywhere."

Londo stood still and gave a friendly little obedient wave as Patti glanced back before disappearing around a corner.

"Now! Let's get out of here before she comes back!" Leigh ran the opposite direction down the hall, then ducked into another one. Londo was on her heels, both of them hooting with laughter.

"I think we lost her," Leigh finally huffed as they zigzagged through the building. An elevator took them to the third floor, where Ed waited. "Good thinking," Leigh congratulated him.

"Patti has her eyes on upper management," Ed told Lon. "She wants to be a supervisor, but HR knows the entire Marketing staff will quit if they set her up over us."

Leigh confided, "We all figure that she must have photos of one of the managers with a goat."

"Remember the time when Marv left and she tried to move into his office?" Ed asked Leigh. "Just being there upped her chances of getting his job in Management's eyes. Lina kicked her out. Lina was almost fired because of it."

"Patti tried to get her in trouble for not being Christian enough," Leigh confided. "Imagine Patti accusing someone of not being Christian enough."

"You can get fired for that?" The idea dumbfounded Lon.

"I'd like to have seen them try. You don't want to go up against Lina when she gets mad. And one of the vice-presidents actually sided with Patti about it!" Leigh shook her head in wonder. "I think she has pictures of them all with goats."

Ed snickered. "I have a Barbie doll hanging in my office, if you want to slap it around a bit. We all do from time to time." He glanced at a large clock on the wall. "Well, except for Lina. Hey, I'm late!"

With that, Ed trotted off to a meeting, while Leigh ushered Londo back to Marketing. "I'll have to leave you on your own. I've got to meet with Chuck the Wonder Boy before he takes off," she said. "Paula's leaving for the airport in an hour, so you can bet Wonder Boy will suddenly come down with bubonic plague as soon as her butt's out the door." She explained to Lon, "Paula's Chuck's supervisor."

This was so different from the jobs he'd had. Londo said, "Lina calls this Dilbertville."

Leigh pointed to a bulletin board across the room that held comic strips that Londo hadn't noticed. "Everyone does," Leigh said. "Nice meeting you, Lon. I hope to see you again before you leave."

Londo studied the yellowed, clipped cartoons. It was all about some guy named Dilbert who was stuck at a job from hell. Downsizing. Inept managers. Crazy management policies. He laughed at one but didn't get the others, even though they'd been posted as the epitome of humor.

Valiant was cut off from the common worker, he supposed, and it bothered him. Could ordinary jobs really be as bad as Dilbert showed them? No wonder Lina had never quit, if she thought that everything out there was this bad.

But she didn't have to worry about that any more, and he was glad for her. He'd had the good sense to bully her into marrying him. She could choose any job she wanted now, or stay home and paint like she'd always wished. She'd be there waiting for him whenever he came home. He congratulated himself and then settled down in her cubicle to examine the MidD catalog and do some power ordering.

He should order for Jae as well. Even though Jae had cabinets full of paraphernalia, Jae might find Terran erotica exotic.

Jae. He had to do something big to make things up to him. The situation had completely changed. Jae knew that. Didn't he? Lon would come up with something.

Who wrote this catalog? Its copy held all the subtlety of a sledgehammer. Every item was hot, hot, hot, and a mere X or even double X rating was not enough. Any video that had a little humor it in was described as "hilarious." He'd seen some of them; they weren't.

And there seemed to be a pattern of trying to avoid saying "penis." On one page every video actor was listed as doing something with his lingam. Lon wondered if the average customer would even know what that was.

At least the female performers were never described by the "c" word; nor, he noticed, were there any "sluts" or "bitches" or– this was strange– no use of the word "tits." He would have thought that would be standard issue around here. Nothing wrong with "tits," an all-American word. After all, the Grand Tetons just meant Big Titties. It was right there on the map. Why wasn't it in the catalog?

Lina, why no tits?

Excuse me?

He explained his question telepathically to her as she sat down the hall in her meeting.

George doesn't like the word, and George is the president. He once told us he didn't want green used in the catalog. That lasted a year. He likes green again, thank goodness. That Christmas catalog was a royal pain.

Oh. What's with all the "lingams?"

That was Virgil's word of the month last quarter. He's one of the copywriters. He goes through phases. I'd made the mistake of discussing some TV show about stone age fertility sites with him, you know, lingams and yonis, and all of a sudden all his copy started using the word. The last I saw, he was using "log" and permutations of same. That catalog hasn't been printed yet, but I bet you can find the 'log' stuff in our online version. I'll try to cut this short.

Do what you need to do. Take what time you need.

Trial tomorrow. Don't we need to get ready?

I've got people working on it. T'inquiète pas; no worries.

Londo checked in via his padd to see how his search for a Level 5 lawyer was going, and was pleased to see some excellent names in the list. It didn't take much coordination to get his chief office assistant to contact and brief Lon's choices. He and Legion Support had trained Moyar well.

Then he settled down to work on those order forms. After he'd filled up ten of them, he peeked through the walls into Lina's supervisor's office to see how that was going. That must be Sharon, the supervisor, a short, harassed-looking woman who might be younger than she seemed.

Sharon expressed concern at the amount of time Lina had been gone. She was worried that production was off, that personnel were getting out of control. Lina offered several alternatives for the personnel problems and reminded her supervisor that not only did she have enough vacation and sick time to cover her absence, but that other workers had been copied on her organizational notes and should be expected to carry on well without her.

He hadn't thought of her that way. She was to marketing what he was to the parahero business, the team leader with the contingency plans. He had so much to learn about her. Londo leaned back in the chair and smiled to himself. He had given her her freedom.

It was just beginning the payback she deserved from him. She'd saved him from a lifetime of abject frustration. She'd smiled and opened her heart to him and overcome her fears to love him. She'd given him full rein over that body of hers. She'd promised him children.

And she'd vowed to stay with him forever.

"But we neeeeeed you," Sharon was pleading. "Look, if you want more money–"

The pleasure Lina was getting out of quitting danced in Lon's mind. She'd never been complimented that much on the job, and now she was getting triple-stroked. Good for her. Speaking of stroking, here was an interesting device… He could drill some holes in the bedroom ceiling for it. Then again, he could rig a couple anti-grav units for even more fun.

Londo wriggled in his chair. Sex was great. Now he could see why everyone raved so much about it. Finally he could as well. He had a very good idea of the feeling all these toys would supply. He could picture Lina when he used them on her. Or she used them on him. And the people in the pornos? He could be one of them now. He'd now been in those positions– well, some of them. And he would be again, thanks to his Lina.

The next page brought him up short. A slender, dark-skinned model gazed sulkily at him from the page. She looked like Aiko.

Aiko was dead. It should have been him instead. Not him dead. If he'd only given Aiko those kids to carry to safety, it would have been he who caught that blast. He could have taken it with little problem. But Aiko wasn't as invulnerable as he.

She had loved him with her last breath. Why couldn't he have loved her in the same way? Guilt had always plagued him that he didn't love her as much as she did him, but he'd always thought that given time, his love would deepen.

And now they were both out of time. Beautiful Aiko had left him forever.

Lon closed his eyes in pain. On the trip home from hyperspace he'd had his computer play a near-constant simulated consultation with his therapist, Adam. Adam told him he couldn't blame himself for the way things sometimes happened, that he alone was not responsible for everything turning out right. He should look to the parts of his life that were good right now, and value those whenever he could.

"You're a good man, Londo," his simulated therapist had told him. "Nothing is going to change that. Everyone has their own path to follow, and sometimes even you can't force them in the right direction at the right time."

Why did Aiko's path have to steer her to death?

Lina returned a few minutes later but came to a stop when she spotted the stack of completed order forms. She set her fists on her hips. "You realize that my name will never be mentioned here again without someone bringing this up," she said. Then she broke into laughter, and he laughed with her.

"Sharon says my discount's still in effect until I walk out the front door. You can pay Kaya down at the reception desk. You give the forms to her, tell them to ship it to us. I don't know what Starhaven's address is."

Londo showed her the address he'd written on the forms: New York. "My American address, since you people don't ship to Canada."

"Don't we get door-to-door delivery at Starhaven?"

"It's a little too far out in the country, *cherie*. I'd show you today, but I don't want to rush your first time there."

"Oh. Okay." She looked frustrated and shook her head again. "Unreality's setting in now that we're back home. We have so much to do. Does Starhaven have a landline? I need to give Sharon the number in case of emergency. And they want me to do an exit interview with the high honchos. Likely they won't listen to a word. We've had enough people point out the same problems through the years. It's a good thing sex sells despite everything, or this place would have gone under years ago."

"Leigh said something about pictures of management with goats–"

"Oh, you met Patti?" She twirled her index finger at him. "Turn around and let me see if she managed to attach herself to you."

"Lina?" Sharon's voice came from down the passageway.

"Twenty minutes," she assured Lon. "Not a second longer."

She was true to her word. Londo barely had time to go downstairs and give his order sheets to Kaya. She laughed uproariously when she saw the pile of forms.

"You won't tell anyone, will you?" he asked.

"Honey, this is what legends are made of!" Kaya wheezed with glee as Londo anxiously watched her belly. "How are you going to pay for all this?"

Lon reached into his wallet for his Sterling card. Kaya stopped laughing. Her mouth dropped open. "I've never seen one of those before," she said reverently as she took the card from him and saw the name on it. "Londo Rand. I thought Lina said Lon Starhart."

"We changed our name when we got married." Lon wondered if–

"Londo Rand… Londo Rand!" Kaya's neck almost whiplashed as she kept comparing the name on the card to him standing there. Her eyes began to roll back into her head, her jaw to slacken, before she bolted straight up in her chair. "Holy shit and a half! It's you! It's you!" She stabbed an accusing finger in his direction.

He didn't like very pregnant women getting overly excited. "Easy. You don't have to point it out to the world."

"Oh shit. Does Lina–? Of course she knows. You know she's psychic, don't you? Jesus christ." Shakily Kaya processed the card, passing the receipt to him to sign. "Could I get your autograph, too? While you're here, I mean? And one for the baby?"

"Sure," he said. "Just keep it down. I don't think Lina wants anyone here to know."

"Why not? Look, if anyone here's been slapped down hard by… well, by certain people, it's been Lina. One of the nicest people here, and least promoted. She's stood up for the employees when *some* people tried to screw them over. Seems to me that those employees would like to know that something good has happened to her." She shook that finger at him again. "You think about that."

Kaya waved at them from within the glass doors by her station as many of the marketing department saw them outside. Some turned to go back into the warm building, but Lina's better friends stayed to say goodbye.

"You be sure to come back. We'll take you two out to lunch somewhere nice," Sharon declared. "And while you're here, we can corral Lina into smoothing out whatever problems have come up since then."

"I'll come back for a few hours one day." Lina assured them and got a better grip on the cardboard box of her belongings. "I don't guarantee that Lon'll be able to make it. He's awfully busy. Now, y'all go back in; it's cold."

"Not that cold." Londo rocked on his feet thoughtfully, another box in his arms.

"It was so nice to meet you," Leigh told Lon. "He's real nice, Lina. A keeper if I ever saw one."

"I'll say," said one of the women. "You got any single brothers, Lon?"

"Not that I know of," he replied graciously. Good people here. "Sweetheart," Lon nudged Lina with his elbow, "Leigh says that my Maximus impression is very good."

"Best I ever saw, ever," Leigh declared as Ed told another marketer, "You should have seen it!"

"But I think my Valiant is better."

Lina almost said something, but then clamped her mouth shut. Londo grinned at her with his eyes and passed her the second box of her things, the one with the potted plants sticking out on top. "Here, baby, you hold this while I try it again. I want Leigh and Ed to say I do the best Valiant ever."

"Yeees, Lon."

He rubbed his hands together, looking around, prepping himself.

"This is going to be good," Leigh nodded to Ed.

4

The audience was eight of Lina's good friends, pornographers all. Londo straightened, using one hand to hold his jacket, Lincoln-like, as he orated. "Mahny people have asked me," he said grandly, "Vaillant, why ees eet we've nevair seen you… wiz a woomahn?"

The crowd tittered.

"Could it be zat parhaps all ees not pairadize in pairahero land?"

"That's good, that's very good!"

"He even looks like him, a little."

"How about you, Lina?" Londo asked her, nudging her again. "How do you think Valiant would answer that question?"

"I sink," Lina replied warily, "zat nowan would evair ask Vaillant zat in ze firs' place."

"That's a rotten accent." They made faces at each other.

"Go on, go on!" Sharon demanded. "You really had me going there for a moment. What would Valiant say to that?"

Ed laughed and said, "I think he wouldn't say anything. He'd just bust whoever asked him that in the chops. So long, jerkface reporter!"

"Maybe he's gay," one of the workers said, and Lina gave a snort. There was enough derisive laughter at the comment at it was. "Yeah, right, Valiant gay!" "You wish, Peter!"

"No, no!" someone else, her name was Meg, Lon thought, shouted through the noise. "He's got this secret identity and he's secretly married. Maybe even with secret kids. I read it in a magazine a long time ago."

Lon scratched his head. "But secret identities are such a pain! He'd have to put on an American accent all the time and wear really tacky clothes…" They laughed at him as he held his tee shirt out for them to see. "And his wife would probably tell him to wear horn-rim glasses or a wig so people wouldn't recognize him. Isn't that right, Lina?"

Londo scooped her and her boxes into his arms and she let out a surprised squeal. "He probably looks terrible in glasses. I think I need to work on my impression some more. Why don't I try this?" He leapt up into the air, his arms still full of wife and boxes, and hovered five feet off the sidewalk. "Does that help?" He asked the crowd.

"Holy–!" "Oh, shit!" "Valiant! It's really Valiant!"

"My Valiant's much better than my Maximus," he told Leigh sternly.

She gulped. "Uh huh," was all that came out of her throat.

"Holy shit, Lina, you married Valiant!" Sharon yelled.

"I did?" Lina blinked at the man carrying her. "You said it was just an impression!"

"A damned good impression."

"Yes, Londo."

Lon turned them both so they hung over the crowd, aware of the faces plastered against the windows of the building, the hands waving other employees to come over and see. "You guys keep this quiet for a while," he ordered the group. "At least until we announce. Which won't be for…" He looked at Lina expectantly.

"Don't ask me," she said. "I thought you could keep quiet for two hours."

"I tried, *chérie,* I tried." He grinned and touched her nose with his.

Sharon hopped from foot to foot while wringing her hands. "Can we tell everyone here?"

Londo considered. "Just tell them that it doesn't go any farther than these doors."

"Yeah, right," Lina murmured. She nodded at Sharon. "I'll give you a call when I can be in town. You have the new number."

"Emergencies only," Londo warned his wife's now ex-supervisor. "And you don't hand out that number to anyone. Eat it if you have to."

"Y-yes, sir," Sharon replied, her face a mask of sincere fear and respect.

"Which way's home, Kitten?"

"Thataway." Lina tried to point with her chin. She wiggled her fingers as she could around the boxes at her friends as they and the ground dwindled below them.

Dairy pastures and forest covered most of the three miles they flew over. Lina alternated clenching her eyes shut and stealing peeks at the view. Her directions came out in a squeak. Humming a silly tune to calm her, Londo aimed for a lane that was the merest sliver of a step above being gravel, winding through the early spring woods. "Passive solar," he noted with approval as they passed over the south-facing window wall of the indicated house. He landed lightly in front of the tiny green cottage on its long-roofed north side.

The property looked to be a little over an acre. It held a neat garden over the septic field, a graveled back patio, and two small fishponds. Forest filled out the rest. The road in front was not well-traveled but neither was it private. Neighbors lived diagonally in both directions across it.

"Not bad," he decided about the house. "Looks cozy." Too cozy for him. He liked much larger living spaces. Still… "It's cute. In a good way, I mean." With her still in his arms, he climbed the steps of the front porch with its heavy-duty trellis extending the roof. An enthusiastic if bare climbing rose had laid claim to it.

Lina shifted the boxes between them to allow her to dig into her jeans pocket. She drew out a key labeled "FRONT DOOR." Likely a copy, as the original had been lost in the fire back on Tiawa. She began to aim it at the door lock before cutting her gaze to him.

"I guess this is yours," she said slowly as she handed it over. She took back the boxes as he released her to stand on the porch.

"Our house now," Londo told her gently. "We'll get another copy made if you think you need one."

Lina's cheeks puffed in a moue. "Give me some time to switch gears," she apologized. "I guess this means we're really married, even after I've been living in your apartment–"

"Our apartment."

She nodded. "For a week. Top goes clockwise…"

"Bottom goes counter. I see it." The locks slid back into the door and Lon turned the knob. He gave the door a push and then blocked her access. Taking the boxes from her, he set them down and picked her up again. Then he carried his bride across the threshold.

"Now we're officially official." Lon touched her nose with his. "Mine," he said, and with a laugh she kissed him.

He still held her as he turned in a circle in the entry. With most of the second floor little more than a loft, the open ceiling under the sloping roof made it all seem bigger than it really was. The south wall of windows let in an expansive view of deciduous forest and light, which also opened up the place. He spotted problems in the wiring and insulation behind the walls, but they were minor. Still, if they were going to keep the place, they'd have to be fixed.

Two cats ran up to greet Lina, their tails straight in the air, and he heard more upstairs, claws on linoleum. "Hey, babies," Lina said as they paused at Lon's appearance. He set her down and looked them over as curiously as they did him. He owned cats now. Lots of them. "Mine and mine," he counted. "Mine, mine, mine…" The others hung back. Even to Lon's unschooled eyes, their body language displayed feline suspicion.

"C'mon sweeties, let's get you fed and pampered for the day, okay?" Lina led the herd into the galley kitchen to pour bowls of dry food. Another cat came through a kitty door farther back.

Lina changed their water and then reached into the fridge for milk. From his position in the tiny dining area, Lon noted the expiration date. She'd been shopping while he was gone. She poured the milk into a bowl that sat on the sill of the kitchen window. A skinny black cat yowled at her, and she lifted it up so it could get at the milk.

"This is Fafhrd," she explained. "She's the grand duchess, twenty-two years old at least. Though one of my vets swears she must be thirty."

"Thirty?" Lon asked, peering at the ancient thing. "I didn't think cats lived that long."

"They don't. I think. That's why she's at least twenty-two. She likes to be helped up to get her milk, but she can make it on her own. She just doesn't like to admit it."

Lina turned to Lon as she replaced the carton in the fridge. "That's acidophilus milk," she instructed. "It's the only kind she gets, the only kind she can digest. The others don't get milk at all. It's just that Faf gets huffy if she doesn't get her milk, she's very sweet otherwise. We have to humor her with this."

"But I always heard–"

"I lost a kitten that way. Most kittens are allergic to milk, and lots of cats are. It gives them the runs real bad. They dehydrate." She paused thoughtfully. "My vet is considering introducing an acidophilus supplement to the others' diet so they have, whatchacallit, good gut flora. We'll have to see about that. But in the meantime, we are milk nazis."

"No milk for you!" Lon shook his index finger at the group on the kitchen floor. The gray tabby of the herd took one look at him and fled out the kitty door. Lon groaned.

"Don't worry about it. Ember's shy. She'll warm up to you."

As Lina completed Fafhrd's meal with nutrient paste and then a thyroid pill delivered orally by a rubber-tipped syringe, she pointed out the rest of the cats and their foibles to Londo: Moose, the burly black cat who was last to come inside for supper, who had been abandoned out here along this country road. Lina said he was a bit of a bully and an adventurous loner. Shy Ember was the one who had taken a shine to Jae but who had few kitty friends. The one with the luxurious dark coat Lina called a "tortie" pattern was Katie Darling, although Lina introduced her as just Katie. According to Lina, it was important that he know Katie hated whichever cat was Molly, and vice versa.

Though he kept his distance from Londo, Obi-Wan the cuddly calico seemed to be team leader here, at least among the cats who wanted to be on a team. Calicos were often female, but Obi was an exception. Branstookah, or Bran-Bran, was the young male tabby dynamo, Obi's best friend, who came right up to Londo and sniffed him out with a suspicious nose before dissolving into a loud purr. Then came plump Molly, the golden girl, youngest of the herd, who knew she was fuzzy and adorable and rubbed up against Londo to let him have the honor of petting her. She hissed at Bran, who pretended he hadn't seen her but then used Londo's leg to hide behind so he could swipe at her, resulting in a spitting fury of a hiss. Bran scampered off, his tail merrily in the air for the trouble he'd caused.

Seven cats. Londo made a mental note to review this section on the floating camera's record as many times as needed. There was no way he could remember all this otherwise. He so carefully tried to pet these fragile little animals that Lina loved. He'd never been around cats before. When he was a kid he'd always begged Hal for a dog, and once he'd been out on his own with a crazy job schedule, he'd discovered he wouldn't have had the resources to care for one properly. Now he wasn't sure how much strength he should use with these things without accidentally crushing them.

At Lina's suggestion, he played with them indirectly using their toys. She gave him a litany of warnings about cat safety as well as lessons on their body language.

These pets really had been neglected for attention these past two weeks, and Lon and Lina tried to make up for it. They stayed an hour, mostly playing peek-a-boo out in the garden. Londo was astonished that the cats not only knew the game, but Katie and Bran in particular, with even old Fafhrd crouching behind a log, peeking out at them, seemed to get a kick out of it, as if they were fooling the humans. Cats *thought!* But though they enjoyed Lina chasing them, and then chasing her in return, they didn't appreciate Londo doing it.

It didn't help matters when Lon was so intent on hiding in plain sight from Katie, that he stepped on Molly's tail behind him. She let out a piercing howl that ended in hisses though Lon immediately jumped into the air.

"I'm sorry," he told her from above. "Ah, Emb— No, you're Molly. Molly, I'm sorry."

The cat backed away from him when he landed an arm's length away, crouching against the ground as spittle exploded from her furious mouth.

"Molly!" Lina ran over but the cat even edged back from her. "Daddy's sorry. It was an accident. It was just her tail, Lon. It looks okay. Aw yoo okay, baby? She's all right, Lon."

Still the cat hissed as if Londo were the devil incarnate.

"She'll get used to you." Lina's expression pleaded with him not to punish her for the transgression of having cats.

Damn her father anyway. "Yes, she will," Londo hastened to reassure her. "And she's going to like me. I'm going to protect her and the rest of her brood."

"Herd," Lina corrected him as he rose into the air again. Molly didn't like that at all. He tossed his jacket to Lina.

Londo darted to a troublesome tree hanging over the far end of the grassy meadow that marked the septic field's boundary. "Maybe she'll appreciate this. Let me fix this while we're here."

"I have a tree guy!" Lina called to him. "He's supposed to come out in a couple weeks to take care of that."

Half the tree was hanging limply, damaged from some winter storm. Londo examined the situation. A long crack ran the length of the tree trunk. Lightning had struck the tree at some point, and the storm had made matters worse. There was no saving it.

Have the cats stay back. You, too, he told Lina. With that, he swooped down to wrench the worst of the damage from the main tree and set it on the ground. He ripped major branches off the remaining tree before giving the base of the trunk a kick, severing it from the earth. Using his knee as a fulcrum, he began snapping the trunk into lengths of about twenty inches. Then he sank his thumbs into the wood, splaying it outward to form neat, fireplace-sized split logs. It took only a few minutes to finish the entire tree and neatly stack the wood.

He returned to his bride to collect his jacket. Her mouth still hung open. "I, ah, think I have a new tree guy now," she finally managed to say.

"*Bon.*"

His reward was tight hugs and electric kisses and her declaring to the world what a fabulous man he was. He could get used to this.

They retreated inside for a quick tour of the upstairs. Here was the art studio he should have expected. Lina's sparse body of work wasn't anywhere near museum quality, but the paintings had a life to them that he liked. Potential. He could see Lina in them.

"I like the colors," Lon decided. "I like what you're doing with the compositions." Definitely he'd make a space at Starhaven for her to continue this hobby. He paused to study what Lina claimed was her bedroom.

"Don't say it," Lina warned him. "I heard it all from Jae."

"And what was Jae doing in your bedroom?"

There it was in her again, that spark of upset when he mentioned Jae. Of course; Jae had been her arresting officer. Too bad. Lon wanted Lina and Jae to be friends.

"Wiley asked to read some of the books I had. He was with us."

Londo studied the full-sized bed doubtfully, crammed into its space with inches to spare, all too close to the sloping ceiling and a skylight. Originally it had been a walk-in closet. The skylight had been added later. Lina had turned the true bedroom into a library for most of her books, the living room into her studio, the vestibule and dining area into living room and client area… It was all quite efficient and logical, but damn, it was so cramped!

"Jae said he thought that sex might be possible," Lina said helpfully.

"I bet he offered to demonstrate," Lon said. He wasn't certain if he found that humorous or challenging. Lina was *his*.

"I doubt it would work," Lina said as she also considered the space as if for the first time. She rubbed Londo's arm. "You couldn't even stretch out in this bed, honey."

"I think the trick is not to stretch out."

Fifteen minutes later, with a large dent next to that skylight and ceiling plaster caked in Londo's hair, they called their experiment a disaster. "Jae's crazy," Londo declared, shaking his head like a dog to get rid of all the gunk. He checked out his hair in the mirror in Lina's bathroom and rinsed his head again, then shook it and rubbed it with a towel until his hair was reasonably dry. Damn, he hadn't any gel with him.

Lina called from upstairs, where she was vacuuming. The sound of suppressed laughter was in her voice. "Maybe Jae gets off by bonking himself on the head when he does it."

"I wouldn't doubt it. Well, at least we broke your bed in. *Our* bed in."

The bookcases downstairs held duplicates of some of his own books behind a small collection of *Star Trek* figurines, mostly stuff on ecology and social science, of all things. Her video collection showed the same doubling, but she didn't have all the action-adventure films he had, and he certainly didn't have all these chick flicks or *Star Trek* movies. How many had they made, anyway? Over here was some X-rated stuff. Hm. He hadn't seen some of these, but he'd ordered two of the titles back at the company. No great loss. These hadn't cost more than a couple dollars apiece.

"Time to get going," Lon called to her.

She came downstairs. "We need five minutes more," she told him, but the sparkle that had been in her eyes all day was gone. What had happened? She led him to her desk and opened deep drawers containing neatly-labeled folders. She showed him folders on her computer, told him her main password as well as where the file was that held all her other ones.

"Why are you telling me this?" he asked.

She pointed at the floating camera. "So you'll know where things are. In case I don't come back here."

"Why shouldn't you come back?" But he knew.

So did she. She took a deep breath and released it quickly. "I read where some mind controllers were punished with lobotomies. There was a story about a whole pack of 'em who had their minds wiped, whatever that means. It didn't sound good."

"You're not going to be wiped. There's no evidence against you. The case is groundless."

"And all too often courts and crazy people in charge punish the innocent. So this is just in case. If something happens to me, it'll be up to you to take care of my estate, such as it is. And my cats. Here, let me make a chart of which cats need to stay together. I know you'll never find someone to take them all."

Londo pressed his lips together. "They're mine," he said. "I'll take care of them." With that he spun the crown of his Legion ring the secret way Wiley had shown him so long ago, for an occasion entirely different from this, and snatched the recording camera from the air. He cupped it within his palms, sealing the edges of contact as only Valiant could. No sound, no visual could get in or out.

"Here's our backup plan," Londo informed Lina. Her mouth opened in shock, but she listened.

Lina gulped and strove again to understand. This was the world Londo traveled in. She was merely a stranger.

The first floor of Affiliated Systems Mega-Legion HQ held many of these small, secured rooms just for such meetings. She and Lon sat on one side of a table, while a woman in one of those bulky, heavy-looking AffSys suits sat across from them. She was taller than Londo, as per usual on this world. Her platinum hair of course was cropped within a whisper of her skull; the AffSys didn't like much hair. Her skin was a beautiful lavender, a shade Lina had not run into yet, and her face looked like someone had pulled her by both ears and stretched her features horizontally. It wasn't a bad look. It was just odd.

"Plible Red Woltrell," she introduced herself. When Lon asked where the rest of her legal team was, she told them that the Legion commander had deemed this security double-five. She was the only one at her firm with that high a rating.

Londo muttered something with a *"crisse"* in it, so Lina knew he was cursing.

"Not to worry, Valiant," Woltrell assured him. "I can handle this. I've dealt with mind control before."

"Prosecution or defense?" Lina asked.

Woltrell shrugged. "Prosecution. But that just means I know how they'll approach this, Mrs… Valiant." It was clear that the marriage of the famous and powerful Valiant had come not only as a surprise but a shock to the lawyer, wrapped up with a mystery. And add a charge of mind control in with it all…

Lina tried to shut off the impressions she was getting from Woltrell's mind.

Lon was sucking on his lips, making his mouth work in all directions as he thought. "I spent a lot of time in hyperspace going through the research, plus a few recent cases," he said.

"Excellent. I see your wife is listed as a fairly powerful telepath." Like a hawk spotting prey, Woltrell's head snapped to her right to hold Lina completely within her line of vision. "Are you a mind controller?"

"No!" Anger flushed through Lina until she realized that this might be what lawyers had to know. "Do we have client privilege, whatever it's called, Lon?"

"Absolute. It even holds with the camera." He tipped his head toward the ever-present recording device.

Lina nodded. "Okay. No, I'm not a mind controller. But I think I might know how it's done."

"Li–"

"It might come up," Lina told him firmly.

"But–"

"It might," Woltrell said, "but we need to avoid mentioning that. You're acquainted with the implants?"

Lina shook her head. "It's hooks. Metaphysical hooks. All it takes is imagination, manipulation of the etheric body."

Woltrell looked doubtful at that. She glanced at Lon, who nodded his head in agreement.

"That's what she says. She says this is a very minor problem on Earth, and she can undo it."

"No one can counter mind control, Valiant. Not without disabling the equipment or the controller."

"Then I guess I must have it wrong," Lina said slowly. "But it just seems to me…"

Lon put his hand on hers. "We'll take this the way the AffSys sees it. Let's not invite trouble by adding another flavor of mind control."

That sounded reasonable. Lina nodded.

"Good," Woltrell said. "We'll need to go over your history, how you two met, and see where they'll claim the control began."

So they– Londo mostly; he took charge of the situation, which was fine with Lina– told a condensed version of how one of Londo's enemies had thought Lina was a match for Lon, and used her to trap him into a situation where he might be rendered vulnerable permanently, or able to be experimented upon, or…

"She wanted to have Lon's baby," Lina confided.

"She did want reproductive material from me," Lon admitted. Woltrell paled.

"Clones? An army of Valiants…"

"Yes, there was that possibility," Lon said brusquely, and continued by telling her that in a battle with not one but two of his enemies, he'd been gravely injured. If Lina hadn't developed powers of teleportation and taken the chance of porting them here to Legion HQ where Wilder Mem-Bazer and Neutrino could render advanced medical aid, they'd both have been dead. After that, they remained in quarantine for well over a day.

"Quarantine?"

"I hadn't figured out how to biofilter yet," Lina admitted.

"And you just… teleported in?"

Londo's mouth actually quirked on one side. "It's a damned quick process. Takes about two, three minutes. Seems like a lot more when you're just hanging there in black nothingness."

But Stoan, whom this lawyer referred to as Commander Magnos, was already accusing Lina of mind-controlling Valiant. When they decided to get married after knowing each other only a few days, his insistence doubled down. He'd tried to stop the wedding, but had relented only when he discovered that the otherwise permanent marriage could be annulled within the first six months.

Woltrell seemed more amazed that their marriage wasn't a limited contract than anything else. She even shook her head before getting back to the subject at hand.

"You were called away to a hyperspace mission right after the ceremony," she prompted Lon.

"Yes. It lasted about six, no, five days. A bit over five days." His right cheek twitched, and Lina knew he was thinking about Aiko.

"Five days continuously within hyperspace?"

He nodded, but then amended, "We took a moment for recalibration for the return journey. Standard procedure."

Woltrell's eyebrows arched and a sly smile spread over her face. "And during this time in hyperspace, did you feel different? Did you act different? Did others comment on a change in behavior?"

"No, ma'am, I was still very much in love with my wife. My attitudes toward my life, the Legion, and my mission were exactly the same."

"That's it then," Woltrell declared triumphantly. "Hyperspace severs mind control. Telepathy can't cross the barrier in either direction. Now all we need are personality tests. Do we have time to put you in a hyperspace chamber?" She finally turned her attention back to Lina. "Ordinarily I'd put you through a truth barrage, either chemical or telepathic. But the commander says we can't bring non-secure outsiders in on this, and well, if you are a mind-controller, you might be able to hide the results by making us think we saw passing results when we didn't." She tapped her chin thoughtfully. "Then again, mind controllers can only control one person at a time. The really strong ones can do two."

Lon cleared his throat. "Ah, you're not up on the latest intel," he said slowly. "We've had reports of controllers who held a dozen thralls."

"A dozen?" Woltrell sat back in her chair, shock playing across her lavender features.

"We don't know how they're doing it. Dr. Mem-Bazer has two teams researching, and Psyche is trying to get Tishana intel for us."

"Any word on the hyperspace disconnect?"

"I haven't seen reports on them breaking that barrier, but that's not to say they haven't." Lon's scowl was grimmer than usual, though when he glanced to Lina he tried to clear it. Unsuccessfully.

Woltrell's expression was similarly sour. "We'll research that before the appeal," she said. "And don't worry, we will appeal."

Lina dragged her feet as they walked down the dark Legion halls hand in hand, the red line high on the walls following her. They passed other people and tried not to notice when some of them turned around to stare, either at them or the line. "First of all," she decided to say, "I'm sorry for causing you all this trouble."

"You didn't—"

"Even though I didn't really cause it. It's all in Stoan's fevered little mind."

Lon grunted. In an approving way, Lina thought. After all, they were being recorded. He couldn't agree that his boss was a lunatic.

"Second, I want to fire our lawyer. Handling a case while believing in ultimate failure is not the way to operate."

"You have someone else in mind?" He sounded resigned, even though Lina could almost feel the gears in his brain working. She'd married a smart guy, she had. He was trying to come up with a plan. Or likely a fourth or fifth plan.

"No," she said. "Third, I want to know something: How many times has someone appealed a Legion case… and won?"

"I could make a guess," Lon grumbled. "Look, they'll have body-reading scans on you the entire time, a souped-up kind of lie detection. Make sure every word you say is the truth."

"I wasn't planning on–"

##Incoming call from Earth, code green,## the air announced next to Lon.

Lon inhaled sharply. "That could be Hal," he told Lina. "He wouldn't want to miss the funeral. Puter, who is it?" he asked as he broke into a trot that Lina tried to match. He explained, "Green means a call from someone I don't want to ignore."

##Michael and Ruth Rand,## the computer replied.

"The gRands! It's about time! Tell them to hold. I want to take this in quarters."

Lina just ported them there, and Lon stumbled before he realized what had happened. "Right," he said and then demanded, "Where are you going?"

"I'm not going to meet your grandparents with my hair all mussed," Lina insisted as she ran to the bathroom.

"Puter, tell 'em we'll be on in a minute." Two beeps. "Lina! They won't care how your hair looks. It looks fine." He caught a glimpse of his own in a mirrored plaque and smoothed it, straightened his jacket.

"Coming!" Desperately Lina patted her hair again as she hurried back from the bathroom and took the seat on the couch next to where Londo had sat. "What do I say? What do I call them? What do we do? Oh, we have to tell them about… They knew her, didn't they?"

"Right. Give me a few minutes to figure how to do this. But let's end the conversation on a positive note," he said grimly and signaled the air. A glow unrolled before them, quickly forming a screen that displayed in startlingly real 3D a couple sitting in a Terran living room just as if they were actually there with them. The room was tastefully decorated in comfortable if high-end furniture. Potted plants and framed photos were displayed on side tables. Though there was still faint light coming through some windows in the background, house lights were on.

"Londo!" the black man, possibly in his late forties, exclaimed. He wore a colorful sweater vest over a short-sleeved white shirt. One arm rested on the back of the couch around his wife. "Keep us waiting, will you? What's with all the messages?"

"Where have you been?" Londo demanded. "Where's Hal?"

"We drove down to Louisiana for a couple weeks, son. Ruth and I got a hankering for some good live jazz, and we had to wait until the worst of the tourists cleared out from New Orleans. I didn't take the cell with us. You know, make it a real vacation. Sorry about that."

"You bet you are." Lon mimed wring-your-neck signs that the Rands waved off with chuckles.

Ruth Rand was of an indeterminate age. Thirty? Forty? Shouldn't she and Mike Rand be in their seventies? She wore a flowered print shirt over neat slacks. She said, "So Londo, what is it? What's so important?"

"Where's Hal? He hasn't been answering my calls either."

"I suppose he's out and about."

Mike Rand scratched his head. "I believe he left a message about a mission that might take a week or two. Or was that a month? I'd have to check."

Londo sighed. "A helluva time for you people to take off," he muttered.

"Hello," the woman said pleasantly to Lina. "Lonnie, be polite and introduce us."

Lon tried to make it all appear casual. "This is Lina Starheart," he said. "Lina, Mama Ruth and Papa Mike Rand, my grandparents."

"So pleased to meet you." Lina bobbed her head. The Rands! She'd always thought the papers used old pictures of them to show them in their prime. Here they were– in their prime for real. These were the people who had helped raise Londo. His family. Hers, now.

Both of them returned her greeting with little curiosity. She was just someone who happened to be in Lon's apartment.

But Mama Ruth asked, "English?"

"I'm from Earth." Lina gave her a smile that she hoped didn't look too nervous. Were her teeth chattering? Then she felt the dark gray energy roll off Londo and her smile dissolved. She turned to him, but held herself back from taking his hand. Not now. Instead she touched his arm as a friend might do.

Lon's mouth worked. "I've got some bad news. Very bad. And I don't know how to break it gently."

"It's not about Hal, is it?" Ruth covered her heart with her hand.

"*Non, non, pas du tout.* It's… Aiko."

"No…" It came out as a groan.

"I'm afraid so." Londo told them about it as Ruth wept. Into Lon's final pause, Mike wiped his eyes.

"She was so young," he said. "So beautiful. I'd hoped… Son, I'd always hoped that you two–"

"I know, Papa Mike." Londo took the tissue that Lina handed him and used it to cover his nose as well as his trembling mouth. When he managed more control, he said, "The funeral's on Threeday. At night."

By now Mike had both arms around his weeping wife. "If there's one good thing, it's that we're still packed. If we leave right now we can be there in plenty of time. We want to be there, if we can."

Lon nodded. "She'd want you to be here, too. I'll arrange it with Security. But you two get some sleep in your own beds tonight. There's going to be some… unconnected business I have to handle tomorrow. Top security. I won't be able to join you. It should take up most of the day, if not the night."

Lina tried not to flinch. What condition would she be in at this time tomorrow?

Lon continued, "We have a new transporter that can get you here. It only takes a few minutes."

"What? Earth to Sarastor?"

"A few minutes!" Ruth exclaimed.

"It may not be working after tomorrow," Lina reminded Lon. If the Legion delivered their punishment immediately…

"It'll work," Londo growled at her from the side of his mouth.

"Since when? Is this one of Wilder's inventions?" Mike demanded.

"Since… about a week and a half ago." Londo drew his hand through his hair. "Damn, I wish you'd had your messages forwarded!"

"Lonnie, stop cursing! Oh, baby, I know you're hurting. But still…"

"Dammit, Mama Ruth, this time I deserve to curse. You were the ones who didn't collect your messages, right? That means you can't blame me, right?"

"What is it? Is someone else hurt, son? Are you all right? Did they let you see anyone there? Doctor Colam?"

"I did a long puter sim with Adam," Lon assured them. "I'll be okay. I *am* okay. Well, as much as can be expected. Wait a minute." He activated the coffee table electronics and searched, calling up a small auxiliary screen that he fast-forwarded through. "Here," he announced. "I know Aiko's death has been a terrible shock, but there's something else I need to tell you about right now. It's something good. I mean, really good. Watch this. You'll like it."

Screen-in-screen showed the two of them and Jae in the holographic Feithi meadow, bedecked in their wedding regalia. Lina held her bridal bouquet as she and Londo exchanged glorious smiles.

"By your vows and by the symbols you wear," Jae as minister intoned, "you show the universe that you are united for all eternity. Now turn and face these people. Who here bears witness to this marriage?"

"I DO!" Came the shouted response from the audience of hundreds of Legionnaires and their families.

"Let the record so show. Now, witnesses: behold husband and wife!"

Londo kissed Lina to seal the contract.

The tape ended and Londo waited, squeezing Lina's hand. She held her breath. Both his grandparents were sitting there with eyes and mouths wide.

"And you missed it!" Londo accused them.

But she's white, Ruth thought as her eyes began to blink again.

There was a quick, similar thought from Mike as he stared at Lina. "Ah," he stuttered.

"You know I've always been partial to redheads," Londo said as he waited for a real comment.

People can't help what they think, Lina told him. **It's unfiltered. This unintentional broadcasting stuff is usually pretty rough. You'll learn.**

Londo explained, "She's Terran. Southern US, even– North Carolina. Papa Mike, don't we have cousins there?"

****_But she's not Aiko,_**** Ruth thought loud enough to hear.

Mike gathered himself though "_married_" and the question of just how much that entailed, leaked from his mind. "Cousins… North… I'm sorry, your name was…?"

"Lina," Londo said gently. "Carolina O'Kelly Starheart. Our married name is Starheart."

"Hello," Lina said again.

****_Married? Married! …Starheart? What's the matter with "Rand?"_****
"Em… I, ah…" Ruth tried to speak and obviously had no idea where to begin.

"Mama Ruth will figure it out about three seconds after we sign off," Londo assured Lina. He turned back to the screen. "I know you two will want to discuss all this just between yourselves, without me being able to hear you through the walls. So you do that, and you get some sleep, and you signal us in three days, Sarastor time, when you're ready to come." He twitched his fingers in a variety of signals. "There. I just sent the whole wedding for you. Don't you dare say a word about this to Hal or anyone, or I'll throttle you both! I swear it!"

"Now, Lonnie–"

"No! This is my news, and I've got three contingencies for how to tell Hal. None of them contain blabbermouths."

"Um," Ruth said.

"You can access the news about Aiko just about anywhere. I'll fill you in on any details you want when you get here. The Legion hasn't announced the wedding yet. We don't want it to detract from… what she's due. So we'll see you in three days," Londo said quickly. "Lina, show them that you can put a sentence together."

"Ah, I'm looking forward to meeting you in person," she managed. "I've heard so much about you. Good. Good things."

"Very good. Starheart out," Londo grinned at the screen and it blanked.

5

Lina called out Londo's name, urging him on as he felt himself getting ready, nearly there. She clutched him, those fingernails digging into his back, the exquisite pain adding to the buildup. "Oh yeah," he gasped in her ear. "Yeah, I'm–"

A soft buzzer went off next to their heads. Lon tried to ignore it. He wasn't sure if Lina had even heard it. He could feel her like a coiled spring, about to loose herself. He clenched his teeth and groaned, sweat pouring off him as his hips strained against her, fighting to gain deeper entry. Don't come until she does. Hold on… Almost. Almost!

The buzzer sounded again. Then again, louder with each time. It wasn't going to stop. "*Crisse!*" Lon finally shouted in frustration, and withdrew. He paused to huff out his frustration before starting to respond. Then he glanced at Lina.

It took her another moment to catch her breath. Then she put her hand over her mouth and nodded. Lon made the quick grab-and-fist gesture.

Stoan's voice was too cool, a hint of cruel humor coming through. "One hour warning, Londo. Actually, a little less than that by now. I thought you'd appreciate a wake-up call if you weren't *up* already."

Lon ran his hand through his dark hair only to rub his face, and gave a black look that missed its target. "Noted, Commander. One hour."

Communications cut from the other end with a blip and Lon collapsed onto the bed next to Lina. "I'm sorry, baby. I'm so sorry. *Ostie de tabarnak.*" He sat up and threw the pillows against the wall in his embarrassment and anger.

Her hand still covered her mouth, but now she stifled a giggle. "Oh, honey... Let's just both beat him up sometime, shall we? I'll find us a dark alley somewhere."

He started to reply, but she crouched next him, using her mouth and hand at the same time that her mind meshed with his, creating a double-feedback of physical sensation. His cells recognized her and only her, lowering their defenses. The double-feedback reassured them both that he'd do her no harm.

"Oh. Oh. Less than an hour, Lina. No time for this. *Ah oui*, that's it..."

What are they going to do, start my trial without me? She lavished attention on her groom. It didn't take him long to shout his approval and then collapse back on the pillows. He promised her payback and more after the trial, but knew that both of them hid the thought that this might have been their last time together.

Londo had come up with a few more plans he needed to tell Lina away from the recording camera. All of them included his never returning here to Legion HQ. Well. Couldn't be helped. He'd make a name for himself somewhere else–with Lina by his side.

"We have been summoned to a Legion meeting," he reminded her. "One hour. *Euh–crisse*, look at the time! Only sixty minutes! We have to get ready."

Lina was used to some of the differences now, such as Sarastoran hours and days being so much longer than Earth's. "What do you wear to one of these things? Oh, I know what you wear."

His black faux leather Valiant uniform. Mm, so sexy. Lina rubbed his chest, imagining the striped shirt there, and then slipped her arms around him, so happy to have him back. She sensed the satisfied ardor that Londo felt. "How about a civilian? I've got tee shirts and jeans and my certified crappy suit. That pareo might be a little too tropical for this, right? Legion Protocol would have a cow."

Lon started to nuzzle her hair, then glanced again at the time and gently detached her from himself. "We'll start with the suit and work from there. You know about Sarastoran body taboos?"

"I got the cover-up fashion lecture, if that's what you mean."

"Right."

Lina watched him get out of bed and rifle through a dresser drawer. Skin like the Mediterranean sun, all brown and toasty. So warm to the touch, rippling with crested waves of muscles. Look at the way his spine curved so regally when he bent. That tightly-packed, round butt.

What had they been saying? She blinked herself back to reality. "I was waiting for you to get back to tell me what kinds of clothes you want me to wear."

He raised his eyebrow at her as he snapped a blue wrap around his waist.

"No, really. I'm your wife now; gotta please my man. To a point. It would be nice to know what that point was."

He shook his head, that slow grin heating her blood. "I like what you have on now."

She stretched out on the bed to tease him. "So I shall become a nudist to please you, my darling Londo. I'm ready for the meeting now. Or do they require shoes?"

He reached out his hand to pull her up. "Time's running out, Kitten. Get in the shower and then your suit. I'd invite you to my shower, but..."

"The time." Lina rose up to rub noses with him over their smiles.

But when she returned (with him still in the bathroom fiddling with his hair) and started to visualize her suit, still in her closet back home, Lina heard, **No.**

"No?" Lina asked her guides as Londo came into the room. He wore his famous uniform and looked like the cover of *GQ* and *ParaWatch* mixed together. Woof.

"No what?"

"*They* don't want the crappy suit," she told him.

His eyebrows rose and he puffed out his cheeks. "That must be one hell of a lot of crap, then."

"What? The what?"

Londo followed her as she retrieved her padd from the living room. "*They* want... Well, it's silly. They keep saying 'DragonCon.' Yes, yes, big dragon breathing fire, I get it."

She showed Lon how, in times of boredom during her arrest, she'd fooled around with cosplay costumes for herself. It was one of those bucket lists of hers:

to screw up the courage to do cosplay at a big convention. "I figured purple body makeup and maybe some wings," she said as he examined her final design. "But this isn't the time for cosplay. This is serious."

"I like it," Londo declared. He gestured and talked to the padd until the design incorporated a capelet that came down to the middle of the back, as well as long sleeves. That done, he handed the padd to Lina. "Your wardrobe, Madame."

A *bing* indicated arrival of the piece in the apartment's delivery bin.

"It's not delivery, it's a replicator," Lon told her. "A souped-up duplication device. Well, most of the time. The food service units are the same thing, but I don't think the food that comes out of them is up to par. People here..." He shrugged his shoulders to say *...literally have no taste.*

"Okay," Lina said doubtfully but she trotted off to the bathroom with the bundle.

First she examined herself in the bathroom mirror. Makeup couldn't hurt. To apply it, she bent over the device she'd been given the other night so its rim sealed with her hairline, and resisted thinking of herself as a powdered Marie Antoinette heading toward *la guillotine.* The process took only a few moments more than a blade crashing to its target.

Then she ported on her new outfit piece by piece, using the *Bewitched*-inspired trick she'd been trying to perfect. At least it wasn't glorified plastic wrap like they'd made her wear the other night.

Oh god, Jae and that other night. No, she refused to think about him, about what they'd done. She'd tell Londo after all this was over. If she came out of this intact. She would. Use *when,* not *if.* Thoughts influenced the universe.

She'd quit her job to create a blank canvas for their marriage. She'd told Jae she wouldn't see him for the next few months to get him out of her mind completely.

This marriage belonged to her and Londo, though at this point she was baffled at how it would progress. Even if she came out of this trial hale and healthy, what was her role? Londo was Valiant. How would he fit the marriage into his life? Legion Protocol had really stupid subservient ideas for spouses that she had no intention of following.

Darn TV Land anyway for not covering these kinds of problems in their depictions of happy Terran marriages! She'd have to come up with some ideas and run them past Lon. There'd be lots of wrong turns, she knew, but they had to learn from them, and quickly, if Londo were to keep to his parahero schedule.

It still took a tug or two after each port to get the clothing in proper place– especially the bra, which was a Terran one because Sarastoran women didn't seem to use the things– she'd have to research on that– but when she emerged for Londo's appraisal, he actually took a step back in shock from where he'd been pouring two glasses of juice in the kitchenette.

"How'd you get dressed so fast?"

She crinkled her eyes at him and twirled. This would not do. Surely he could see that. One did not wear Halloween costumes to high court.

The costume was a simple dress with a gauzy handkerchief skirt that billowed and flowed like a ballerina's when she moved. The bodice was cut straight across, which accentuated the curve of the top of her breasts without being the show-all neckline too many female cosplayers wore. A mottled pattern of spring green and cream was designed to invoke leafy shadows. It darkened to a graduated, dappled forest green on her soled tights.

"We should order the fairy wings," she said as he studied her.

"It's good," he concluded. "You look beautiful in it. They'll be impressed. *Bon,* we are dressed. We'll get breakfast there."

"Eat during the trial?"

"We still have items concerning the… funeral… to deal with before that."

"And I can listen in?" Oh right, they were going to mind-wipe her or somesuch afterward.

"They are not. You remember what we talked about."

She glanced at the camera that hovered next to them. Lon had assured her that he'd set it for privacy mode when they'd had sex. It still recorded, but the security required to view that part was practically impossible to crack. It would take a high court order.

Were there courts higher than the Legion one?

She went back to the bathroom to give final attention her long auburn hair in front of the wide mirror there.

Londo leaned against the frame of the doorway to watch as she caught it back in a loose braid.

"I love your hair," he said. He moved over to stroke it softly, taking in the reflection of the two of them together. Lina leaned against him, gazing into the reflection of his brown eyes. "Braided or loose. Both have their–"

The buzzer sounded again, followed by Stoan's voice. "Valiant!"

"*Crisse,*" Londo said, taking Lina's hand. "We're going to have to run–"

Picture it in your mind, Lina told him silently.

She ported them to his opera box of a cubicle, overlooking a broad stage. ***See, I told you I'd get faster with practice,*** she smugly declared.

I'm impressed.

Down on the main floor, Stoan stood braced over some kind of communications console, his eyebrows knotted together.

"We're here, Commander. On time," Lon said into his ring.

Stoan startled up at them, and Lon gave him a little flip of a salute as they both sat down.

Londo took one chug of the juice she ported in as the special meeting began, then set the glass to the side of the built-in desk in front of him. For himself he ignored the breakfast pies that popped out of a slot, but offered them to Lina. She didn't seem to have an appetite either.

To her he seemed calm enough on the outside, nodding and giving a little half-smile to people who checked in privately via monitor to this cubicle, but between calls he ran his fingers quickly over keyboards. Three page-sized monitors floated in the air to his view, filled with small text. It all looked very legal, and he frowned at the screens as he read them.

"Problem?" Lina whispered to him and got a quick, jerking shake of his head in response as he queried for more information. "Don't worry," was all he said.

So Lina looked around the great theater or auditorium ("Main meeting room," Londo whispered to her out of the side of his mouth), then around the cubicle to see if she recognized anything there among the lit signs and screen triggers on the desk. Though it held one wide flat area with little on it, there were also two different angled levels to allow for better use of the all the keypads.

The side and far edges of the desktop ended in a number of permanent vertical screens. Two of them were larger than the rest, one now showing a closeup of Stoan down in the spotlight on the main floor and the other, someone responding to him: the meeting's official participants. Some screens didn't appear until called for, materializing out of thin air to float in an orderly fashion that didn't obscure either of the permanent screens or the view.

More surfaces displayed a confusing constellation of lights, abbreviated labels and buttons. As if there weren't already an information overload, a constant info stream scrolled just above the top tier of monitors.

One text screen caught Lina's attention. She squinted at it, trying to decipher the writing, and thought it was the meeting agenda. Yes. A yellow rectangle highlighted a line of type: updated casualty reports from the *Travern*. They were talking about that now. A little way down the list, Lina saw her name. "Inquiry of Carolina O'Kelly for mind control of Valiant," it said in Panlingua.

Lon must have noticed the troubled look on her face. He squeezed her hand. **It's going to be all right. Whatever they come up with, we can take it. And if worse comes to worst, well, I do have a bit of a reputation we can lean on before we have to resort to Plan B.**

Just a bit? She summoned a smile for the most famous megahero in the galactic sector. **But Lon, going on the run is not a solution.** Plan B had a few variations, but it still boiled down to that. **It looks cool in the movies, but reality doesn't work that way.**

It won't come to that, chérie. *Besides, I have three more contingencies I'm working on.*

There were preliminaries to be expected from a formal meeting of any large group: brief summaries of goings-on, oddly with no word about the scuttled planetary invasion of the past few days. Lina wanted to ask Lon more about what they were talking about down there, but he told her, **Later.**

Stoan announced the agenda for Aiko's funeral. It would be telecast not only to all member worlds of the Affiliated Systems but the Unaffiliated Worlds of the sector as well, and of course all pomp and ceremony would be given to honoring such a great hero. A timetable of those events ran on one of the cubicle's screens. There was Lon's name; he would be giving a eulogy. The room was quiet for some time after that. Then Stoan straightened at the podium.

"Carolina O'Kelly," he proclaimed. He pointed to a spot lit chair in the center of the stage. From the side, Ms. Woltrell walked in to take a podium next to it.

I'm coming, too, Lon said. He scooped up a portable padd the size of a credit card that he'd synced to his monitors. They ported down and she took the chair, Londo standing beside her.

"Valiant–" Stoan began.

"I stand beside my wife," Lon declared, stony-faced. He placed his left hand on her shoulder.

"Permitted." Stoan referred to the informational monitors of his podium as he addressed the convention of Legionnaires. Lina could see hundreds of faces in the hive that ranged above and around her, all watching her curiously under their dim lights, compared to the spotlights on the stage.

Quite a few of the windows were empty. Some members must still be on missions; the Legion currently had about 500 on its rolls. Let's see, thirty per-cent– or was that more?– were assigned to the Legion stations elsewhere in the sector. A lot were stationed on AffSys worlds. There were several space outposts as well. Lon said that usually another ten percent were out on medical leave at any one time. That left…

Most of the missing members are watching this wherever they are. It's a compulsory meeting, even for redlined members, Lon told Lina. Redliners were those who were hospitalized. She nodded.

Holding a holographic screen in the air, Stoan announced, "I have here testi-mony from both Dr. Mem-Bazer and Neutrino as to the mysterious circumstances leading up to your marriage, Valiant."

Lon was scanning the audience. "Both of whom seem not to be here today, Commander."

"We need all witnesses present," Woltrell declared. "Statements can't be cross-examined."

"They are otherwise occupied," Stoan stated as he turned to Lon. "It concerns the Aldierra situation."

"Ah yes, Aldierra. I'm afraid I can't tell you about that, Ms. Woltrell." Lon politely nodded at their lawyer. "My wife played a major role in that mission, which concluded– How *did* it conclude, Commander? I don't see any new flags around here, so I must assume–" His eyes sparked at his commander, daring him *not* to include it as part of the record.

Stoan addressed his remarks to Woltrell. "The counsel will note that this matter is not to be discussed in any manner with anyone under Level Four within Legion HQ and Level Five outside. Dr. Mem-Bazer and Neutrino and… Ms. O'Kelly… stopped the invasion fleet, without Planetary Defenses help. Mem-Bazer and Neutrino are now in diplomatic discussions, as Aldierra has not only called off the invasion but is going to be closely allied with the AffSys, at least in terms of requiring interplanetary aid and assistance."

"Invasion fleet?" Woltrell asked. Her head jerked to regard her client.

Londo didn't try to hide his satisfied smile as he turned to Stoan. "So my wife told me. I just wanted to remind everyone here of the stakes and who it was who performed a Legionnaire's duty. And if any of you don't know about it, look it up now. If it weren't for work my wife accomplished, we might not be holding this building today. It seems to me that this should score a helluva lot of brownie points. Maybe even a thank you. We're waiting."

"Too much coincidence, Valiant. She suddenly appears and all of a sudden you're lying dead for a few minutes in the lab, and then there are… lights… and you're married, and then this invasion–"

"I've had coincidence up to my ears and beyond for the past week, St– Commander," Lina interrupted as she stood. Must remember to call Legionnaires by their cape names only. "I can't speak for Lon, but this is not something I'm used to either. Up until now I've led an ordinary life."

"Then you have no proof to stand in your favor."

"Commander Magnos," Woltrell said, "I contend that the Legion has no proof to bolster your argument either. My client does not control minds. I have submitted a preliminary list of mind controller characteristics which the Legion has already tested her for. According to the records to which I was given access, she has not demonstrated any of them to a degree the law would accept."

"The threat has changed radically in recent months," Stoan declared. "The old way of discerning mind controllers no longer stands."

"Then this court must furnish defense with updated and specific profiles used for testing."

Lina glared at Stoan. "To you I'm some plotting Terran witchdoctor telepath who's latched onto Valiant. I know you–and some of you–" she widened her arms to take in the entire audience, "are thinking mind control. I don't know how to begin to disprove it." She turned to Londo. "So tell me what's the basis here: innocent until proven guilty?"

"*Non.*" He regarded her levelly. "Security needs to be absolute within these walls. Presumption of guilt until innocence is proven."

Woltrell grasped the sides of her podium and leaned forward. "I expect examination of this case to be of direct concern to the charge, with time allotted concerning new guidelines for us to format a reasoned response."

Stoan just stared at Londo. Londo held his silence.

So it was up to Lina to break it. "Swell," she said, and turned to Stoan. "So what's the program?" she asked, hands on her hips, her mouth set into a defiant line.

"We have questions for you. Sit."

She did.

They asked her everything they could think of, trying to establish the basest of motives on her part. How did she meet Londo? That alone caused the coincidence flag to stand at attention. She had to explain about her new clients, and then about her clients in general, what she did moonlighting as a psychic advisor, then about people who called you out of the blue to offer you free vacations to Tiawa in the South Pacific from an agency that had been recommended by those new clients, and how Londo had been there caught powerless after fighting Terry Rhodes–

Who was Terry Rhodes? At least Londo could answer that one. He'd known and battled Terry and Dr. Menlo for years. Was she affiliated with any interstellar activity? Had Lina known her before?

"Terry said that they'd had to use people fourth-hand in order that Lina wouldn't catch on to the plan," Londo told the group. "She had to hire people who hired people to see her."

Terry and the infamous Dr. Menlo had trapped the two of them on Tiawa. Using experimental devices, Menlo had ripped away Londo's powers for a few days and Terry set an army of mercenaries at their heels, forcing them to run. Lina's powers had come upon her suddenly, probably the result of a brick hitting her and doing *something* to her brain, and then they hadn't had to run. They'd ported across the island and gained a few days' safety before Terry had found them in the end. The entire scheme had been to study Londo's powers as they regenerated. Maybe.

Why did Terry say that she'd suspected Londo of being a telepath? Did she deal with telepaths? Maybe mind controllers?

Lon was trying to cooperate with his commander, but he scowled through most of this. "I might have mentioned a few instances that could have been construed as telepathy. Terry likes to theorize. She would have latched onto anything odd. Of course, it did turn out to be true…"

Quiet consternation in the gallery broke out.

"Yes, I'm a telepath now," Londo said to the people who did the talking.

"Is this a side-effect of mind control?" someone asked.

Suddenly a flurry of loud conversation erupted in the audience, quickly narrowing to four people who began to speculate about mind control implantation and catalyzed telepathic abilities.

In spite of all the talk, they didn't seem to be making progress with specifics and proof, so Lina took advantage of the diversion to satisfy her curiosity. **Did Terry or Dr. Menlo know how your powers work?** she asked Londo privately. He turned to her as Stoan controlled the discussion around them.

What do you mean?

If they knew that, then maybe it would make sense to think of you as a telepath, or to use a counter-telepathic means to take your powers away

What are you talking about?

"You don't know, do you?" Lina vocalized in her shock.

"Order! What are you doing over there?" Stoan barked at them. "Keep your conversations on an audible level for everyone to hear."

"One moment, Commander," Lon told him, turning back to Lina. "What do you mean?"

Your powers are psionic in nature. You knew that, right?

Psionic? Lon's brows constricted in confusion.

Wiley never told you, at least?

"He's never been able to figure out much about them. Are you sure?"

Lon, maybe we shouldn't be discussing anything along these lines here. Lina's gaze darted around this army of powerful strangers. **Just how secure is this place? Do you trust every last one of these people? If Menlo knew and used that knowledge to make that bazooka-thing, then Out Here there could certainly be others with the knowhow...**

"Speak," Stoan commanded. "Vocalize. The recorders can't pick up telepathy. I'll hold you both in contempt, if nothing else."

"Valiant. Mrs. Valiant," Woltrell urged.

Lina shook her head resolutely. **Recorders– I'm not going to endanger you, Lon. I'm not going to say anything like this where someone could use it against you.**

"Stop recording for a few minutes," Londo ordered. He looked up at Stoan, their eyes a battle of wills.

"Why?"

"I'll tell you when you stop recording, Commander," Lon told him.

Stoan considered for a moment. "Computer," he finally said to the air, "stop recording until told to resume. Deadman switch set for five minutes. Privacy curtain around the counselor. Stand by, remote members. Pause transmission." Double beeps of acknowledgment followed each order.

"Okay, Valiant, what's up?"

"Lina..."

"Are you sure about this?"

"I'm sure. Tell them."

Lina sighed and turned to Stoan. "I didn't know that Lon didn't know that his powers are psionic in nature, that it's really no great wonder he's a telepath when he's got so many other psionic abilities going on."

"And what psionic abilities would those be?" Stoan crossed his arms over his chest.

"All his parapowers," Lina said. The gallery stirred. "They're all psionic."

"How is invulnerability psionic?" Lon asked.

"I told you before; maybe you didn't understand. Your cells– they're all emitting a psychokinetic kind of force field. Equals invulnerability."

"Strength."

"Same thing, basically. Psychokinetic in nature, mind over matter on a cellular and holistic level."

"Flight." Lon answered himself. "Same thing?"

"That's probably why you can fly so fast." Lina smiled as she saw comprehension slowly lit his wonderful face. "Speed of thought, and all that."

"Vision," Lon said triumphantly, knowing that he'd stumped her.

She shook her head at him. "Clairvoyance. It doesn't operate the same way mine does, though. I need an anchor, a starting point to get mine going. You seem to start here…" she put her hand in front of his eyes and then moved it away. "And then you sort of telescope it, working your way out, moving through the distance and peeling it back layer by layer until you see what you need to see. At least I think you do. There are all kinds of ways to accomplish remote viewing. Is that how it appears to you? The telescoping, the peeling?"

Lon frowned. "Well, yes. It's clairvoyance?"

"At least all this explains why you told me you weren't clairvoyant. That had me stumped."

"It would account for the instantaneous nature of it, not having to wait for the speed of light to slow things. But how about… heat breath?"

"Psychokinetics– speeding up molecules to heat something. You use your breath to cool things off, too. Same thing, done opposite. The breath is often used to garner more psychic energy. And as for your hearing: clairaudience."

"Never heard of it."

"Very funny. I listen to my guides all the time. You seem just to hear things on the physical plane. Your endurance comes from linking into universal white light. It strengthens you, lets you operate longer than others. You're a psychic nova, Londo."

The galley stirred before a single voice rose above the murmur. "How? Why do his powers seem to mimic Maximus's so much? The Lectori seem to have wanted to match him as closely as possible."

The alien Lectori had kidnapped Londo when he was a child and experimented on him for years to give him the powers. "I don't know," Lina responded. "Maybe Lon was influenced by Maximus's being able to do it all. After all, they'd only developed the flight and strength in you before you met him, right?" She turned to him for confirmation.

Lon considered. "A little of the vision, too."

"Maybe those Lectori chose you because you had a lot of psychic vibes they could use. You know that their plan somehow involved Maximus. Maybe they wanted you to appear to have all his powers. In fact you do; they're just psionic in nature. Besides, has anyone ever figured out how Maximus does what he does? Maybe the Lectori had a few theories of their own, and used you as a guinea pig."

Stoan still had his arms crossed. "Just how do you know all this?"

Lina gave him a steady gaze. "I've trained for years to be a psychic healer. Shouldn't you all have this information in his medical records? I'm surprised that Wiley– Dr. Mem-Bazer hasn't tested Lon for this. Of course he's rather dubious about metaphysics. I notice that the technology here isn't set up for much of that kind of thing." She looked at Lon. "Is Terry a telepath? A psychic– no, she couldn't be too psychic."

"Why not?"

"You have to have achieved a certain level of… I don't know, harmony with the universe, in order to get very far up the psychic ladder. I really didn't get the impression– as she was giving orders for the both of us to be chopped up– that she was incredibly spiritual."

"I agree." Lon smiled at Lina. "I think she's just been watching too much *Star Trek*."

Lina gave him a hard look and then relaxed when she saw he was kidding her here in front of the entire Mega-Legion.

Lon looked over to Stoan. "So. My powers are psionic in nature. No wonder I'm a telepath. There's no need to talk about side-effects from mind control," he said matter-of-factly. "I don't see Dr. Mem-Bazer here to confirm or deny."

Stoan rolled his eyes ever so slightly and took a breath. "Computer, resume recording. Transmissions back on. We'll fill you in when you get back," he told the monitoring members before he dismissed Ms. Woltrell's privacy curtain. The barrage of questions continued.

What kinds of guns had Terry used to take away Londo's powers, to kill him? What about Dr. Menlo?

"He's dead," Lina told Stoan.

"What?!" Londo exclaimed.

She turned to him. "We found his body a couple days ago. Wiley has a re-cording. We called the ParaNet about it."

Lon looked a little dazed at that. Dr. Menlo had been a considerable, almost unstoppable menace for years.

"A recording?" Stoan demanded. "Where is it?"

"Wiley made it; ask him."

Stoan gave a frustrated *harumph* that the mega-Legion's renowned scientific genius wasn't there.

When had Lon's telepathic abilities begun? What kinds of guns and lasers had been used on Lina? When had her teleportation come into play?

"A brick hit her hard in the back of the head when the hotel exploded," Londo told them. "I was afraid that she'd concussed. Hell, at first I was afraid she was dead. But Dr. Mem-Bazer said that it was a brain injury, and that it probably caused the porting."

"A brick. How convenient," Stoan sneered. "And Wilder has this infor-mation, too."

Lina spoke up. "Riz checked it out, too. She says that I was brain-damaged when I was a kid, and apparently it hadn't healed up properly, but this second time it did. I was born with this power. I just had an injury that prevented me for years from using it."

Lon squeezed her. "So it really is permanent?"

"Looks like," she beamed at him.

"*Bon.* Very, very good. Now, who's this Riz?"

"Who is Riz?" Stoan echoed.

"Dr. Riz Gorgeon, Chief of Legion Medical," Lina stated clearly for the record.

Stoan wrinkled his nose. "Oh, Gorgeon."

They had to call up Riz in the Legion medical wing and get her to testify over the screens. Every time now that Lina had to say something about Riz, she called her "Dr. Gorgeon." These Legionnaires liked their own titles, but they didn't like to use those given to others. Riz deserved the title of Doctor just as much as Wiley. Might as well rub the fact in their faces.

Finally that line of questioning was over.

How long had Londo and Lina known each other before they'd had sex?

Lina opened her mouth to utter a blasé response and show these so-called society betters that she could be as cold as they were, but stopped when she felt Lon's great consternation.

"Privacy," Lon said. "Keep your questions to the pertinent facts, Stoan."

All his adult life Londo had been teased about his virginity.

"Sex would be the easiest way for a telepath to gain access to your mind," Stoan said in a rough voice. Apparently he didn't like asking these kinds of questions in public to his good friend.

"I object to this line of questioning!" Londo thundered. "I won't have it!"

Ms. Woltrell looked thoughtful for a moment before she objected at a more reasonable level, citing Legion procedural law.

"Objection noted," Stoan told them. "I regret to say that we must continue along these lines. You had sex without powers, but now apparently still can, even though you are at full strength?"

"I refuse to answer this line of questioning," Londo persisted.

Woltrell said, "We invoke the right of privacy."

"I don't want to cite contempt," Stoan prodded. "I just want to know how–"

"Of course we can still have sex." Lina jumped to her feet. "And Londo does it pretty damn well, too. Do you need a demonstration? We usually don't start this dressed. Lon, that floor looks a little hard. Could you–" Lina started to peel off her capelet as loud speculation broke out in the stands.

"Contempt of court!" Stoan roared, slamming his fist down on his podium. "Stop that now!"

"Just trying to cooperate." Lina smiled sweetly even as Woltrell whispered to her that theatrics wouldn't help. Lina began to refasten the cape but stopped as whispers filtered through her mind. "What?" she asked.

"This court will find any further such actions from you contempt," Stoan warned.

"What?" Lina asked again.

"I said–"

Lina motioned him to be quiet. "Please. I'm trying to– He *what?!*" Her mouth flew open and her hands balled into fists as she shook in rage. "You… pervert!" she shouted at Stoan. "You stinking pile of–"

"Lina!" Lon exclaimed. He clamped his palm over her mouth. "Honestly, Stoan, I don't know what's–" Lon paused, staring at Lina before he released her. He advanced on Stoan. "You *what?!*"

"He filmed us!" Lina hissed. "*They* say he filmed us night before last. What, Stoan, don't they have good enough porn here for you? You have to film your friends and watch? There, Lon– he admits it!"

"I heard," Londo growled and kept striding toward his commander.

"Valiant, don't!" Woltrell called, though confusion and fear crossed her face.

Stoan was indeed thinking about the things he had seen. He'd left a tiny min-icam hovering in their bedroom the night he'd broken in, waiting for whatever happened to be recorded. Lon halted inches away from Stoan. A gray wall of force field appeared between the two of them, triggered by the subcommander.

"I'm not going to kill him, Andri," Lon's quiet voice was the rumble of far-off thunder. "I want to know why. I want an apology. I want these proceedings to end. I want him punished!" He whirled on his heel and returned to stand with Lina, his back to Stoan.

Silence filled the great chamber. Woltrell's lips flapped soundlessly. Lina was scarlet with embarrassment. Londo's face lined with anger. "Subcommander Nurunori!" he called. "I invoke Article Six!"

"Yes, yes, Valiant. I agree." Andri pushed Stoan aside and took his place at the podium. Sullenly, he let her. "Commander Magnos, did you make a recording of… intimate matters that happened in the Rand rooms two nights past? If so, you were violating every Legion privacy reg in the book."

"I researched it thoroughly during hyperspace transit," Stoan declared. "There's direct precedent in the investigation of a mind controller who gained access to Legion Headquarters almost a hundred years ago. Recordings were made then. They were the only concrete evidence that could be gathered, to bring the Tishana in to finish the investigation. There have been dozens of other cases, not connected with the Legion, in which such surveillance was undertaken. They all involved mind controllers. And sex. What was done needed to be done. I'm on solid legal ground here."

"How convenient for you," Lina spat. "Perv!"

6

"Quiet." Andri's face was set in a grim mask. "And this recording you made, Magnos, what did you hope to accomplish?"

"I wanted him to see that… that what she was doing was all in his mind. That she was tricking him!"

"And is that what it showed?"

A couple of heartbeats went by. "No," Stoan said quietly. "It showed nothing of the kind. The record has been destroyed. There were no copies made. Nothing remains of it. I took personal pains to make sure the data were completely dispersed on both a quantum and programming level."

Andri nodded. "I've known you a long time, Commander, and when you say you researched this, I have to believe you. Although I will double-check. The threat of mental control is such that sometimes extreme measures have to be taken." She gestured to people standing along the sidelines, who then disappeared behind a flurry of research screens.

"I apologize, Valiant. Mrs. Valiant," she said. "I know this is embarrassing for you, and I hope you won't hold this against the Mega-Legion."

Woltrell looked about to say something, but Andri waved her down and instead looked up at the balconies. "Vote of censure," she announced, and stepped back from the podium.

"What's going on?" Lina whispered to Londo as proceedings seemed to stop.

But Londo gestured. "One point for further consideration," he told the chamber. "Commander Magnos waited until I had departed into hyperspace to have my wife arrested. She was kept under arrest for the entire time of our mission, and I was never informed!"

Andri nodded. "Point added," she said. "Now vote."

Lon gestured twice, voting, Lina guessed, and then crossed his arms, cloaking himself in bitter rage.

Woltrell stepped back to stand on Lina's other side. "They're voting as to whether the commander has the right to continue to preside over this affair," she told Lina wonderingly. "If the tally goes against him badly enough, there could even be a no-confidence vote to temporarily suspend him from office."

Andri read the results on her podium screen. "Commander Magnos may remain… on the sidelines," she announced gravely. A nod at Woltrell had the attorney joining her. "We'll take a short recess."

"It's not enough to call for suspension," Londo whispered to Lina as the large wall screen showed the results. "I didn't think it would be. He has an outstanding service record." Even so, Lon let out a low growl.

"Jae said he goes crazy about mind control," Lina whispered back. My god, that man had seen her and Londo having sex! She could hardly bear to look at him!

"Crazy. Huh." Londo's stare at Stoan was black. She'd never seen anyone as angry as this. It frightened her. Sometimes she had to step back and remind herself that her Londo was Valiant, too. He could turn rocks into dust just by crumbling them in his hand. His slightest actions could have dangerous consequences.

"Just think," she tried to joke, "now I've been in my first porno."

Mistake! He hissed under his breath and Lina rubbed his arm anxiously. "Calm down, honey. If you're like me, you can't think straight when you're angry."

Lina pulled the chair out of the spotlight and made him sit down. She had Londo drink some water while she made "magnetic" passes around him, trying to detach some of the anger. He watched her without saying anything.

"Feel a little better?" Lina asked hopefully. "Can I get you an aspirin?"

That did cause the barest of smiles to twitch at his mouth, and Lina felt cheered. "This can't go on forever," she said. "I got the impression this was going to be a quickie, one, two, throw the girl out kinda thing. It's going to be over today, isn't it?"

He nodded. He was looking at his glass now, not at her.

"Well, then, that's something positive. Now march in place and touch across your opposite knees with each step." She did it for him. "Think of an X. C'mon, Londo."

"They'll think you're insane," he murmured as he slouched.

"And they'd be absolutely right." She grinned at him. "I let my body march for Londo," she chanted as she marched, touching knees. "Think of an X. Get those brain hemispheres working as a team."

For some reason Lon felt like shaking the anger out of his arms. He could almost feel the worst of the cloud leaving him. He could think coherently again.

"Mind control," Lina said cheerily as she watched him recover.

"Don't even joke about it in here," he warned, and took her hand. "C'mon, let's get this over with." He led her out to the stage again.

"We're back in session," Andri announced. Woltrell returned to her own podium. Stoan sat in the open cubicle where Andri had been during the first part, close to the center stage.

"I hate to harp on this, Valiant, and please bear with the court," Andri said, "but these things must be discussed. I tend to agree that with you especially, if a mind controller were going to target you, some kind of sexual trap would be the easiest course."

"Possibly," Londo said, his mouth tight again. "But a mind controller wouldn't stand to be raped."

"Rape?" Andri gasped.

"Rape?" Woltrell echoed, blinking at Londo. She made a gesture in the air that would shut off her personal recorder.

"I tried to rape her," Londo said. "She fought me off. If she'd been controlling me, she could have stopped that situation from the start."

Lina stared at him in shock. "Don't listen to him!" she finally cried to the subcommander. "There was no rape." She pulled ineffectively at Londo's arm. "Lon honey, don't go there!"

"I just went crazy at one point." Londo brushed her aside. "She wouldn't let me touch her and there I was, powerless, and it would be the one day in my life that–" He swallowed. "So I tried it. She fought me long enough for me to realize what I was doing and stop. But a mind controller would have taken a different tack. Be quiet, Lina. I'm telling the truth here."

"He didn't rape me," Lina insisted. "He didn't come close. He snapped out of it very quickly. He'd been under a lot of stress that day. There were hundreds of gunmen in the forest after us and he didn't have his powers, and no one knew what was going on. He was the perfect gentleman after that. He must have apologized a million times. You can't blame him!"

Lina turned to the audience. "Look, I don't even know what this mind control is that you people are talking about. If someone could just explain it to me, maybe I could think up some hard fact that would prove that I'm not a controller. I mean, I've been Out Here for a few days now and I haven't seen the first–" No, that wasn't true.

"You haven't seen the first what?" Andri prompted.

"Um." Lina looked wildly at Londo. She'd stuck her foot in her mouth. She didn't want to get anyone else in trouble. She grimaced at Woltrell.

"Defense requests a short recess," Woltrell said quickly.

But Andri ordered, "Denied. Mrs. Valiant, continue."

"Ah, just forget I said anything," Lina said weakly.

"What is it, *chérie?*" Londo peered at her worriedly. "Mind control? You saw someone–?"

"I said, forget it!" Lina exclaimed. **Please be quiet, Londo!**

From the sidelines, Stoan stood up. "What?" he asked. "Did you control someone? I thought you said you couldn't do it." Stoan flashed a savage, triumphant smile, and Lina couldn't see any way out of it without implicating someone. She couldn't do that. What to do?

"It was innocent enough," she began. "It's probably not even the same kind of mind control that you're talking about. No one was harmed–"

A wide screen popped into the air next to the subcommander's podium, flickering on to show Erik Gallad's face, paler than normal. "Look," he said nervously, "it was me, all right? It wasn't her, Commander. Subcommander." Obviously, he'd been monitoring the meeting from wherever his team was. The other three Legionnaires on his mission sat behind him on the screen.

"Sunstorm," Andri acknowledged. "What, are you claiming to be a mind controller now?"

"No!" he replied before his forehead creased. "I mean, well, maybe. I don't know. Lina said that I have a bit of telepathy and I use it… well…"

"What?"

He looked abashed. "I use it to get girls."

The gallery was silent for a long moment before some parts of it exploded in laugher.

"Influence them," Eric corrected himself quickly. He passed a nervous hand through his coppery hair. "In a very minor way. Extremely minor. That would be sexual assault. I would never think of using any kind of mind control on anyone. You know that, Subcommander."

"Mind control?" Lon mouthed at Lina.

She shrugged and shook her head. **It was psychic hooks. Is that mind control?**

Eric's chin jutted as he sat straighter. "Look, Subcommander, Mrs. Valiant told me what I was doing– and I don't think it was mind control, not at all– and she told me to cut it out. Then she tricked me into doing it again so Dr. Mem-Bazer could get a record of it to see how it worked. I don't know if it registered or not. He'll tell you it's not real mind control. He will confirm."

"He's not here."

"We seem to be missing an important witness in all this," Londo declared. "Can't we get him?"

"These diplomatic talks are at a delicate point," Andri stated. Her mouth twisted in the smallest of smiles. "All right, thank you, Sunstorm. We know you… influence minds now. All the women here will be watching you in the future. But we still don't know if Lina, I mean, Mrs. Valiant controls minds or not."

Stoan said, "It boils down to the sex."

Londo grimaced. "*Tsé,* ten years from now we'll all look back on this and be mortified by these questions. Maybe you should keep that in mind."

Andri nodded. "Then one more embarrassing question: How?"

"Do you want the actual mechanics?" Londo said from between clenched teeth.

"No." Lina tried to be as forthcoming as possible, tried to be as calm as she could to offset Lon's agitation. Tried to remember that they had hired a lawyer to handle all this. If Woltrell was too afraid to stand up to the Legion, Lina wasn't. "She wants to know if it's mind control. It is telepathically based, yes. Neither of us could do it if the other weren't a telepath. Or if one weren't a psychic healer."

"More coincidence," Stoan grumbled.

Lina decided to ignore him, and addressed Andri. "I performed a psychic healing during which I was in tune with Lon's cells and then we got the idea—"

"Privacy, Lina," Lon murmured.

"Well, I'm trying to phrase this delicately. Let's just say it's a telepathic dual…" She paused because she couldn't find the Panlingua word for it. Londo provided it telepathically. "…feedback system, okay? I think Wiley's writing a paper on it that he doesn't plan to publish, thank goodness. He might let you see it. I hope he doesn't."

"Wiley again," Andri muttered, scratching the back of her pink-haired head in consternation. Then she placed both her hands firmly on the edge of her podium and faced Lina. "Did you ever force Lon to love you? Did you telepath love to him?"

"I was the one who forced her," Lon butted in harshly.

"Oh hush, Lon," Lina pulled him back from where he was advancing on Andri, and the action didn't escape people's notice. Mouths opened around the hall: a slip of a human restraining Valiant.

"Of course I telepathed love to him, just as he did to me. Telepaths must do that naturally. I'm sure that regular people do it, too, just not quite as blatantly. As to how we fell in love… well…"

"Ah, I get it," Londo announced to the hall. He began to walk in a wide circle to address his audience, his hands behind his back, his chest thrown out, as he considered them. "Falling in love equals mind control. No one ever explained that to me. I must have missed that day's briefing."

Londo turned slowly before them all, linking gazes. "I met this very beautiful, sweet, clever girl on the few days of my life that I could actually end decades of unwanted celibacy. And then it turns out that I don't have to endure that celibacy ever again. Was it mind control that made me propose to her, or was it common sense? Maybe it was even love, something that I wonder if some of the people here know anything about. But Legion Protocol does indeed allow for love. They allow marriage also; I've seen the regs. Are we now going to investigate every married member here? Is marriage going to be deemed a security risk? Is sex?"

He scowled at the audience. "Let's see how you like it when sex is forbidden to you! When the people you love are subjected to embarrassing public trials. When someone records what goes on in *your* bedroom."

"Enough," Andri said as Lon returned to squeeze Lina's hand. "Let's get something here we can put our finger on and say either yes or no on the mind control question. Anything."

Woltrell held up her information padd, scrolled to a listing of mind control characteristics. She held it high, its screen facing the gallery so the members could link it to their sub-screens.

For twenty minutes she went through the list, dismissing each item with evidence that had been gathered during Lina's incarceration.

"Very good," Andri said when a vote had been taken to tentatively clear Lina of those specifics. "Now Kembril's compiled a list of suspected mind control advances. Explain them to us, Kembril." As the debate on that began, she stepped down from her podium and approached the defendants to speak privately. "Londo, I just want you to know that this isn't about the marriage itself."

"Then what the hell is it? With this kind of accusation, anyone can accuse anyone else and not be held to account. What shred of–"

"She's *Terran*," Stoan called from behind Andri.

"Go back and sit down, Commander," Andri ordered. "This has nothing to do with ethnicities. This has to do with–"

"Coincidences," Londo said.

Lina put her hand on his arm. "Not coincidence. Not for us."

Andri massaged her forehead and closed her eyes.

Quietly Lina addressed Andri as some woman in the hive of watching Legionnaires spoke to the group and Woltrell answered her. "The basic question for me isn't about mind control at all. In the past week and a half I've changed in ways that I doubt mind controllers must need to, well, control people. It's been a string of crazy things, like the universe is building up to something. Unless this is what it's built to, and this is as far as it goes. Which is just fine with me. Well, not this trial.

"I met Lon, and he's the best thing that's ever happened to me. He also helped me get rid of some pretty severe phobias. I became a teleporter. I'm able to travel just about anywhere, even other planets. My ability at psychic healing increased, at least where Lon is concerned. We got married. I got arrested. A planet used me to speak to twenty billion people– individually. And I know songs now."

"Songs?" Londo asked her.

She nodded. "It's like a gigantic musical library locked inside my head. What kind of mind controller would need to know that, unless they needed to drive someone crazy with 'It's a Small World'?"

Lon snorted. "I don't think that's on Kembril's list."

Lina counted on her fingers. "Whatever's happening, song or singing comes into it, clue number one. Clue number two: it's got something to do with Londo and me being together."

"Clues?" Andri asked.

"We get enough clues, we find out what's going on. Oh."

"What?" Lon asked.

"I just remembered. When I was doing that first healing here on you, I was in the salt water tank talking to this world, and she said, 'We've been expecting you.' She wasn't using the royal 'we.' She meant someone else."

"What does that mean?"

Lina shook her head. "I have no idea, but I know it's very important." She looked at Lon and held up three fingers. "Clue number three: Sarastor is in on it, with at least one somebody else." She turned toward the floor. "C'mon, Sarastor, what's going on here?" She stamped her foot impatiently. "Damn, she's not going to talk."

Stoan jumped to his feet, jabbing his finger in her direction as he trotted to them. He'd been paying attention to them instead of the debate. "A planet? You're implicating a planet?" Stoan exchanged fed-up glances with Andri.

"And that night when I proposed," Lon remembered. "The voice said, 'Two of the three have accepted each other.' Who's number three?"

"Lon," Lina said. She started singing softly, "*Irsta winter meil ur vinte…*"

"*Yail un wirste, dall a mar…*" he continued, confused. A song about communities of people working together.

"That's the way it started with me, being able to finish a song that I didn't know. This is an ancient song of Sarastor. Excuse me," Lina addressed the audience, and Woltrell paused. "Can anyone finish the song Lon just sang? No? Then the third isn't here."

Lon shrugged. "That makes sense. Of all the worlds represented by the Legion, only Earth has a culture accepting song." He paused as he realized…

"You're wrong, Lon," Lina said slowly.

He nodded. "Feith did."

"Just because Feith's dead doesn't mean its culture is."

Londo looked around. "And Jae's not here."

"And… oh dear." Lina touched her mouth with a finger.

"What?"

"Um, we figured out– three days ago?– that Jae's gone telepath on us."

"Jae– telepathic?"

Lina nodded. "He's been playing his guitar and singing in public. Protocol didn't approve."

"Are you trying to say that Neutrino's in on this too?" Stoan demanded. "Are you trying to implicate him or just mislead us? Did you control him as well when you were under arrest?"

"Commander Magnos, go sit down," Andri said.

"I'm just trying to figure this out," Lina hissed at Stoan. "Give me a break."

Stoan bared his teeth at them. Trotting out of the spotlights, Andri conferred with a small group of people and screens. Around them the larger debate proceeded.

But on center stage it was just the three of them. Lon started, "If we can get Neutrino over here, maybe we can prove other coincidences."

Lina added, "At the very least, we've brought up the point that there's something strange going on here, and it's involving more than just some teleporting psychic and your most powerful member."

"Neutrino could also be considered such," Stoan declared.

Andri interrupted, calling from off-stage. "Commander Magnos, I am ordering you to sit down. You will respect my authority. Everyone, let's suspend the debate. Give us three minutes over here and then we'll continue."

Lon stood before Stoan, his hands balled into fists. "Stoan, I've been in her mind. Deeply. I can tell you for a fact that there's no pretense in her, no craving for power, no mind control."

"Valiant, don't engage him," Woltrell cautioned as she returned to their area. She glanced curiously from one to the other.

Stoan snapped at Lon, "As if we could actually believe anything you could have to say when it comes to this."

"So what's the real reason behind all this?" Lina demanded. "If Lon and I had waited a while, would you have supported us then? How long would a decent engagement have been for you?"

"I'm asking the ques–"

"Mrs. Valiant, don't en–"

"How long?!"

Lon took her arm. "It's not the quickness that bothers him, *chérie*." He looked at Stoan as if he were looking through steel. "It's the choice. Stoan regards himself as a matchmaker of sorts."

Stoan stood silent.

"You obviously disapprove of Lina," Lon said. "*D'accord*. Whom would you have chosen? Whom could I have married that would suit your standards? The standards of the Mega-Legion?"

Stoan was still silent.

Lina looked at him. He was broadcasting on purpose this time. "Oh," she said quietly.

Lon shook his head. "It would never have worked, Stoan. And she's dead now. No way to bring her back."

"She's dead, and you died, and *she* brought you back." Stoan pointed his accusation at Lina. "A… witchdoctor from Earth, of all places."

Londo braced himself between them, protecting Lina. "I'm from Earth, Stoan."

"But you've risen above it. You're a Legionnaire now."

"Ooo, a Legionnaire," Lina said so softly that even Lon could barely hear it. He reached back to squeeze her hand as a warning. **Not now, Lie.**

Stoan had seen that she'd made some kind of comment, but he continued. "A Legionnaire who's supposed to be better than ordinary people, above them all, setting an example. Not running around with some person who… *sings*… and performs shamanistic ceremonies and thinks they deal with… with angels, by the orb. Use your common sense, Lon. All of a sudden things are happening that we can't even begin to find explanations for. It all centers around *her*. And now you're married. Can you really be sure that it's of your own volition? That she hasn't taken over some part of your mind? Maybe it's just to secure you, and maybe it's a way into the Legion and its defenses. Can you be sure?"

"I can. One hundred percent."

Stoan gave him a sour look. "Well, I can't. This is a matter of galactic sector security now, and–"

Lina scowled and ignored Lon's squeeze. "Listen, I may be a nobody from a backwater planet, but even I can see when something of cosmic proportions is beginning. Planets talking to their people, mind powers appearing, *angels in the architecture*… This kind of thing doesn't happen every day, even here at the esteemed headquarters of the high-and-mighty Affiliated Systems Mega-Force Legion, does it? I think you all may be caught in the trap of not seeing the forest for the trees. Step back and view the big picture. Give whatever it is time to come to fruition and reveal itself fully."

"While you have time to ensnare more of us? I think not."

"So it all boils down to a Catch-22," Londo said sourly. "Anyone who knows Lina enough to testify in her favor is obviously under her mental control, which means that she's controlling anyone who can testify in her favor. Circular logic. Witch hunt."

In this recess the auditorium lay deathly quiet as people listened to the conversation. Stoan faced down the two of them. "In your best interests, Lon," he hissed, almost nose to nose, "I'm going to move for an annulment so we can get rid of the emotional baggage and investigate her more thoroughly, away from Headquarters where she can do no harm."

"Did he just call me baggage?" Lina asked softly, dangerously.

"Don't worry, Lina," Lon told her just as dangerously. "Between the two of us, they won't be able to do this. We're a team now."

"Forever," Lina agreed. And paused, realizing the importance of the Legion to the galaxy, to Londo's life. She wasn't going to embarrass him or diminish him, ever, so she added, "Or at least until you meet my parents. Don't divorce me because of them, Lon."

There was a soft stir of laughter in the gallery that broke the tension. Londo looked at her and quirked his lips, realizing what she'd tried to do.

"And you haven't met *my* father yet," he said.

"Oh gawd."

Lon let out a huge laugh and hugged her to him. The gallery echoed him. Everyone knew the vast legend of Maximus.

Stoan didn't like what they were obviously doing. He opened his mouth, but Lon interrupted, a smile still lingering on his face.

"Andri! Excuse me– Subcommander Nurunori! Call for a vote, please. Now."

Andri looked back sharply at him, startled to see that Stoan was still over there.

"Get Dr. Mem-Bazer and Neutrino here, have them testify for or against, as they will, and call for a vote. Let's settle this. Let us get on with our lives, in time for me to take my wife out for a quiet dinner at the Boko Rash."

Andri stepped back to her podium, pointedly gesturing to Stoan, who took his secondary place in her cubicle. "And if the vote goes against her?" Andri asked.

Lina looked at Lon. **What kind of sentence are we talking?**

"It won't," Lon said with force. "Things like this don't happen without a reason. People who get in the way of the cosmic game have a tendency to get run over by it."

Lina tilted her head at her husband. **The cosmic game?**

He smiled back at her, put his arm around her shoulder. **You're catching, love.** She laughed softly, and they faced Andri together.

The subcommander frowned at their obviously silent conversation, their confidence. Andri was quiet for some time. Then she spoke. "Get Dr. Mem-Bazer and Neutrino over here. Interrupt the talks." She turned to Lina. "And take Mrs. Valiant away while we hear their testimony."

"What kind of holding cell could hold me?" Lina asked. "Besides, in my country the accused has the right to hear their own trial."

"This is not your country," Andri replied mildly. She looked down at the board in front of her. "And I think you can be restrained very easily within a force field somewhere. It will only be an hour or two. Holding cell 3-FF–"

"Force… Oh. I wouldn't bet on that," Lina said slowly, and Andri glanced up. "I'll voluntarily stay there, but I don't think a force field will stop me. I did a little research on them the other day. I think I might have been put in one already."

"*Chérie,*" Londo murmured, but the microphones picked up his voice clearly, "this isn't science fiction. If you'd been in one, you'd know. Force fields are real."

"Oh, I have no doubt," she told him. "But everyone's making the assumption that I travel through space when I port. If I did, then a force field might put a damper on things. But I don't think I *travel,* at least linearly."

Londo considered. "And Wiley says…?"

"Wiley's not committing himself to anything that outrageous. Yet," Lina smirked.

"Let's test that, then." Andri played with her podium's controls. "Puter, raise primary force field around Headquarters in fifty seconds. Three-quarters power."

Yellow lights immediately flashed along the lines of the ceiling of the room. Two strident beeps made even Londo jump. A genderless voice announced the raising of primary force fields in forty-eight seconds, everyone to clear away from force field area. The message repeated itself four times, then from nowhere came a subtle but real whine, and static crackled through the air.

Andri pointed at her. "Teleport," she ordered. "You stay here, Lina. Port in something through the force field."

Suddenly Lina held a salt shaker in her hand. "From the Pares Restaurant," she said, displaying the logo engraved there. "They serve very good hamburgers, but the music there sucks."

Lon laughed softly and squeezed her. She let the shaker return.

"Force field off," Andri said to the air. She frowned in concentration. "We'll take another short recess."

"So far so good," Londo whispered to her as a group of members gathered around Andri's podium. "Maybe." They kept their place, listening to Woltrell detail possibilities and how they should act with each one, until the group at Andri's podium seemed to reach a consensus. Andri waited for the room to quiet down.

"We believe we've come up with a solution," she told the gathering, not looking at the two of them. "The prisoner–" Lina tensed to hear the term– "will be taken to the hyperspace holding area. She has already shown that hyperspace blocks her kind of telepathy, so perhaps it will block her teleportation as well."

Lina's breath caught but she stood as straight as she could to combat the trembling in her legs. "Even if it doesn't, I'll stay there voluntarily. A hyperspace chamber it is."

Two large Legionnaires appeared out of the darkness to lead her away.

Lon faced the walls of cubicles. "Since none of you will accept my further testimony as a witness, I'm going with my wife. I cast my vote in her favor," he said, and turned to catch up to her.

Andri started to say something but then lowered her chin to stare at her podium.

The doors to the main meeting auditorium thudded shut behind them. The two guards– walking fortresses– stood more than a foot and a half taller than Lon and twice as broad. They flanked the two of them down the restricted corridors. Lon introduced their guards to her: green-skinned Boroh and blue Minzier, but their responses were clipped. They were obviously uncomfortable with having to escort their comrade Valiant to a holding cell.

And edgy thinking that Lina might very well be taking over their minds.

Formerly forbidden hallways opened to her now. Too few light-colored walls punctuated the black acrylic back here. She'd called the Legion's dark decor depressing before, but now it was downright suicidal.

Everything blinked or hummed. Small machinery toddled out of their way as they strode by. They came to one section with thick picture windows through which Lina could see several people working with straw-like torches on trailer-sized machinery. Like the machinery, they were dressed in metal– at least Lina thought so until she saw one of them unscrewing their arm to put on another. She clutched Londo's hand tighter.

"It'll be all right," he told her. He noticed where she was looking. "They're just Legion employees, love, nothing to be frightened about. Voluntarily-made cyborgs. You know what cyborgs are?"

She nodded quickly and looked away. Voluntary!

"It's not like the science fiction back home, *chérie*. Cyborg implants provide the same experience as the human body here. They can feel everything normally." He pursed his lips as he considered. "Wiley's a cyborg of a different type."

"He's got implants," Lina recalled. "Communications and data. He has five minds, so he needs the extra input, right?"

"Right."

"Oh. I guess that's… okay then."

"The cyborg implants let them accomplish more than they would as pure human. They're here; it's very prestigious work."

"Oh."

The corridors became busier with purely artificial life as they progressed. Now they almost waded through a waist-high sea of robotic vehicles scurrying to and fro. "Make way, you *skurny* midgets!" Boroh bellowed, and the robots tried to keep a distance clear in front of them. Two minutes more and they were through the worst of the swarms.

"Repair bays," Londo explained to Lina. "We're almost there."

A waft of hot food drifted by as they passed a small group of those cyborgs eating in a cul-de-sac. They weren't talking to each other. Their food came in a form that could be sipped through straws. They didn't look at it, but rather tipped their heads down, staring at…?

Lon answered her silent question. "Part of their sensory input is direct hookup to Sarastor's internet. They're playing video games." He made a sound that was halfway between a grunt and resigned sigh. "The way they do their repairs is by gaming. Wiley's staff designs games that are really repair processes. They put tab A into slot B and get points."

"So they don't have to think about it? They don't find their own solutions?"

Again that sound he made, this time louder. "They don't have to think," he finally growled.

They passed hallways labeled "Medical Supplies," "Construction Supplies," "Food Supplies," "Auxiliary Weaponry," and "Civilian Exit– checkpoints ahead."

"Let's take that one," Lina whispered to Londo.

"Not today, *chérie*. Look, here we are."

"Hyperspace Bay, Level 26," the sign over the towering warehouse doors read. They rumbled open and the group entered a space lit like an underground garage, with an orangey spectrum that left no shadows, though it seemed dimmer than it should be. Sound echoed harshly, and a smell Lina could only identify as bitterness overhung it all.

They passed several gray ships of aerodynamic design. She supposed that once these ships were out of hyperspace, whatever that was, they were capable of maneuvering in planetary atmospheres. But here were others shaped like short railroad cars, and she wondered what they were used for. Maybe the three different levels of hyperspace called for different kinds of vehicles.

The group continued to a large circular vault-like door. Instead of motioning to a computer, Minzier spun a wheel to release it. It whooshed open. Lon and she stepped into a long corridor facing a similar door. They had to keep to a narrow pathway that dropped off on either side to bottomless depths. Weird yellow lights from all around provided no help in figuring how far the walls were from them.

"When you come back, give us a second or two warning, will you, Bli?" Lon asked Minzier. The Legionnaire nodded but didn't meet his eyes.

It was some kind of airlock. Or maybe, Lina guessed, a doorway between regular space and hyperspace. Their guards stepped back into the hangar. The first door closed behind Londo and Lina with a thump and a blue light flashed on the door ahead of them.

Londo nodded at it. "Blue means clear, okay, go– the equivalent of green back home. Red means the same as red. Yellow means caution or that something's about to happen. Green means pay attention to directions that will be available nearby." Lon took the wheel and spun it for the inner door.

A normal room lay beyond. As Lina looked around, he secured the door behind them. Almost immediately the sign next to it flashed: "LOCKED FROM OUTSIDE."

Then the world went blank.

It felt to Lina as if she had water in her ear, blocking her hearing, but this was in her mind. She shook her head but it didn't help. The only point of life around her now that she could sense was Londo. She wrinkled her nose sourly.

Lon turned to her. "I know. It happened to me on the trip to the *Travern*. That's why I asked Bli to warn us when they open up again. It hit me pretty badly when I came out of hyperspace." He looked at her measuringly. "Can you port out?"

She tried to picture Lon's apartment. Odd. She could imagine it, but she couldn't form a perfect vision of it in her mind. It was fuzzy, just a spot or two of crisply-remembered clarity. That wouldn't do at all.

She shook her head no at him. "It might help if I knew what hyperspace was. I mean, I took some quantum mechanics in college, but they never got much into, well, science fiction. I have a good idea what it isn't, but not what it is."

"I've got some books and videos you can look at." Londo took her hand and led her to a sofa. This chamber was set up as a large entertainment room with familiar furniture: the sofa, chairs, and a kitchenette that was larger than the one in Lon's apartment. To one side sat a round gray table with chairs around it, as well as a wall-sized area of neutral color, akin to things Lina had seen in her books. It was an older-style TV screen in inactive mode.

"Are we being recorded?" Their camera hadn't followed them since the trial began.

"*Mais oui,* I'd assume that. But it's not instantaneous. They'll have to examine the record after the chamber is re-opened. There's no communication between hyperspace and conventional space."

She put her arms around him to calm her nerves. Londo was safety. He turned her so she sat in his lap.

"It's all going to turn out well," he assured her. "Promise."

"So tell me, what's the Legion's punishment for being a mind-controlling villainess?" she asked.

"You'll be cleared."

"No, really, what–"

"We don't talk about that now."

"But–"

Londo shook his head. "You are not to worry about this. Stoan's jumped the gun. He was too eager to prosecute, too quick to bring this to trial."

"And we can always appeal, as Ms. Woltrell said. Is that before or after the execution? I hope we're not paying her much."

He didn't even crack a smile. Instead he locked her in his steely gaze. "There will be no execution, no punishment of any kind. You don't have anything to worry about, Kitten."

"But you're worried. Are you sure–"

"I'm not worried. I'm mad," Londo told her. "Mad at myself. I allowed myself to lose control on this. I took it too personally. I'm a professional. I'm a Legionnaire."

"I tried to get it taken care of before you got back," Lina told him. "I almost got through to a lawyer, but they caught me."

"Did you know this lawyer?" Lon asked and she shook her head. "Do you really know the extent of the law they're accusing you of breaking?" Again she shook her head.

He scowled as he chewed on the inside of his lip. "My fault," he said. "I did research– a lot– while I was traveling through hyperspace to get to the *Travern.*

I thought they'd allow a few days to process it all after we got back. Didn't know they'd gone ahead and arrested you."

His mouth worked before he gave his shoulders a shake and lifted his chin. "We shouldn't lose today. Stoan has failed to prove anything and the circumstances are too circumstantial to get a conviction, even for mind control."

"Are you sure?" Lina asked. "The crime includes being a Terran as well, and I'm very guilty of that."

He frowned at her joke and then grimaced when he realized it wasn't. "Good point," he said. "Prejudice. And probably some reflected jealousy from some. I've had to call out a few members in my time and they haven't appreciated it. Some might want to get at me through my wife."

"So." Lina clasped her hands in her lap and pursed her lips. "Maybe it's time for me to hide. Get people to forget about me for a while."

"No. This may be your trial, but it's my command. We play this my way." He touched the tip of her nose with an imperative finger. "I'm familiar with the laws. I'm familiar with the culture and the organization. Woltrell's rep seems to have been overblown, though it's true enough that she didn't have much time to prepare, we have to give her that. I know some great lawyers. I can get their security rating upgraded. If we lose today there are at least five more levels we can appeal to, with prep time built in to the schedule. Do not worry. That's an order."

"Are you–"

"Don't question team leader. If they order confinement they probably won't let me see you for a day, maybe two, while I'm examined for mind control. I'll have Jae check on you."

"Haven't he and Wiley been contaminated?" Lina asked. "Won't they be detained as well?"

Londo gave a "hmmf" at that. "If that's the case," he decided, "I'll have my team members do the job. Two of them haven't even met you yet. They're due in tonight. I'll leave them instructions as soon as we get out of here. In the meantime, Stoan hasn't called even one Tishana expert. He's not going to get a firm conviction without someone who can pin down exact, current symptoms of mind control and prove them. He's still off-balance from Ai– Aiko's death."

"Poor Aiko." Lina sighed and rested her head on Lon's shoulder. "I'm sorry to be such an embarrassment to you, Londo, especially at a time like this. The last thing you need is a scandal."

"You're not an embarrassment. What is this? Are you sorry you married me?"

She looked up and gave him a smile. "If you want, I could prove to you how happy I am, cameras or no cameras."

He managed a small laugh, rubbing her arm and then linking his fingers through hers. "You're something else."

"Lon, don't ever tell anyone this…" He looked at her expectantly. "They'll take away my card from the Stubborn Women of America Club." That made him smile. "But when I'm with you, I…"

"What?" he asked softly.

"I just want you to hold me in your arms and protect me. All of a sudden I'm waiting for you to run my life."

"It scares you."

"No it doesn't. Well, maybe. I've never felt that way before. I've always had to provide for myself."

"But you're not on your own now, not ever again. We're a team; you just haven't found your equilibrium. One thing I'm an expert on is teams. And I don't think that Stoan would say you've lost your stubbornness." He chuckled.

"Oh god. Stoan," she said. "What is it with him anyway?"

"I think you've just caught him on a series of bad days, as Mama Ruth would say." Lon paused and considered her. "And I think it's because, as you said, *as you said*," he repeated, pointing at her nose, "you're a nobody from the wrong side of the tracks."

"To make it worse, those tracks are on Earth."

"Right. A place Stoan considers backwater. And you've stood up to him, you've met him on a equal footing."

"Why shouldn't I?"

"You should, you should. But Stoan's been used to being treated as commander of the Mega-Legion for years now. How would I define that position?" Londo bit his lip as he looked up and to his right. "Oh, I know. It's like being God."

Lina laughed.

"Maybe a step or two below that. Stoan's a real nice guy, real down-to-earzth if he'll pardon the expression, but now he's used to being seen as two steps below God. If he ever loses a reelection, he'll automatically assume that everyone will treat him like a regular team leader again. But you've come along…"

"A nobody."

"And you just haven't shown him what he feels is the proper respect. Or maybe it's not the amount of absolute respect he receives as a matter of course from other people."

"So maybe that comes across as being disrespectful," Lina said thoughtfully. "Though he's the one who started all this. I can't stand disrespectful people."

"*Voilà.* Plus Stoan hates mind controllers especially. He has–" Lon's eyes darkened with the memory, "a bad history with them, going back decades. Stoan's another member of our group."

"Ah, which group is that?"

His brows knit together. "The 'We Had a Really Bad Childhood' Society," he told her. "Stoan was born into a slave marriage."

7

"**D**o you know what that is?"

Lina nodded. "It's one of those horrible three-ways, with one of the partners a slave. Londo, did you know that the Legion actually condones slavery?"

"Ah *oui*. They know enough not to have me get up in front of a press conference and back them on it, though. I'll tell you about some of that later. Back to Stoan. Since he was born into the marriage, that meant that he was born a slave."

Lina considered. "They said slave marriages were contracted for a limited time like the other marriages Out Here. Did that mean he became free after the marriage was over?"

"No. He was born into it, not contracted. He was to be a lifelong slave. He hated his father for that– his father was the slave– but he hated his masters more. When the marriage dissolved upon completion of the contract, his father was emancipated and took off, but Stoan stayed with his masters. They worked him hard." Lon heaved a sigh.

"But…?"

He shrugged. "Stoan developed the powers. That's why he'd been bred, you see. They'd hoped the genes would come up in the right combination. It's a high felony to construct paras in the lab, so some people breed for them. There were electromagnetism paras on both sides, back a few generations. Once Stoan showed his powers, though, they were mega and not just para, and he used them to make money and buy his freedom."

"Oh." Somehow Lina couldn't imagine Stoan being a slave, not being in control.

"He was arrested almost immediately for the murder of his parent masters."

"He murdered them?"

"And some other relatives. He did it under mind control. Some entrepreneurs on his world wanted to own him without the possibility of him being able to buy his freedom, so they arranged for a mind controller to take him over and commit the murders through him. He was found guilty– the motive was obvious enough– and sold for life to the highest bidders. Who were the actual killers."

"No."

"Yes. But Stoan was clever enough to gather evidence while he was bound to the killers. And let me tell you, it's damned difficult to get evidence about mind control. One day he managed to break free long enough to deliver it to the authorities, and the sentence was revoked. That's why he goes ballistic about mind controllers. So you've got to cut him a little slack in this, Kitten. Try to see him as part of the big picture."

She looked at him with admiration. "You're a pretty good shrink, you know that? You ought to hang out a shingle, Dr. Ran– Dr. Starhart."

Still, Londo needed counseling himself. As he and Lina avoided talking about punishments today's trial might order, he started to drift back to another problem, closely aligned in his mind. Lina could see the image of Aiko in his arms, dying by impalement. His misery rolled off him in great, bleak black waves.

"Back massage," Lina ordered, and went to work on him. It seemed to help. Afterward, Lina shook the sour energy out of her arms. Funny how though there didn't seem to be a planetary presence here to receive it here in hyperspace, it flowed from her as if something was willing to suck it up and recycle it to good use.

"I mean it," Londo was telling her. "I'm taking you to a nice restaurant to-night. A relaxing one, far from Legion HQ. Somewhere we can talk honeymoons."

"Can we get someone to feed the cats for us if we can't go back?" Lina asked. "I should have thought of that before we…"

Londo straightened, rolling his shoulders as he did so. "Ah *oui*, cats. That shouldn't be a problem. If you're… unavailable, I'll put a call through to Earzz–"

"Try that again, dear."

"What? Not call?"

"What planet are we from?"

The comers of his mouth quirked up." Urzzh," he slurred.

"Ear*th*."

"Urzs. So I have a lazy *th* sometimes. Sue me."

"Now, Lon, remember that you're the sole Legion representative of a planet that apparently has no standing Out Here. We need you to remind the good people what a terrific place you come from, in a way that they'll be able to look it up if they're interested. It shouldn't be a scandal to come from Earth. Now, I wouldn't change your accent for the world. It's the sexiest thing going. But there's got to be this one exception. What planet are we from?"

He touched his nose to hers. "Urzz," he said clearly. "*La terre. Terra firma.* Third rock out. Sol IIIa."

She frowned at him, her eyes dancing. "We'll work on it," she promised. That is, if they had a future that allowed them to. With that thought, the day became depressing again.

"Let's get out of this mood. We can play a game," Londo told her as he pulled on his gray-striped shirt. "This is the Alpha teams' official non-official hiding place, where we go when we don't want to be found. There are lots of great games in here. I've taught more than a few people how to play poker. There should be a pack of Terran cards here somewhere." He rummaged through a drawer under the game table.

"I hate to tell you this, Londo, but these poker games you're so fond of?"

He looked up at her, questioningly. "Yeah?"

"You can't do them any more."

"Why, don't you like– Oh. Oh."

"Uh huh. Telepaths sort of spoil the odds. And even if you can shield yourself from the other players, they won't believe you."

"*Merde.* You're right." He'd found the deck and dropped it on the table. "Man, I really liked poker, too." He considered for a moment and gave a crooked smile. "I wonder how long it will take for them to catch on? I mean, I might have a few good games left in me."

"A larcenous Legionnaire. You'll give Earth a bad name, Lon, if it could get any worse than it already is. Do they have any games out here that don't rely on anything that telepathy could spoil?"

"Just solitaire, I guess. How do you play solitaire with two people?" He shuffled the cards and laid out the cards for the game.

They tried for a while, but Lina favored cheating when they got stuck, while Londo didn't mind starting another game. "It's not like we're in a time crunch," he said. The game or maybe its monotony seemed to absorb him, so Lina let him play without interruption.

Finally she decided that underneath the terror of the day she was bored stiff. And getting hungry. There was nothing in the kitchen here and no replicator, so she walked around the great room to see if anyone had left anything interesting lying around.

So many famous trials had resulted in verdicts that she'd never seen coming. Were juries always that stupid? Would a Legion jury be stupid– or vengeful, seeing this as a way to avoid the scandal of Londo marrying a Terran? A simple lobotomy, an annulment… and the Legion could continue to survive in its own upper-crust society, the marriage never announced to the public.

All this did have a silver lining, though. Amazingly enough, Londo was also worried. Lina had never had anyone care about her before. The thought warmed her through her fear. Londo was the most wonderful man ever– and he'd be by her side the rest of her life. Life could be very sweet.

She called out game titles as she checked cabinets, but Lon's descriptions of them seemed too much for her to handle now. Instead she suggested, "Maybe we should discuss that honeymoon, assuming they aren't going to burn me at a stake. It is permitted to have a honeymoon, isn't it?"

"Of course it– Aw, someone botched the deck. How did that happen?"

"Hm?"

"They slipped in a card from another deck here. I'll work around it. It'll be a wild card when things get down to the wire."

"What, you can't cheat a little and toss it?"

Lon pointed the edge of the card at her sternly. "Sarastor has rules."

"So I've noticed." She cocked her head at him. "Somehow I don't see you following rules. You don't seem like a Stepford to me."

He gave her that slow, sly smile of his. "So maybe I don't run by the rules all the time. But I'm not going to give specifics when there are cameras around. I'll tell you later." He pointed. "Try that cabinet," he told her. "There should be some mazes in there."

"Oh no, not more mazes!" She sorted through another stack of games and educational programs, while he let out an angry grunt.

"*Maudite marde,* another one!" And then: "Lina, come here a minute, will you?"

She walked to him and looked down at the cards.

She couldn't contain her sharp intake of breath. "Where did you get those?" she demanded.

In front of Londo, face up on the three remaining tableau stacks, sat the same card with different writing on each.

"Have you seen this card before? I just realized that the words on this last were in English."

"It's from the tarot. 'The World,' Waite-Smith deck." Lina stared at the three cards, all of them showing a colored drawing of a naked woman floating suspended in space.

She pointed out the significant parts of the card. "This represents the end of the Fool's Journey, as he gains experience in the world. She is the triumph, the completed knowledge of the descent into matter and ascent into spirituality. She holds the scrolls of knowledge both of spiritual and worldly truths in her hands. These four," she pointed to the figures in the corners, "represent the four archangels."

"Good card?"

"Very good. The best, if you can compare tarot cards. You're encouraged not to, but with some cards you just do. Completion, triumph, graduation with honors, all things coming together, mature spiritual being… just good, good, good."

"Too bad we don't have four in here for a complete set." Using his paravision, Londo peeked in the stacks under the three cards. They were all normal playing cards.

"Lon, there's only one in a deck. You have three here. One in English. Do you recognize the language from these other two?"

"*Euh,* oh, that's Samarran, the native language of Sarastor there. 'The World.' This other one. Nope, I don't know the language, but I bet it says 'the World,' too. Okay, what does it mean?"

Lina stood up and addressed the ceiling. "You know, it might be helpful if you just sent someone to tell us what was going on, instead of giving us all these clues. We can't help it if we're slow."

"I hope *they* heard you," Lon laughed. "Okay, these cards. What would you tell your client if they got these in a reading?"

"I told you, there's only one card in a deck. There's no way anyone could get a reading from this. The cards are supposed to be taken in context. There's no context here. There was no question asked."

"All right. How about if we take the cards literally? Three Worlds. What does that tell us?"

"Three Worlds." Lina sighed helplessly as she sat next to Londo. "Three planets." That stopped her. She had mentioned to someone about three planets lately. Who? And in what situation?

"*Eh bien,* you're the one who talks to planets. You just had one speak through you a couple days ago. Surely that's related to this." Londo tapped a card on the table as he puzzled it out.

"Maybe, but how?" Lina propped her chin on her fists, staring at the three cards. "Three Worlds…"

Without warning, the door to the hyperspace chamber whooshed open. Lon let out an agonized cry as Lina crumpled next to him, clutching her head. All the telepathic impressions of the outside world crashed upon her. It squeezed her brain. She fought her way out of it, struggled for balance, and opened her eyes. Lon held her by her shoulders.

Baby, are you all right?

"Yeah, now." She let her breath out heavily. It was like standing under a summer thunderstorm, not yet broken: the pressure of all the minds of this world suddenly present, buzzing around in the background of the ether. "That was… a surprise."

"Sorry."

She looked behind herself even as she recognized the voice. Jae.

Oh god, Jae. She'd forgotten. She had to keep away from him. Even now with Londo by her side, she was too aware of the way he could hold her gaze and make her forget to breathe–

"I'll know enough to give you some warning next time." The tall, blond Legionnaire held out his hand to help her up. She didn't take it. "Come on, something's happening in the meeting room."

Lon came instantly to alert. "What? Have they taken a vote?"

"No," Jae said hurriedly. "When I finished the song that you and Lina had started, the discussions became very complicated. There's something else going on now, and I thought you two should be there."

"You're breaking the rules," Lon growled as he helped Lina up.

"It's not the first time."

"Good. Let's go."

Once out of the airlock, Lon scooped Lina into his arms and the Legionnaires flew like darts through the connecting corridors to the meeting auditorium. They landed lightly in the middle of the stage and Lon set Lina down.

Above the buzz among the cubicles, Lina wondered why a choir was singing. It sounded very far away, the voices almost discernible. Violin-laden music played accompaniment. It definitely wasn't an electrical hum of machinery. She brushed a strand of hair away from her eyes and looked where Londo stared.

A fuzzy patch of light fogged an otherwise empty cubicle. Wiley and several others pointed sensors at it from the main floor. Stoan and Andri stood in the space behind the light within the cubicle, measuring it from that side. Two Legionnaires hovered just outside and above the cubicle to get that angle on their sensors.

Now and then Lina could see an image within the flickering light, and the image was:

"Aiko," Lon breathed.

Jae turned toward Lina. "I thought you might be able to… do something about her," he said.

"She seems to be doing fine on her own." Lina pointed.

The light definitely coalesced into the form of Aiko now, sitting there as if she were alive and perfectly whole, wearing the caped gold and white costume she'd made famous in life. She rose and gracefully leaped from her station into the air as the two floating Legionnaires scrambled out of her way. She landed in front of the three new arrivals. A cloud of light hung about her like an afterimage, a soft glow of golden white contrasted against her dark skin, and twinkling in her short, metallic-tipped hair.

"So you are all here at last," she said in a voice that rang throughout the hall. "Lon. Jae. Lina. You should know that you three have been chosen. I was sent to tell you."

"Aiko," Lon said again, his voice cracking. "How–?"

"Be at peace, Londo. Have faith in the universe." She turned a beatific smile upon him and then at Jae and Lina. "All is as it should be, even as the universe is playing a cosmic game, as you put it. What have you learned today about yourselves, about what is happening?"

"That we three are involved in… something," Jae managed to say.

Lina said, "That whatever it is involves three worlds." As Aiko gazed at Jae something dawned in her. "Maybe four."

"Feith is dead now, Lina, but you are right; she still figures in this but from a secondary position. But the three primary worlds are…?"

"Sarastor," Lon said immediately.

"Aldierra," Jae added. Aiko nodded.

Lina thought. What could be the third planet if it weren't Feith? Oh, of course. "Earth," she said.

"Very good," the ghost of Aiko said.

Behind her images of those three worlds appeared in mid-air. Earth's blue and white made Lina homesick. The others were brown and violet-blue under the clouds, and brown and green. The latter she recognized. The jeweled Soul of Aldierra looked just like it, in miniature.

The now-familiar spirits of each world reached out to greet her. The violet-blue planet was Sarastor; the green one, definitely Aldierra. Earth was there as well. Below each world appeared its written symbol. Lina was not surprised to see that they matched the symbols on her wedding dress. The symbol for what had to be Feith had also been there in the background. When Lina looked out of the corner of her eyes, she could see another globe behind the three, barely visible. She could feel the resonance to it in Jae: Feith.

The ghost of Aiko spoke: "You three are the chosen ones of these worlds. The humans living on them have altered the balance too far for the worlds to bear any more. You are offered new responsibilities, if you will take them.

"Restore the harmony. Heal the worlds. Bring the yin back to balance the yang. Promote peace and community. Remind the humans that they are part of the whole, that they are members of a family that not only consists of all the life on their own world, but these Three Worlds and indeed the entire cosmos.

"There are many worlds that are similar to these three, worlds with people much like the humans of the Three Worlds. These three have banded in an alliance. We could also call it an experiment. Many world entities will be watching. Many, perhaps, will want to follow suit or even enlist your help if this proves a success."

Aiko quirked them a little smile. "But for now, you are requested to focus on only the Three Worlds. Let us see how far you get with them individually and as a group before you broaden your horizons. There will be tests and great difficulties, but it will be worth it to win through. It will be worth it for ages to come.

"We hope that this lifetime of effort from you three will affect not only the life on these worlds now, but all their future generations. Your work should spread out like a ripple and in turn influence other worlds, creating more ripples."

She moved between them in a gliding motion, meeting their eyes as she seemed to take their measure. "There are dangers involved. You can easily think of some, but others will appear that you could not imagine. If anything happens to any of you, you are instructed to find a replacement. The Worlds will guide you in your search.

"These plans have been in the making for hundreds of years. There are a number of viable alternates for the Chosen. But the Worlds are extremely pleased that their first choices, you three, have all survived your own harsh tests and training to make it this far.

"We ask that you make the decision, yea or nay. Jae and Lina, you are released from your priestly vows for this purpose only, so that you may make the decision with total free will."

Londo felt he was stumbling as he took in all this new information. "How would we accomplish all this?" he asked. Was this truly Aiko here, or an otherworldly construct?

"It is up to you to create your own solutions. The Worlds will help in any way they can. You are the co-creators. Now decide: will you be a part of this?"

She glided to Lon. "Londo Falcon Rand Starheart, my dearest love when I was incarnate. Will you build and protect these worlds? Will you accept the charge?"

"I–I've been trying to help all worlds since I was a kid. Would I be barred from them now?"

"No. But it is hoped that you would concentrate more on Sarastor and Aldierra, in addition to your responsibilities on Earth. You may consider yourself…" her eyes squinted to find the metaphor "…a shepherd whose flock contains three very special sheep. Guard the entire flock, but watch the three especially well."

Shadows of considerations swept across Londo's face before he nodded. "Then I accept. If I understand this correctly, this would give me leave to solve the roots of problems instead of always acting like some kind of bandage."

"Yes it would, Lon. Oh, excellent." She glided to her right. "Jaeson Rheoboth Rallene, the living heir of all that was Fcith, will you share with these worlds the legacy of your late world and accept the charge?"

Jae opened his mouth once and closed it. Then a slow smile bloomed. "Of course. It would be a very great pleasure. And honor. I should never have held back in the first place. I accept." He glanced at Lina. "Like a ton of bricks, you said."

"Very good. Those who gather around you are pleased and proud." And though the recording of the event never registered it, all three clearly heard her whisper, "And I was never as tight-assed as you thought."

Jae's smile broke into a broad grin. "Great *skurny* orb, it *is* you," he said. Did Aiko give a little sniff and toss her head? He chuckled at that.

Aiko now moved to Lina. "Carolina Angelina O'Kelly Starhart, to whom the universe has seemed to heave in these past few days. Timing is not always set at a comfortable pace during life. Lina, will you teach the inhabitants of these worlds about themselves? Will you accept the charge?"

The ghost of the preeminent heroine of vast star systems stood before plain little Lina. How could this be happening to her? "I, ah, wonder that the Worlds would offer this to me. I'm new to all this."

"The Worlds apologize to you. You were held back in order to obtain training that you would not have otherwise gained. Be that as it may, you are ready now. Do you accept?"

A song washed through Lina's mind about a wish for adventure, a wish for love as well.

Aiko had a faraway look in her eyes as if she'd heard the song, too. "Be careful what you wish for," she said with a distant smile. "You may find yourself living a happy life."

Lina had to share in the smile at that. "I accept, with thanks. Great thanks for everything that's happened. I'll do my best."

"Good." Aiko rose into the air to hover above them. Lina could hear the buzzing of dozens of sensors and cameras taking down everything. "Then I shall name you to your new responsibilities."

She paused over Londo. In her hand she held a small cruet that she tipped so light flowed from it in a blazing stream down to Londo's head. It poured over him like water, flattening his hair for a moment, and he caught his breath in surprise. He raised his left arm to touch it, but now a glowing, golden shield fastened on that arm. Aiko righted the cruet. The stream of light stopped. Tearing his eyes from Aiko, Londo peered at the shield quickly, then back to her.

"Protector of the Three Worlds," Aiko intoned.

She slipped above Jae and poured the light onto him. To Lina's eyes, a rainbow blossomed where it intersected the outer boundary of his etheric aura, but the white light fell straight and true onto his hair also. It slid down him to drip in runnels down his right arm and hand. He held a great staff of authority.

"Minister of the Three Worlds."

Lina: the light penetrated the very core of her self, blending and strengthening her so suddenly she gave a small cry of astonishment. It was as if she'd been standing in the cold all her life, and now finally found the warmth of shelter.

The heat spread out from her heart and the soft whisper of singing that had been in the room now rang from all directions around her, lifting her mind with it.

For one infinite moment she saw the Whole of the cosmos, the fundamentals of the Plan of Creation, still under construction and utilizing input from every spark of life there was. Love, joy, and creativity were the only things that mattered. Then she stood back in her body, knowing that she was individual again. Even so, the knowledge that she and everything else played a vital part of eternity electrified her. The entire universe sang to her, sang *with* her soul. In a moment she realized that she held a beautifully engraved golden flute in her hand.

"Speaker for the Three Worlds," Aiko announced over her.

Aiko retreated to view them as a group, and nodded approval. Their new signs of office disappeared, but Lina could still feel her flute ready to appear at her command.

Aiko said, "The ceremony is over. I can return home now. But there is one, no, two requests that I make for myself of you, Lina. It's not often that people on the Other Side are allowed to do so."

"Ah, that's true enough," Lina agreed. She still didn't feel quite real, so why not make a deal with a ghost?

"First: sing at my funeral. Isn't it strange how I can hear the entire universe singing all around me only now and not when I was incarnate?"

"I'm so glad you can hear it. I will be honored to sing if it's permitted. And the other request?"

"Take care of Londo. He is very dear to me. I have watched over him for a long, long time. I held on to physical life waiting for you to come and take over for me."

Lina's eyes blurred with tears. She locked her arms around Londo's strong right arm. "I will try, Aiko. I'll do my absolute best."

"Jae, I ask you to do the same. It is selfish of me, perhaps, to care for one more than I care for all. I know I don't ever have to ask this of you for you'll do it anyway. But I do ask."

"I will, Ko-Ko," Jae managed to say.

"That's all I wanted to hear. Dearest Londo…" She paused as she considered him, love shining like a beacon in her eyes.

"Aiko… Are you happy? Are you all right?"

She smiled reassuringly at his pained face. "I am as right as one can get, dearest. You can't begin to realize how happy I am. I'm home, with loved ones all around me. Everything is love and joyfulness.

"Don't think of me as I died. Try to forget that. Remember me with joy and not sorrow. I will always love you and care for you. I will remember you always."

Her fingers may have touched his cheek and might not. They were ethereal, fading. She took one more glance at the three of them and then regarded the hall, the people there transfixed at her presence. "Farewell and take care of yourselves, all of you. Trust in the universe. Trust in yourselves." She saluted those in the room and disappeared, leaving the ceremonial Legion auditorium seeming ordinary and dull.

Silence ruled for a minute. Two. Only the sounds of electronics recording. Lina hugged Lon fiercely, and he buried his head in her neck. **God, I miss her so,** he said.

Do you want to go back to your apartment?

No, just give me a minute. Eventually he straightened up, and they looked in each other's eyes. He gave her a little smile. Lon turned to face a concerned Jae and they hugged. No one else noticed because now everyone else was shouting, running for playback machines, directing others to check tapes. But within the spotlight that held the three Chosen, peace reigned.

Lon looked at Jae and reached out to brush Jae's bangs off his forehead. "Did you know you have a tattoo?"

"What?"

But Lon and Lina were gaping at the hand Lon had used. "It looks just like this," Lon said, showing Jae the mark on his right hand, just above his knuckles:

a triangle enclosed in a circle with a starburst close around it, all in a metallic gold that shimmered in the light. It was the size of a quarter, and blended in to the skin tone until the light hit it. It was also the same symbol that appeared on Lon and Lina's wedding rings.

They both turned to Lina. "Where's yours?" Jae asked, raising an eyebrow with an expectant smile.

Lina's eyes widened in innocence. Lon, however, let his eyes roam up and down her for a half-second, using his special sight to look through her clothing. "Found it," he said with a grin, staring at her left breast. "Heart chakra, I believe." She almost brought a hand up to see if the spot felt different, but stopped herself.

Lon took her hand and then reached out for Jae's. Lina held her hand out for Jae to take, uniting them in a circle. As their fingers closed on each other the world around Lina faded and another scene flashed through her mind in an instant although she saw it in its entirety:

They had been in quarantine still, after just one day on this new world. She had been asleep under Wiley's healing ray treatment, and Lon had watched her for a long time, she knew. But now he looked across the room to Jae and motioned him to the break room of Wiley's laboratory. He hadn't put up a privacy screen. That would have flagged Wiley's attention.

Lon programmed some drinks silently, then turned to Jae.

"You've been my closest friend for so many years," he said slowly. "You've always been there for me. I don't know how to say this. I know how you feel. But Jae, I love her. I'm going to ask her to marry me."

Jae started to collapse but he caught himself on a chair before Londo could reach him, and sat. He licked his lips as he shook his head slightly. "And, and her? Will she accept?"

"I think she will. I know her mind now. Jae, I know what we've had has been so special."

"But it's over now."

"I'm sorry. God, I'm so sorry. I wish…" Lon paused. He didn't know what to say. "Please don't hate me because of this."

Jae turned toward the wall. "Do you love me, Londo? You always said you did."

Lon swallowed. "I still do."

"In spite of her?"

"In addition to her. We've shared minds. She's actually a part of me now. Jae, I love you, but you're not a part of me. I can't live without Lina. I have to marry her. There's no other option."

Quiet anger flared across Jae's face as he faced Londo. "You'll kill her. Marriage to you is an automatic death warrant. Everyone will be after her. A norm, Lon. A norm!"

"She's not a norm. I wouldn't even consider this if she were. She's not invulnerable, but still a para. It looks to me like she might even be a megapara. Her power is sensing danger and escaping. It's perfect, it's like the universe programmed her just for me."

Lon gritted his teeth at the onslaught of the emotions Jae's mind was throwing at him: fury, betrayal, loss, fear, hopelessness… It was almost embarrassing to read him so clearly when Jae couldn't do the same to him. "I'm tired of being alone," Lon said. "This is my chance, and I'm taking it."

"You were never alone with me," Jae snapped.

"Of course I was alone. Us being so close made me even lonelier, knowing that I couldn't get closer to you. We shared hearts, but not bodies. And not minds. With Lina I'm not alone, not ever again."

Jae turned from him, burying his head in his hands against the wall. A long silence hung in the air.

"Jae. Jae, *chéri*. I will always love you. I'll always treasure the time we've had. The times we're going to have. This isn't the end of our friendship, love. We can always be the best of friends. Can't we?"

Jae turned to him desperately. "But us? Us as more than friends? Surely you can think of options for us. I can."

It took a beat for Londo to realize. "What, cheat on my wife?"

"I believe it's called an 'open marriage.' With the other spouse consenting."

"We can never have sex. Not real, anything near all-the-way sex. With Lina, I can."

"Have you told her about me yet?"

Lon took a breath. "I'm afraid to."

"Or ashamed?"

Lon didn't answer for a tortured moment. "Afraid," he finally decided. "This will make her stop and think when I propose." He tried to laugh and failed. "When she has to stop, she takes her royal time making a decision. I want her to jump into this. I said I can't live without her. I mean it."

Jae's jaw worked before he spoke. "Will you tell her afterward?"

"Of course I will."

"Then… maybe she can decide on that, too? An open marriage?" Jae gazed at Lon earnestly. "It may not be the same, Londo Rand, but you're a part of my life, too. I don't think I can live without you."

"Don't say that, Jae. You'll be fine. Give it some time."

"Look, I'm not threatening suicide."

Lon's voice hardened. "So don't make it sound like you are."

"I just… Things haven't been going that great lately. This isn't helping. I need you to be here for me."

Londo checked to see if they could be seen by Wiley, then took Jae's hand in his. "I love you and I always will. But we both know we can't make it official. And the physical aspect just isn't possible. It's been frustrating for you; it's been frustrating for me. Now I've found someone it is possible with, and miracle of miracles, I'm head over heels in love with her. I am going to marry her, Jae. When I do that, I'll be wishing with all my might that you'll find someone who'll do the same for you. You certainly deserve it." He drew Jae into a soft kiss. "I do love you. Never doubt that."

"So consider telling her. See what she wants to do." Jae kissed him defiantly, used to the lips that didn't mold to his own. "Tell her about us. I don't care if it's before or after you propose. Just make it soon. We've planned something like this for so long…"

"I don't guarantee that she'll say yes."

"To you or to me?" Jae's eyes were challenging now.

"To me, she'll say yes. To you… I don't know. I don't really know her that well."

"But you're planning to marry her, Lon."

"Details. I just don't know the details."

"And how many times have details tripped up plans?"

Lon glowered at Jae. "Are you trying to dissuade me?"

"Great orb forfend. Trying to stop Valiant from marrying someone he doesn't know well…" Jae grinned at Lon, but his heart obviously wasn't in it. "You're letting your hormones run amuck. You've always been a boob man."

"You've been looking at my woman." Lon grinned back.

"They're hard to miss." The grin faded to a sickly half-smile. "Look. I've known her for a whole day now, and I can see that she thinks that you're the beginning and the end. She's got a crazy slant on life, and you've always liked people with that. And *skurn,* she brought you back from the dead. Who am I to beat that?"

"She reminds me a lot of you," Lon said softly.

"Great," Jae said without enthusiasm. "That'll keep me warm on cold nights." He blew out a breath. "This is craziness. That's how some people will call it, you know. Correction: they'll say mind control. By the longest road, I love you, Londo, but I want you to be happy. And if she can make you happier than I can–"

"It's not that. It's not a comparison here. I love you both in very different ways. It's just that I literally cannot live without Lina now. I'd break down completely."

"That would be dangerous for the universe."

"Yeah. Just as it would be if you broke down." Lon looked at his hands and then back up to Jae's face again. "I will talk to Lina about us, as an open marriage. I don't know when, but I'll make it soon. And if she says no…" He steeled himself. "I'm going to have to give you an old line, but I mean it. If she says no, then I want us to remain friends. I don't think I can live without you in my life, either. If Lina doesn't like you, that's tough. We're still friends."

"But just on a lower level then we've been," Jae said slowly. "Shards and splinters, this is so sudden."

"The quick cut is the kindest."

Jae took a shaky breath. "So it is. Go ahead and do this craziness, Lon. But you'd have my eternal gratitude if you didn't put off telling Lina too long. Certainly before the marriage."

"That would be fair." He took Jae's hands in his. "Thank you, Jae-Jae."

Jae tried to smile. "So, when's the big event going to be? You've got it planned, I can tell."

Lon said, "*Eh bien,* June on Earth is the traditional month. That's about ninety days away. It should be enough time to get things organized, and Montreal will be warm enough for an outdoor ceremony. *Mon dieu,* it's going to be a media circus…"

CHAPTER

8

Lina's vision faded and she stumbled backward. How long had it taken? A moment? An hour? The bustle in here was the same as it had been, despite the fact that the universe had just turned inside out.

Londo was in love with someone else.

With Jae. Jae was in love with Londo; Londo was in love with Jae. The only reason Lon had married her was because they'd shared minds and could have sex.

How was she still standing? The room spun around her.

Lon glared poisoned daggers at Jae. **You made a pass at my wife?! You made more than a pass at her–!** Lon must have seen something different than Lina had.

Jae's shocked expression froze, then reformed itself into one of the infuriatingly uncaring masks he used to hide himself from others. He glanced around the hall to see if anyone was watching them and then returned his attention to Londo. He was still new to telepathy, so he had to form his silent words carefully. **We'd just saved the world against impossible odds. You know how it feels, like you're dancing with Creation. You want to celebrate.**

You wanted to celebrate with my wife.

I... Yeah. Londo, I'm attracted to Lina. Look, it wasn't her fault. None of it was her fault, not a moment of it. If you're going to be angry, be mad at me, not her.

Don't worry, I am!* Calisse, *Jae, how could you do this to me? To her?! If it were anyone else, I swear I'd kill– The teeth Londo flashed at him were those of a predator, poised to attack. "*How–**

The same way you could almost rape an innocent girl in some jungle and then try to abandon her after it was all over.

Londo blinked at that. Jae had seen something different than he had. ***It was… I was… a little crazy.***

Lame excuse. It was a good thing she could slap some sense into you. If she'd been on stims and crashed, you would have been all over her. And then you bullied her, tricked her into falling for you. You knew precisely what you were doing. Some hero, Valiant!

Their mental shouting turned into unintelligible gibberish as Lina retreated into the safety of her own shattered heart. She had married someone who didn't really love her. She was an accidental second choice to Jae. Londo– wonderful Londo, who'd pledged himself to her– had lied. He'd only married her for the sex after all. It could have been anyone, as long as he could touch them.

Jae's thoughts came to the fore. ***And then when it was all over, you were going to dump her like garbage.***

***Stop it, stop it!** Lina cried. Emotions crashed on top of each other in her mind. The two of them were fighting over things that she should have been in control enough so they never would have happened. She couldn't breathe. How could it all have gone so wrong?

They were in public; they couldn't make a scene. Mustn't embarrass Londo even if… Even if–

There had to be a way out of this. ***Londo, can you ever forgive me for what I did? Honest to god, I–***

I saw it all. He took advantage of you. He can be a sneak. He can stab you in the back if you don't watch him.

I swear, Lon, I didn't plan–

Shut up, Jae. You and I are going to have real words in private as soon as we can be alone. More than just words.

Lina felt so dizzy. ***We should get out of here. Not to kill him, Lon. Can we just leave?***

Lon crossed his arms over his chest, glaring at Jae. **We have things to discuss in private. We seem to be partners now. Let's get everything out in the open.**

Yes, Lina agreed helplessly. **Anything. Just let's go.**

An unequal partnership. Jae's thoughts dripped with bitterness. **Are you going to agree with everything he suggests, Lina? Make excuses for him every time he's wrong?**

I don't—

I saw you then. I see you now, and what I feel from you is that anything Londo does is right, everything is perfect, no matter how wrong it might be. Lon's going to protect you from everything you fear, and you're afraid of everything. Isn't that right?

Lina swallowed, fighting through the vertigo. **Yes. I'm afraid of everything, but I'm willing to make excuses for you, too. Haven't I already? I look back and I see that you were flirting with me, and I was too damned stupid to pick up on it. You wanted to drive a wedge between me and Londo, didn't you? It was only when you actually got caught that you got cold feet.**

Jae frowned and looked away from her. **Damn it, it wasn't cold feet.**

Then what? Londo demanded. **Lina, port us out of here. I know a very private, soundproofed place.**

I don't care if it's soundproofed.

Jae pulled at his earring. **I was just sounding you out, that's all. It didn't seem like flirting at the time. But once I realized that it had been, that's when I realized that I'd taken it too far.**

Her head throbbed, her eyes burned. **I believe him, Lon.**

Yeah? Jae asked hopefully.

Lina's chest constricted and she tried to breathe. **I guess. I don't know. But suppose he's telling the truth?**

Lina, what he did—

Just for a moment, give him the benefit of the doubt.

I—

You can go back to disbelieving him later.

Lon's eyes narrowed as he considered. He held Jae in his hard gaze. **Tell me.**

I was crazy, Lon. It wasn't me trying to get back at you. It was… just crazy. I don't know what you saw, but if you stuck around long enough, you saw that I stopped.

Lon wiped his mouth slowly with the back of his hand. His eyes cut to Lina's. **And you? How do you feel about Jae?**

She swayed in the confusion of the room. **Lon, you told Jae you'd tell me about you two before we got married. Before!**

That stopped Lon cold. His gaze went to Jae and back to her. **You know–?** Did he blanch? **But… we got married in such a hurry.**

Lina's eyes went wide and unfocused as the mammoth presence of Aldierra washed through her. Her back arched to ride with the power. **Hear me, my Chosen,** Aldierra told the three of them through her. **Let me remind you of your immediate concerns.**

The message that Lina had communicated to each and every citizen of Aldierra, began again:

I am Faun. I am Aldierra. I am your mother, your nurturer, the source of your life. I have loved you for eons but you have tried to destroy me. No more!

…I am an advanced being and I need to evolve. I can do this with you or without you– Make your choice. Stand by me; support me and love me, and I will continue to support you, too. You will receive my bounty in abundance. In turn you will evolve, become more loving toward each other. Happiness will come within your grasp.

But continue to forsake me, to destroy me and the creatures who live upon me without remorse, and I shall have to destroy you. Lovingly so, for you are my children. But I say I will not take this abuse any longer!

…I have enjoyed your presence until these last few centuries. I wished to be your home as you matured. But sometimes you have to cull the herd, thin the seedlings so that others may survive. I will do this if you force me to.

DECIDE. By the equinox after next, DECIDE!

Inform my Chosen and I will know.

This time, when Aldierra pulled out of her, it did not leave her weak. Lina did indeed feel that she was going to be sick– here in public and in front of cameras and Legionnaires– but it wasn't from sharing the Aldierran Ultimatum with Lon and Jae. This was something more important than the lives of twenty billion people.

God help her, Londo was in love with Jae! All her father's slurs rang through her mind. *Unlovable! Stupid Muttbutt! Whore! You'll die in a gutter where you belong, and no one will ever care!*

Lon had lied to her. Now she recalled Terry the Bitch calling him a liar. He had told Lina a number of small, reassuring lies in the time they'd been together. It looked like he didn't mind telling big lies as well. After all his declarations, Londo didn't really love her.

The two Legionnaires wanted to be together. Them, not her. They'd be the ones to throw her out into the streets, out of their lives.

She's been thrown out before and she'd survived. But she didn't think she could survive this.

"You three certainly seem to be taking this well." Dr. Wilder Mem-Bazer strolled up to them, a recording padd in either hand directly inputting data into his nervous system. Short violet hair stuck straight up all around the crown of his head. He must have been scratching in consternation during the entire event. Equipment hung out of his pockets, draped across improvised belts, clipped to the pockets and edges of his yellow lab coat/uniform.

As if that weren't enough data-gathering capability, his eyes moved independently of each other as he examined each of them. All five of his minds must be processing at top speed.

Wiley walked around them in a circle. "Do you feel any different? Any tingling? Any mental aberrations? Any new powers pop up in the last few minutes?"

Lon reached out to steady himself on Jae's shoulder. "Aldierra," he croaked, then regained his voice. "It… She just gave us the Ultimatum again. So that's how it was. The other day, it went out to everyone, Lie? Every Aldierran, no matter where they were?"

With a palm over her mouth she could only nod, trying not to look at him.

Jae's dark tan seemed paler than usual as he passed a hand across his forehead. His eyes came back into focus. "What the orb was all this?" he demanded. He tried to see Wiley's screens. "What kind of readings did you get from Aiko? From the Worlds? Did you get anything just then? It was Aldierra herself, a world talking just to us."

Wiley frowned at the question. "I don't think I'm prepared to put a hypothesis together yet." He waved one padd around Lina and then peered at her with both eyes. "Your blood pressure's dropping," he accused her.

"I'd like to leave, if that's okay," she managed in a voice just above a whisper. She felt like she was being torn in two. Her heart was disintegrating and pulling the rest of her apart as it withered and died.

"Is this an aftereffect of the event?" Wiley asked her.

"I'd like to leave, please," she repeated. She blinked hard. She was not going to cry, not in public. "Choose a place. That hyperspace thing or Lon's apartment." Not theirs. Not anymore. "Fifteen minutes. Please."

"Are you all right, *cherie?*" Londo asked. "You're white as a, a..." He reached for her arm and she drew back ever so slightly as he touched her.

Traitor! She wanted to shout at him. But not here, not in public. *You lied to me! You said you loved me!*

Jesus, wasn't this just like the real world? They'd come down to reality at last, where love was a sham, where people hurt you after you made yourself vulnerable to them. Where people destroyed you and laughed.

"I'm leaving in thirty seconds," she told him. "Give me a destination that I'm allowed to go to or I'll pick one myself."

"Lina." **Snap out of it, baby. We're in public.**

That's why I want to go to someplace private.

"She'll be okay," Londo told Wiley. "She's not used to this kind of thing."

"And who is?" Wiley asked him. His azure face was positively radiant with the unexpected day and its new events to study. "What were your impressions of the event, Londo? Did you think that was really Aiko, or was it some outside force? "

"You're taking subjective opinions, Wiley?" Jae asked.

He stood so close to Londo, his hand on Lon's arm. The boy Legionnaires, growing up together. Powerful. Important. Both so handsome and charismatic that you practically had to squint so you weren't sucked in by their presence. They belonged with each other.

"I'm trying to get a complete record from all perspectives. The, ah, entity seemed to solidify as soon as you three appeared together. She looked amazingly well to me. Do you agree?"

Lina wrapped the lines of planetary force around herself. Hide. Where to go? She could feel her lower lip quivering and she bit it to make it stop. Lon's apartment. That was still in Legion HQ. Maybe she wouldn't get him in too much trouble if she did that. She ported.

And just in time. Her legs gave way and she fell on the rug. She cried in fury, wept in pain. She hated when people lied to her, and she had trusted Londo with every inch of her being. Loved him with all her heart.

A voice inside herself accused her of adultery with Jae. No! That had been the stims! But she had been so attracted to him. No, that was an echo of Londo's feelings, captured during their sharing of minds. His deep feelings for Jae had shadowed Lina's mind.

Ah god, Londo loved Jae and not her.

She slammed her fists on the floor. Damned if she was going to let this beat her! Days ago she had decided to guard her heart and she hadn't. Stupid Lina Muttbutt! She had fallen completely.

The old Lina would have cried like this and let herself be destroyed. But she had changed. The new her was strong. She could get through this. Decisions would have to be made– but not now. Not with the destruction of her heart tearing her apart.

Lina? What's wrong?

Get out of my mind, Jae! She slammed the door shut against him, but could still hear them faintly.

Londo, Lina's gone.

She's what? Where– Lina? Lina! Get back here.

Her mind shied away from his. Who was he, anyway? He'd had her fooled completely. He was a stranger to her. **Leave me alone, Londo.**

Why'd you take off? Get back here now.

She ignored him as she dragged herself to the bathroom. She got sick there and then lay next to the tub on the floor, feeling its coolness beneath her as the kol-vanasche cleaned up. Her tears ran sideways across her face, puddling against her cheek on the tile.

She hadn't changed at all. She'd lied to herself.

Separate from the body completely this time, maybe? She could do it, the ultimate Out of Body Experience. Snap the cord. Things wouldn't look so dark from the Other Side, would they? There'd been another time when she'd come so close, back when she was ten. There were a few times later just thinking about it, but by then she knew there was another solution.

She'd taken two steps back from life. Since that first time, she'd cut herself off from the world and others. It was lonely but it was protected. She could still function like that. She could still help.

They were business partners for life now, avowed to the Three Worlds and their mission, whatever it would entail. She'd given her word. She couldn't just run away. She could be professional.

The Three Worlds would have to come first, above anything else. Maybe that was it: she could devote herself entirely to the Worlds and drive Londo and Jae out of her mind. Maybe that way her soul could remain intact instead of like it was, lying here in shreds on the bathroom floor.

Aiko had called her Lina Starhart, but that only showed how much spirits knew. She was Muttbutt Lina O'Kelly. Of Podunk Town, Earth. Not Starhaven. Not Sarastor.

A bitter laugh surged out of her like a sob. Damn, things had really gotten out of sync. She'd thought she was in some kind of faerie tale.

The fantasy she'd lived for these last few days would have to be enough to last for the rest of her life. It was time to get up and face the world again. She was in charge of three worlds now, given the public directive to shape their future in whatever ways she could. It was what she'd always wanted to do and she should be looking forward to this.

The door to the bathroom opened. "Lina? Are you all right?" Londo stood there, her worms-eye view making his a hulking, powerful silhouette. Valiant. Who had she thought she was, to try to come close to Valiant's heart? Idiot!

She tried not to sniff and didn't succeed. "Yes," she said as she sat up. She couldn't look at him. "Yes, I'm fine now. I'm sorry to have ducked out on you like that."

"Why'd you leave?"

"I said I would. I just had… some stuff to clear out."

"I asked you to stay."

"You told me to stay. I couldn't. It won't happen again." She tried to slip by him without touching him, without looking at him, but he grabbed her arm. She instinctively drew away from him, her skin shrinking from his touch.

"What's going on?"

"I said it wouldn't happen again, Lon. Please let go. Didn't Wiley have some more questions for you?"

"He's got questions for you, too. Jae's talking to him now. I told him I'd come get you."

"Well, we wouldn't want you to break your word, would we?" Ice dripped from Lina's voice. She glanced around the bathroom: there was her brush, her things. She'd really moved in here, but it wouldn't take that much effort to move everything back. "Give me a minute." Lina shook off his hand, then rinsed her mouth, dabbed her red eyes with cool water. She reached for her brush as he stood there.

"What's going on? Why are you closed to me? Is it about this Three Worlds thing, or about Jae? I told you, I understand about whatever happened between you two."

"I don't even know what happened between us," she said, smoothing in short, quick strokes. "Just the beginning. I was drunk on stims. You should ask Wiley about the effect."

"What?" Londo squinted at her. Who was this woman standing here, so aloof, so cold? "I'm not going to mention any of this to Wiley, and neither are you."

"Whatever you say, Londo. You're always team leader, aren't you?"

"Lina, don't do this. Look at me. Look at me."

Her gaze met his. They were stranger's eyes, lackluster and distant.

"What the hell is going on?" Londo whispered. For a moment he considered that maybe she was possessed. The afternoon's events might lead to something like that, mightn't they? Spirits and possession and priests dressed in black.

"Didn't you say Wiley was waiting for us?" she asked.

"Let him wait," Londo growled. "What's the matter, Lina? You don't like gays? I would have thought you were more open-minded than that."

"Wiley will notice if we're too late," she replied coolly. "You wouldn't want to have to explain too many things to him, would you? Or do you lie to him, too?"

"You think I lied to you?"

"What would you call it?"

"I didn't exactly lie—"

"Lon and Lina, Main Lab, please," Wiley's voice came from the air. Almost immediately afterward Stoan's voice blared on an official circuit: "Debriefing in one hour. Debriefing in one hour."

"I do not lie!" Londo exclaimed. "At least, not to people I love."

Lina calmly put down her brush and turned around. "That's the problem, isn't it? You lied to *me.*" And she ported them to Wiley's familiar lab even as Londo drew breath for his reply.

Damn it, Lina—!

"You wanted to see us, Wiley?" Lina purred while Londo fumed behind her. Let him try to see if he could be half as mad at her as she was at him!

"I want complete physical readings," Wiley declared as he approached them. Behind him a cabinet followed, appendages unfurling. He directed it to an open area of the crowded, warehouse-sized laboratory that had become so familiar. "Lina, you first. We detected minor radiation in there. Let's see if it was focused toward you three."

Lina stood obediently where he pointed and turned when he told her.

You think I lied to you?

She ignored the presence of her husband.

Apparently you lied to me, too.

She couldn't ignore that. She glanced at him.

His look at her was hard. **You promised you'd love me forever. A week is not forever.**

Wiley waved her off and Londo stepped forward to be examined. She could feel Jae come up beside her, but she didn't look at him. He'd tried to warn her, hadn't he? He'd told her that he loved Londo more than anything. She should have realized. She should have realized! She could be so incredibly stupid.

Women had always warned her about men: all they cared about was sex. They mixed up the concepts of sex and love. So Lon liked having sex with her. He took that for love. But he loved Jae.

Lina sat down suddenly and concentrated on not crying. She never cried! Why did she feel like crying for hours now? She could handle this. Shut it off, hide from it. Deny.

Taking those two steps back was harder than she remembered.

Jae touched her shoulder and she twisted the chair so that his fingers fell away. "Come out of it," he whispered to her. "Can't you see what you're doing to Lon?"

What she was–? How dare he! Anger rolled off her in a deep red-black cloud. Jae stepped back warily.

I know you're mad at me, he began.

You didn't bulldoze me into marriage by lying to me.

Oh. Ah. Jae regarded Londo standing there in a dark auric cloud of his own in the middle of the lab. **So you don't hate me?**

She started to say something, but bit her lip instead. Jae saw how very pale she was. Dark circles rimmed her eyes. **Lina,** he finally asked, **when was the last time you ate?**

"You do not exist," she managed to whisper.

"What?" He crouched down to be at eye level with her but she kept her gaze averted from him.

If she couldn't take her two steps back, she could make them do so instead. "Londo does not exist either," she informed the air beside her.

Jae rolled his tongue inside his cheek. "So. So you made a promise to Aiko to care for a figment of your imagination, did you?"

Lina stopped breathing. She'd promised.

"It's so easy to break a promise when it was all to someone who doesn't count, isn't it?"

Oh god, what was she going to do? She'd promised to take care of Londo. She'd promised, she'd promised, she'd–

Lina's lower lip quivered violently, no matter how hard she tucked her upper lip in to steady it. She wrapped her arms in a death hold around herself.

"Use the break room," Jae told her. "Get something to eat while you're in there, but turn on the privacy curtain. You remember how?"

A jerk of her head told him she did, though she still didn't look at him.

"Go."

She dashed to the small room at the front of the lab, keeping low so that Wiley wouldn't notice her. Jae saw the subtle shimmer of a privacy curtain immediately appear over the entrance.

Now he turned to watch Londo holding still for Wiley. It always took the instruments longer to read Londo than anyone. Then it was time for Jae to be examined. Lon headed towards the darkened break area as Jae unfastened his white cape.

"Hey, Lon." Jae raised his voice to get his attention. "I think it might be interesting to contrast and compare Legionnaire and non-Legionnaire reaction to all this, don't you?"

"What?" Lon turned at that.

"I mean, here we are. We're used to the blazing orb itself breaking loose. Sure, this was a little over and above normality today, but just think about it from Lina's point of view. Today added to everything else she's been through in the past, oh, two weeks. Not even that. Are you going to do a psych study, Wiley?"

The doctor looked up long enough to scratch his scraggly head. "I could, I suppose. She did appear to be a little upset."

"I can't even begin to imagine what all this is to her," Jae swept his arms out to take in the experiment-filled room, futuristic even for Sarastoran technology. "A norm from a barbaric world suddenly imprisoned on Sarastor for a week. Or you could look at it as an average person who suddenly was taken against their will to trial at the AffSys Mega-Legion, locked up for a couple hours while the fate of their very mind was discussed, and suddenly they're granted– What were we granted, anyway?"

"Godhood," Wiley grunted. He produced new equipment to run around Jae's tall silhouette as Londo returned to his path toward the break room.

Jae laughed. "Quite a few levels below that, Dr. Mem-Bazer. But still right up there, right up there." Jae's gaze followed Londo. **Or you could look at it as an untouched virgin with big, innocent eyes who'd never been close to anyone in her life, suddenly falling head over heels for some famous schnook and him rushing her into marriage before he can tell her that he loves someone else, too. And suddenly she finds out, but it's not from her husband. You told me, Londo. Why didn't you tell her? Give her some time.**

Londo stopped, but didn't turn around.

"Maybe dictatorship then, if not godhood." Wiley grunted again as he studied his findings. "Something peculiar here, but I'm not sure what," he finally surmised.

With a jerk, Jae whirled to face Wiley. "What? What?! Tell me: am I going to live?"

Wiley reached for more equipment, which moved within his reach. "Did I say it was something bad?"

"You didn't mention anything good. Maybe you should assign mind number five to creating a calm and reassuring bedside manner."

Londo returned. He examined the readouts, his face reflecting puzzlement as he tried to understand data a handful of levels beyond his understanding. "C'mon, Wiley; is Jae okay?"

Wiley shook his head and rubbed his chin. "Look there: there's activity with his RNA-activants. A slight increase."

"What does that mean?" Jae demanded. He tried to push Lon out of the way so he could see, but of course he couldn't move Valiant. "How slight?"

"Slight. As for what it means…" Wiley blinked, thinking, and changed the screen. "No," he said, "delfic levels are steady. White blood cells show no abnormalities." He scratched the back of his head for a moment and then called up Lon and Lina's charts.

"There." He tapped the screen on Lina's side. "RNA-activants."

"But not Lon?" Jae asked.

"Not Londo."

"So what the hell does it mean, Wilder?" Londo grabbed one of the screens and pulled it closer, peering at it. "RNA has to do with memory, right?"

"If you want to be extremely simplistic, yes. Memory on a cellular level. But we're talking RNA-activants here, not RNA. It's very strange. It should be starting to affect the delfic systems even at this low level, but it's not."

"Delfic systems. I skipped class that day."

"Delfic is the one that keeps the body in condition, the plasticity of form and function. It aids in DNA replicating uniformly."

"Those game pieces–" Jae said suddenly and the two of them looked at him. "The game pieces Lina ported in when she was first trying interstellar ports. The one that dissolved…"

"Interesting that you should tie porting to this and not our supernatural event," Wiley said slowly.

"Lina and I have been doing a lot of porting lately. Londo hasn't."

"Are they dissolving?" Londo slapped his hand to his chest to wring his shirt's placket. "Devolving?"

"Easy, Lon. I don't know what they're doing. This is an incredibly small increase. It's not reacting the way I would think it should, but there's been very little research in this area. It's just something we'll keep an eye on. Let's see, who's been porting around lately? Puter, have Ion Emperor, Multiplex and Sunstorm report to me at their earliest convenience." Two beeps. "Let's see if they're showing signs of this, too."

"Should Lina stop porting?!"

"Londo, you're ruining my furniture again."

Lon's fingers had dug creases into the tube arms of Wiley's chair. He hastily released. "Sorry. Should she? Tell me."

"Easy. I shouldn't think that this signals anything really wrong with the process. Perhaps if it causes problems she can fine-tune her porting. I'll perform a weekly check of her if you want to bring her back."

"Of course I'll bring her back," Londo growled. "Lina is my wife! If she needs medical help, of course I'll bring her here!"

"Well, if I can't figure it out, we'll just have her ask those guides of hers." Wiley looked at Jae strangely. "That's right, she got that right."

"Got what?"

"When she told you that you'd get a new job, a new home, a new love," Wiley said. "You just got a new job today, Mister Minister of the Three Worlds. You will keep me informed on the other things if they happen, won't you?"

Jae spread his hands and gave him a grin. "Only if you keep me informed about my RNA-activants."

"Deal. Lon, let me run a questionnaire by you and Jae. Where has Lina gone now? Oh. Did the event really shake her up that badly? I want her to answer questions, too. Maybe I should toss in some psychological ones as well."

"I don't think she's eaten today," Jae said, catching Londo's eye. Jae crossed his arms across his chest and lowered his chin to give Lon an accusing look.

Wiley pored over his readings. "Very low blood sugar; yes, here it is. Dehydration. That's bound to add to the stress of the situation. We know she doesn't deal well with starvation." He shook his head over other readouts. "Stress, lots of stress here." He made a little noise to himself as he cross-referenced some more screens. "Does this have something to do with the RNA-activant levels?"

Lon was angry, but he didn't know at whom. Lina or himself? Or Jae?

Don't be mad at her, Lon. It wasn't her fault.

Yeah, let's find a private place and have a little chat about that, Jae. Right now.

We've got debriefing in twenty minutes. You don't want to have to drag a dead body in there, do you? Jae flashed Londo his most winning smile, wiggling his eyebrows.

Jae, you've got too many balls. I can take care of that problem for you. Making a play for my woman– What's the matter, you can't get one of your own? You have to steal from me?

I wasn't stealing. I was just... just teasing her and it got out of hand.

It got a hell out of hand. What happened when she woke?

She declared her true love for blonds over brunets. We're running off this weekend, Londo, leaving your sorry ass behind.

What really happened?

Jae couldn't meet Londo's eyes. He stuck his tongue in his cheek, then worked his jaw, before he replied. **She yelled at me. She called me names I'd never heard before. She cried. She thought she had betrayed you. It tore her up, but not half as bad as she's torn up now. Just now she told me you'd lied to her.**

I didn't think she'd be against homosexuals.

The word is "gays." She's been teaching me a lot of things. Rainbows and petitions for gay rights. She signed one while we were on Earth. She has lots of gay friends, did you know that? She wants to introduce me to one. His name's Mace. He's an old friend of hers.

Londo eyed Jae warily. **You seem to know a lot about Lina.**

You know her from the inside out, Jae said. **I know her from the outside in.**

And you want to know her better.

Just like we planned.

Londo turned his back on Jae.

The privacy field gave a shimmery rustle as he stepped through. Lina sat there with her face in her hands, a steaming cup of soup untouched on the table next to her. "Wiley wants us both to take a questionnaire," Lon told her.

She nodded without moving her hands.

"Debriefing in a few minutes. I think they'll want you there."

"Tell them I'm Terran." Her voice was muffled through her fingers. "I'd probably contaminate their precious meeting chamber more than I already have."

He sat down and took her soup. "Do you mind? If you're not going to?"

One of her shoulders shrugged, pointing him at the soup as well as giving her acquiescence.

He took a good swig of it. What to say to her? He was angry at her for being angry at him. He was angry at her for withdrawing herself from him. She couldn't do that. She was his, and he would not allow this. And though he knew it wasn't her fault, he was angry because of what he'd seen her doing with Jae. But something in the waves of anguish washing off her kept him from saying it.

"Wiley says that your RNA-activants are at higher levels than they should be."

"They're going to get higher."

"Do you know what RNA-activants are?"

She shook her head.

"Lina, look at me."

"I'm doing reiki."

A soft gong sounded: fifteen minutes to debriefing.

"You're going to have to look at me sometime. At least tonight when we make love."

She raised her head. The circles under her eyes were gone. "You're back," she said hollowly, "and Jae's here. What do you need me for?"

"Here!" Wiley burst in through the privacy screen and threw two note padds onto the table. "Fill those out before the meeting. You can make your answers brief for now." He went over to the replicator and signaled for *tarn*. "Quickly!"

Lina picked up the device that was the size of a business card. A screen triggered over her hand and she tried to decipher its Panlingua through her crying headache. "English usage," she finally said, and the writing changed.

She went through the questions. *What was your impression of the entity presenting herself as Aiko? Give a description of what you saw. Did you feel any kind of power flowing from the area she was in? What were your impressions of the Three Worlds' offer? How did your gift from the Three Worlds feel? Where is it now? What does it feel like when it isn't there? Did your telepathy change in any way during the ceremony? Are you telepathically linked, and if so, how deeply? Did recording the event seem to change its character in any way? Do you think it would have been different if it hadn't been recorded and measured?*

Wiley looked over their shoulders as they scribbled. "You could just postpone the meeting for fifteen minutes or so and get some longer answers," Lina told him.

"Scheduled times are scheduled times. Now shut up and write! Dictate if you can structure your answer well. Hurry up. We can get longer answers later."

So she wrote in quick phrases and impressions. At the end with Wiley standing over her, impatiently holding out his hand for the padd, she wrote, "They say don't worry about the RNA stuff or the pre-plasm (spelling?), which you haven't caught yet. Levels will increase and it's nothing for you to lose any sleep over." She handed the padd to him and flexed her fingers.

"It's about time," he grumbled.

"Debriefing is now taking place," Stoan's voice echoed slightly over the intercom. "Dr. Mem-Bazer, Valiant and Neutrino are late. Get the blaze down here!"

"Come on, Lina." Lon reached to take her hand.

"I didn't hear my name called. I think I'll stay here and get something to eat. I'll go back to quarters later." Start transferring things back home.

"Nonsense," Wiley declared. "You're needed as a primary witness. Londo, I want her in my box. She's the closest thing we have to an expert on the supernatural. It will make an interesting contrast to our scientific records. Everyone who's anyone at the primary Tishan Institute is asleep now, and when I suggested that we wake someone Stoan said he didn't want anyone there to think that we'd all gone mad. He said we had to wait until after this preliminary investigation." Wiley made a frustrated face. "Stoan can be so immovable at times."

"Rand! Mem-Bazer!" Stoan's voice bellowed from mid-air.

"We're coming!" Wiley replied.

9

They had Lina port them to just out of the spotlights on the main floor. "I'm here, I'm here," Wiley grumbled to Stoan as he fumbled with the handful of note padds. He took his place at a podium that had not been there that morning. It contained a sizeable workstation area. Immediately a life-size hologram of the Aiko apparition appeared in mid-air, surrounded by various charts measuring ambient phenomena.

"Come on." Londo grabbed Lina's hand.

"I thought I was sitting in Wiley's cubicle."

"No. You're coming with me."

He pulled her along and she let herself be led. Two flights up of dark stairs behind the cubicles brought them onto a narrow, steel frame balcony. The sixth door down carried a small sign with Lon's Valiant name, and it opened onto a familiar cubicle. He motioned with his fist as they sat down. In answer, a privacy screen appeared to obscure the cubicle's window onto the main floor.

At first he didn't say anything. Lina wasn't going to volunteer. He didn't exist. Instead she watched a small muted screen with Wiley's face on it.

Lon slapped his hand down to cover the screen in front of her. "I want to know what's going on," he demanded. "Why are you doing this to me?" The privacy field sputtering off startled him, and he looked up.

"Cut the privacy crap and pay attention, Londo," Stoan ordered on a private circuit. His eyes flickered over to take in Lina's presence, but he didn't say anything about it.

"We haven't had a chance to discuss any of this in private yet."

"Good. I don't want to hear edited reports." The circuit cut off.

There were too much data being given, too many sub-circuit conversations going on, too many requests for Lon's quick opinions, for them to converse telepathically. Just as well; Lina didn't feel like talking to him.

Instead she sat and numbly watched as Wiley reran the afternoon's proceedings. He had angles from all directions, measurements and commentary on the extraordinary phenomena. He used technical words that she was unfamiliar with, nouns and verbs that were not part of everyday language. She let them roll past her and just watched it all again.

Londo pushed a cup of something in front of her.

She managed to say, "Thank you," just as she would for any stranger.

He reached for her left hand then, laying his fingers on top of hers. She pretended to watch the floor show. Close off from him. *Protect yourself. Survive.*

She eased away from him when he released her to address the group with his expertise. He came from Earth, after all, a place where some scientific research into paranormal phenomena was taking place.

But Valiant's experience with psychic events had been superficial: third-hand accounts of hauntings, of possessions. Stories that had made the news, but that he'd never personally witnessed. He'd never even watched an episode of *Long Island Medium.* Oh, there were beings like the Green Mage, vampires and such— but they were products of the Timeless Realms and more magical than psychic in nature.

Of course Valiant would be accustomed to magic. He was a megaparahero. Lina? She was a nobody. How far had she overstepped herself these past few days pretending to be worthy of being Valiant's wife? Besides, Valiant didn't want a wife. He needed a temporary make-do until he could get what he really wanted: Jae. He just wanted a "beard."

She was no man's beard. She would not live a lie.

Another screen came to life in front of them. It was Wiley, who by now had gone to his own cubicle. A bar of type across the bottom of the screen said that this feed was for the entire membership and not private. "Mrs. Valiant," he said, "you seem to have experience dealing with these kind of entities, if indeed this is a true ghost. Was this truly the essence of Orenya?" "Orenya" was Aiko's hero name.

"Of course it was," she said. She took a breath to organize her thoughts. It was time to sidestep her feelings and be professional. She'd lectured in workshops before.

"Unless you people have found a way to give a false presence of soul to holographic images, the real spirit of Aiko, I mean Orenya, appeared today. She wasn't a stuck ghost; she'd gone all the way over. She had access to universal knowledge. You don't run into many human spirits who've had that. Usually people are just as ignorant on the Other Side as they are here, at least the ones you can contact, or maybe that's the way they can contact us, that they communicate with their incarnate personality and knowledge so as to appear familiar. There are layers to the human soul. We incarnate beings seem to be the bottommost, but still connected to them all."

Lina thought through the possibilities for a moment, comparing the kinds of presences she'd talked with over the years. "Aiko said that she'd been taking care of Londo for a long time. She may have been doing that for longer than one lifetime. She might have been a guide who incarnated, maybe one of Lon's personal guides."

"Doubletalk," someone in the audience said. "I really do not want to turn this into some kind of hoodoo party. Let's keep this rational."

"The explained is a tiny amount compared to the unexplained," Lina countered. "Just because you can't explain something doesn't mean it doesn't exist."

Someone else interrupted, "Do we really want to tell ghost stories here?"

"If that's where we have to begin," Wiley said, "that's where we start. Lina, you mentioned studies in the supernatural on Earth."

Lina told them about parapsychology, running them through a brief history of the science from England's SPR, through the Rhines and up to modern research. She tried hard to remember details from that lecture on ghosts she'd attended at the Rhine Research Center only a couple months ago. Ultra-low frequency sounds, temperature changes, magnetic fluxes…

Wiley adjusted some of his scans. "Yes," he said, "look at the room temperature. A distinct bubble of cold air followed the phenomenon, fifteen degrees difference, and climate control even tried to compensate. Lina, you say that the presences of the world entities were present?"

"Yes. They were going along with what Aiko said. Confirmation, if you will. Of course you'd have to believe in the worlds as beings to believe the confirmation."

"You've mentioned speaking to worlds before. I've recorded quite a few comments from you about that even before the Aldierran Ultimatum. These worlds have true intelligences?"

"They're very old, very advanced and wise, but they talk to you like you'd talk to a friend, or maybe a grandchild."

"Why hasn't anyone on Tishan ever mentioned anything like this?" a Legionnaire asked. It was one of her big guards, Minzier. "This wouldn't be something they would keep secret."

"The Tishana keep everything they can secret, Bli," the red-haired Brügz Sikrichat answered by remote monitor from whatever planet he and Erik were on.

Conversation switched to focusing on Brügz, who had once been married to the Legion's resident Tishana telepath, Psyche. She was on a secured mission at present and couldn't be reached. Too bad it seemed she hadn't told her husband much about her business, though Brügz was certain that his ex had never communicated with ghosts or planets.

Wiley broke in. "All right. Lina, when you say Orenya had completely passed over, what does that mean?"

"That she's… Some ghosts are souls that are stuck close to our plane of existence for one reason or another. They're unhappy or confused or just leftover emotional energy from a single event. But Aiko had gone on, and she'd either regained knowledge that she'd already had or she'd tapped into the universal knowledge."

"What does that mean?"

"You know, like in Near Death Experiences."

At Wiley's blank look she had to explain the typical NDExperience. She finished by saying, "Most people, once they reach the stage of experiencing the ultimate light that is love, are allowed to tap into some kind of absolute, all-knowing bank of knowledge, past and future. I got a taste of that this afternoon, but it's gone now."

"And you think that this is what happened to Aiko."

Lina considered, licking her lips, weighing possibilities. "Yes. But. It's my gut opinion that Aiko was one of Londo's guardians or spiritual mentors who incarnated for a time. That feels right. If this is the case, she normally exists on a higher level than most humans. I'm not familiar with scientific studies about those, just what psychics have written on the subject."

"These are the guardian angels you've spoken about."

"Yes, entities who guide and protect. These can include Higher Selves, those upper layers of incarnate souls."

Some brave member respectfully brought up the fact that Aiko had not been a perfect angel and before Lina could break in, Jae explained that higher spiritual beings, the ones Lina referred to as "angels," were also climbing the ladder of self-improvement. Incarnation was a process of putting oneself through tests.

Everyone silently pondered the Last Feithi's words. One person asked him if he communicated with such discarnate beings.

He sat perfectly still a moment before he answered. "I can sense them some-times," he said. "And I regularly communicate with, shall we say, first cousins to such entities." He did not elaborate, nor did anyone suggest he should. The secrets of the Feithi were sacrosanct.

Lina mulled his words. She had caught Jae talking to devas, or something akin to them. In general, devas ruled non-human things and concepts while some families of angels watched over humans. Jae seemed to do it differently from her, not quite ordering, not quite persuading, but some way that forcefully di-rected devas. It was how his power over the very matter of the universe worked. He wanted to keep that technique secret.

Why did this bother her so now? Why did this knowledge loop in her brain?

Londo shifted in his chair, rising momentarily to the realm of existence. She shoved him out of her mind and concentrated on the discussion at hand.

Andri asked her, "So you're saying Aiko was just alive to learn lessons? That's all?"

"I don't know why she incarnated. If she was one of Lon's guardians, she was here because he needed someone to be here for him on a physical level. That could have been a very minor reason why she chose to live. I've done past-life regressions on people who didn't start out as human. I remember one woman who had been various natural things: a pond, trees mostly. She saw humans around her and was fascinated by them, so she incarnated as a human just to try it out, and then got stuck in the cycle of human lives quite against her will."

The discussion wore on and wove itself away from Lina. She leaned back in her seat and watched yet another replay of Aiko. This time Aiko asked her to take care of Londo and she agreed.

He was looking at her.

Why couldn't Aiko have asked Londo to keep his promises? Just a few days ago he'd promised Lina that he loved her and would cherish her forever. Why had he lied to her?

He was a proud man who was tired of being publicly celibate. He would have taken anyone, anything that could offer him relief. He would have promised anything.

He would have lied until his tongue turned black.

A message flashed across the screen for her: a reminder that she'd missed an event with Legion Protocol, of all things. She ignored it but wondered what Protocol's Ms. Yency would think of her marriage if she knew.

Yency would say to smile to the cameras and never, ever say anything negative about her Legionnaire husband, no matter what he did wrong. There must be no hint of scandal within the Legion's ranks. Since Lina and Londo had been married the Feithi way, with no possibility of divorce and a lifetime contract, they had to live this sham for the rest of their days and smile to the public about it.

So many promises made these past few days. Lina had promised Londo that she'd never embarrass him. She'd promised Aiko that she'd take care of him. And at the wedding, she'd promised her husband that she'd always—

"So, Lina, in your opinion," Wiley was asking, "what does it all boil down to for this alleged Aiko today?"

She hoped she hadn't turned red from being caught with her mind elsewhere. Taking a long breath in preparation to speak gave her the moments she needed to organize her thoughts. "She was an honest-to-god apparition from Beyond, with knowledge imparted from the same," she told him and the room. "That's my 100% gut opinion. I also think she is one of Londo's guides." She couldn't ask her guides for confirmation, as upset and disconnected as she was.

She had to be able to think about everything rationally. No one ever made good decisions when they were overly emotional. "Now you people can argue about what kind of equipment it would take to come up with the events of the afternoon. Good luck in trying to pin it on me." Lina sat back in her chair, determined to shape up.

"Give 'em hell, Lina," Jae said from a small, private side screen.

"Commander Magnos," Wiley said, "we have to talk to people on Tishan. Let's get some of them on the screens."

A dozen people echoed him.

Jae appeared on the main screen. "Whatever we do," he told the group, "we can't lose the overall picture. If you take a recording of a human voice and break it apart, study every tone and inflection, what the vocal cords are made of and how language evolved, you can figure out how it works. But you've lost the message. We can't lose the message here. Aldierra is in dire straits, under a death threat, and Sarastor and Earth are worried that their worlds could follow."

Jae was right. With all this unholy mess to fight through, Lina couldn't lose sight of the new responsibilities she'd been sworn to today.

"I don't see how Sarastor could be involved in all this." This time Lina recognized a Legionnaire: Excell. She couldn't remember what her powers were, though. "I think we'd all call Sarastor the best world around. It leads the galactic sector in civilization. There's still poverty on other worlds, but everyone here is provided for."

Londo leaned forward. "Everyone is provided for," he agreed. "Everyone gets their anti-depressants so they can deal with life. Everyone has their video feed. But some don't get enough. Call up suicide statistics for Sarastor and compare them with, say, an Unaffiliated World of their choosing. The stats should shock you. Go down into the streets of Sarastor sometime. Anytime. They're empty. When you consider how many people are here, how many streets there are, those streets are empty. Everyone's sitting in their own apartments, hooked up to their monitors. Never interacting with the real world, living vicariously through their screens.

"Here at the Legion our job requires that we be out and about. How many here have close friends native to this world? Very few. That's because there are so many people out there we haven't met because they're only connected to the nets, every moment they're awake and often when they're asleep. Because they're alive they get fed, they get shelter. But do they live a true life? They only imagine they're alive."

Now Jae joined in. "On a planetary level Sarastor is a joyless world. I remember a world filled with laughter. On Feith everyone danced, everyone sang, and everyone loved. Here so much is gray and lifeless. Sometime long ago someone told others how they were supposed to live efficiently, and apparently people took it to heart. I saw all this when I first came here, but I forgot." His voice choked. "I forgot. Now I remember. Sarastor is a sick society, and probably dying. No wonder the planet is calling out for help."

From his podium, Stoan frowned at Jae's image. "I haven't found anything wrong with Sarastor," he said. "It's a quiet world, not a sick one."

"That's because all you see are the exceptions," Jae said quickly. "You meet the few who are trying to do something in the world. It's everyone else who's so quiet– because they're dying inside."

"No wonder there are so many suicides here," Londo said. "We have to import everyone of any importance. When was there last a Sarastor native in the Legion? It's been over a century. Teachers, politicians, engineers, sports teams– everyone who's doing anything here is an immigrant.

"Life here is so much like death that people didn't ever bother to come up with ideas about what happens after you die. They've already got it. Life is hell."

"Can we spare the philosophy and get on with examining the event?" someone asked tiredly. "Unlike Sarastorans, I do have a life."

There was mild laughter at that, and discussions went back to quantum analyses of every frame of what Wiley labeled "the Investiture." People kept asking Lon and Jae what had happened at certain points, so they were busy replying and carrying on personal asides to Legionnaires and each other. Wiley would interrupt on personal circuit with snide comments about some speaker or another and his estimate of their intelligence level.

Lina tried to access the screen on her side of the desk, but it flashed ACCESS DENIED at her. Lon reached past her without saying a word and touched the side of it. It cleared, and she called up explanations of technical terms as they came up. Many times she had to specify layman terminology, and once or twice she had to go below that, practically to kindergarten level or so it seemed, to get something she could understand.

Londo scowled into her silence. This was no possessed person. He'd seen this part of her in her mind but she'd never acted this way before in his presence. She'd been a caring, sensitive and passionate woman. Yes, he'd seen her hide from the world, but it was just a reaction, wasn't it? Not a basic way of thinking.

Now she was hiding from him. He didn't like it. He'd teach her differently once this was all over. She was his wife. She'd made promises– and if there was one person in this universe who thought promises were as holy as vows, it was Lina. He'd remind her of that fact– later.

This Investiture thing was tied into the Aldierran Ultimatum and the attempted conquest of Sarastor. On his cold side of the cubicle Lon called up what Legion cameras had managed to catch of that: how Lina, Wiley and Jae had discovered the cloaked invasion fleet. Jae's crazy plan to confuse them and make them think that Sarastorans as a race were powerful, all-knowing… tour guides.

Londo stopped the video where Lina had ported back in from the Aldierran ships to Wiley's lab to get supplies. God, that dress. Her in that clinging, almost-there dress, the same one he'd seen in his vision: Jae stripping off that dress in a hotel room, taking off his own robe and then caressing her as if she'd been his.

Lina stood in that dress on his screen, flowers in her hair, her face a little flushed from what, he didn't know. Wiley was about to give her a stim that would leave her drunk and hallucinating when she came down from it. He remembered the unfocused look in her eyes that Jae had seen too, and not noticed, the wobble of stim withdrawal. Jae hadn't wanted to see that. All Jae could see was Lina in this dress.

Slow anger burned within his gut. Lina was his. His! His alone, to decide what happened with the two of them. If the Three Worlds wanted the three of them to "accept each other," as they'd put it, they'd have to go through Londo to get his permission. He would be the one to allow Jae into bed. Jae couldn't invite himself, couldn't help himself to Lon's wife. He'd have to explain that very carefully to Jae in a way that Jae would never forget. Jae didn't like to play by the rules, but he'd have to learn that there were some rules you just didn't break. Lon's rules.

So you'd put yourself above the Worlds? Jae's mind whispered to his. *That voice you heard wants us all together.*

So maybe that's what we'll do, Londo replied. *Only you have to ask permission.*

Jae paused. *All right,* he finally said. *Just let me try her alone first. She's furious at you now. She doesn't want you in her bed. Let me have her tonight. I'll say nothing but nice things about you the whole time, love.*

She's not angry with me!

Hoo hoo, talk about basic denial. Crying her eyes out. Shards, even Wiley saw that something was up, and he never notices personal things unless they're at the thermonuclear level. You don't act like a general with women, Londo, ordering them about and withholding important information. At least not with women who aren't Legionnaires. And certainly not with women you marry.

The man of experience speaks. I haven't seen you with that many women.

If Lina were mine, there wouldn't be any secrets. There wouldn't be any orders, and I'd tell Stoan what he could do with his ideas about mind control.

Damn, you're hot for her. Don't you know that she's a one-man woman? I thought you were a several-men man, Jae.

It doesn't seem to me as if you're the one man she particularly wants today, Lon-Lon.

She wants me. She'll be under me tonight, begging for more. Bet you.

Without bullying or orders?

I am not a bully. Bet.

You'll drive her to me.

****She's not interested in you.****

****She's interested enough to be afraid of me. A good push from you and–****

"Lon, I want to take more readings," Wiley said over a private circuit. He seemed irritated. "Come down here so I can get at you."

"You've taken enough."

"There's no such thing as enough readings. And I haven't scanned for pre-plasm levels. When I'm done with you, I'll get Jae and then Lina."

When Londo returned he was startled to see Lina upside-down in her chair, kicking her legs in the air over the head rest. She quickly pulled herself back up to proper position, a padd in her hands.

At least she acknowledged his presence now. "You aren't paying attention to the discussion?" he asked as he sat.

She shrugged. "One guy says it was a fake, and another guy says no it wasn't, and the first guy says was too, and the second guy says was not. They've come to the conclusion that there's not the right kind of equipment here to put on the show, so now someone's trying to say I ported in some kind of huge something-orother generator to stage this. But they haven't been able to figure out where I hid it."

"So what are you doing there?" He pointed to the padd. It looked like one of Wiley's. "You know how to use it?"

"Jae showed me."

She pushed the padd's screen at him. She hadn't looked him in the face yet, but now she was talking to him. By tonight she'd be over it.

"There's almost nothing out there in non-fiction on the supernatural. Every time I think I've found something, a great seal of Tishana Regulated Information comes up. Do you think that if they put a trademark on thought they could stop all thinking in the AffSys? And I'm not going to get over anything until you give me a lengthy and honest explanation. Look here, this is ancient stuff."

Londo blinked at the change in subject, but looked. Very old info indeed, by maybe five or six hundred years. Psychic studies concerning discarnate beings.

"It's like something Duke University might have done sixty years ago," Lina complained. "Elementary, although very scientific and controlled. A bit anal retentive; they didn't account for the importance of attitude. You can't work well with right-brained things in an entirely left-brained way."

"Let's see how fast Legion priority can crack a Tishana InfoShield," Londo muttered at the screen. His hands flickered over fields as they came up, and he pressed his ring against the screen three different times, penetrating data layers as he went. Finally he pressed his ring again, but a circular seal came on the screen. "Tishana Regulated Information." He pressed his ring against it and the screen blanked completely.

"Thought police," he growled. He reached out to touch the main viewer screen. "Can anyone tell me why Legion Priority doesn't get through Tishana InfoShields?" he asked.

"Can't get through?" Stoan's face appeared on the screen. "What were you trying to access?"

"Research libraries: experiments from a few centuries ago in contacting the dead. I got in far enough to see that the categories were there, and then they booted me out."

Someone else came on the screen. "Are they saying their security's higher than ours?"

"What if we needed information for an emergency?" someone else asked. "Who's the InSeCentral on Tishan? We need to talk to them, find out what the blaze is going on. Commander, it's time to get some Tishana on this, get their opinions on Orenya's ghost."

"So they can classify it so the Legion can't watch it any more," Lina murmured. Lon grunted.

"Wiley," he said to his screens, "you can get past their security."

"I'm busy." Wiley's face came up with someone's arm in the side of the picture: Jae's, obviously. "They have blazingly difficult security walls to get through. They change every five minutes, so you waste half your time getting past the new security system and then trying to figure out where you were. I think that once you hit certain levels they have telepaths scrambling your thought processes. If I want to get into Tishana secured files– and let's face it, everything on that planet is secured– I wait until Psyche's available. She's allowed in, but not to all levels. And sure enough, Jae's pre-plasm levels are up. Lina, let's have a look at you next."

"What's this about pre-plasm levels?" someone asked. "Something to do with ghosts?"

"At present I have no idea what it's related to," Wiley said as Jae exited his cubicle. "All I know is that Neutrino and Mrs. Valiant register some anomalies. Valiant doesn't. And unfortunately no one else who's been ported many times is here for me to check against to see if this is a result of porting or of this Three Worlds business. I knew I should have ported more."

Lina got up to leave. "Here, let me show you," Londo said, quickly swinging his chair around as she went out the back. He put his arm around her and she eased it away from herself. The door to the cubicle closed behind them. The balcony outside was empty.

"Do I have to break through this again?" he asked sharply.

She looked past his cheek, not at him. "Lon, we need to talk. All these interruptions aren't helping at all. I am trying to put things on hold until we can find some privacy. Please don't push things until then."

"Push things?" He pulled her chin up, but her gaze would not come around to his face. "Baby, do you remember a few days ago? A little wedding ceremony? And a couple days before that? 'I'll love you forever'? Where are they now?"

"Is this private enough to talk?" At last her eyes met his, but hers were blazing green. "Do you want to have our discussion here? In the open? How many cameras are on us?"

"There are no cameras," Lon said, and somewhere below them a cubicle door opened. They stood still as Boroh stepped out, moved down the hall and through another door. "So we'll make it–"

His ring buzzed. "Londo, I see neither of you are in your cubicle. Have you both lost your way?" It was Wiley.

"We're just trying to have a private conversation. Give us a few minutes."

"Don't upset her. I don't want anything to interfere with these readings. Electrolytes must be perfect."

Londo frowned and his frown became deeper when he saw Lina striding off in the direction of Wiley's cubicle. She had to look at the door labels. He trotted to catch up. "Damn it, Lina! I'm trying to get all this straightened out, and you're running away."

"Let's just drop the whole thing until later and be professional about it now, okay? Neutral."

"Neutral?" Londo took her roughly into his arms. "Is this neutral? Is what we've been doing, what we've been feeling toward each other, neutral?" He pressed his lips on hers, holding her head so she couldn't get away.

She didn't kiss back. Instead, she pummeled his shoulders with her fists.

Lina finally freed herself from his mouth but he still gripped her in his arms. "Do I have to slap you again?" she demanded. "Have you go back there with a big red mark on your face? How will you explain that?"

"I don't need to explain anything."

"I think you need to explain a helluva lot!"

"I think that you already knew. You're the big telepath around here. How is it that you don't know everything?"

Her mouth worked before she could speak. "And you're the big parahero with the big reputation. How is it that you can't tell the truth when it really matters? How is it that you like to hurt others just so you… so you can keep them under your control?"

"Says the woman who can read minds."

"Is that going to be your excuse from now on? Not telling me anything and then saying that I should have known? Am I supposed to scan you every time you tell me something important? Or are you going to lie to me about the little things as well?"

"Some people would be intrigued by this, Lina. I thought you would be. I'm disappointed in you."

"Disappointed?" The word hit Lina like a knife, echoing her father's words: *Clumsy, stupid girl! You should be ashamed of yourself!* She turned her head from him. Break away. Run. "I don't want to talk about it now," she told him, blinking hard.

"Hide from it, like you do everything else?" He shook her.

"And you just… assume that you can drop these thunderbolts and I won't say anything about it, that I won't question it because you're team leader. The great and powerful Valiant. No one questions Valiant on anything! Lon, how could you lie to me like that? Have me make a vow when you hadn't told me the truth?"

"This has nothing to do–"

"This has everything to do with that! Can't you see? This is the very foundation of what we are, and you're, and you're–" She choked. "My god, what have we done?"

"You can't run from this. You made that vow, Lina O'Kelly. You can't leave me. You have to stand and face the problem."

"I am not running away!" Again she tried again to push herself free from him and couldn't.

He shook her. "I don't like it when someone tries to take away something that's mine. I won't stand for it."

"Perhaps you should have made a list of your possessions for me before we got married," she hissed. "You pretended–"

"Look, Lina. People do this every day. It's not like it's something brand new. You above other people should know about things like this."

"Things like–" What was he talking about?

"I don't see why you couldn't have–"

"You're trying to blame this on me! Well the game doesn't work that way, Londo Rand. You have to start taking some responsibility for your own actions. I'm not the one at fault. This is way, way too big. I would never have–"

"Waitaminnit. I seem to recall seeing a little something myself." He towered over her, his hurt and anger overwhelming him. "My sweet bride of… how many days? How many hours? And I see her with another man–" He stopped when he saw her turn white.

"No," she whispered.

"Yes." Damn her anyway! He spread his fingers around her throat. For an instant the impulse to squeeze swept over him and he snatched his hand away from her before he could do any harm. "Did you even think of me? Did you just forget about me?"

Tears streamed out of her eyes and the vision came back to Londo: her lying there naked under Jae, whispering Lon's name, the haze of stim withdrawal heavy upon her. Yes, she had thought she was with Londo, but the reality– It was Jae there, not him.

He couldn't think straight. His world tilted completely out of his control and he scrambled for any way to make sense of it all. To put it back where it should be.

She trembled in anger– or was it fear? "How can you say that?"

Londo wanted to be cruel to her and hurt her as she'd hurt him. That would work. "It sure looked that way to me, baby." She clutched at the railing as she reeled. "That's loyalty," he sneered. Somewhere he heard a male voice whisper, "Whore," to her, and wondered where it came from.

Lina shook her head, trying to silence the accusing voice that was always there. *Whore! Liar! Slut! You bitch of a worthless girl!* But Dad was far from here. He'd ruined her life. She didn't need him trying to ruin things now– they were bad enough. She fought to smother her anger and shame, and wondered if she'd get sick over the railing.

You ugly tramp. No one could ever want you! You'll wind up in the gutter some day, and see if I just don't keep walking when I find you there!

"Don't," she gulped. She couldn't handle this, too many things coming at her all at once. She tried to shove Dad away. Dad wasn't here. Dad wasn't real. One thing at a time, goal A first. Focus.

Londo and the big problem with him loomed, blanketing out everything else. Make Londo go away so she could find her balance and figure out things. If Lon could be pushed two steps back, she could concentrate on these other things that had to be done right now. Finish them, then face the Londo problem.

She didn't want to think about him as a problem. Her life was wound around and through him, embedded in the idea of him. She had to pull herself away somehow without tearing herself apart in the process.

But not right now. If she didn't come through for Londo with this investigation she'd embarrass him as well as mess up the beginning of this Three Worlds project, and that just couldn't be allowed to happen. She'd promised.

"I refuse to be confused," she said. "Don't try to cover one thing up with something else. This is not the place for this, Londo. Let it drop. We need to get out of here and talk. Later. *You* need to talk. You need to do a lot of talking, and every last damn word had better be the truth!"

"I–!" He was temporarily speechless, livid. "You can't talk to me like that. I am your husband now. I deserve some respect, if just for that. I am not ordering you to do this. It's just the best thing; anyone can see that. We've had this planned for years. Don't be stupid."

Stupid dumb bitch! Go away, Dad! "So I should trust you?" Londo pulled her to him again, and she pushed away. "You were the only person in this entire universe that I trusted. And now I find you lied to me. What an idiot I was!"

Her fist pressing against her mouth was the only thing keeping her from breaking down. She would not. She would not! *You'll rot in hell, Lina! You'll end up in that gutter and no one will ever care!*

"Damn it, Lina! You're getting everything mixed up. I can't even read you, things are spinning around in there so bad. You're living in the past with the Victorians. Time to grow up and join the rest of the Twenty-first Century. We are faced with a situation that it's in all our best interests to–"

Londo looked up. Wiley stood fifteen feet away from them. How long had he been there?

"I hope you don't mind if I interrupt," Wiley said tiredly. "I requested her delivered in good condition, and now look what you've done." He walked toward them. "I don't know what kind of fight you're having. Jae won't give me a hint about it, although it seems he has a clear idea. Londo, why don't you go back to your territory and Lina can come with me? Maybe you two need time apart."

"We've had too much time apart," Londo growled at Wiley, scowling at Lina. "What can we do to get this meeting dismissed? They're just going round in circles in there."

"It is inefficient, but it will culminate in convincing Stoan to get some Tishana in here sooner rather than later. I'm glad you brought up Tishana Security. That should speed things up as well, as Stoan sees the lack of respect given to the Legion. Maybe we can even gain access to Tishana records after this incident is resolved. Now back with you. Lina, what do you know about pre-plasm?"

Londo watched the two of them disappear beyond the curve in the wall.

10

"**D**on't let him walk all over you," Wiley told her as they entered his cubicle. He didn't like her pH. Had she been this pale at the trial? Still, she lifted her chin defiantly.

"Who said I was?"

"Jae made it seem as if you were upset because you hadn't been taking care of yourself. But this is an argument."

"How observant you are, Wiley Five-Minds." She distracted herself by picking up and setting down the instruments that were scattered messily here on his desktop.

"Don't touch. Did this start before or after this Investiture?"

A striped cloth ribbon with was attached to a hitch pin on his *hecter fip*. She pulled on it. "It's none of your business. Stay out of it."

"Just tell me when it started. As part of the scientific investigation." He eased the pin away from her and she took his *yiris* instead to pick at it.

"Ohh… Oh hell. He started it, days ago, and I didn't find out about it until right after the whatever it was. There at the very end."

"Hm. I take it he wasn't the one to tell you?"

"The Worlds showed us all… things. Things we hadn't told each other. We all saw different things. Look, Wiley, I want to go home. I have some stuff to think about. You understand that: thinking. I only have the one mind. It comes a little harder to me than it does to you, I'm sure. Please, say I can go home. Now." She wiped the corner of her right eye hard with the heel of her hand.

"And what thing hadn't he told you?"

"None of your business." There wasn't a second chair here, so Lina sat on the floor, fighting herself to soothe her pounding heart, to slow her breathing to normal. She sniffed miserably. She'd made vows and promises. She'd always tried to keep her word. And now…

"Are you sure it was a true sending? That somehow filtering through your consciousness didn't color it, distort it somehow?"

"I'm sure. Drop it, Wiley." She ported in a tissue and blew her nose, then ported in the entire box.

"I don't think I want to. If you don't want to tell me what you saw, then tell me what Jae and Lon saw."

"Ask Jae and Lon. You're not getting anything more out of me. When the hell is this meeting going to be over? I want to go home!" Alone, to her quiet home in North Carolina.

"I haven't gotten my readings yet. Stand up and let's see if all this stress has left you with anything my sensors can pick up." Reluctantly she stood for him and he pointed a pistol-like scanner at her. "So you don't know what pre-plasm is?"

She turned slowly for him, her arms out as if she were having a dress fitted. She dabbed a new tissue to her nose. "No," she hiccupped. "Or RNA-whatsises. They're just going to go up, and it's okay."

Wiley frowned at his readings and now turned the scanner to himself, running it up and down his body, showing his armpit at it. He looked at the screen floating next to it and frowned again. "Maybe a difference on me. Very, very slight."

"Well, congratulations," Lina said, sitting on the floor against the rear wall even as she reached for another tissue. "Now you know it's porting and not Three Worlds."

"I want you back here once a week to keep track of this. And I want you to eat something. You still haven't."

"I can't seem to swallow today."

"Do you want me to give you a trank?"

She took a long, shuddering breath. "No, I do not want you to give me a tranquilizer." She blew her nose once more.

"What's the big argument–"

"Next topic."

"All right. Let me see the instrument."

"It's called a flute." She held out her hand and the flute appeared, fading-in as opposed to the suddenness of a port.

"Where has it been?" Wiley asked. He reached, but his hand went through it as easily as if it had been a projection.

"Cool," Lina breathed. A beautiful magic flute that the Worlds had given to her as a gift. They liked her, but Lon…

Wiley passed a new sensor, what Lina thought of as his tricorder, over the surface, and frowned at his readings. "Jae, get in here," he said to the air, then, "This is the same as that other instrument you played?"

"Yes. I told you, it's a flute. I haven't tried this yet."

"So try it."

"Here? Isn't there a meeting going on?"

"What's up, Wile?" Jae came in the back door.

Wiley pointed at the flute. "How cold does it seem to you?" he asked.

Jae touched the flute. "Room temperature," he said.

Wiley shook his head and scribbled a note on his padd.

"You weren't supposed to be able to touch it," Lina stage-whispered.

"No? Touch this then." He made his staff appear. Lina ran her fingers down the length of it. So beautiful. It exuded a presence of power.

"It's wood," she said. "Is that a ruby? Or just colored glass?" The head of the staff held a palm-sized red jewel.

"It's a ruby," Wiley said as he reached for the staff. Again, his hand went right through it. "There are assorted quartz crystals as well as Herkimer diamonds–"

"Herkimer diamonds?" Lina looked for them. There they were, large double-pointed quartz crystals set into the staff. An intricate weaving of fine golden net encased much of the wood, a crochet of the three symbols, holding all kinds of stones on it, some dull, some bright and jewel-toned. She'd seen wands made somewhat like this and walking sticks for New Age friends, but none nearly so elaborate and intricate and damned awe-inspiring. This was something a king or an emperor used. He would sit on his throne and use it to point so grandly into the crowd…

"Herkimer," Wiley confirmed. "Also real diamonds and citrine and aquamarine, turquoise and obsidian… all kinds of gemstones of precious and common types. Very fancy. Some people would consider it a phallic symbol."

Jae wrinkled his nose at his friend. He'd bet it was mind number five that had made that comment. Number Five didn't seem nearly as serious as Wiley's other minds. "I wonder if this does anything," Jae said, studying his prize. He suddenly thrust it out like a weapon, a staff, and whipped it through the air, stopping an inch from Wiley's nose.

"Using an intricately-crafted object of potential power as a bludgeoning object," Wiley said dryly. "Very good. Too bad it will go right through me." Wiley was so difficult to impress. The blue-skinned man shook his head, so Jae swung again, this time lower.

"Ow!" Wiley rubbed his shoulder and looked at Jae, puzzled. "That hurt."

"Sorry." Jae straightened the staff to examine it again. He stamped the staff on the floor once in his embarrassment. So he didn't know. He wouldn't make that mistake again.

All sound in the great chamber stopped. All private conversations, all official orating, even the subtle buzz of the electronics, seemed to die out for a moment.

There were a full ten seconds of silence. Heads swiveled to Wiley's cubicle and monitors trained on the scene there. "Did you want to say something, Neutrino?" Stoan finally asked from the floor.

"What made you choose Jae to ask?" Wiley asked Stoan.

Jae gave Lina a small conspiratorial smile. **Oh, I'm so going to enjoy this,** he told her.

Wiley asked Stoan why had everyone stopped talking? They had just felt like it. Stoan's attention had just turned to Jae.

"As well it should have," Jae declared. "I wanted Lina to play us a little song on her new flute. You feel like playing, Lina?"

"I—"

Stoan crossed his arms as various Legionnaires let their opinions be known. "We do not need any music!" "This is ridiculous!" "There's a time and a place for Terran–"

Jae motioned to Lina and she held the flute ready. He tapped the floor very lightly with his staff.

Silence.

Into it Lina played the first song that came to mind: the theme from *Titanic*, recounting a love that had once burned hot but had died except in memory. She kept it to one verse and a chorus, her heart tied into the song. She didn't think she could play any more without weeping.

No one spoke for a second or two after the last note died. Someone nearby was sniffling, and Jae gave Lina a sad smile. "Very nice," he said. "I understood it."

Wiley sighed and then sat up with a start. "I didn't record that!" he exclaimed.

"Powerful stuff, Wiley. Three Worlds stuff," Jae smirked.

"Use the overall record to study it, Wiley," Stoan said from the floor. "Jae, no more of that in here. I will not have my meetings disrupted because you have a new toy."

"I'd hardly call it a–"

"Excuse me, Commander," Wiley said as he signaled a woman Legionnaire. "Sorbens, what was the song about?"

The screen brought up her image, her cheeks colored with embarrassment.

She's on a Gamma team, Jae explained to Lina. **She's in the cubicle to our right.**

This must have been the snuffler they'd heard.

"I thought…" she began hesitantly, then sat straighter in her chair in proper Legionnaire attitude. "I received the distinct impression that the music was concerned with lost love," she reported.

"So did I," Wiley said. "Who else had that impression?"

Writing washed across his desktop screen, and he nodded. "Almost everyone," he considered. "I also received an impression of death, that one of the lovers was dead. Who concurs?"

Again, the votes tallied on the screen. Lina had to give the story of the song. Some of the Legionnaires had even sensed cold water or a sinking ship, something that had never entered Lina's mind as she played. "Perhaps," Wiley said, "and perhaps not. The subconscious is a powerful tool. Perhaps this is some kind of amplifier."

Down on the floor Stoan directed space to be cleared and Legionnaires moved quickly to his commands. "Valiant, get down here. Let's see that shield of yours."

Two Legionnaires fired their personal energy blasts at the shield as Lon stood scowling against them on the floor of the chamber. They'd had to erect three layers of force fields between the mock battle and the wall of cubicles. Lina couldn't see through the hellish blaze of fire, but when everything had died down and she dared take her hands from her eyes, Lon's shield still stood intact, as did he. The Legionnaires came up to touch it, to see if it had heated up from the barrage, but they couldn't put their hands on it. Only she, Jae and Londo could.

"Ladieees and gentlemen, the Threeee Worlds!" From the main floor, Jae bowed expansively to the galleries.

Someone up there spoke: "I thought I was hungry, but suddenly I've lost my appetite."

Jae stuck out his tongue at them.

Stoan called for silence: "All right. People. Legionnaires!" Stoan saw that Jae was about to tap his staff against the floor and he pointed warningly at him. The staff disappeared in a slow fade and Jae wiggled his empty fingers in a display of innocence.

"Order!" Stoan called. "All right. I'm bringing in some Tishana authorities on this." There was a distinct cheer from all sides. "They'll take a few hours, maybe more than that, to look at it all and give us a preliminary assessment. I would say we'll meet on this tomorrow or the next day, but no one's going to be in the mood."

Lina perked up at that. This was the first she'd heard Stoan make excuses for human emotion or needs.

"So might as well just get back to this at the next regular meeting on Fiveday unless these people pull something before then." He frowned at the three of them.

"No more of the unexplained, at least for three more days. That's an order. Meeting adjourned."

Everyone stopped what they were doing when Jae entered the Alpha team members-only café, located four floors above the medium-security levels of Headquarters. At least thirty Legionnaires congregated here. At first Jae tried to ignore the stares and sudden hush, but then he nodded at them and nonchalantly went about his business. A private screen gave him his nutritional readout and suggested menu.

"Neutrino, what the *kick* was that all about?" Bove finally called out. He was echoed by others and Jae turned toward him.

"You saw as well as I did," Jae said.

"So what, are you going to take over here? Are you going to ask the government to step down for you?"

Jae gave him a withering look. "Some of your brains are leaking out, Bove." He swept an errant lock of hair out of his eyes, and a woman nearby gasped.

"What is that? Is that part of it?" She turned to her seat mate. "Look, he's got a tattoo."

"It's a mark of one of being one of the Three Worlds' Chosen, we think," Jae told her. "Valiant and his wife each have one, too."

"Valiant?"

"Yeah, you remember him. You didn't notice it? Right hand."

"A tattoo on *Valiant?*"

"Where are they?" another one asked, craning his neck to peer around the room dividers. "Downstairs? You'd think that after all that they'd allow *her* up here for one meal."

"I think not!" his teammate said quickly, echoed with variations by others. "Mind controller! Terran!"

Jae barely noticed as one of the almost-invisible human servers bowed to him before proceeding across the room with drink refills. "They're in quarters, and I thought I'd give them some space. They're having a fight. No, I wouldn't call it a fight, it's just a little disagreement. Not even that. Just a small… difference of opinions. Not even worth mentioning, it's so minor."

Bove had turned all the way around in his seat, resting his crossed arms on the serving line partition. "Mention! What's it about? C'mon, Jae."

"It's private," Jae said. "Give 'em a break. They jumped the gun on some things and now they're catching up. I figured it was a good time for me to get dinner for everyone."

"What, you're going to interrupt the fight?"

Jae gave Bove a one-sided grin. "What else are best friends for?"

Speculation erupted in pockets around the dining area.

"So tell us," Kembril said from the fifth seating down. "What's she like? How Terran is she?"

Jae motioned for today's menu and scrolled through. "Terran. Do you realize," he said, "I don't even know what that means any more. I've been to Earth a lot in the past week, at least once a day."

The statement met with sputtering astonishment.

"It's not what you picture when you think of a barbaric world. Of course it's not like Sarastor, but that's not necessarily a bad thing. It's very back-to-nature with tiny cities and lots of wilderness, forests from what I saw. Lon's told me about it over the years, and he says that globally it ranges from stone age in a very few isolated places to where most of the AffSys was, say, three hundred years ago. Maybe less. Maybe a lot less in some areas of technology."

Yullowei sat near him. He waved his glass in a wobbly path through the air to make the "Tishana hoodoo" gesture familiar to everyone. "Apparently they're on a level with Tishan when it comes to Tishana kinds of things."

Jae frowned. "I don't know about that. Does anyone besides a Tishana have a clue what the Tishana know? And just remember, Lina's not a typical Terran."

"So we get the atypical ones together and find out what they know. Break the Tishana monopoly on this *parapsychology*."

"What are the people there like?" Excell asked. "They sing."

"Yes. So do Lon and I. So does Maximus; I never told any of you that. So what? I don't think there's a square meter on Earth where you can't hear some kind of music. They even have *choruses*. That's where a group of ten or twenty people get together and sing very complicated music."

There was scattered laughter at that. "So, are all these atypical Terrans witch doctors, too?"

"As far as Wiley and I have been able to tell, it's a very small minority, almost an underground movement or clique. It's semi-illegal, what she does."

Someone guffawed.

"No, really," Jae said. "There are a lot of people who claim to do what she can, but who can't and still charge people for their services."

"Ouch," came a reply.

"Exactly. Lina's found legal ways to work around the laws. How's the *surry min* today?"

"A bit on the sour side. What's she like?"

"Lina?" Jae considered. "She's nice, a little crazy. Emotional. Too damn honest sometimes, maybe. She doesn't know the technology, but she's clever and she's willing to learn. If she can't tell you how to jury-rig a *beater bam* yet, she'll still be able to figure a way to out-pace it. I'll lay you odds she's running the betting boards before the year's out." There were hoots at that. "Of course, she gets her information from sources a little different than we're used to."

"What, you believe in it? In whatever she's doing?"

"Whatever she's doing works, in case you hadn't noticed. And yes, Kembril, I am." He looked around. "She wanted to know if I'm really a telepath now. Who recommends the *kahil?*"

"Londo, I just want a straight answer out of–"

"Straight, is that what you want? As opposed to bisexual?"

Pulling her hair, Lina stormed around the territory she'd staked out behind the couch, while Londo stood in the center of the living room, arms crossed high over his chest– very Valiant-like. Nice try, but it didn't count for beans now.

"There you were saying that I was the only *woman* you loved, and you forgot this one itsy-bitsy little de–"

"I was going to! Jesus god almighty, Lina! I tried."

"When did you even mention this in the least?"

"In the lab, just before the ceremony. Remember? I tried–"

"I don't remember anything. You must not have tried too hard. All those jokes about doing it quick before I changed my mind– You were serious."

"Like you'd really have married me if you'd known."

"Of course I wouldn't have! Knowing that you were in love with someone else–"

"But it's you I want."

He wanted her because she was the only one he could have sex with, not because he loved her. She clenched a sofa pillow to her chest to protect her heart.

"Lina. Lina, *chérie.*"

"Don't call me that!" Jae had been right. Jae had been trying to tell her the truth about the situation all the time. He'd told her that Londo liked to lie. Terry the Bitch had called Londo a liar. Wiley had said that Londo used people.

Lina wrapped the pillow around her head and ears so she wouldn't have to hear his lies. She plopped into a tailor position on the carpet facing away from him.

Unreasonable woman! Londo let her hear that thought. She tightened her grip on the pillow as if that could block him. He walked around to her front and she shifted away, but then he hung upside down in the air, his face in front of hers. "Liiina," he cajoled. "Honey love…"

"Go away." She shut her eyes.

Londo righted himself and paced in front of her, changing his path as she scrunched around in a tiny circle on the carpet, avoiding him. She was an ostrich! Hiding here in plain sight. Such childish behavior! Time to put a stop to this. Nobody backed out on *him.* No one quit his team.

He told her that at great length as she sat with her eyes clamped shut. He detailed the many teams he'd led and the successes he'd had when they'd followed his lead. Everyone had benefitted from it. In this marriage, she would as well.

His words ran together into a meaningless buzz between Lina's ears. She should just port home, shouldn't she? She needed time alone to think. She wasn't a team type of person. Lina Muttbutt was a loner.

Kind of like Jae. But Jae was a team leader here, too, just like Londo was. Why had she thought that?

Because Jae was alone in every other part of his life. He might jump from bed to bed each night, but he'd never been with the one he truly loved.

Maybe now that Jae was a telepath he could commune with Londo's soul. Would that satisfy them or make the physical matters worse? It was surprising that his telepathy had lain dormant for so many years, when he talked with devas on such a high level.

If Lina left, Jae could take care of Lon to a point. They could share minds. If Londo ever got hurt, Jae could probably heal him as well as Lina. Surely Jae could commune with–

Lina's heart constricted.

Jae could speak to Lon's body. He loved Lon so much. Of course they could have sex now. All he'd have to do would be to convince Lon's cells not to put up any resistance to him, the same thing she had done.

Ah, god.

The universe must have arranged circumstances so that Lina could learn the technique and then pass it on to the person who truly deserved to be Londo's lover.

Jae.

Sometimes she could be so stupid! She pulled the pillow tighter around her head, wanting to pound some sense into herself.

Lon's gung-ho speech must have taken a new tack at some point. He crouched next to her.

"What can I tell you to make it better, Lina? What can I say besides I love you? You are the only woman for me. And Jae's the only man. Jae and I can't have sex–"

She lowered her pillow slowly. "But now that you can, you're bringing him into the picture again and throwing the *baggage* into the trash."

That stopped Londo. "Now that I– What are you talking about?"

Lina slapped the pillow at him and glared. "It's obvious, isn't it? You and Jae are both telepaths, and he can talk to cells. He loves you so much he could do the whole shebang. At least he's honest about it. So you and he can have each other forever. Happy ending, and the bride goes off to live in a convent for the rest of her life. Shit. Why did you do this, Londo?"

"Jae… talks to cells?"

"Of course he does! How do you think his power works? He talks, and the devas listen to his commands."

"You know how his… Jae talks to devas?"

Londo sat on the floor beside her with a thump. It took his brain more than a few moments to completely process the revelation. So many people had theories but… but Jae could talk to his cells, the same as Lina had? He could have sex with Jae? He could touch Jae like he touched Lina? He could hold him, really hold him…

The possibilities flooded his mind. The suddenly-undammed craving for Jae began to spill out of him. He scrambled to his knees. "Would you teach him? Would you show him how?"

"Oh, now I have to furnish printed instructions on top of everything else? This is where they came up with 'adding insult to injury,' isn't it?"

Londo took hold of her upper arms. "Lina, you are my wife and now you're going to listen to me. You are going to sleep in my bed every night of our married life. You are going to stay by my side every day of our married life. You got that?"

Lina sat silently, her eyes flashing. But at least she was looking at him.

"And through it all, you are going to consider that perhaps, just perhaps, Jae can join us in that bed. I'm going to invite him. Even if you don't teach him, I'll still invite him, and he'll come."

"How very cozy. Are you sure you two wouldn't rather be alone? I could arrange that very easily!" The last thing in this world she wanted was Londo having sex with her while he was fantasizing about Jae. She couldn't live that kind of lie!

She wouldn't allow it. She was New Lina now. She had her pride.

He slammed his hand against the impervious floor and the sound thunderclapped through the apartment. "*Crisse!* You are the stubbornest woman I've ever met!"

"I told you you'd get tired of me! Two days out, and we have to do a patch and repair job on the marriage," Lina said. "All because you couldn't take five minutes–"

"Five minutes? Baby, you would have told me where to go in three. I couldn't take a chance on that."

"So you get me to make a lifetime commitment and then you spring this little secret on me."

"And you have a little secret that you kept from me."

"…How dare you! I told him to stay away from me. I *ordered* him to."

"I don't want him to stay away from *me.* You promised before we got married that Jae could have his time with me."

She covered her face with her hands. "God. I did, didn't I? I didn't know." She'd agreed to a sham marriage and hadn't known it. Somehow she'd been tricked by them both.

"You agreed. You *promised.*" He sidled up beside her as she trembled on the floor in confusion. More gently, he said, "Jae's my friend, my more than friend. Give him a chance."

She lowered her fingers to look him straight in the eye. "What else, Londo? What other secrets are you keeping from me that I need to know? Who else do I have to worry about?"

"What–? There's no one else. A handful of old girlfriends, but they weren't serious. Just Jae."

"Does… Did he stand above or below Aiko?"

"Above. Way above her, and she suspected… No, she knew it. *Chérie,* there's just Jae."

"Just Jae." Lina's head hurt and her eyes burned, but she was damned, damned, damned if she was going to let him see her cry again!

Londo wrapped his other arm around her. "We'll give this a little time," he murmured. "We'll figure this out, win-win-win."

"You're the one who win-win-wins. How does this happen in a marriage? That three people are happy?"

"Lots of people do it, Lina love. It'll be very liberal, an open marriage. Not a hint of scandal. It's very private and on the side."

"Which one of us? Jae or me?"

"Come on, be reasonable, Kitten," Londo made sure he was talking behind her ear, letting his voice resonate in the way she'd said was so seductive. He nuzzled at her neck.

All right, maybe he'd screwed this up royally. It wasn't remotely how he'd planned to tell her. And he had been about to, he reminded himself. Tomorrow. Or maybe the next day. But by then for sure.

He hadn't figured out just how he'd do it. That was what had been holding him up. This had to be done delicately so as not to hurt her. He wasn't good at "delicate," but Lina couldn't be hurt. She was his to protect in all ways.

But now the *merde* had hit the fan, Lina was hurting, and for one of the few times in his life, he had no idea how to handle it. He was floundering. He had to show her that an open marriage would be best for them all. Lina *and* Jae– how could things get better than that?

He stroked her coaxingly. "It's all going to be all right. We'll be fine. All you need to do is calm down. Relax."

But she jerked away. "Don't do that, Lon. Not now."

"Come on, baby…" He slid his hands on her, caressing that warm skin of hers. She was so vulnerable to touch. He could convince her just by this if–

He could feel Jae in the outside corridor. Surreptitiously he made a quick fist in the air and pumped, signaling the puter to lock the door even as he stroked Lina with his other hand, breathing softly into her ear. Was she relaxing?

"Code Neutrino!" Lon heard Jae growl to the door outside and kick it as it unlatched. He stomped into the living room, the door whooshing back behind him.

Slamming three covered food trays down on the coffee table, Jae pointed at Londo. "Tell her about the baby now, Lon, how I want a child of my own. Tell her how you promised *me!* Does that open discussions again or not?"

Lina pushed away from Londo in one startled motion. "A baby?!"

"*Calisse de tabarnak,* Jae, I almost had her calmed down." Lon gritted his teeth. "We can discuss that later!"

"We discuss it now."

Londo stood up, his feet apart and braced, and stared Jae down. Or up, considering the height difference. "I said later."

"And I said now. You wanna step outside, Londo love?"

"You can't hope to–"

"I think I could. I think that I'm one of the few people in this whole miserable universe that can take you down a few pegs, Londo Rand! And believe me, you won't like the way I do it!"

They stood there a foot apart, fuming at each other. "What's this about babies?" Lina demanded. "Londo, what else haven't you told me? How big a hole are we in here?"

"We are not in a hole."

Jae fumed, "You were going to gloss up everything, weren't you? Just bull your way through. A child, Lina. Not an adoptive one."

Lina sank back to the rug as the room spun around her. "You're saying with you and me?" she asked, fighting for composure.

"That's what I'm saying."

The man was serious! "And how do we present this to people? Oh yes, she's married to him, but she's having *his* baby. Aren't they good sports! Why no, there's no touch of scandal there. No reason to bandy the word 'bastard' about. Or 'whore.'"

Jae braced against the back of the couch, staring down at her with a terrible need. "Londo promised me," he told her. "For years he's said that he'd bring home a wife someday, and I'd be the one to bed her, and in return for my duties he'd make sure one of his children was mine."

Lina caught her breath. So it had been discussed far more than the one time. It was a solid deal, a verbal contract that she hadn't been in on.

"Things have changed," Londo growled at Jae. "The entire universe has changed. That plan is no longer in effect. You've got a half-dozen sectors of females drooling after you. Pick one of them for the mother. Pick a hundred."

"I choose her. Lina. She's the only possibility."

"The last Feithi has spoken," Lon mocked.

Lon and Jae stood toe-to-toe as Jae's jaw jutted. "Yes he has. I want her. I could probably get legislation passed to enforce the decision if I had to."

The last Feithi. Jae was the final one unless he had offspring. Lina blanched as she thought of his notoriety, of the public attitude toward legendary Feith.

People would go crazy if they thought Jae was considering having children. They'd do anything he wanted. But… they'd do the same for Valiant, wouldn't they?

Londo and Jae argued as Lon tapped Jae angrily on the shoulder. Jae slammed the bottom of his fist against Lon's chest. Jae was getting the worse of the deal.

"Don't I get a say in any of this?" Lina shouted above the din. "Do I just sit here and let the two of you plan my life for me?"

"We're just straightening things out." Londo scowled at Jae. "Sometimes Jae isn't too smart. He needs things explained to him."

"And sometimes Londo just lies his way out of trouble," Jae sneered. "His plans don't always work, but he always wants to look good."

"I deal with reality."

"Oh yeah. Lon and reality."

Londo started to say something and stopped, then began again. "The reality of this situation is that Lina and I are married. I seem to recall you doing the honors. Are you going to recant it all?" He paced between the two of them for a moment and then stopped. "Look, Lina; listen for a minute," he pleaded. "I've been thinking about this for days now."

"Days," Lina muttered, crossing her arms. These were not the honorable and caring men she'd thought she'd come to know.

"Well, what the hell kind of telepath are you that you didn't pick it up?" Lon asked.

"Again you try to blame this on *me*," Lina spat back.

"Calm the hell down!"

"You sound like my father!"

Londo sucked in a breath. "Let's all take it easy. I've got this figured out now. Well, for the most part." Arms outstretched, Londo patted the air, as if laying the landscape for a story. It was finally forming for him: the plan. "Jae comes to live at Starhaven with us. There's more than enough room there. And it's extremely isolated. When you get pregnant and the baby's a blond, well, you said once that you had a blond nephew."

"What?"

"So now we'll say that blonds run in your family."

Lina glanced at the now-fuming Jae and back to Lon. "A secret love-child," she jeered. "This is your idea of figuring it out? Well, Londo, pointed ears do *not* run in my family! Why not just hire a host-mother, Jae?"

"Maybe I don't want a host-mother. Londo, shut up. You're digging yourself in deeper every time you open your mouth." Lon began to retort when Jae said, "No! You've made a *kicking* mess of all of this. And Lina, you listen."

He took a few moments to gather himself. "There are ways to approach this. But okay, the Three Worlds want us to work together. That means us together in all ways. Lon's all for this idea, obviously, any way he can get it. I… I want Londo. And I'm very willing to give you a try, Lina. You know I like you. And I want that child."

She started to say something but he pointed at her. "Your time for rebuttal is not now. Hear me all the way through. Let me just throw this idea out: the Feithi dual-triune."

"The what?" Lina asked and saw that Lon's mouth had opened in surprise.

Jae planted both hands earnestly on Londo's shoulders. "Dual-triune; you remember. That's my solution. We could do it right before we commit to my child. You got a better idea?"

Londo blinked, his mouth trying to say something. He glanced at Lina, sitting there with her knees firmly against her chest, hugging a pillow to herself, and then back to Jae. "I'd forgotten about that."

"Remember it."

"They… Ah *seigneur,* dual-triune? No one would go for it. Feith is dead, Jae. I'm sorry, but it doesn't exist any more. No one's going to recognize–"

"So you're saying your Feithi marriage ceremony wasn't legal?"

"No!" Londo scratched the top of his head. "No, but it was… normal."

"It was Feithi. This is also Feithi."

They didn't seem to be arguing any more. They were discussing this whatever it was. Lina hid behind her pillow. They were deciding her life and treating her like a womb with legs.

Childbearer to the two Legionnaires who loved each other. That was all she'd been to Londo: someone who could have sex with him, someone who could bear him children. Jae hadn't been able to do either. In the Great Pageant of Life, she was Miss Congeniality, the loser who got a nice title to take home with her, a framed certificate for a cold and empty wall.

"I am not a baby-making machine," she finally growled.

Londo turned as if he'd forgotten about her, the impediment to his plans. "I never said you were."

"You corral me before the wedding, when you knew I couldn't think of anything beside you, and you made me promise two babies. And now you've promised *him* I'll host a baby for him! What other requirements do I have to fulfill?" she argued. "Did you make up a list? What happened to the 'You don't have to be anything but yourself,' line you handed me?"

"But Lie–"

"And what the hell's this dual-tricycle thing?" She squinted at Jae, Jae who thought he could get away with anything. Spoiled Legionnaires! Spoiled boys!

Controlling, bullying, arrogant, egotistical…

Jae stood straighter. "Dual-triune. Don't make fun of things Feithi."

"I'll make fun of anything I want to," Lina countered. "I may not be a big-shot Legionnaire, the son of Maximus or the last Feithi, but I am a citizen of the by-god United States of Amer–"

"Lina," Londo said sternly.

She scowled at him. "Be quiet, Londo. I want to hear this. Jae? Dual-triune. Go."

"It's our way out, when we want to go public," Jae said quickly. "It's the answer to everything."

She crossed her arms and glared. "Terrific."

"It's a type of marriage. You have monogamous marriage, then you have the triunes. A dual-triune had three people in it. I was born into a dual-triune. My mother was the tertiary."

"The tertiary." Lina rolled her eyes to meet Londo's. "Polygamy. What a *fabulous* idea. What, no slavery or prostitution angle? I thought that's how they did it in the AffSys. Jae, are you proposing?" Her voice dripped with as much irony as she could manage.

"Not if you're going to take this attitude."

"Oh, I'm sooo sorry. I should have said, Jae, are you proposing to Londo? Is this your way to finally get him for your own?" She turned from the both of them as the air rushed out of her. Time to admit defeat, turn tail, run for home and hide. Who was she to stand up against Neutrino and Valiant? Miss Congeniality.

"Yes," Jae hissed. "This is my chance. This way we could realize what Lon and I planned– until *you* came along. This way I can still have Londo." He paused. "And you. This is a great idea."

"It is?" Lon asked.

Jae gave him a hard stare. "It is."

"Yes. It's perfect. Lina…" Lon's cool voice matched the hand sliding along her hip. "You can see that. When we need it, we can pull it out of the hat."

"Mind control," Lina muttered.

"Just calm down, think and listen. Jae, dual-triune was pretty common on Feith, wasn't it?"

"Yes, maybe sixty percent of the marriages were dual-triune, maybe more. But it was only on Feith," Jae said. "Only a telepathic culture could truly support a relationship like that. And just think: here we are, all telepaths, and you two already married by Feithi tradition."

Lina whirled on him. "Did you plan that?"

"I… don't think so." Jae's face was troubled as if he truly didn't know for sure.

Lina balled her hands into fists and turned away from the both of them.

"It solves all our problems, *chérie*," Lon said softly.

"It solves yours." Sarcasm was in order. "And the liberal population of Earth will certainly approve."

"We aren't asking for their approval. We don't need anyone's approval." Lon reached to touch Jae's arm. "She says that we could probably have sex."

Jae took a beat for that. "What?"

"She thinks it's possible. I think it's possible."

Jae's eyes burned into Lon's. All these years of yearning, all those frustrated times… **You're mine, not hers. You've always been mine.**

11

You're mine, Jae, but she's mine, too.**

"Out loud," Lina groaned. "Say it out loud."

"I love Jae and I always will," Londo said, "the same as I love you, Lina. Get that through your thick head. I love you."

"And this dual-triune would let you have Jae, legally, for the rest of your life. Legal on Earth?"

"It would be, if it were done the traditional way. We don't have to go through with it until it's necessary."

Lina faced Jae but couldn't see through the bitter betrayal that was the world. "Tell me about the dual-triune."

Jae looked lost for a moment. "It's… It has two parts. The primary marriage, between two people."

"Same sex? Opposite?"

"Either. And then there's the tertiary, orbiting them as if he or she were a moon. The primary couple are bound within the marriage. The tertiary is free to have casual partners as they will, but is still pledged to the primaries. Not as closely linked as they are, but still very close.

"Children are raised by all three together, all property is shared, but with slightly lesser provision upon death given to the tertiary. The primaries were favored over the tertiary in some ways, I'm not sure how. Certainly, the primaries were the focus of the marriage."

Lon had been tapping two fingers against his lips as he tried to figure things out. "What if the tertiary sires a child not with one of the primaries?"

That stopped Jae. "Why plan a child outside of marriage?"

"An accident," Lon offered. "Unplanned."

Jae shook his head with the smallest of smiles. "You're reminding me that I'm talking with barbarians. Children are planned, that's all there is. You're married, you plan a child for that marriage. You wouldn't go outside it for–"

"What if you had a genetic disease?"

"No genetic diseases on Feith. Londo, it just wasn't done."

"So, is it an add-on deal?" Lina asked. "A monogamous marriage that adds a third? Is the first marriage always the primary?"

"Most of the time; maybe not always. I was so young when– It can either occur in two stages or in one event. And there's no divorce."

Lina knew that in such a set-up she'd be the tertiary, the unimportant one. That way Londo could still claim her as a wife when he needed to. Society wouldn't accept this. In order to lessen the scandal, sometimes he'd have to drag her along where people could see the two of them. She wouldn't have to worry about being totally cast off when they were on Earth. Maybe they'd keep separate houses. Could this actually work? Should she live such a lie? Was there any real need to go through these kinds of hoops?

"And the Legion?" she asked them. "They'd recognize it?"

"I don't–"

"How about the people of the AffSys? They're liberal enough to recognize a three-way marriage? Slavery or prostitution– Three-ways aren't respectable. I've learned that much. Protocol wouldn't stand for it."

Jae shook his head. "Not a three-way marriage, not for a Legionnaire. But a dual-triune, Lina– that's totally different."

"Anything from Feith is considered above AffSys society," Lon added. "But there it was everyday, ordinary, PTA stuff, Lie," Londo told her. "Nobody even blinked at it."

"Too bad there are no Feithi around not to blink anymore," Lina bit back. She jerked her head around to catch him in her glare. "What is Maximus going to say about this?"

He recoiled as if she'd struck him.

"Does he know you're bi, Lon?"

"He won't like it at all," Jae said bitterly. "Not for the apple of his eye."

"He never learns about it," Londo commanded them. His right eyebrow arched in fierce determination and his fist ground into the palm of his other hand. "No one ever learns about it. When we go dual-triune we keep it a secret. That's an order."

"Then what's the point?" Lina blurted.

"Secret?" Jae asked. "Why?"

"Valiant being bisexual is something some people may not like," Lina explained quickly.

"I'm just thinking about what's best for us," Londo said. Lina laughed in derision. Make him hurt like she was.

"I mean it," he declared. "Now that I've had a few minutes to consider, I can see that even a dual-triune would reek of scandal. People wouldn't understand." He urged Jae, "We could get kicked out of the Legion."

Jae's eyes searched his. "Even Stoan wouldn't… If he knew it was Feithi… Damn it, there's nothing wrong with a dual-triune!"

"You know Stoan hates polygamous marriages," Londo said. " I suppose we could always re-apply when Stoan steps down as commander."

Jae grimaced. "I don't want to re-apply. I don't want to leave. The Legion's the only family I have."

"Feith was never a member of the AffSys," Londo mused. "If it were, we could sneak through under intra-AffSys cultural compliance."

Intra-AffSys cultural compliance. Lina snorted to herself. They were talking polygamy. She knew there was polygamy on Earth, but it was obviously a primitive concept catering to the idea of male superiority… Except that here Lon and Jae were talking two men, one woman.

She shook her head to herself. They were trying to escape the hole they were in by digging it deeper. No, the answer was to climb out, figure where they were, and travel in the direction they needed to go, toward the truth. The direction the two of them took would need to be different from the one she took, that was clear enough now.

Lina could feel the doors closing around her, clanging shut as her skin numbed. And she still loved him so much! It was as if her entire universe revolved around Londo Rand. How shallow she was! God– how like her mother, caving in to the man's wishes.

"Lina?"

She shook her head. "I'm sorry, I didn't hear," she said, and the world seemed very far away, beyond a long, dark tunnel.

"Let's just sleep on this tonight," Londo said gently. "It's been a day for a lot of strange things to happen. Let's put this aside and think about this Three Worlds thing after dinner."

She nodded, so numb, and pulled in protective Sarastor energy hard, angry with the universe. It was two against one. What could she do?

Lon's voice came to her from a distance. "Why are you hiding? Come on; eat something. We don't bite."

Jae laughed. "Speak for yourself, Lon."

"Eat something, Lie," Londo said, pushing her plate towards her. She picked at it, pushed things around so that maybe they'd think that she was eating. They only had eyes for each other. They wouldn't notice.

Maybe she owed them babies. She'd promised Londo two, and Jae was the last of his race. Was she a breeder mare? Scarlett O'Hara was right: sometimes tomorrow was another day. She'd be able to think more clearly tomorrow. This afternoon all she could come up with was one answer to this entire mess that would leave at least two people happy. Two was better than none.

She'd shared minds with Londo. Apparently you could keep secrets even when doing that, but she'd seen the truth at his center: the steadfast devotion to the decency of the world. How he loved helping others. How lonely he was despite his fame. He had solid ethics. He was proud and believed in living an honorable life.

And yet he was a liar.

They weren't paying any attention to her. Jae and Lon were digging into their dinners as they spoke briskly back and forth, arguing and then agreeing, then arguing again in the way of old friends. Lovers.

Once Londo reached out to smooth Jae's hair away from his eyes, brushing his cheek at the same time. Clearly it was not the first time he'd done that. Such an intimate gesture, just like the way he did it with her. Their voices echoed through the far-off air as Lina sat opposite them, hiding away in the thick Sarastoran energy blanket. They laughed at something and she flinched, coming out of her daze.

She ported in her padd and searched it for Feithi marriage customs. All information directly from Feith was locked— forbidden knowledge, by order of Jae. So Lina searched through the AffSys libraries for what information about Jae's world had leaked out over the centuries into common knowledge. At the wedding, something had been mentioned…

There was the listing for dual-triune. It was real. And here was the monogamous marriage. No rules were listed as to what kind of genders were required for that, but these weren't laws she had found, but word of mouth. She queried the computer to double-check what she'd been told: was there any way to divorce, annul, otherwise get out of a Feithi marriage?

No divorce. Separations of not over two seasons allowed. After that by law the couple was required to attend marriage counseling, and it seemed such counseling was always successful. Feith had been an odd world, an advanced world.

Annulment: Just as Wiley had said at the wedding, if the participants were under sixty years old and thus deemed rather immature, a priest could annul the marriage within the first half-year only.

Lina knew some priests.

They hadn't even finished dinner when Jae and Lon were called to a conference with people the Legion had managed to rustle up from Tishan. Lina wasn't sure if they were in person or by phone. It was practically the same thing with the communications systems. The only aspect the equipment missed was taste, if that.

As soon as they left, she ported home. Dutifully she fed the cats but didn't talk to them. She didn't pet them. She lay down on the rug and spread her arms and legs out as if she were floating on water. She was far too numb for tears. A decision had to be made— now.

There was only one answer.

She had made vows to Londo, but those were bound up in the marriage and its false foundation. She'd promised Aiko to take care of him and she would, by giving Jae to him. Making sure he wasn't saddled with her would help him as well. Jae had also promised, and he could fulfill that from within a Feithi marriage with Lon.

Personal promises she'd made to Londo– maybe she wouldn't break them, but she wouldn't remind him of them. As if he would remember her now that he had Jae.

Jae! She tried to snarl at the mental picture of him, tried to beam anger at him, but in her mind he laughed at a joke he'd just made. He whirled her around in his arms and then gazed at her as she sang a love song for the crowd at the Terran Zone.

Ah. She could see how Londo would love Jae. Jae probably made Lon feel happy, too. She sucked in a shuddering breath. Sometimes the universe asked you to make sacrifices for the greater good. She could do this. She could do anything if she set her mind to it.

Back on Sarastor they still hadn't returned, so Lina picked up the dishes from dinner and carried them into the kitchenette like an automaton. This was what Hell was. It had been Heaven last night, welcoming Londo into her arms. She stuffed the things into the recycler.

Forgive me, Earth! Forgive me, Sarastor and Aldierra! But all she cared about were the shards of her broken heart rattling around in her chest. A choked sob came out of her throat, surprising her and then making her furious. She was not going to cry! She wouldn't give him the satisfaction! How could he be so… inhuman?

This was his fault. Making her fall in love with him, deeper than anyone ever had in the universe, when he didn't mean it. Never confessing first that he loved someone else. Terry had been right, Terry the Bitch who had called Londo a liar.

They had six months to annul. She gritted her teeth. Stoan would really like that, and she hated the thought of making him happy. Jae would jump at the chance to be the priest to annul, wouldn't he? No, she wouldn't use Jae. She had friends who were also priests of Uriel. One of them could do the job.

She found herself in the bedroom, her head whirling between anger and denial, her skin flushing and then cool as the emotions ebbed and flowed. She unpacked her drawer and moved Lon's things back the way she thought he had had them. There were some unworn nightgowns here in the closet that she had bought to entice Londo to their marriage bed. She stood and stared at them. Could he return them? There hadn't been any receipts that she could recall.

She'd need a nice dress when she went to the priest to get the annulment. Should she order one from the nets before she left? No. She could wear her crappy suit. She'd leave everything she'd bought with his money here, take what she'd worn with her. She could repay him. She'd squeeze the last of her savings accounts to do that, even as she searched for a new job.

Lina swiped her eyes with the back of her hand. He could send her a bill. She turned back from the closet, clothes clutched to her chest, and he stood in the doorway of their bedroom. His bedroom.

"Lina, what are you doing?"

"I'm… I'm…" Her throat closed up. Her lips quivered too hard to speak. The black hole that was her chest ate her words before they could escape.

He took a step forward and she took one back. Stay away from him. His mere presence held power over her.

"Why don't you get ready for bed?" he said as he took another step. She backed into the wall.

"I…" She had to say something! She had to be brave, to face this situation and get them out of this disaster! Instead, "I need to take a walk," were the words that came out of her mouth.

"*Si tu veux.* I know a nice park in the northern hemisphere we can go to."

"Alone."

"No," he said. He stood over her now and she looked at the far wall, not at him. *Be strong, Lina.* She swallowed.

"I need some time to myself, Londo. I need t-to think this out." *I need to run away from you.* With one hand she clutched at the wall behind her to hold herself up as her legs trembled. "I'm… going home."

"I said no." His voice was very gentle, but she could hear the steel in the words. "You promised you wouldn't leave without me, remember?"

"That was for before you got back."

"I'm back now, and the promise still holds. You keep your promises, don't you? There are a few other promises you need to remember, too. Promises about love. Promises to Aiko."

"Yes." Her nod was shaky as he took hold of her wrist. "I promised to do what's best for you. But–"

"Look at me."

She didn't. "It will work out so much better this way," she said. "Feithi marriages can be annulled if the people are young enough."

"Annulled?!" His grip on her tightened. "Do you think this will help with the mind control charges? Did Stoan get to you?"

"No!" She shook her head wildly. "I looked it up, double-checked what Wiley said. It would make it so much easier for you." She whimpered at the pain on her wrist and he dropped it. She hugged her wrist to herself, still unable to meet his eyes.

"How the hell does it make things easier?" he demanded. "How the hell does any of this tantrum you're pulling help things?" He slammed his fist against the wall and it boomed like low thunder.

"Tantrum?" Bastard! How dare he? "Listen, for once in your life! We get annulled and then you're free to marry Jae in a Feithi marriage. They allowed same-sex marriages there. It was absolutely legal. It would stand up on Earth. It would stand up here. You could be…" her anger suddenly dissolved, leaving just the misery, "happy."

With both hands he leaned against the wall, slowly turning to look at her. "What? Jae and I? Jae and I happy? Is that what this is all about? I don't understand."

The tears were welling to the surface again despite how she fought against them. "You two can be together now. You don't have to settle for me. I know that you thought… you thought I was the only chance for you. It was a mistake. I… understand. I mean, you didn't mean…" Her voice failed her for a moment while she blinked back tears. "I don't think you meant to hurt me. You just grabbed the first available life preserver and held on. I shouldn't blame you for that. I," she hiccupped with an unvocalized sob, "I hope you'll be happy. I know you will be."

"Settle for you?" Lon's mind tried to shift gears, but they slipped, not quite meeting. "I thought… I thought you didn't like… men loving men. I thought you couldn't bear the idea of…" Londo looked around the room at the little piles of clothing that she'd gathered. She was moving out, out of his life. "You think I don't care for you."

The neurons snapped into place for him as she rubbed her eyes as best she could while dropping more clothes on the bed. Lina had never been loved in her life. He was the first, and now… Now what did she think? The lie she'd been talking about. It wasn't that he'd lied about not loving Jae; she thought he'd lied about loving her! Ah *calisse de tabarnak,* no wonder, no wonder!

"We can make it quick and p-painless," she was saying, taking up three tee shirts and reaching for the stack of underwear and jeans. "I think I can w-work with you on this Three Worlds thing, but you're going to have to give me a while t-to adjust."

Her breath came out as a sniffle. "I know I can be happy for you two. I will. You're wonderful men, and that won't change. I don't know how long it'll take, but I told you, I won't cause any t-trouble. Tell your friends… Tell them that you realized you'd made a mistake. Tell them whatever you want."

"Can I tell them that you still love me?"

That made Lina look at him. His image blurred through the film of tears over her eyes. "Of course I still- love you." The way her throat tightened, she could hardly get it out. "I'll always love you, Londo. Don't worry about me. I'll be all right."

He was reaching out to her. She shook her head to focus, focus. Think of home, get the picture in her mind. "I want you to be happy."

He took Lina's hand and pulled her over to the bed. He sat next to her.

"Here," he said gruffly. "This makes me happy."

And he opened his mind to her.

He opened it all the way, wide open, spreading himself out so that she could see, if she wished, the innermost depths of him. Terror spilled from him at letting another living being see him like this.

"See my secrets, Lina. See every last damned one of them."

Fear. Self-hatred, self-doubt, self-loathing. Shame. Guilt. Enemies he had killed. Lies he had perpetrated, plots he'd planned. People he'd hated.

It wasn't right to see that far into a person's soul. Lina turned away. "Stop, Londo. Please."

"Then look here. Just here."

He showed her the place in his heart he kept for Jae, all the love stored there alongside the frustration. The respect, the lust, the gentleness, the trust, the loneliness, the unspoken vows.

And then he showed her where she stood within him, within his heart, within his mind, within the very cells of his body. Love and protectiveness. A different kind of tenderness than he'd ever known to give or to feel. A magic, a sweetness of being that only she could make him see in himself. The hope for a family, the sense of home that she embodied for him. Lust, yes, and the holy bond of matrimony to make it a sacred lust, a blessed love. A bond to last through eternity.

"I love you, Lina." His whisper was soft but fierce. "I love you forever."

Lina wrapped her arms around him and sobbed on his shoulder. "I don't usually cry," she managed to say between all the tears. "I never cry."

Oh god, she loved him so! And he loved her. Truly. Deeply. As if she'd been a plant kept in parched darkness for years, but now grounded in rich soil under a bright sun, she bloomed within the light of his love.

They were one and yet different. Complements to each other and yet the same abiding, eternal font of love and caring. For all eternity, she wanted this man. In all the universe, she wanted this man.

This man was her husband, now and forever. He would be the father of her children, the other half of her soul. His home was now her home. His steps were now her steps. His wishes were her joy to fulfill.

Whatever he wanted was perfect with her.

Londo heard someone's feet padding up the hallway toward his bedroom. He jerked full awake– intruder!– and was flinging the sheet off himself, scrambling to be ready for battle, when Lina appeared at the doorway.

She blinked at his wary, naked stance. "Breakfast," she told him. "Fresh from Earth." She was dressed in tee shirt and jeans, and held a large bed tray heaped with eggs, peppers and cheese, fried potatoes and onions, toast, baked apples with whipped cream, and glasses of juice.

"Um," Londo looked around. He was married. There was another person living with him, sleeping in his bed now. "I just wanted to get washed up before you came back," he lied and sat back down. "Breakfast in bed?"

"I think you deserve it after last night," Lina smiled at him, enjoying the view. She cautiously settled the tray around him as he scoonched back in the pillows, and gave him a kiss on the forehead. "I'm sorry I was such an idiot."

"I don't want to hear you put yourself down, Kitten, not ever again." Lon drew her to him for a long kiss, a tricky thing to do while keeping the tray steady. "We were both in the wrong. Okay, I was a lot in the wrong. I set records for being in the completely, crazy wrong, and now we're both in the right. We are never going to fight again, not ever, understand?"

"Yes, Londo." Last night he'd vowed never to lie to her again. She believed him… to a point. She didn't think any more big lies that could hurt would come through. The truth that he loved her was the only thing she really cared about. "But we do have some important things to discuss today."

He caught his breath and nearly choked. Then he grunted. "Yes. We will figure things out."

"Not as a team," she said. "As a partnership. An equal one."

He played with the eggs. "I don't know if I'm good at that."

"You will be. So will I." She gave a decisive nod. "We'll have to learn and do it quickly. Practice will likely help." With a blown-out breath of wonder she added, "We're in something called a marriage."

"This is where that 'compromise' stuff comes in?" He patted the bed beside himself, and she carefully curled there, watching to see she didn't disturb the tray.

"I think so."

With a sigh he said, "Okay, we'll try it. I take it we need Jae in on the discussions? At least some of them?"

"I… It would be fair to him."

"I agree. Now, is this all for me? You think I'm a pig? I promise you, I will eat it all."

She leaned against him and smiled. "I was hoping to scrounge leftovers."

"You can cook." He scooped a pile of potatoes and onions onto his fork. "Um, you can cook great," he said around his food. He took another forkful and held it in front of her lips. "Eat," he ordered. "I want you to keep your energy up for later today. And tonight. Lots of energy for tonight."

"Not in a few minutes?" she asked coyly. Still, she ate the offering.

"Work. Legion-related. No rest for the weary."

"I didn't think you ever got tired."

One side of his mouth went up. "Last night would have left most men dead. Me, I'm looking forward to another night just like that. Kill me, sweet Lina. Kill me every night and bring me back to life."

"You were wonderful," Lina purred in his ear and he chuckled delightedly. "I love you so much."

"You're my every dream come true, *chérie*." At her silent blush, he asked, "You do know that now?"

"Yes, Londo."

"Good. I mean to remind you of that several times every day. And this breakfast isn't some kind of give-and-take thing? 'Thanks for all the sex, now here's a breakfast in return that will make you weep with joy'?"

"Silence.

"No. No exchanges for love. Love is freely given, and our love is beyond price. I thought I'd gotten you over that."

"I'm one sick woman, Honeybear."

"So we'll work on it. I don't want you sweating in a kitchen anyway. Though you look so sexy when you sweat. Next time I'll do breakfast and next time we'll go out and next time we'll just open a box of cereal."

"I *wanted* to do this for you." She held up a long, dangling onion in front of his mouth and he caught it in his teeth. "It's not against the law. It's a minor infraction. Or will I have to go to trial again?"

"No more trials." Londo considered his plate, considered his bride. "Cooking is a talent," he finally decided. "We can't have you squandering your talents–

any of them. You can cook every now and then, but not as a trade-off. And only if you enjoy it. You don't cook one bite unless you enjoy doing it."

She broke into a warm smile at that. "Yes, Massa Lon, honey."

"I am not a dictator. Listen, love, we'll have to postpone the honeymoon for a few days."

"The funeral." Lina sighed.

"Yes."

"Lon, was I ever cleared of charges?"

"*Euh,* ah, I don't know. One would think you were." He waved his hand and a screen appeared before it. "Nothing on here about a continuation. I'll check with Stoan to make sure. And Woltrell."

"I think she should give us a refund. Partial at least."

"*Peut-être;* maybe. We wait until I get something pinned down about the verdict. Today. Puter, schedules for the day, for both of us."

Two beeps sounded in mid-air and a much larger than normal screen unscrolled with a timeline down the left side for two matched columns, one for each of them.

"I have a schedule?" Lina asked as she scanned the alien writing. "Ah no, not a meeting with Protocol. I hate Protocol."

"Your first spouses' meeting." Londo smiled and had to catch a drip of egg at the edge of his mouth with the tip of his little finger. "I hear they're something."

"What's that supposed to mean?"

"Look." Lon pointed at the screen. "We've both got Legion PIC afterwards…"

"Which is, um…" Lina tried to remember.

"Public Information Center. PR and such. They'll prep us for interviews about the marriage."

"Must we announce?"

Lon leveled a gaze at her and she rolled her eyes.

"Okay, we announce. But surely no one's going to interview us before… before the funeral. We shouldn't mix these two things. It's not proper."

"No, it's not. Aiko should get her final spotlight without any competition. I bet Stoan has the announcement planned for the day after, maybe two." Lon scrolled through the next day's schedule, and the next, frowning. "Nothing."

"Maybe he doesn't want us to announce."

"Maybe he's got too much on his mind right now to remember. I'll remind him, Kitten. I'll be seeing him and Andri this morning. Hey, this apple is great. I've never had baked apple for breakfast before. Here, eat some and see."

Lina entered the fairly normal-looking auditorium, clutching her note padd like a shield as that nice woman with the dark orange skin and fuzz of platinum hair waved to her from the seats. What was her name? Crazy or Loony or…

"Derainjt," the platinum-haired woman said to her without prompting. "You probably don't remember."

"Things have been confusing," Lina told her as she settled into the roomy seat next to her. Two screens popped up in front of her and she jumped, which made the chair back flip backward in a forty-five degree angle. "Awp!" From below, leg rests raised separately so one leg angled high above her while the other leg was level with the seat.

"I don't know… How do you…"

"Here." The woman reached over and waved peculiarly around Lina's armrests. The back straightened before the leg rests retreated. The screens popped back out of existence. Lina held her breath.

"I'm afraid to move," she admitted. "Does this thing come with an instruction manual?"

"I don't think so," the woman told her. "It's just an ordinary chair."

"Not for me."

"Right. You're from Earth. I forgot." The woman made more movements. "I've shut off all chair functions."

Cautiously Lina raised her compressed neck to a normal position. She looked around with just her eyes before she dared turn her head. "You're sure?"

"I'm sure."

Lina resettled herself, this time cautiously, and glanced about the auditorium. There were a few hundred people in here already, over three-quarters of them women. "I'm sorry. Rainj, was it? I'm Lina." How she hoped Rainj didn't expect her to remember who her husband was! How she hoped Rainj didn't think she was an idiot! "I, ah, usually don't make a fool of myself. At least, not all at once."

"Don't worry about it," Rainj assured her. "We've been trying to tell Protocol that we need to do these meetings the modern way, remotely from our quarters, but no, they insist on being old-fashioned."

"This is old-fashioned?"

Rainj frowned at her chair. "They want us to function in the traditional Legion way, like they did two hundred fifty years ago when it was first founded. They expect us to show up at all functions in person. At least we got modern furniture installed."

"Oh." Lina thought about that, tried not to hear the titters that had risen around her. "I did introduce myself, didn't I? Lina."

"Of course. Everyone's been talking about you. Is it really true that you were a prisoner? And what about what happened yesterday? Jigger said—Well, sometimes the Legion makes up stories about—" Rainj snapped her mouth shut and jerked her head towards the stage. A green-haired, middle-aged woman in triple-layered parachutes, the latest in current fashion, like the outfit Rainjt wore, was walking up to the podium, flanked by another woman and a man in similar ugly clothing. "Later," she whispered.

Someone had let that biddy Yency be in charge of this thing. Lina knew that these weekly meetings would not become a favorite.

Ms. Yency called the meeting to order. Briskly she announced the proceedings for tomorrow's funeral, and where and when the spouses would appear during the ceremonies. They'd be seated just behind the officials, who'd be seated behind the Legionnaires. Yency gave the order of procession.

"Excuse me." Lina put her hand up.

"Don't attract her attention!" Rainj hissed.

Yency looked up from her podium screen and revealed a moment's scowl when she spotted the young Terran witchdoctor. "Mrs. Valiant," she identified Lina. "You have a question? It's against the rules otherwise to interrupt. And one should signal before speaking."

With some gesture or button Lina didn't know. "Yes, I have a question."

Yency nodded. "We have yet to welcome you formally," she said. "Everyone, this is Mrs. Valiant. She is from Earth." There was a disagreeable murmur at that, though almost everyone here must have been at the wedding. Surely they all knew that Valiant had married a barbarian Terran.

Lina distinctly heard someone back and to the right stage-whisper, "Mind controller!"

"Everyone please note that she is not using 'Rand' as a surname, but rather 'O'Kelly.'" Bong! Strike against her.

"Actually," Lina said, "we've changed it to 'Starhart.' For both of us."

Yency looked doubtful at that, but pressed on. "We missed her at the reception for the Tikkee ambassador three nights ago." Bong! Another strike. "And the luncheon yesterday for the society newsmedia," Yency noted as she glared at her. "You were absent." Bong! Three strikes.

"I'm sorry," Lina said. "No one told me I had a schedule. I was a prisoner for a few days, you know that, Ms. Yency, and then yesterday I was on trial here– I mean that was official Legion business, certainly it supersedes your social schedule. I was sweating out a possible lobotomy about the time you were starting on your appetizers. But I don't think I can be where you want me in this funeral seating thing."

Yency waited a beat. "And why is that?"

"Well, Aiko wants me to sing at her funeral. I promised her I would if they'd let me. I don't think anyone's asked yet." **Lon, have you scheduled my song at the funeral?**

From wherever he was, he answered, **Crisse, *I forgot. Give me a minute here.***

"And who is Aiko?" Yency asked coolly.

"Aiko. Orenya," Lina replied.

"The Legionnaire Orenya?"

"The one who's having the funeral," Lina snapped. Was this woman just playing dumb or truly an idiot? Maybe she was trying to make a point about only using Legionnaire names in public. Was inside Mega-Legion Headquarters considered public? "Yesterday she asked me to sing, so I said yes. I don't think that with a ceremony this big, I can sit out in the audience. I'll need to get up and leave or port out at some point, and that could interrupt things. I'd better just stay on the sidelines with the other presenters. Oh, Lon just said he'd put the song in a tentative spot on the schedule. Did your screen update?"

"And the dead Orenya asked you to *sing*. Yesterday." Yency couldn't withhold a sneer and sidelong glance at her companions on stage.

"Yes. The Legion's got it on record in about fifty thousand different versions. Please check your schedule."

"I know what the schedule is. You should learn that here on Sarastor civilized people don't go around claiming to talk to dead people and…" Yency glanced down at her podium, at the screen there. "Oh." She studied the screen.

There the entry was, near the end of the scheduled events of the ceremony. "A funeral song, sung by Carolina Starheart, Speaker for the Three Worlds."

"I just think it would be disruptive and dishonorable to Orenya's memory if I had to climb over everyone in order to get to wherever they need me," Lina told Yency.

"She didn't like that at all." Lina told Lon about Ms. Yency as they made their way to their appointment in the lower levels of HQ. Today there were no flashing red lights following her. That must be a good thing, though Lon said he hadn't found a definite dismissal of her charges. "She worked in a few 'We are the Legion's and huffed and puffed before she got back to telling everyone that they weren't perfect enough to be at this event, but they had to fake like they were and not bring scandal to the Mega-Legion. She should have been a drill sergeant."

"Maybe she was, before she came here," Lon said. "You know the Legion has a lot of ex-military in it. Many of our support staff came from the military as well."

Before their advance, doors opened to a conference room where seven Legion PR staffers awaited in their crisply-draped, multi-layered suits. Suits were Suits, Lina learned, no matter what planet you were on. They had no sense of humor, it was difficult to tell one from another, and their idea of their own self-importance was inflated beyond the norm. The Legion was the highest level of society in this galactic sector, and theirs was the responsibility to keep everyone to that level– and make sure that everyone else respected that.

One of the Suits interrupted Londo's introduction of her: "She's Terran?! Can we say she's from some unnamed Unaffiliated World instead? Valiant, married to a Terran! That will never do."

"I'm Terran, too," Londo said, but the Suits dismissed that, just as Stoan had. Londo had "risen above" being Terran.

"Say it," Lina whispered to Lon as the Suits conferred.

"Earzz."

"Practice, dear."

Her hair! "Who ever heard of hair that long! What can we do with it?"

"We'll just cut it to normal length. Unless you want your head shaved, Mrs. Valiant. It would look very lovely that way, very lovely indeed, Valiant. We could do that very quickly, eyebrows too."

"Her hair stays the way it is." Lon's voice was quiet thunder and the Suits clucked in dismay.

"Those clothes…" Lina was in jeans and tee shirt, with her favorite sweater added for decorum.

Londo crossed his arms in front of his powerful chest. "I'll get her proper Sarastoran clothing."

"We'll schedule some designers to come around this afternoon. When is your schedule open, Mrs. Valiant?" They consulted the Official Legion Schedule for All Personnel, and reeled in shock when they found that not only was Lina the Barbarian supposed to appear in public tomorrow, but that she was scheduled to be part of the ceremony.

"Poise lessons."

"Etiquette lessons. Speaking lessons."

"She's too short. Floater boots for her. Something to wear that's long enough to cover the floaters."

"A script– Someone start working on a script for her. We want no ad lib comments to the press." One of them peered at her. "How fast can you learn lines?"

She peered back. "Does that mean I have to know how to read?"

That set them off again. Lon looked at her and she batted her eyes in innocence.

She fumed. Apparently anyone associated with the Legion thought they were Hot Stuff, even the people who shined the Legion's many boots and hot-waxed their spaceships. When would people learn that they were all the same?

One of the Suits suggested that Lina should dress in a black faux-leather feminine version of Valiant's uniform, to make them seem more like a matched set, and so Valiant's secure societal position would rub off more easily by association onto her. He ran out of words when he saw the look on Lon's face.

Eventually they started discussing the inevitable press conference that would be held when they announced their marriage: what to say, how to say it, and what not to say. Which questions would be planted (which was most of them), and how they should answer. Londo should do all the talking he could, since he was Above Being Terran, and orb only knew what the Terran witchdoctor would say in front of reporters.

What should they list as her profession? An artist? Who the orb was an artist these days?

Thank goodness they don't know what I really do. Did, Lina whispered to Londo and he squeezed her.

Porn's not that big a negative Out Here. "Gentles," Londo smiled at the group as he extended an arm to indicate them all, "my wife quit her job day before yesterday, so all you need to announce is that she is unemployed or between jobs, or whatever the politically correct phrase is. Or you could announce her as the Speaker for the Three Worlds and let people guess what that means. We haven't figured it out yet, but it sounds good."

The Suits liked that.

But they couldn't say anything about the Investiture into the Three Worlds.

"I don't believe the Legion has any say over that," Londo replied testily, beating out even Lina's quick retort.

From behind them came Stoan's voice. "The Legion has control over everything that takes place within these walls."

Everyone turned as the commander entered the room. The Suits hushed while his hallowed voice uttered the sacred words: "Nothing about Three Worlds. Not yet." Thus sayeth the Lord. "Inside Legion HQ makes it Legion business."

"A lot happens inside HQ that's none of the Legion's damned business," Londo countered. "This happened here because Neutrino and I are both members, because of the appearance of... Orenya," his voice strained on her name, "and because it needed absolutely unimpeachable evidence, which only the sensors here in HQ could provide. Other than that, we appreciate having had the hall rented for us, in effect, but we are the Chosen of the Three Worlds and we decide what's announced and when."

"Valiant–"

"Don't worry, Commander, we won't announce today." Lon gave his crooked smile– a little tight under the circumstances– to his friend. "We'll give Orenya her full due. Let the galaxy focus on her while we get her buried and honored. But the next day, or maybe the day after that to let everyone catch a breath–we're announcing. Have security lifted about the event so we can talk about it. We'll need to show the tapes. We'll need to offer at least partial evidence to the reality of the event."

Stoan just stood there, his face unreadable. Finally he said, "I'll consider it," and left.

12

J ae gave his white cape a little flip so it wouldn't impede him as he slid onto the elegant chair beside Londo. A waiter followed him with his lunch on a gold tray. "What a day," Jae said after the server had gone.

A baby at the table behind them started to squall and was quickly hushed behind a privacy screen. The noise level here in the main Legion family cafeteria was that of the average restaurant: a continuous murmur, although there was no background music. Narrow islands of beautiful narsaws separated the tables into their own semi-private spaces.

"What have you been up to?" Londo asked.

"Just got off honor guard duty."

Lon checked out what Jae had on his plate, speared one of the little square things from a corner and then ate it slowly. "It's for Aiko," he explained to Lina, who was trying hard to ignore Jae. "We're standing honor guard over her… coffin while the public comes to view."

"Except they're viewing us as much as they are her." Jae picked at his food. "How can they claim to be feeling such grief for her, when they take their selfie vids with us in the background, and bow and giggle? It's horrible." He pushed a pile of brown layers around. "How can people act like that?"

"They live on Sarastor," Londo said. "The media teaches them that we're gods, so of course they're excited to be around us."

Jae grunted and tasted the brown stuff. From his expression, it wasn't what he wanted.

"Say hello, Lina," Lon told her.

"I don't think I should talk to him."

"We need to work on this. Today."

Lina dropped her voice so only Londo could hear her with his parahearing. "I told Jae that it was best if we didn't see each other for a month or so, Lon. You and him, fine. Take some time today. But please don't expect me and Jae to hang around together." She couldn't even pretend to eat, because the food suddenly looked unappetizing. This was happening entirely too often. She needed to grow a backbone.

Jae regarded Lina from under his thick blond bangs. Then he turned to Londo. "Is she talking about what I think she is?"

Lon and Lina exchanged a variety of facial expressions. His final one had both eyebrows up and his chin tipped at her expectantly. "She just said that it might be convenient if you escorted her this afternoon while I stand guard duty. Somewhere in there you two will have time for a nice conversation, and we three will have another one later. I think that one might last a while. Plus we're going to Earth at thirteen, when I get off."

"I've got some interviews at thirteen."

"So you won't come to Earth with us today. We're only going to feed the cats. How many times a day do they have to be fed, Lie?" Before she could answer, he told them both, "We should meet with the Aldierran delegation. Most of tomorrow I need to finish my eulogy. Today I can rough it out in my head while I have duty."

"The giggling will interfere."

"No it won't. You treat Lina well while I'm gone. Do not upset her."

Lina laid into her lunch with much clacking of golden flatware, glaring at Londo.

"Keep it up, Lina," Jae muttered. "There are already rumors about you and Londo having a terrible fight."

Lina stopped chewing. "And who started those rumors?" she demanded. "Good god, Lon, isn't anything here private? First they shoot home movies of us in bed, and now–"

There certainly were enough people staring at them, at the barbarian woman from Earth who was already having marital fights with the revered Valiant. The barbarian must certainly stick out here in this stately restaurant-slash-cafeteria with its fawning waiters and draperies and golden sforks and crystal goblets and beautiful piles of seashell narsaws.

Lina drew her index finger across her plate, gathering her food into a great glob, and theatrically sucked her finger dry for the benefit of their audience. Sound in the room stopped.

Silent laughter shook Jae's chest. "Thanks," he said. "I needed that."

Lon stopped her when she tried for an encore. "You've made your point," he said. "Whatever you do, don't lick the plate clean. The one-time joke is the subtler one. It shows finesse."

"I'll remember that."

"Good. I need to check on a couple things before guard duty, so I'd better run now. Jae, you take care of her this afternoon."

"Define 'take care.'"

"Use your own judgment." Lon turned to Lina. "I trust him. You do, too."

"He says I should never trust him."

"He doesn't mean it."

"Then he shouldn't say it."

Lon regarded her, then Jae. "Can I leave you two alone? Will there be anything left when I get back?"

Jae made a face at him.

"Good. *Chérie,* I'll see you in a little over two hours, Sarastoran." He gave her a quick kiss.

Lina grabbed his ears and brought him back for a long, long kiss.

"So much for rumors." She grinned triumphantly at him.

Lon's grin was just as big. "I do like this girl," he said. He took a swipe from her plate as he left.

"Go away," Lina hissed at Jae.

He nodded to a Legion spouse walking down the hallway as they entered the lift. In return he got a reverent bow.

"Where are we going, Sweet?" he asked Lina as they stood there. On those lower stories of Legion HQ, the lift had an actual, if transparent, floor to service those without the ability to fly.

"I don't know. I don't have anything special on my schedule. And don't call me 'Sweet.'"

"Tenth floor," Jae told the lift, and it took them there in a second. "I figured the first time would more comfortable in your quarters than in mine."

"What would be more comfortable?"

"The sex, of course." Again, Jae nodded at a passerby as they stepped out and again he was bowed to. "And the couturier will expect you to be there. Your schedule said something about–"

"I don't want a fancy couturier. I can get something off the nets a lot cheaper and it'll be just as good."

"And we'll have more time for the sex. Good thinking."

"There will be no sex." The door to Lon's room opened for her when she signaled. "Goodbye."

"Let's see what Lon's got to drink." Jae butted in front of her to make his way to the liquor cabinet.

"Why are you still here?"

He glanced at her a moment and went back to searching through bottles. "I'm making a drink."

"Out. Now." Lina pointed to the door in case he'd forgotten the way.

Humming to himself, Jae selected a glass and poured from two bottles, then added a dash from a third. "Anything I can get you?" he asked.

Lina threw her hands in the air with a wordless exclamation of frustration. Turning on her heel, she stalked into the living room and flung herself onto the couch. She needed something to do. Lon had a stack of magazines here featuring himself and his father, so she picked up one and flipped through it.

After a few minutes Jae came in and sat bump-up beside her with the large drink in his hand. It reeked of alcohol. Lina wrinkled her nose in distaste.

"Back off," she told him.

"You slept with him," Jae said. "You made up."

"Move over or I'll move you."

"He said you would, you know. He bet me. Yesterday."

Lon had been bragging to Jae about them? Making bets?

Jae continued, "I asked him for permission to have you for the rest of the day, and he said no, he was going to be having sex with you last night, no matter how mad you were with him. I believe he said you'd be begging for it. Were you?"

Coolly she turned another page. "Are you still here?"

He put his arm around her shoulders and took a sip from his drink. "It's not really true that Lon and I could have sex, is it, Sweet?"

How casually he asked that, and yet Lina knew his insides were churning over the question. He was wearing that damned mask of his that hid his emotions from the world. How Lina hated that beautiful mask! "So now you stoop to cheap bribery."

"I don't consider myself cheap. Do we have the sex here or in the bedroom? Or would you prefer the guest bedroom? I like the decor better in there. It's more homey. Of course, Lon's bed has more bounce. I picked it out for him."

"Did you know that gays don't suddenly convert?"

"I didn't know sex was a religion. Or is it only straight sex that's sacred? Turn the page."

Lina slapped the magazine down on the coffee table and used the movement to scoot away from Jae. She folded one leg under herself. That way he'd stay at least a knee's worth away. "Why are you still putting moves on me?"

"Londo pretty much ordered me. You were there; you heard."

"And Londo is team leader."

A crooked smile. "Yes."

"It's all because of Lon, isn't it? You love him so much. Jeez, I must have been blind not to see it before. You'd do anything for him."

Jae looked down to his drink. "Yeah," he finally said. "Anything."

"Even make yourself believe that you and I could... Jae, gays don't suddenly become bi. It doesn't happen that way, you know that. You're fooling yourself." She straightened her spine and looked him straight in the eye. "I can accept it. I want Londo to be happy, but I also want you to be happy. I'm… okay about you two."

"So we'd have your permission to have relations outside of your marriage?"

Lina bit her lip. How would it be years from now, waiting for Londo to come home because he was off with Jae? Still, even to have a part of Lon's huge heart was so very much more than anything she'd ever dreamed of before. That he could love her was light-years above any wish she'd ever made. Lon loved her. He loved her deeply.

It would be lonely when he wasn't there. Maybe this way he wouldn't ever get tired of her. Maybe this way she'd be valued for the variety she could bring to his life. Lina nodded to Jae. "Yes. I'm giving you permission, you and Londo."

"How about you and me?"

"You don't have to be untrue to yourself. Just remember as time goes by to maybe let me have him now and then."

"Now and then." Jae cocked his head at her wonderingly. "You're the legal spouse here. Don't you think I should be the one begging you for time with him?"

She gave him a weak smile as she got up to replace the magazine and search for a new one. "We'll have Lon set up one of his schedules. I– I've heard of marriages where people have these kinds of arrangements. It's just a little… strange to do it so soon after the ceremony. I had hoped…" She'd hoped that she would be enough for Londo. He'd promised that he would never get tired of her. She was not going to cry! "Gah! Ever since I met Lon I've been a crying machine!"

"Here now, here now." Jae rose quickly and gathered her into his arms to rub her back like a brother. "Now you know what I've been through all these years. Now you understand why I brought up the dual-triune. It solves a lot of these problems."

She knuckled her eyes, commanding them not to leak. "It does? Not ethically."

"Maybe not. Maybe so." He finished the hug with some pats, as it seemed she was coming out of it. "So nice to have someone to talk to about ethics around here. Usually they're left outside Headquarters."

"Who would be the tertiary, Jae? Which one?" Lina asked him anxiously. It took him a while to answer.

"I don't know." He didn't look at her.

They'd cancelled the couturier and were watching Londo's interviews from two nights before when Lina received a call from Legion Comm. "Legionnaires requesting port back to HQ," a female voice informed her.

"Rallene here. She'll need clearance," Jae told the intercom.

"Clearance has been granted for Lina Starhart for porting purposes, Comm only."

Jae nodded. "The Comm Room looks like this." His jaw worked as he chewed over forming a good picture in his mind.

Lina tried to neaten her hair by touch. "I don't want to read your mind, Jae."

"Well, you don't have clearance for the floor the Comm is on, so we can't go by the lift," Jae declared.

With a frown, she searched for the image he was concentrating on, and then ported them into the Command Central of Mega-Legion HQ.

The Legionnaire on duty, a surprisingly short, black-haired woman wearing a lilac and black costume with a repeating triangle emblem, gave a startled jump at their arrival.

Lina turned in a circle to take in the huge bubble of a room, covered floor to apex in a mosaic of active screens. At the end they were now was a narrow desk with an uncomfortable-looking high chair meant to keep one awake, where the woman was seated. Better-upholstered chairs and stools were placed in front of communications screens along the perimeter of this level.

A lower level, open to this one, held businesslike seating for twenty or more around an oval conference table with larger screens. Three Legionnaires were seated at it, working solo.

"This is Viret," Jae told Lina. "Not her real name, but that's what she goes by. Aka Shockwave."

"Hello," Lina said as Viret nodded at her. "I'm starting to sort out names and faces."

"This is the core of Legion HQ," Jae explained. "This floor is comprised of team meeting rooms, debriefing rooms… and rooms that you don't need to know about." He turned to Viret. "Who's coming in?"

"A half team." Viret pulled up a screen midair in front of them all. There stood Brügz, Dellen, Erik, and that woman from the other day who had turned out to be Brügz's sister, Eila. They were all in their flashy, thick spandex costumes, duffle bags slung over their shoulders.

Ex-Legion commander Brügz was obviously the team leader as he stepped up to the monitor on his end, but Erik surreptitiously waved hello from behind him. "Good afternoon, Lina," Brügz said, "or is it morning there?"

Jae spoke for her. "It's afternoon, almost thirteen."

"Good. We'd like to take the quick way back, if you would. We had to talk Shockwave into letting us do this, so don't let us down. Eila's transport is already set on automatic return."

"This I've got to see," Viret mumbled, and Jae patted her back.

"Sure," Lina said. "Give me a moment." Four people at once. After feeling out the space they took up within the cosmos, she ported them into her local space, letting them hang just outside of reality for two minutes as she brought them in tune with Sarastor. They popped into the room.

Eila seemed a trifle pale. She was hanging on to Erik's arm. Erik didn't seem to mind.

"It doesn't take as long as it seems," Jae assured her. "Plus, I think Lina's getting faster."

"How about that," Viret said.

Brügz grinned. "Thanks, Lina."

Dellen gave a huge, sinuous stretch and smiled at Jae. "It's good to be back so soon," she said. "It gives me time to get caught up on personal matters."

Jae gave her a non-committal smile in return and the corners of her mouth slumped.

"How about that," Viret repeated in a dazed tone. She checked a minor screen. "No contamination."

Brügz quickly sat at a nearby station, reporting in and assigning debriefing files. "So, Jae," the distinguished, copper-headed man said over his shoulder, "are you still on prisoner guard duty? When are you rejoining your team?"

"Lon just asked me to keep her company this afternoon. Which I have. Team meeting tomorrow, but earlier than usual. Check your schedule. I'm scheduled for interviews in a few minutes. Lina, you should port back to quarters–"

"No need." Everyone turned to Londo as he strode in. "I heard my wife was in the Comm for some reason. No one's made her a Legionnaire, have they?"

"Not yet," Jae said, "but give us time."

"No. No Legion for Lina. I mean to keep her safe and pampered. One Legionnaire in the family is enough, right, *chérie?*"

Her husband was the reason why someone coined the word "dashing," Lina decided. Londo in his black faux-leather uniform: awe-inspiring. Yummy.

"Yet another subject for the betting boards," Brügz smirked at Dellen.

"Another?" Lon drew Lina to him and gave her a quick kiss. "See us in an hour," he ordered Jae. "I want to meet these Aldierrans and get fully debriefed on the situation." He ticked off a quick, "thanks for your duty" salute to him, which warranted a crisp return nod as the Feithi left for interviews.

"There's a section that's filling up quickly," Viret said of the betting boards. "You may want to check on it, Valiant. The last I saw, a discussion about underwear was trending."

"Underwear?" Lon signaled for a screen, and one unscrolled in the air in front of him. Type scrolled by too quick for Lina to read. "What's all this about Legion membership?" He signaled and announced (the screen entering what he said), "My wife is not going to be considered for Legion membership. Period. So stop making bets about it."

"Yeah, right," Brügz might have said over at his station.

"What's that, Lon?" Lina asked, pointing at a section.

Lon cleared the screen and it disappeared back into the ether. "Something about your underwear having my name embroidered on it," he said sourly. "'Lina, property of Valiant.' I am not some kind of possessive dictator," Londo declared to her, to Brügz, to the room at large. "Why does everyone keep saying these things?"

He paused as he noticed Erik there. "Sunstorm," he said. "Thanks for coming to Lina's rescue yesterday. That took courage."

"Thank you, sir. I felt it was my duty— and only fair to her."

"His name is Londo," Lina told Erik, but he gave her a "give me a break!" stare.

"I'm sorry my mouth got ahead of my brain yesterday. I hope you weren't unduly embarrassed," Lina said sincerely. "He won't be punished, will he, Londo? It was really very minor stuff, easy to break through. It can't be this mind control everyone's talking about."

"There will be no punishment," Londo proclaimed.

"Subcommander Nurunori has ordered me to report to her as soon as I get back, sir," Erik said.

"I'll have a talk with her myself before midnight," Londo assured Erik. "I believe Dr. Mem-Bazer had an appointment with her this morning concerning the matter."

"Have you been practicing your visualization?" Lina asked.

"Yes, ma'am," Erik replied carefully. "I'll be good."

"How's your shoulder?"

Erik put his hand on it and rotated it. "No problems, no *thwunks*. Feels like new, thanks. And maybe my little confession will… interest some of the ladies around here." His attention settled on Viret, who raised an eyebrow and then smiled to herself, settling back to her work at the boards.

The others had watched part of this, and now Brügz stepped up to Lon. "We need to institute this porting as a permanent service."

"Stoan won't approve it," Lina said.

Brügz shook his head. "No, probably not." He turned to Londo. "But it wouldn't hurt to insist. It's extremely convenient. We couldn't be back in time for the ceremonies if it weren't for this. We wouldn't have been able to contain the riots on Rimhold without it."

Lon looked at Lina, who shrugged and turned the decision-making over to him. "We'll consider it."

From her console, Viret asked, "May I tell the other teams that it's available? Everyone wants to be here."

Londo chewed it over. "I don't want this to become a habit," he finally said. "This does not fall under the classification of 'pampering.'"

"I'll be happy to take as many as I can," Lina assured Viret. "Could you have some stims standing by, just in case? *They* say there's a lot who want to come back before the funeral."

"Can do, Mrs. Valiant."

"Lina. My name is Lina."

After they'd fed the cats and returned to Sarastor, Londo worked on his eulogy for some time, mumbling darkly. He wasn't pleased with what he'd come up with. Honor guard duty had not allowed him the atmosphere he needed for this. His grief and attempts at trying to summarize what Aiko had been to him as well as the AffSys had been interrupted time and again by the strolling audience, who too often did not hold to dignified silence.

Lina tried to tune him out as she sought a suitable funeral song for Aiko. She had the idea to search the song database from Aiko's home planet of Feen, but along with the other worlds of the AffSys, that culture had abandoned music a century ago. Still, there was a history of music from before that. It was just taking forever to sort through it all, and it didn't help that after all these days apart from Lon, she had ideas about better ways to put her time to use. First things first. Goal A. She sighed heavily and went back to work.

After a long while, Londo checked his schedule and then changed into civilian clothing. It didn't look remotely like fashionable parachutes, nor did it cling to him like plastic wrap. Knickers over boots made him look more like a Depression-era newsboy who'd just co-starred in a modern anime fantasy.

AffSys fashion confused Lina, so she closed her eyes and pointed at a selection on her padd, hoping for the best. It was one of those parachute styles, but not as bulky as she'd seen others wearing. Still, she felt clumsy in it.

Londo approved Lina's final result and reassured her that she looked beautiful, but added after hearing her complaint, "That's what a Sarastoran couturier would do, find something you'd be comfortable in, yet still be chic. This'll do for this afternoon. Neither of us will be in the spotlight."

"Maybe I need a barbarian Terran stylist instead," she joked.

Lon let out a surprised grunt. "*Exactement.* And I know just who we should get. But not today. When we get back home."

A stylist. For real. Lina didn't know what to say to that.

They found Jac— also in civilian wear that alternated between being skin-tight and oversized— waiting impatiently when they joined him at his apartment. He dragged out 3D star charts to locate Aldierra for Londo, and the two men had to overlay boundaries and callouts to show Lina how the borders of empires, confederations and unaffiliateds lay in this sector and its neighbors.

Isolated in its own stellar neighborhood, Aldierra was a long, long way from Earth. But it was a long way from Sarastor as well, well into the next sector.

Lina asked, "Why the hell did they come this far for an invasion?"

"Easy pickings, Kitten. Way too easy, with practically unlimited rewards to the victor. The Affiliated Systems and Sarastor have depended far too much on the Mega-Legion for their defense, and they came a hair's breadth from paying the price. Thanks to you and Jae and Wiley, the sector's safe, but if any of you hadn't been there…"

"Maybe another few billion wouldn't be here as well," Jae said softly. "We came too close. That can't be allowed to happen ever again."

Londo nodded. "Now the government knows better. They've got every official organization scrambling for weapons inventories, personnel recalls, retraining. The AffSys will be safe for a few more years… until it becomes complacent again."

"How can it be complacent with the Empire right over there?" Lina pointed to a shared border between the AffSys and the Yanist-Glory Empire. Just behind that– rather, to galactic east– was the Terran sector, fairly empty and small for a sector, with only Earth and a few other marked inhabited planets occupying it. The border with the Empire was very, very close to Earth.

"Gloryboy's not one for invasions," Londo told her.

"The emperor prefers to collapse governments from within. There's less backlash that way. Fewer bodies to bury."

Lina looked at Jae. "You mean with mind control."

He nodded. "And other things. Mind control is difficult but a very efficient way to accomplish his goal if he insinuates his controllers deeply in the right places. Lately he's been doing it more often. At least, that we've been able to prove."

Lon said, "He's found some easier way to make controllers. That has to be it."

"Maybe. There's some evidence that he's found a way to increase the capacity of psychic implants."

Lina shivered. Voluntary cyborgs and psychic implants. What a universe.

They packed up their padds and grabbed a taxi from a few stories up the side of Legion HQ to avoid paparazzi below, who had arrived along with tens of thousands of mourners who stood in line to file past Aiko's coffin. A temporary viewing stage had been set up in the plaza outside HQ. The saucer-shaped taxi had to maneuver tightly through crowded airspace.

Almost immediately upon arrival at the Aldierrans' plush hotel suite Londo noted the incredible deference given to Lina by the would-be invaders, how they insisted on calling her "Speaker." He examined the officers with their hungry eyes on his wife and dismissed most of them as being too stupid, too uncreative to plan an insurrection against anything of note. Space Fleet Admiral Bracken, on the other hand, had a keenly intelligent manner about him. Londo didn't trust him for a second.

Lina took a breath. "Admiral, this is my husband, Londo Rand Starhart."

Londo strode forward and shook the beefy admiral's orange-tinted hand. "I'm known as Valiant," Londo said.

"Valiant?"

"Valiant!" The aides looked at each other, then edged away from Londo, inclining their heads.

Lon gave them all a tight smile. "I take it you've heard of me?" Good. Very good. A little awe always helped when big jobs had to get done.

"We've heard the legends, even on our world," the admiral said. He squinted at Londo, as if not quite believing. An aide handed him a padd and Londo knew that his face was there as a member of the Legion. The admiral nodded. "Of course, legends have a tendency to grow," he said.

"No legend can be larger than the facts about my husband." Lina twined her arms around Londo's solid right arm. "He's the greatest hero there is. And now he is Protector of Aldierra."

"I will be there to guard your world, Admiral," Londo said, so pleased with this wife of his. He briefed the Aldierran delegation about the Investiture of yesterday, and Jae dug out a formally mounted crystal that contained a hard recording of the event. The Aldierran group watched it with them, and discussion of what this meant, what this would entail for their overpopulated world, was laced with fear. It did not help the Aldierrans to link this with their defeat in war. They were doubly vulnerable now.

Londo's forte had never been negotiations. He felt like he was tiptoeing around these people who had ultimately been responsible for Aiko's death. He'd much rather give them a show of strength, let them learn who was boss, and have them obediently fall in line. Things were made more complicated because the Aldierrans didn't have a firm grasp of Panlingua, and Lon's translator hadn't been programmed for their language yet.

"We three will be keeping close watch on Aldierra until the planet makes her decision," Lon told them carefully. "I'll do whatever I can to aid your people, to help them in the projects they come up with to see you through this crisis."

"And I'll be available as well, Admiral Bracken," Jae told him. "I may not have the legend that Valiant and his father have, but I get things done all the same."

That brought a smile to the admiral's face. "Indeed you do. Stopping my entire fleet. Very clever, Neutrino. I am with two legends here: Valiant and the Last Feithi."

"His name is Jae, Admiral," Lina said softly.

"Three legends." Bracken studied Lina. "You are Speaker to our world, the only person who can tell us if we are saved or not. And you are married to Valiant, and betrothed to the Last Feithi?"

Lon opened his mouth but Jae beat him to it. There'd been lies told to help stave off the invasion and keep Lina safe. "Yes. We're engaged. Does that disturb you?"

The admiral blinked and thus missed the confusion on Lon's face. "Three legends united in marriage. This is a fearful thing if you mean us evil."

Lina touched Bracken's wrist. "We don't. We want to help, that's all. Tell us, what plans have your people come up with? How can we help you right now?"

"I'm afraid that is still up for debate." The admiral shook his graying head. "There is opposition in the Great Council to us doing *anything*. There is even one faction that is moving to transport the upper houses off-world by Final Equinox into space stations so as to evade the Doom."

Lina said, "That's not going to protect them, sir. Aldierra can track down everyone. She found everyone to deliver the Ultimatum, didn't she?"

Bracken's swallow was audible. "Yes. That is what a number of people have reminded them, but they are not listening. Others say that we can trick the planetary entity, we can pretend that we are following her instructions right up to Final Equinox." The thought from his mind was clear: *Should I be telling her this?*

"Aldierra won't be fooled."

"No, I did not think so."

Jae took a seat. "You're a wise man, Admiral. You want what's best for your people. Use this Ultimatum as an excuse to execute real changes on your world, make things better from the bottom up."

"We need information," Londo told him. "We need to know what resources you have, what the worst points of social as well as ecological abuse are, what your people think of all this, where the opposing factions are."

"And why they're opposing," Lina added.

Bracken held out his hands, fingers spread helplessly. "The opposing factions are everywhere. People are confused. They are frightened. They are angry. Some think it was all a trick."

"So we'll just have to convince them differently." Lon nodded to Jae, who nodded back. "We'll hold some press conferences, telecast information to the people of Aldierra."

"We'll hold town hall meetings," Lina said. "We'll get opinions from everyone. We'll explain what we're doing as we go along, keep things transparent, and that way if we start to make a mistake, people will be able to stop us in time. I'm sure most Aldierrans have a good idea of what's wrong with the world. They must have ideas about how to make it right, too."

Jae and Lon explained how they'd begin making regular rounds of all the Three Worlds in addition to helping out on long- and short-range plans to improve them, with the emphasis, of course, on Aldierra until Final Equinox. Jae stressed that Aldierra should consider herself a part of the Three Worlds and not alone any longer. Comparing experts, they promised an exchange of knowledge.

As the meeting wore down, Admiral Bracken expressed his remorse at the loss of Orenya without quite accepting guilt for the deed. War was war, and they all edged around the fact that for a few days, Aldierra had been at bloody war with Sarastor.

There were a couple of personal questions that finally got answered. The admiral confirmed that symbol number three on their Three Worlds emblem was indeed an ancient symbol for Aldierra. Londo surprised Lina when he fished the three World tarot cards out of his pocket. Sure enough, the third one was in the primary language of Aldierra, Farrani.

The admiral looked at the card. "If this is so important, why is it a woman?" he asked.

"Why not?" Jae wondered.

"We do have games on my world with pictures of people as playing pieces. If you're going to have an important piece, it should be a military man, a conqueror."

A thought suddenly struck Lina. "Admiral Bracken," she asked, "why are there no women among your staff?" She realized, "There are women on your ships, but none of them are military personnel, are they?"

He smiled indulgently at her, even though she was the Speaker. "Why should there be? A woman's place–"

Londo surreptitiously held Lina's arm. **Don't say it,** he warned.

"–Is serving men in a woman's manner. Or taking care of the children at home."

Lina smiled sweetly. "How very interesting. So your culture recognizes people. And then it recognizes women. Not quite people, even though they are born the same way as men."

"We all know the differences of the sexes." The admiral opened his arms and spread his hands in innocence. "A man has the power and drive to get things done in this world. What shall we call a woman? A nurturer, the soft structure of the family unit that lets the man operate to the fullest extent of his ability. She is the relief valve for man's more primitive nature."

Londo increased his grip on Lina. Jae turned to study the pattern in the room's wallpaper.

"Very interesting," Lina repeated. "So tell me, what do you think of the Legionnaires, that some of them are women? Or that the president of the Affiliated Systems is female?" Or she was if the tourism tapes Lina had studied so hard had been up to date.

"Obviously, the women are different here. They have more maleness in them. Our Aldierran women are soft and sweet and much loved. They tend toward superstition, whereas the men are more scientific. Of course women cannot understand the sciences. Which is probably why our planet chose you, a woman, to speak for her. The entire process is quite unscientific, most unprecedented."

"And yet it happened," Lina mused. Unobtrusively she patted Lon's hand and he released. "I wonder if anything in your science could match it."

Jae was interested in this. "Do you educate them? Send them to school?"

"Of course," the admiral was proud to say. "There are girls' schools everywhere to teach them how to run a household, raise children, how to look pretty for their menfolk and please them in bed."

Londo was about to say something, but Lina spoke instead. "So very enlightening. Thank you for telling us about it. But." She took a breath. "If we're going to get this thing done, that's going to require everyone on Aldierra working together. Men *and* women."

One of the admiral's aides turned to another, whispered something and snickered. The admiral gave them a dark look and they became serious again

"One final question, then." Bracken addressed Londo. "The Minister– Neutrino– said that both you and your father had legends that had spread across galactic sectors. Excuse me for asking, but we know so little of worlds so far from our own. Who is your father?"

Londo relaxed at that. At last someone who wasn't acquainted with the practically demi-god Maximus, someone who wouldn't automatically link his name behind that of Hal's, forever in eclipse. "My father is known as Maximus–" he began.

"Maximus!!" The admiral gasped. His eyes searched Londo's face as if trying to see a spark of divinity there. The admiral's aides all suddenly looked at the floor, holding a hand over the left sides of their faces in some sort of show of humility.

"Maximus!" The admiral said again. "He exists? You do not lie to us?"

Damn. "Yes, Admiral, he exists. He raised me, adopted me as a son."

The general bowed low before Londo. "The son of Maximus. Truly, great things will happen on our world."

13

"O kay, Jae," Lon said as his apartment door secured behind him. "What was all that about? The fiancé stuff?"

"Problem? I thought we had been talking dual-triune," Jae said as he made his way to the liquor cabinet.

Lina wrapped her arms around herself as she watched the two men from a corner of the living room.

"Yes," Londo said. "Talking. I didn't think we'd decided on anything yet, and that the decision was still a few years in the future."

Jae emerged from behind a cabinet door with a bottle and jar in hand. "The admiral had already been introduced to Lina and me as fiancés," he said. "He's suspicious enough already. We've told him enough lies that have been revealed as such. He needs to be able to trust us now. Why not continue with the story?"

"Because it's not true?" Lina asked.

Jae pointed at her for emphasis. "He didn't even blink when he heard," he said. "I think polygamous marriages are more normal than not on Aldierra. Our Admiral has two wives, did you know that?"

"Now you've painted us into a corner," Londo said. "What if Bracken finds out? What if he mentions this to a Sarastoran? Or a Legionnaire?"

"The Legionnaire will just suppose that the war facade is still in effect. They'll go along with it."

"Or they'll automatically tell him that it's untrue, and there goes our reliability rating with Aldierra."

Jae shrugged. "Guess I'll just have to feel my way around the topic when I go there," he said.

"We'll all have to–"

"Londo, I'm off to Aldierra in two days. By myself," Jae said as he slammed a bottle on the counter. He glared at it before pouring a second drink for Londo.

"Two days! But the funeral–"

Jae began to search for a non-alcoholic brew for Lina. "Is tomorrow night, yes. Then I'm off as official Legion observer with the fleet the next morning. The admiral refused a suggestion that someone could go over early, faster than his navy. I didn't mention Lina's power in particular. He wants the entire fleet to arrive at the same time. No stragglers, no early arrivals."

"A show of power?" Londo asked as he accepted the reddish-brown drink.

"Sounds like it." Jae leaned on the counter with his elbows, rubbing his own glass with his thumb. "I wonder what kind of hell-hole this Aldierra is anyway. Lina, any hints from Her Aldierraness?"

She sniffed at the liquid Jae had given her. "Huge overpopulation, massive destruction to the ecosystem. I already told you that war vibes hang over every-thing. Other than that, I've only asked about solutions."

Jae shifted to watch Londo, who stood thoughtfully in the center of the room. "I'm going to be gone for a week, maybe more," Jae said. "I want tonight, Lon. I deserve it. I've waited too long."

As least Jae had the decency to glance at her, Lina thought. So, this was it. Her husband had a lover now and she was expected to go along with the deal.

But Jae's look lingered on her instead of Londo. He checked her expression and then his gaze slipped downward before returning to her face.

"Let's make it easy," he offered. "A threeway to get me started. We could go all night and sleep in. We're on skeleton staff tomorrow until after the funeral."

"When was I part of this deal?" Lina asked.

"You were always a part of it, Sweet. We just didn't know your name," Jae replied. "Now you've changed our plans, and I think I like the direction they're going." He raised his drink in a salute to her but paused when an alert beep sounded from his and Londo's rings. An accompanying male voice announced, "Neutrino. Valiant. Bruin. eMage…" The list continued with a few more Le-gionnaire names. "Report to Comm immediately."

"I'll be back when I'm back," Lon told her as he set down his drink. He did manage to give her a quick peck before he and Jae raced out of the apartment.

He was gone for quite some time. Lina ported home to play with the cats, and then returned to discover Ms. Yency had more lessons for her, this time in Yency's office. Joy.

Between these Lina experimented with the food replicator to get a snack, expecting to eat with Lon when he got back. Experiment: fail. But those PR suits decided they had some additional things to say, especially about the song she had to sing, and Lina really needed to figure out that song so she could explain things better to them, and during it all Londo contacted her to say that he had to eat with his team to finish discussing their role in tomorrow's funeral. By the time she was able to return home she could sense Lon's imminent arrival and after that… Well, dinner was not her primary goal.

He'd returned to her and not to Jae. She nearly swooned with relief, if not love and desire. Lina tried not to remember that a reason he was there had been that Jae had been called to the commander's office for another briefing on his Aldierra mission. In two days he'd be gone.

Now Lina crept out from under Londo's arm, carefully rearranging him so that he'd sleep. She didn't really want to leave his warmth. He was so hot in so many ways. She kissed him on his lips and cheek and jaw.

"Arum? La."

"I love you," she murmured. Ooh, his shoulders were heaven to stroke.

"Wuvvu," he managed.

"I'm going to get something to eat. You want something?"

But he had already returned to his dream, his face little-boy innocent, her love forever.

Lon's– no, *their*– kitchen held no acceptable food. She didn't want to take the time to train on the replicator. She didn't want chemical-tasting cookies or greasy chips, or even the random cans she had ported in the other day from home. How long had it been since she'd had a real meal? Here were the remaining crumbs of the chocolate cake they'd had three nights ago. The cold, plain beans and rice she'd made the other day while she was still under arrest– ick. She dumped it into the recycler. She'd have to find food elsewhere.

Before she left she paused at the door to the bedroom. Lon was lying on his back, his arms splayed over the sheet. That seemed to be a favorite lone sleeping position. Standing there she studied him, a god in repose. Broad of shoulder, layered with hard muscle, cafe au lait skin as warm to look at as it was to touch. Wide, sensitive fingers and full lips that could be surprisingly soft and sweet. That all-Canadian guy-you-wished-lived-next-door face. Tousled deep brown hair, almost black until the light shone on it.

She laughed to herself. Someday he'd probably find a way to keep his hair perfect even when he was sleeping or making love. But she liked it tousled. It made him look like the rambunctious boy he'd never been allowed to be. His dark eyelashes were so fine and soft, showing off those liquid brown eyes when he was awake, the eyes that turned her legs weak every time he looked her way. The strong jawline, the determined mouth used to directing battles. The mouth that whispered such lovely things into her ears. That courageous heart of his, so starved for love, so loving.

Her husband.

So he had a few emotional problems. He'd explained to her that yesterday he'd been thrown off-balance by emotional barrages coming from too many directions, and instead of dealing with it calmly and piece-by-piece like he'd been taught by his many psychiatrists, he'd gone back to his old ways. "I just freaked. I exploded," he admitted. "I haven't done that badly in years. It won't happen again. I think. I'm so sorry."

"And I imploded, after I'd just become New Lina," she said. "I went back to being the old one who hides from the world."

"We both need a little more work."

"Maybe a lot."

"But now we'll help each other," he assured her. "That's part of marriage, right?"

"I believe that was in the vows, darling." She'd settled on his shoulder, feeling so *right.*

Valiant.

They'd even heard of him on distant Aldierra. Now she was wife to him. She wondered how Maximus' wife handled things. Maximus did have a wife, but

Lina couldn't recall ever seeing a picture of her, not even a distant and blurry shot.

Just a few years ago Maximus had come out with the announcement. Lina remembered it clearly: the thunderbolt that hadn't quite crashed into anything because there was such a feeling of non-closure about it. He had said that her name was Something. Other. Else. That was it, Else, and that she was not from Earth.

Lina supposed that she lived off-planet, but it was certainly odd that he'd never brought her to Earth– or at least never that she'd known. Maybe Else just wanted her privacy and Maximus was fooling the press. Maybe Else lived right in the middle of Portland, Oregon and no one even knew.

Maximus attended so many affairs and ceremonies. How odd, now that she thought about it, that he never escorted his wife. Well wherever Else lived, she was still wife to Maximus, and the Big Blue Max's reputation was even bigger than Lon's, if that were possible. Lina wanted to meet her to compare notes. Was that presumptuous?

The hallways of Legion HQ were black acrylic and metal and sparkling tiny lights. She wondered if three-quarters of them really had a function besides impressing people. They all looked alike. Which way was–?

"Puter," she said to the air, hoping that it operated out here as well as in quarters, "show me the way to the main family cafeteria, please." On *Star Trek,* a lighted path would appear on the starship's walls, leading the way.

Instead a map appeared in the air in front of her, making her jump back. It had a little "You are here" 3D three-dot symbol (the AffSys didn't use arrows) superimposed over the floor layout. Multiple floors, transparently layered, fanned out behind the map. Oh yes, the cafeteria was four floors down, to the right as she got out of the Jetsons tube lift thingie that was down this way, not that, then left a ways.

"Thank you," she said and the map disappeared.

Though it was still an acceptable dinner hour, there was no one else in the cafeteria, just as there'd been only two people in the residential halls. Maybe the approaching funeral had driven everyone to quarters for the evening. There were still food service personnel on duty.

Just today Lina had been informed that having personal service was a sign how high the strata was that she now occupied. Ordinary people worked with automation.

Sitting in the empty dining hall over a small plate of mystery food, she realized how much she still had to learn about the basics of Sarastor. It was a big planet out there, an alien culture and technology, and somehow she was supposed to help bring it around to a path that was better for it than the one it was on now. Teach the people about themselves when she'd only met one native Sarastoran face-to-face so far. Round up the unwilling herd of strays and turn them back onto the trail, she and her two cowboy companions.

Two.

Where did Jae fit into all of this? She might as well get used to the idea that he was going to have relations with Londo. She'd have to learn to share.

Jae was nice. Extremely nice, at least when he wasn't being manic. Having Londo closer in his life could only help him through his depression.

Would they make a schedule? Jae got Lon Sundays through Thursdays, and Lina got Lon for Fridays and Saturdays? That would sure beat the wondering-which-one-he-was-going-to-be-with-tonight anxiety that had gripped her a few hours ago.

At least Lon had been with her tonight. That meant she'd been able to put off having to leave Londo with Jae for one more day. But Jae would want him tomorrow. It would be only fair. They should be together after the funeral and before Jae left.

Would the Rands be staying overnight in the guest room? How would she explain it?

Listlessly Lina pushed the food around on her plate, then stared at it. She needed to take a walk. She put her food in the recycler herself instead of leaving it for the service staff, and tried to figure her way out of here on foot, as she ported on her climalon jacket.

The clear tube elevators were easy to find again. Hesitantly she stepped into that seemingly bottomless space. "Ground floor," she said, and the fall was not terribly far. Quarters were close to street level, just above the almost-public civilian levels. The higher you went, the more secure areas there were, and at some point there was no floor in the lift. Passengers were then supposed to fly on their own, which meant they'd be Mega-Legionnaires using their handy ring anti-grav system.

The Mega-Legion lobby was also empty, complete with a soft echo of her steps. There was a section of wall containing a flashing "call for security escort" panel, but she didn't touch it. She wasn't a celebrity. She bypassed the security corridor's sensors by porting the short distance to the front doors. She needed to be alone.

Against the late evening beyond the electronic "windows" of the building, bright lights blazed. Lina stepped outside, wondering what it was, and then realized–

It was Aiko's viewing stage. It looked so different from this angle. A great pool of white light focused on a platform draped in black and white. An ornate, oversized black and white chair sat empty and stark while six people stood around it in formation. They were Legionnaires. She recognized Leenduk and next to him Wiley, who was dressed in a black, fitted version of his lab coat, almost like formal tails. There were four others, two of whom she remembered being introduced to, standing alert with ceremonial lances in their right hands.

At the front of the stage hovered a horizontal, man-sized black capsule. It offered no reflection to all the lights and thus seemed unreal. In front of it stood an oversized still holograph of Aiko. She gazed nobly into the sky over the heads of her mourners.

The long line of them stretched down the block, as far as Lina could see into the darkness. Tiny blinking lights kept people in line and stopped them from wandering the plaza.

Unlike what Lon and Jae had reported, the people filing past the coffin seemed quiet, although she could hear crowd noises in the distance. Additional people in twos spoke to the people in line while baseball-sized globes– **Cameras,** her guides whispered, while the image of a quill pen denoting reporters came to mind– floated over their heads.

Legion Plaza was really no place for her. Lina turned and almost stepped into one of those camera-couples, a woman and a man. The man made funny gestures and squinted at her, controlling the camera and maybe whatever mikes it had built in. Two screens floated next to him, one a monitor for them to see the broadcast video, and the other a text screen with notes, pictures of Legionnaires with their names underneath, and info-dots to get more information: a public, floating cheat sheet.

The woman's face showed her disappointment that this was not a recognizable Legionnaire coming out of Legion HQ. She managed a sad but brave smile for her audience. "Reja Lemain, MegaNews," she told Lina, blocking her way. "Are you anybody? Are you affiliated with the Legion?"

What to do? "I'm not on your Legion lists," Lina told her, nodding to the cheat sheet. "Now if you'll excuse me–" She tried to push past, but this Reja woman wouldn't let her.

"You've been inside Headquarters," Reja told her. "How are they reacting in there to the death of such a great hero?"

"The death of a hero?" Lina asked. "Aiko was their friend. I'm sure that if you asked any Legionnaire, they would acknowledge the tremendous respect that was due Orenya, but first and foremost, she was their dear friend. They've lost a member of their family. I hope you'll consider that in their time of grief."

"But this is news; you don't stand in the way of that. Who can we talk to in there? Can you get us inside?"

Now it was Lina who blocked the woman's path to the door. "The news is that Orenya is no longer with us. She lived a legendary hero and died the same, and her memory lives on along with her spirit. The news is that Legionnaires are grieving. Anything beyond that is idle curiosity that impinges on the rights of privacy for these people." Lina then moved around the two of them but they quickly caught up with her.

"You called her 'Aiko.' Did you know her?"

"No. I only met her. Twice."

"Twice, meeting the great Orenya! You must have been honored–"

"I had never heard of her before. I didn't realize the honor involved. She seemed like a very nice person, and now I've begun to realize how much she deserved her reputation."

"Didn't know–!"

"I'm from an Unaffiliated World."

"An Unaffiliated World that doesn't know about Orenya?"

Lina turned to face the woman. "There are those out there. If Orenya isn't known on my world, then… certain projects she was involved in will be. Soon. Her legacy will live on. I hope her family and friends can find some solace in that."

"May I have your name, please?"

Lina paused for the slightest of moments. "Ms. Starhart." That was anonymous enough. Soon it wouldn't be.

"Are you one of the Legionnaires' lover, Ms. Starhart?" The cheat-sheet screen scrolled through pictures for the reporter to compare.

The accusation caught Lina by surprise. She half-laughed and stopped herself. "You really don't want to hear anything from me. Please do have some consideration for the Legionnaires."

"But these are Mega-Legionnaires. They gave up the right to privacy when they became celebrities."

"Did they? Did they sign some contract that said that from now on it was all right for any…" *yutz* "one to stick a camera in their face and post it? I don't think so. I think that Sarastorans must be pretty bored if they need to live their lives through the lives of other people.

"That's something you should think about reporting after all this is over. I'm hearing more and more about Sarastor's crisis of being, of not having a full and involved life. That might be a very ironic story at a time when a woman who rose so far above the level of ordinary living now has her body lying dead. Consider that." Lina walked between the two and stalked off deliberately in the direction away from the crowd, down the darker stretch of street.

The reporters didn't follow her.

Ah shit, if Legion Protocol had seen that, Ms. Yency would be on the screen to her tomorrow to chew her out. Maybe she shouldn't have shot her mouth off.

But at least she was finally alone! She strolled aimlessly down one of those empty, canyon-like streets that they had here, a long New York block and then another and another and another, stopping sometimes to turn in circles, to wonder at the new sights:

Buildings that stretched endlessly up, their facades plainer than that of a warehouse. A blinking grating of light that peeked out of the sidewalk every now and then. If she stood still she could feel the pavement vibrate softly under it as if dozens of subways lurked underground. A short strip of stores with large street-level windows that advertised lobbyists seeking votes for sale. That reminded her of home, though this was more blatant. People inside one large window chatted earnestly around a large desk, unconcerned that anyone was watching them.

When Lina got within twenty feet of another window, it became a pathway pointing into the building with holographic video of people welcoming her and giving her a sales pitch for something called *"orjesstika,"* which was either a land-use bill or retirement property. Another window displayed a touchable directory to display demo videos of various self-medications being enjoyed by patrons, and how their minds reacted to each type. The videos were awkward and obvious, like commercials from the Fifties.

For a moment Lina rested on a bench until a loud screen popped up in front of her offering information and a business directory of the district. She stood to get rid of it but had to duck: a small vehicle screamed in off the rooftops, dropping to street level before zooming down the road away from her. It stopped three blocks up, then lifted vertically with a high-pitched squeal that didn't reach her for a good five seconds.

Only one or two other people walked the streets. They clutched their cloaks around themselves as they scurried through the night cold, their footsteps sharply echoing in the metal canyons of the city. Were they offworlders, to be outside like this? Where was everyone else? At least the chances of getting mugged were slim.

It wasn't that late here. Lon and she had gone to bed very early, but this place was deserted. It would have been silent except for the rush of constant traffic— mostly large transports— flying just above the skyline, and the occasional taxi that swooshed into the street sections.

A park lay ahead. Now Lina had a destination and she aimed for it. It was primarily a flat stretch of green with a few sidewalks. Skywalks interrupted the rectangle of sky overhead. What trees there were had been planted in a spaced geometric pattern. They weren't close enough for the trees to whisper to each other like she imagined they did at home. The chill of early spring hung in the air, magnifying the night's emptiness. City lights and low clouds hid the stars that must shine somewhere above her.

Lina sank to the grass under a tree so she could ground herself as she tried to sort things out.

Her world had turned upside-down from what it had been ten days or so ago. Touching. Sex. Love. Marriage. Powers. Promises.

Being loved was an incredible feeling, and being loved by Londo was the best thing there could ever be. That was what marriage brought her.

It brought sex, too, which was heady stuff. Touching would always be a miracle to her, and sex was touching and warmth and doing crazy things and being as close as two people could get. And then you added in the sharing of minds. Angels must do that, that's why angels were always smiling and radiating love. Londo was Lina's angel and she smiled just thinking his name. Marriage was an excellent, excellent thing.

Londo brought with him safety from the universe. It was a relief to be in his arms, knowing that she could let down her defenses at last. Londo was her refuge.

Sure, the marriage brought some bad stuff with it. Lon had his issues, but now she thought she understood him better. They'd work through them. His sporadic schedule seemed like it might be a problem they'd have to address.

There was Legion Protocol, all those people with their thumbs up their– well. She could side-step them. She didn't have to play their games. And the people out to hurt Londo by trying to hurt her– she could port away from them now. She was the best at running away. She could do that, no problem.

So there remained just this little thing with Londo and Jae.

Anything for Londo.

A wet, frost-tipped breeze began to pull at her hair and sting her nose. Jae sounded like he wanted to do this dual-triune setup sooner rather than later. Londo? She doubted that Lon would truly go for it, no matter what he'd said about a vague future event.

So it came down to Lon having a lover on the side and being perceived as a cheater, or having a husband from within a non-conventional and uncomfortable but legal marriage. Could there really be any difficulty deciding which was better?

Of course Lina knew what the real problem was: Londo. Lon had to be in the middle of a bright spotlight where the masses could cheer and love him.

Scandal meant being thrown into the dark, dirty gutter while people laughed at you and tried to kick you when you were down. It would destroy him.

Her? She couldn't care less what people said about her, right? Lina chewed her thumb tip as she tried to figure out if she was fooling herself on this. It did matter what people said– to a point. Words could hurt her. She often believed things that people said, though she shouldn't. She took insults to heart.

And being the wife who permitted her husband to play around would not be a flattering role. Who else could understand what Jae was to Londo? Damned few.

Item: Jae.

Okay, so him being with Londo would mean less time with Lon for her, but the time they had together would be quality time, right? Yes. And she'd always been an independent kind of person. When she got her emotional balance back, she'd be wanting some space of her own. In the long run, this would probably work.

It was just a tiny bit of hell in the short run.

At least this way she wouldn't be around Jae as much. When Jae was with Londo she wouldn't be near, and when he wasn't around she'd be with Lon. She didn't want to be around Jae. The more she kept away from him, the better. Just as well that he was going to be gone for a few days until Lon and she could join him on Aldierra to check out the place.

Above her tree limbs creaked in the growing wind and she scooted around, letting the trunk of the tree block the wind and its cold.

How much of the other night with Jae was just her imagination? How much of it was true? Poor Jae, throwing himself at her because she reminded him of Londo.

Poor Jae. Longing for Feith and knowing he would never have it again, always deprived of the one thing he wanted more than he wanted Lon.

Was his loneliness what had made her feel the way she had while Lon was away? Had she sensed an echo whose answer was also Lon?

Jae was so courageous. No, he was afraid, like her, but he put up a wonderful show of bravado. You could forget how hidden he kept his true self from the world.

And he was so beautiful. He moved like a great cat, all strength and danger and grace. Sleek and muscular, with a mane of blond hair like that of a proud lion or maybe a sun god, the light stubble on his cheek so dangerous. Those cool blue eyes, stripping away her secrets. His hands on her, exploring, hungry. His mouth on hers, hot and demanding. Or had that been the stims and her fevered imagination?

She refused to face what her heart was demanding she consider. She pushed the thought off, though it kept buzzing around her.

A single drop of icy rain spattered on her cheek. Lina pressed her finger against the spot. Human touching was just as electric. Seductive. Confusing.

That buzzing thought slammed into her like a physical thing. She was infatuated with Jae. This went beyond mere friendship. Was Dad right: was she truly a whore? Did being around Jae and wanting him make her one?

A few stars continued in their peekaboo waltz across the cloud-flocked sky. A presence… She brushed the hair out of her face as she felt someone land lightly behind her tree.

"You've got to become more aware of your surroundings."

"I knew it was you," she said.

Jae grunted and then came around to squat beside her. He was dressed in his black Terran-style jacket, its collar turned up against the cold with his white cape attached, a strange combination. The rest of him was clothed in night colors. Tight night colors. He considered her.

"You're making decisions."

"I'm sorting. Things have been confusing."

"Funny, I thought things were finally straightening out. The fog was clearing, the light was shining at the end of the tunnel, the wheels were turning again—"

Now Lina grunted and Jae chuckled, bracing his forearm against the tree above Lina's head. "You have no sense of humor for what the universe throws at you. No sense of the ironic."

"Is it ironic?" She eased away from his closeness. "I cried more yesterday– more this past couple weeks– than I have in my entire life. I feel like someone's been twisting my insides for their own amusement."

"These Three Worlds of yours?"

"Of ours, now. All I know is that it's too much in too little time. I thought I asked you to stay away from me? We settled on three months."

"You settled, not me."

"I need that time. We have a big problem."

"Not that big." He removed his hand from the bark and wiped it on his leg, then sat down in the grass beside her. "There's a simple solution," he said.

"Simple for you; not for me."

They sat there in the darkness in silence, the occasional *pit* of a raindrop on the grass or sidewalk the only sound beyond that of the traffic far above them. Lina heard Jae take a breath as if he'd come up with something profound.

"I bet your butt's getting cold," he told her.

She had to laugh. It was true; the ground was like ice under her jeans. And it didn't help that Jae being so near sent a different kind of shudder through her.

"I don't like cold butts," he told her. The sprinkle was becoming an earnest one now, adding to the chill.

"Fine. You go back to where it's warm and I'll stay here for a while longer and think."

"I don't get cold easily. You can think where it's warm. I'll warm you up."

She licked her lips. "I think you should go now," she said slowly. "You and Lon… You have your time together. But please, Jae, stay away from me. Okay, not for three months, but for a little while: a couple of weeks. We'll see how it goes."

He leaned in to her. "And what if I don't want to stay away?" he asked. "Remember that reading you gave me? I'm supposed to stay close to the two of you, not just Lon."

His lips were dangerously near. Lina pushed herself away from him, and then bounded up. "Then I'll go," she declared. "Please don't follow me. Please don't–" Her mouth worked but nothing came out. Lina spun on her heel and walked away quickly, deeper into the small park. And then she was running through the night rain, away from the temptation that would turn her into something she didn't want to become.

Like a hawk he swooped down from above, blocking her exit. With his strong hands he grabbed her shoulders as he landed. "Don't run from me," he ordered, standing firm in front of her. "Don't treat me as if I don't exist."

"My god– what do you want from me, Jae?" Lina cried. "Whatever it is, I can't give it. Please– just leave me alone!"

She covered her face with her hands, determined not to cry, and his arms encircled her, clasping her to his chest. He made clucking noises to soothe her. Then he stroked her hair, brushing the rain off it as he could. She shook her head against him, determined not to give in to the evilness of her heart.

"Don't be afraid of me, Lie-Lie," he murmured to her. "I won't hurt you."

That had been what Londo had promised her, and he'd hurt her badly these few times, straight through the heart. Now that she and Londo were right again, she wanted the universe to remain just as it was, and that universe did not contain the idea of– The idea of–

"Please, Jae." She lifted her head and discovered that he'd been shielding her from the rain. It was a downpour now, Lirravon's scheduled every-fourth-night rainstorm.

Jae was an elemental in the rain, the city lights catching his drenched hair from behind, creating a raindrop-emblazoned golden halo around his head. And yet his eyes seemed to glow endless blue from the darkness of his face.

"You remind me of home," he said so softly to her. "You have a Feithi way of seeing the universe."

"I'm not Feithi. And I'm not Londo."

"You are Londo's and I am Londo's as well. There have been worse matches made in the history of the sector, but not many better ones."

"Terran barbarian," Lina reminded him and he nodded.

He said, "And yet Terra has played such a part to me. The Terran Maximus rescued me after Feith died. When I thought my own soul was dying, the Terran Londo came and brought me back to life. And now you. You brought my Londo back to life for me. You showed me a world that has such promise, this Earth, Terra, so much like what I imagine Feith was, so long ago. And you–"

He let his eyes roam her face as his hands strayed on her back. "The universe sends me a woman unlike any other I've ever met. A woman who understands me. A woman who could have my child. We would enjoy making that child, Lina. And we could have lots of fun even when we weren't making one. You are totally uncivilized. You'd like it all."

That elfin grin appeared on his face. "I figured it out. It's not that you always look like you want to be kissed– it's that when you're near me, you want to be kissed by me. Admit it. You got a taste of a vintage that appeals to you the other night, and you can't get it out of your system."

She tried to protest, but the words wouldn't come.

His eyes held hers. "Your heart's pounding," he told her triumphantly. "No more mistaking me for Londo tonight, girl. I've had enough of that game. He's asleep, right? I can sense him. We'll go back to my room and–"

She squirmed in his embrace. "I will *not* betray my husband!" she cried. "Now let me go, you crazy Legionnaire!"

"You need to listen to your heart more, Green Eyes. You should listen to what your worlds tell you. Follow your heart: *Shalla dyem.*"

"*Shalla* what?" But she'd heard that phrase whispered to her before. How did Jae know?

"*Shalla dyem.*" Jae ran the side of his thumb down her cheek and she brushed it off. "It was what you told me after the Ultimatum. You hadn't come out of it yet, but your voice changed. It was the voice of Feith that you were channeling, I could feel it. You said, '*Shalla dyem, ta fal,*' to me."

"Feith?" That whisper the other day. It had been Feith speaking to her.

"It's Feithi. It means, 'Follow your heart, my child.'" His eyes held the fire of triumph. "You heard something like that before from Sarastor, and you married Londo. Now hear it again. I heard. I listened. Why aren't you listening, Speaker to Worlds?"

"I'm married to Londo," Lina said defiantly. "Even though it was a Feithi marriage, it was between two Terrans, and there it's a matter of being totally committed to each other."

"But you admit it was a Feithi ceremony." He was fiddling with her collar, tickling her neck, and she squirmed. "No vows of that kind were sworn."

"Even Londo has a problem with this," Lina said, trying to brush him off.

Jae shrugged. "So he wants it kept secret because it doesn't follow Sarastoran rules. I can talk him out of it."

"No, it's more than that," Lina insisted. "Londo has a big problem with his sexuality. Just think, all these years of being taunted by everyone because he was a virgin, that he couldn't be anything but a virgin for the rest of his life. It was okay for him to be bisexual because he couldn't express it. No one had to know."

The fiddling stopped and the smile slowly drained from Jae's face. Lina detached herself gently from him, and he let her.

"Londo's always wanted to fit in, to be loved," Lina explained to him. "He does everything he can to be the image he thinks is lovable. Hero protector. Well-dressed. In charge. What's preyed on his mind has been his virginity. He thought it made him look less manly, and it's thrilled him that that's no longer a problem. He even went to great lengths to get married immediately and to have everyone witness it, so he's an acceptable, manly married man. But bisexuality–"

"Bisexuality," Jae whispered. "It's not accepted at all. It's clandestine, a pariah of the personality… Or so the people here think. The *civilized* people." His voice took on a bitter tone. "How could he think that? What does he think of me?!"

"He loves you, Jae, from the depths of his heart," Lina soothed quickly. "He showed me. He can celebrate his bisexuality with you. But he can't celebrate it in himself. He's ashamed of it because he knows that if others find out, some of them are going to love him less. Some of them are going to hate him."

"No…" The sound tore out of his chest. Jae raised his head to the heavens, and the rain beat down on him. "No! He can't!" He sank down to his knees, bowing his head down until it touched the ground. "He can't!"

14

Lina knelt to steady him. "He loves you. He wants you. But I don't know if he can deal with a marriage. It would force him to face the truth about himself in ways that he doesn't want to. Others would find out. There's no way we could keep it a secret from everyone forever. And I think that if he kept it from Maximus, that knowledge alone would kill him eventually. He doesn't want Maximus to stop loving him, but he doesn't want to be dishonest with him either."

Jae clawed at the soaked grass, at the mud. "*Grigach,* Lina, what do we do?" He pushed himself up and looked at her miserably, his hair hanging down into his face in running streams of rain. Gently she swept it back.

"I can start with some things that I do know," she said. "I know that you and Londo belong together. I know that Londo and I belong together, and we have a marriage unit. Anything more than that…" Again she tried for words and came up with nothing.

"Too fast," Jae said. He shifted and sat down hard in the mud, drawing his knees up. Lina sat beside him companionably, despite the icy wetness.

"I told him he was rushing," Jae said. "He should have slowed down when I said to and thought this all out! He should have told you and we three could have–"

"That's a good game, Jae. Woulda, coulda, shoulda. I love playing that."

He frowned at her. She frowned back until he sighed in surrender. They sat in the cold and Lina tried not to shiver. Now was not the time to run out on Jae.

"All right," he said after a while. "Think if you must."

He pulled his cape under them to make a groundcloth and kept a flap out that they could hold over themselves like a stadium blanket. Together they watched the sheeting rain sparkle around them in the distant lights of the city. It was beautiful but cold. Lina trembled.

"Never sing to the icicle about the summer sun," Jae said softly.

"What?"

"Old Feithi saying. It means that it's damned cold out here for you. Even I'm starting to feel it."

"You go, then. I'll be back by and by."

But he remained next to her in the darkness. After a while he began to drum his palms on his thigh in a beat, nodding his chin and shoulders to it. He muttered a silent, inner tune.

"Am I boring you?" Lina asked.

"Go ahead and think."

"I can't make any decisions tonight," she said. How could she think when Jae was so near? "The world is spinning too fast."

He nodded and stared off into the distance. "There have got to be some conclusions we can come to. One: what do you think of this Three Worlds stuff? I like it, I like the idea and I like the possibilities. It's exciting."

"And scary, to have that much responsibility. Twenty billion people on Aldierra alone, Jae. Twenty billion!"

"So handy that you've met them all."

"I'm serious. How are we going to do it? Where do we start?"

"I think we've already started. All we have to do now is keep going." Jae smiled at his thoughts.

Lina considered what she'd learned through the years about setting goals. "Steven Covey says to start any project with the end in mind. We have to get a clear picture of what we ideally want everything to be when we finish. Then we have to remain flexible to change that goal as circumstances and new information warrant. And Zig Ziglar says—"

"Too logical," Jae mused. "I wouldn't have thought that of you. Me, I already know what the end result is."

Lina mouth opened as she realized it. "You're to share the legacy of Feith."

"And thus we efficiently arrive at our goal," Jae told her. "We are going to have to be very efficient in our work, what with only three people over three worlds. What is that, an overall population of thirty billion? More or less. Ten-billion-to-one odds. That makes it interesting."

She snorted at him. "I'll make you a crown. You'll like that. It'll go with your new toy."

The staff materialized in Jae's hand and he stroked it in wonder. The rain passed right through as if it didn't exist. "Isn't it something, Lie-Lie? It's right out of one of Lon's faerie stories."

Lina reached out to touch the gold net wrapping the staff, glistening in the glow of the city, and Jae placed his hand atop hers. **When you said you wanted us to be friends– that still stands?**

She slowly withdrew her hand, and he let the wand disappear. "It will have to, won't it? I mean, how else are we going to get all this work done? I've had to work with enemies. It's no fun."

"I never want to be your enemy." Again he laid his hand on top of hers, this time on her knee. It covered hers and then some. "We are good friends."

Lina didn't draw back her hand, but she stared at his. His fingers twined with hers. "Jae–"

"More than friends." He put his other hand around her waist. His cheek touched hers.

You want to be a... husband to my husband. A father to my child.

"We are lovers," he whispered in her ear.

"I must have missed that."

He gathered his cape around them to make a more intimate space against the rain. "The night's still young, Sweet. Who knows how dawn will find us? At the very least, my bed is warm and dry. Oh yes, we both can do a lot of deep thinking there. Very deep."

He was temptation itself, but she could still remember the husband who was sleeping so trustingly in her own bed. He had expectations of her. And she had heard enough stories about Jae now to know that his feelings about others– besides Londo– weren't as important, as permanent, as Londo's for her.

He turned her face toward his with a finger under her chin. Their eyes met, dark in the night. **You feel something for me, Lina.** "Tell me I'm wrong."

"Jae, what happened night before–?"

"I'm not talking about the past. I'm talking about now." **What do you feel now?**

She could only feel her heart trying to beat itself out of her chest. He leaned forward and brushed her lips with his.

"My place," Jae whispered to her.

"Londo–" she began.

"Uh uh," he smiled at her, leaning into her neck to whisper. "We'll have none of that again."

"He's asleep," she said. **Maybe it is a good time for us to talk privately. Where it's warm.**

And what if I don't want to talk?

You might as well put that out of your mind. I won't ever go behind Lon's back.

So we let him watch. I could show him some things.

She pushed him away as he chuckled. "We will talk," she commanded.

"Uh uh." Jae leaned in for another kiss and was pushed away again.

"I do not betray my husband."

"That's good to know." Jae bent down to nibble on her neck right under her ear.

"Stop that!"

A fresh downpour drenched them, catching them by surprise. Jae snorted out water that had gotten up his nose. "My place, Lie. Now."

It was decidedly wet out here. And cold.

"My place," Jae repeated insistently.

"Just to talk," she finally decided.

"Yes, yes, just talk. Get us out of here."

She did, but neither of them noticed the figure standing on the far side of the park.

They dripped in the vestibule to his quarters. The sudden warmth sent a spasm of shivers through Lina, even as Jae gestured something about heat to the puter. Another gesture, this time to focus his powers, and they were both dry. He swung his cape off them to drop it on the floor and reached to help Lina with her jacket.

"I-I think I want to keep it on f-for a while," she said, but he took her into a close embrace and said something silently, something she couldn't quite catch. She warmed up rapidly from the inside out. The heat didn't all come from his power.

"Is that better?" He released her.

"Um, yes. Thank you." She eased away, taking off her jacket. Then she tried to smooth out her hair as she looked everywhere but at him.

Where Lon's apartment was furnished with furniture whose geometric lines were so crisp she sometimes thought she might cut herself on it, Jae preferred large pillows and other soft surfaces. In places potted fernlike plants hid the walls. His main sofas were actually masses of arranged pillows that somehow maintained their positions.

"Soft lights," Jae commanded the air as he took off his jacket in two graceful motions and dropped it to the floor. The room lit dimly, more from a glow from the false "windows" in the living room than anything else. "Are you still cold?"

He was looking at her chest.

Lina blushed.

"I could warm those up for you." He reached and she knocked his hand away, but he caught her arm and took a step toward her.

"No," she said. "Forbidden territory." She pushed him away. "I'm going to clean up."

"You don't have to."

Lina turned around so he wouldn't have her chest to look at, and slapped at the seat of her pants. "These jeans are filthy. I'll get your furniture all muddy."

"So take them off. I won't mind. I've seen you in less."

"Let's just forget the other night, shall we?"

"So good at lying to yourself."

"We came here to talk, is that clear?"

Jae inclined his head to her. "For right now we talk, Speaker. You're safe with me."

"Good." She similarly nodded to him and then trotted off to the bathroom.

When she emerged, her hair brushed and hands clean, wearing new jeans, new shoes, and a new tee with a plaid shirt over it, Jae was just coming out of the kitchenette with two wide goblets like margarita glasses.

"Ratchets," he announced. "I make the finest in the known universe."

"So I've heard. All of Erik's raving has made me a little curious."

"Try it," Jae urged her. "I'll deactivate the alcohol before it can affect you."

Hesitantly Lina took a sip. It reeked of alcohol, the fumes as sickeningly sour as alcohol usually smelled to her. But the drink itself was rich, almost thick. Creamy. It went down warm all the way. Even her fingers and toes felt the effect.

"Like it?" Jae asked.

"If it weren't so alcoholic, it might be a nice drink. Does it come in choco late?"

"Chocolate? Lon had me try some once. I wasn't impressed."

"Londo probably brought the gourmet kind. It's not as good as regular. Is it really warm in here now?" She blinked. This time the heat was coming from a furnace inside her. By god, this drink had a wallop.

"Here, let me," Jae said. He burrowed under the plaid overshirt and placed his hand at the bottom of her rib cage. "The stomach's about there," he murmured, as his hand slid up to butt against the bottom of her breast. "No more alcohol. Begone. Poof."

She edged away. "Thank you," she said.

"What are you wearing under that?" Jae stayed with her, his index finger tracing the band of her bra through the tee shirt. "It doesn't feel very comforta ble."

"Which is an opening for me to make myself a little more comfortable. Jae, you are not being a gracious host."

"I can't imagine how wanting a guest of mine to make herself comfortable could possibly be misconstrued. Here, let me be the first." With one hand he unfastened his wide belt and dropped it.

"Jae. Jae, let's talk about everything."

He set his drink down, took off his overtunic and draped it across a sofa cushion, then removed the thick band at his left wrist. "There's a lot to talk about. One hell of a lot of things have happened lately. They're going to keep happening. Maybe something tonight." His right wrist band dropped to the floor.

"Will you please stop stripping?"

Jae paused before he started to pull his tight-sleeved shirt off where it fastened to his tights. "Stripping? When I strip for you, you'll know it. I am merely making myself more comfortable. It *is* warm in here."

Lina frowned at him as he pulled the shirt over his head. "Puter," she said to the air, "What's the temperature in this room? In Terran Fahrenheit degrees."

#Eighty-three degrees.#

"What's the temperature usually maintained at when there are people here?"

#Seventy-one degrees.#

"Puter, bring temperature down to seventy-one degrees."

Beep beep.

"Spoilsport." The grin Jae gave her was unremorseful. The tip of his tongue stuck out from between his teeth, and his nose wrinkled in deviltry.

Now he was clad only in black tights and boots over that dangerous, lean physique. "I did it just to warm up those cold *places* of yours. Well, the host has established the mode of dress for the evening." He cocked his head at her and gestured. "Why isn't the guest following suit?"

"Protocol might do a room check with their fashion police." Her mouth was dry. Lina leaned down to pick up her glass and realized it had that alcohol concoction in it. She tried not to look at Jae as he stood there, a god of a man, beautiful as a statue but warm to the touch.

She wanted to touch him to see just how warm.

"We'll compromise," Jae said. "Just the shirts off. Whatever you're wearing underneath seems substantial enough."

"Underwear is not to be worn by itself in public. You don't have to pull this number on me. Lon showed me how much you mean to him. I've got a pretty good idea how much he means to you."

"Yesterday you were shouting at him, then you were in shock as far as I could tell, and now you don't have a problem with us?"

When she didn't answer and turned away, Jae heaved a loud sigh. "Let me see if I have anything here for you to eat. I know you haven't eaten much these past couple days, even though you tried to fake it."

"I can get something later."

"I wouldna be a good host if I let you do that, would I?"

She followed him to the kitchenette. It held only superficial differences from Lon's. Jae leaned down to investigate the top level of a stack of chilled drawers.

"You're checking out my ass," he announced.

Lina spun away from him. "Am not."

Jae chuckled as he sorted through the contents. "Ain't telepathy fun. I'm having a marvelous time with it. Wiley– isn't he an interesting read? All that buzzing around. It's a wonder he can think straight."

Apparently Jae didn't like what was in that drawer after all. He went to the next.

"It's not polite to read others," Lina told him. "You wouldn't want others doing it to you."

"Give me a break. It's a new power. Let me have a little fun before I settle down."

"Don't get bad habits."

"Yes, Mother. Here." He passed her a bowl of rainbow-colored, grape-sized globes.

"I don't want candy."

"They're not. They're *lopa*."

"*Lopa*." The noun clicked into place in her mind. "A vegetable. They don't look like it."

"Whatever." Jae took her free hand to lead her back to the longer pillow couch. Their drinks sat a low coffee table. "In public you'd use fingersticks, but I hereby declare that here you can eat them the barbarian Terran way, with your fingers. You eat while I drink and we talk."

Lina sat and popped one into her mouth. Hm. It wasn't too sweet at all. Chewy. "Lopa," she said. "Not bad."

"And they have a fair amount o' fiber. Kuttr's always telling us that we need more fiber. Personally, I think he eats rope four times a day. Make way," he said, and fell backward toward her. She lifted the bowl so it wouldn't spill.

As he settled his head on her lap, Lina said, "I am not playing this game."

"We're just bonding," he said. "Eat. Many things happened today; many things loom in the future." He pointed at his mouth and she popped in a lopa. He chewed and considered, then swallowed. "We must make quick choices, particularly in basic personnel and duties thereof."

"By personnel duties, you mean personal relationships? Not on how we handle the Three Worlds?"

"You saw yourself yesterday, Lina. Paralyzed because of those unresolved personal relationship issues. Orb, I'm talking like Saichan. He's my therapist. If he were here, he'd tell you that you've got issues, too."

"You must allow me a little while to get over the surprise."

"Surprise? Your mind was screaming betrayal."

"I–"

"I can understand that," Jae said around another lopa. He shook his head as he considered the ceiling. "Londo can be infuriating sometimes, keeping secrets that shouldn't be. This was a monumental secret that should have been revealed before you vowed yourself to him. You understand vows, Lina. You are a priest too."

"Yes."

"The only way out at this point would be…"

"There will be no annulment."

Jae perked up at that. "You discussed it. While I was gone– annulment?"

Lina bit her lip. "Yes," she confessed. "I thought that back on Earth I could find a priest to annul very quietly, so Lon wouldn't be unduly embarrassed."

"You were going to do this for you? Or for him?" Jae took her hand and rubbed it. "For him. And me. You'd have done this for us."

"Lon showed me…" Lina's eyes welled up. "He's so brave! I'm a part of him now. The link is unbreakable."

"And he is a part of you." Jae's eyelids closed halfway in thought. "Do you think there's a possibility of that ever happening to Lon and me?"

"You two are already linked," Lina said. "It's not the same as Lon and mine, but it's there."

"Are you saying that I don't love him as much as you do?"

"I'm saying that it's different," she snapped. "Do you want me to figure calibrations?"

"No, don't do that. Don't be cross, Sweet, and give me another."

Lina frowned as she popped another lopa into his mouth. "Why are you still coming on to me? It's not my imagination, is it? No. Normal people don't do this. You're half-naked. Coming on, yes."

He gave a crooked smile as if to himself at that.

She said, "I thought we'd decided that Londo is the one with the problem that's causing the most trouble. You should be concentrating all this energy on him."

Jae nodded. "Oh he is, he is, and I will. It's just that you're a problem, too. And you're going to be so much easier to convince in your problem than he is in his. Solving the simpler problem first will help in approaching the harder problem later." He gave her a quick devil's grin. "We are well-trained in battle strategy here," he said. "You keep forgetting: I am a Legionnaire."

"You just think again, Legionnaire. Jae, how much do you drink?"

He blinked at that. "Just because you're a teetotaler—"

"*They* say that there was no genetic cause for alcoholism on Feith. But they also say that you get out of control with it by your own choice."

"You are too nosy even for a Terran." Jae's mouth set in a bitter line as he sat up, facing away from her.

"Drinking covers up fear."

"You over-simplify."

"I do. Jae, I don't want to be partnered to a drunk in Three Worlds or in some… other way."

"You want me to give up just alcohol? Or other hard drinks? Londo says you just have alcohol on Earth."

"We have drugs as well. Light drinking, drinking so long as it doesn't change your mood drastically— I can live with that. I've been around too many people who think they're hardly drinking, but they turn into annoying, ugly versions of themselves."

"You've never seen me drunk."

Now was not the time to contradict him. "Everyone around here holds you up on some kind of pedestal. The last Feithi, plus a Mega-Legionnaire. It must be tough."

Jae didn't say anything.

"Maybe there are ways around the stress. I don't know. Maybe all it'll take is someone you can talk to. What I was thinking is that maybe… If you and Lon have each other, maybe the way we can see this Three Worlds thing through is if you and I become good friends. I'm a good listener, Jae. And now I can give pretty good hugs."

"You kiss well, too." He twisted to face her. "We haven't discussed that."

She edged ever so slightly away from him.

"What else do you do well, Lina? Something that you might be able to do with me?" He swung all the way around to sit beside her and gave her a hunter's smile.

She made a move to stand up, but he grabbed her wrist.

"Don't go. Not yet."

"This isn't a good time to talk."

"It's perfect. Lon's asleep, and you don't have to worry about what he might think if you speak the truth."

"The truth? We're friends, Jae. The other night wasn't real. You can't believe–"

"It could have been. If Wiley hadn't hopped you up on so many short-term stims, you wouldn't have conked out on me. It would have been terrific, baby. It still can be."

"No." She shook his hand off her wrist. "I love Londo, and for me, that's all there is." That was how it had to be. She was neither whore nor traitor.

"You're so stubborn!"

"The word you mean is 'sensible,'" she sniffed.

He *harumph*ed in frustration, sprawling on the couch. It displayed him in delicious, half-naked glory. "Look, Sweet," he said. "I am not a patient man, so let me lay it out straight. I'm infatuated with you. You're infatuated with me; don't deny it. I want to have sex with you, and I don't think that's too much to ask, not with the position we're in now. So to speak. You tried sex with Londo before you married him. I think it would be *sensible* for us to do the same thing. To bind us together as partners, if nothing else. I mean, if you were like that when you were falling asleep, I'd love to see what you were like when you were wide–"

Lina clapped her hands over her ears and clenched her eyes shut. "I do *not* want to hear this! I am out of here!"

Unconcerned, Jae rose to her side. He pried one hand from her ear and whispered, "But how do I do it? How do I go up to my best friend and say, 'Hey, Lon, I want to have crazy sex with your hot little bride?'"

"Maybe you just ask," Londo's deep voice replied. He emerged from the dark entryway, dressed properly in his black costume, although his hair was tangled as if he'd rushed. The door shut behind him. He eyed Jae up and down, taking in his half-nudity.

"Londo!" Jae cried, a blush blooming across his face and chest.

"You took your time getting here!" Lina almost ran to hug her husband.

"You two were having a very interesting conversation." Lon took her in his arms. "I didn't want to interrupt."

Jae threw a pillow at Londo. "You listened–!" He threw another at Lina. "And you called him!"

"Damn straight she did." Lon's eyes roved over Jae's body. "So you take off half your clothes, you attempt to get my wife drunk, you try to feel her up, and now you're pulling out everything you've got to seduce her."

Lon surveyed the room, the epitome of composure, before he focused on Jae again. "And yet you didn't manage to get her into the bedroom. Jaeson Rallene the sexpert, the seducer supreme, champion of all things carnal." He grinned at his semi-naked friend. "How is it that you didn't get my Lina?"

Jae made a rude noise, and Londo laughed.

"And *never* wear black around my Lina again."

"Black?" Jae regarded him, then Lina, with interest.

Lon squeezed Lina. "He does look good in it, doesn't he, pet? You can see why I like looking at him, can't you?"

"I'm not your pet."

"Yes you are. You resisted that blond-haired devil for me, didn't you? Even though he's slobbering after you."

"He is not, Londo."

"Yes, he is." Lon grinned at Jae as he played with Lina's hair. "Can I pick 'em or can't I?

Defiantly, Jae crossed his arms across his chest. "Let me sleep with her, Lon."

"I don't think she wants to sleep with you."

"If you give your permission, she'll do it. She wants me."

"I don't," Lina said quickly. Lon patted her waist in reassurance.

"We made plans all these years," Jae urged Londo. "All three of us would be in bed. Me with your wife. I planned my life around that– *my life,* Lon! It's time to set our plans in motion."

Lon was silent for a moment. Then he said, "You started to work on them prematurely, *chéri.* I don't appreciate that."

"That was a mistake. I've apologized. I'll apologize again, as many times as it takes. You're here now; you have a wife. Time to turn her over to me. Tonight." Jae stood up quickly and Lina slid around Londo so he would stand between Jae and herself. "I'll take good care of her, Lon-Lon." Jae's tone was urgent. "I need her tonight. You know how it is."

"I've known how it was for years. I couldn't do anything about it. You can wait."

"Oh yes, wait!" Jae threw up his hands in derision and fell back onto the couch. "Wait while you two share minds and have sex and become so close that no one could begin to join you! Where are our plans then, Londo? What have you done with my life? Where does that leave me?"

Londo didn't say anything.

Lina murmured to Londo, "What if you stay with Jae the rest of the night, darling? Seal him to you." She ran her fingers over Lon's cheek as he regarded her. "I can wait. But he's right. Every time we're together, we get closer. If he's to have you, he needs to be with you. Now."

"You'd teach him?"

Her mouth made the movement, though it took another try for the sound to come out. "Yes," she whispered, her face pale.

"What are you two talking about?" Jae demanded.

Londo closed his eyes wearily. "We are talking about how precious this woman is to me," he told Jae. "There's no one like her anywhere. You don't deserve her. I don't deserve her."

"We were talking about you staying with Londo for the rest of the night," Lina managed to say.

Jae gripped the edge of the couch. "I can't believe it's true. I could really... with Lon?"

Anything for Londo. "Yes."

"Londo..." Jae's voice held such longing.

Lon's arms tightened around Lina as if she were Jae.

Jae said, "How? What do I do? When– Are you sure? Londo?"

Lon's words were a rasp of tight emotion. "Let's give it a try, Jae-Jae. Lina? A massage? Is that how–?"

"Yes. Yes, a massage." The world spun around Lina so she took a few breaths and looked around. "Here, or–?"

"The bedroom," Jae said immediately. Fire burned openly in his eyes but he didn't reach for Londo. He held himself back now as he had for so many, many years.

When Lon hesitated, Jae bowed and gestured to the hallway.

15

Londo trembled in Lina's arms. **Are you absolutely sure about this, chérie?** he asked.

It will work. He loves you so much. She hugged him before giving him a push in Jae's direction. Still he hesitated before taking Jae's outstretched hand. She followed them to the bedroom.

It was… *voluptuous* was the only word she could come up with. Plushly upholstered in dark fabrics, it had a New Orleans atmosphere of decadence. Draperies surrounded the bed. Ropes hung in their shadows, though they didn't tie anything back. Pillows of various sizes and shapes had been scattered around the room, particularly in a corner of the bed where they formed a small mountain.

A wide mirror dominated one wall. Another one was embedded in the ceiling. What Lina supposed were dressers were cushioned as well. There were very few hard surfaces in the entire room.

Jae had switched so quickly from trying to seduce her to focusing on Londo. Surely that demonstrated where she stood in Jae's eyes. She was merely a means to an end. Or was she pencilled in somewhere on his official Legion schedule as just another two-week fling?

She watched him as he moved to the other side of the bed, walking as if he were surrounded by danger: supple and alert, not quite mortal. He was taller, leaner than Londo, his muscles sharply defined with all the training he had to maintain. He wore those unsoled tights, unlike Lon's leather pants, and it was like watching an acrobat or ballet dancer, able to see the muscle masses rippling through the fabric.

How many had he seduced before this?

Those elf ears that peeked through his hair begged to be examined. A lover could drown in the bright blue of his eyes. His lips were thinner than Londo's full lips, yet still soft. Jae's cheek was more rounded than her husband's. Lon had those handsome dimples, if you could give that dainty a term to the masculine lines of his face, and Jae's face had that sexy stubble.

Londo slipped onto the sheets. She took his vest and shirt as he offered them to her. When he lay on his stomach, she caressed the muscles of that broad back of his. It wouldn't be entirely hers to enjoy any more.

Lon held out his hand and she took it in both of her own.

Lina, I just don't know. It's all happening so quickly. Are you all right with this?

Even unto eternity, love. How much more permanent can you get?

But I just found you. I don't want you to think that I'm abandoning you.

I know that now. I love you like no one's ever loved anyone.

He shifted to his side and his eyes shone at her. **So what did you think when Jae told you he loved me?**

Lina considered. **I was surprised. But Lon, you're the most lovable person I know. Who couldn't love you?**

She heard his mental laugh along with his physical one. "D'accord," he said. **And what did you think of me when you found out I loved Jae?**

You know. But Lon, now I can see why you would. Growing up together, both of you needing each other. Jae's so funny and sweet–

Sweet? Jae?

It's perfectly natural for you to love him. I'd think it was unnatural if you didn't.

So why is it so terrible for you if you might love him?

Lon!

He smiled at her and stroked her cheek. **I said "if." Just imagine. Start to think about it.**

I never want to hurt you, darling.

He brought her closer to kiss her lightly on the mouth. **Kitten, you won't.** There was a tension around his eyes that only Lina could see, but he turned around and casually called over his shoulder, "How the hell long does it take, Rallene?"

"Just a minnit, right," Jae said. He'd been rummaging through drawers around the room, laying out provisions.

"Becoming Irish has slowed him down," Lon shared a conspiratorial smile with Lina.

She realized: "You gave him that English linguatape with the accent."

"He's a leprechaun," said Lon, "or hadn't you noticed? Though I've never heard him say more than three English words in a row until now."

"Found it," Jae announced from across the room, brandishing a bottle of something. "Genuine Nound massage oil. I was saving it for a special occasion." With a bound, he landed on his knees on the bed next to Lon. "Where do I start? How do I begin?" He handed the bottle to Lina and rubbed his hands expectantly.

"As I recall, the masseuse takes her shirt off," Londo said, looking around at Lina.

"Don't push it. Jae's the masseur tonight and he already is quite shirtless."

"So he is."

Lina tried not to bite her lip. She was going to share this secret with someone else. The unique bond between her and Lon would be unique no longer. Jealousy and fear rampaged through her and she had to take a breath to fight it.

This was Jae. This was Lon. They'd wanted each other for so many years. They'd been through such pain. She didn't have the right to stand in their way. Maybe this was another beginning instead of an ending.

"Massage is hard work," she said.

Jae stretched in preparation. Londo's face was to the mattress. Lina's eyes traveled on Jae's displayed body, and they locked gazes. He gave her a slow, wily smile and she finally had to turn her eyes away. Her skin had started to tingle.

Jae knelt on one side of Londo with Lina on the other, to give instructions. Jae said, "Lon, you want to warm this?" He made a motion to Lina, and she held the bottle of oil to Lon's side. Lon blew on it.

"There," he said, and turned his head back to the mattress.

Now Lina poured a generous dollop on Lon's shoulders. She gave a quick initial rub, just to get Lon ready for the more thorough massage from Jae. "Oh!" The oil smelled like sex… sex and something darkly spicy. Just inhaling it was exciting her.

"Nound oil," Jae repeated. He'd rubbed his index finger across the top of the bottle as he'd unstoppered it for her, and now held the finger under Lina's nose. It made her dizzy, and his eyes narrowed speculatively to see the heavy-lidded arousal on her face. "It's a little illegal," he said. "Just a tad."

"It's illegal for an unmarried person to own it." Londo's voice was muffled in the mattress. His breathing was deep and regular; the oil was getting to him, too.

"Unmarried person? They can legislate like that?" Lina's confusion broke her from the spell.

"Different rules," Lon said.

"Discriminating rules," Jae said. He nodded at Lon's back to Lina. "The technique?"

"You communicate with the cells," she explained to Jae as he listened closely. "Start with just one muscle, and then move on when that muscle starts to really relax. You'll get the feel of it."

"And what do you communicate?"

"Just tell the muscle, the cells, that you love them. That they're doing their jobs wonderfully, and you love them and you love the owner of this body. Tell them that it's you who loves them so much, and that they should recognize you. They don't need to put up any defenses against you. Just beam them all the love you can."

"I think I can do that," Jae said softly, tracing a design in the oil on Londo's back. Perhaps it was the Feithi symbol for a heart, or for love.

Jae swung his left knee over Lon so he could straddle him, and then began. He approached it with obvious Legionnaire determination. Lina could sense his concentration narrowing to a hard focus on Lon's shoulders.

"Love," she whispered, and he gave the slightest of nods.

The hardness mellowed and warmed. Lon's cells noticed Jae's presence. They bathed in a brilliant pink ethereal light, the color of a spring dawn. Like flowers to the sun, they turned toward it.

Lina showed Jae how to siphon off the fear toxins Londo's cells threw up in self-defense as his influence upon them grew. After a while she eased off the bed and left the room, closing the door behind her so they could be alone.

They'd call her if they needed her, but she didn't think they would. This was the culmination of well over a decade of frustration for them. They'd be the rest of the night at least.

Back in Londo's room, she held her hands up to her face, breathing in the Nound oil that coated them. She wanted it on herself. All over. Porting off her clothes, she stretched and rubbed it everywhere, even through her hair, groaning as if her hands were someone else's. The Nound was like a phantom lover's touch. She spread herself to it deliciously, adding her own unique fragrance.

"Ah god," she murmured. Hurry, Londo. Jae. Someone. Anyone. Hell, if Stoan Kinrol came through the door now, she would throw him on the floor, rip off his clothes and mount him.

The idea made her laugh and she realized that she'd been caught up in the aphrodisiac. Good one: *eyow*. But she needed a clear mind to make decisions tonight. Jae would be leaving day after tomorrow for Aldierra. He would have to know how she would vote in all this. Maybe she could come up with an alternate plan that Londo could live with.

So she showered leisurely, making sure all the oil came off. Its effects must still linger, for she couldn't bring herself to practical thoughts yet. Nound oil: could you buy it on the Nets? She wanted a bottle for just her and Lon.

Somehow instead she found herself in the clothes sections on the Internet, scrolling through selections until she found what could be turned into a slinky short dress. Take away the sleeves, add a little cleavage… Would Londo like it? Maybe it would make him forget about Jae for a while. Mm, maybe it would make Jae crazy, too.

She shook her head hard. She was not after Jae!

Scrolling down, she found a cute black dress hiding in the nightwear section. Too naughty for Sarastoran tastes, it came with a little jacket-cape to cover up things on top. On impulse, she ordered it in a cinnamon red. Matching stay-up stockings she finagled through the system.

She added a tiny red lace thong and bra, referring to her previous programs of lace for the order. Sarastor fashion had never heard of lace, much less bras (for some reason Sarastoran women didn't use them), and she'd had to furnish some samples as patterns a couple days ago for her nightgowns.

It must have been because it was a complicated custom order that the clothes didn't appear in the merchandise unit for five full minutes after she hit the send key. She stared at them for another minute before she touched them. *Wake up, Lina. Get sober, Lina. Clear and logical head.*

Still when she tried them on she did so without porting, sliding the material over her skin while imagining Londo's sure fingers peeling it off her. She got goosebumps thinking about him. There on the edge of her consciousness, she could sense his deep passion rising. Too bad it was rising in Jae's direction.

Music would cover them up.

Jae had some of her favorite CDs. She ported quickly to his apartment, thankful that his bedroom seemed well-soundproofed, and rifled through the large stack of CDs that he'd accumulated in the past few days. This one and this one…

She tried to tune out in her head what was happening back in the bedroom. It was impolite to be here. They might think she wanted to intrude. Did she? *Leave.* "Puter," she instructed, "lights off in here, please." *Beep beep.* A bump of her toe brought one of the stacks of CDs tumbling. She knelt down to straighten them—

And heard the apartment door opening without a knock. She crouched lower. Her view of the door was good, but she'd be hidden from whoever it was.

And it was Stoan.

He picked up Jae's cape and jacket from the doorway before dropping them again, turned and gave Jae's discarded tunic and shirt a little kick.

Heads up, guys, you have company, she beamed to the two in the bedroom.

Jesus H. Christ! Lina— can you stall him? Give us three minutes, maybe five.

Stall? Lina looked around quickly. Stall with what? She drew the lines of force in to hide herself and ported Jae's rachet glass into the kitchen, above the sink. It fell, tinkling as it landed and rolled around. Stoan trotted to investigate, which gave her a few more seconds to think.

Should she just port Lon and her back to his apartment? He hadn't said to. She took her capelet off and draped it on the floor. "Puter, send the kol-vanasche to pick up Jae's clothes in here," Lina whispered. Those two acknowledging beeps were excruciatingly loud, but maybe Stoan wouldn't notice them.

He emerged from the kitchenette and started down the hall to the bedroom, of all places. Why? She gave a little muffled groan, as if she were waking up. He stopped where he was.

She groaned again. "Um, isn't it a bit late to be sneaking around? Or are you just trying to find someone new to film?" she asked from her place in the living room.

He whirled around. Surprise and then anger washed across his face. "Puter, lights on full in here."

Silently Lina thanked all her lucky stars. Good thing she'd showered off that Nound oil!

Stoan glanced around the room as if he expected to see someone else there. But all he had to see was her lounging on the pillows. Alone. She rose up slowly, showing more leg than she would ever normally think of doing, and reached down for her capelet, revealing an eyeful of cleavage. *Forgive me, Lon,* but this was the only kind of stalling she could think of off the top of her head. Too much Nound oil tonight!

"You like invading people's privacy," she said, remaining seated as she tied the capelet around herself. She brushed her hair back with her hands, letting the capelet reveal her again, and then decorously adjusted her skirt to modesty. Let him come to her. Let him have his back to the bedroom doorway so they could assess the situation.

"And you have made yourself quite at home," Stoan said, striding forward to stand over her. She made a great deal of stretching as if she were unused to falling asleep on Jae's stacked-pillow furniture. She flounced and punched a few of the pillows as she replaced them.

"Where's Jae? Where's your *husband?*"

"Ah, I suppose I might have fallen asleep. What time is it?"

"It's a little after nineteen."

That would make it ten-thirtyish back home. Still that early? Sarastoran nights were long.

Lina hid a delicate yawn behind her fingers. "I was waiting for Londo so we can go to bed. They were in back doing something." She waved her hand vaguely and brought it back to tangle in her hair so his eyes would remain on her. "Your Sarastoran technology; I just don't understand it." She looked up at him. Should she play the French maid again like she had for the Aldierran invaders? Stoan was a jerk, but was he a dumb one? "I take it you're not satisfied with the results of yesterday's events."

He braced one leg on the couch in an arrogant pose as he towered over her. "I don't like things I can't understand," he said.

"Sometimes you just have to go with the flow and figure out things as you can."

"Too many unexplainable–" Stoan began.

"Stoan, what the hell are you doing here at this time of night?" Londo demanded as he stalked out of the bedroom in his uniform. Jae was right behind him, fully dressed in his.

"What were you doing in there?"

"Jae's thinking about putting in a sound system for music." How smooth was his lie! "What are you doing here? Did you have a meeting scheduled, Jae?"

"None that I was aware of," Jae replied curiously, clearly giving Stoan the once-over.

Stoan frowned at him. "I was just checking in… to hear Jae's thoughts about what happened yesterday." He glanced at the entryway floor, but the clothing was gone behind the crystalline pancake of a retreating kol-vanasche.

Lina got up to join Lon. He put his arms around her and held her close as she lay her head against his cheek The newlyweds. She knew they made a sweet picture.

He sneaked in without knocking, she told them.

Jae said, "What, I get a promotion and you don't expect me to be pleased? It sounds exciting. We've been talking about it ever since. Well, just a few short breaks here and there. I'm about ready to turn in now, though. It's been a very long day. Can this conversation wait until morning?"

Stoan looked at each of them. "I suppose so. Sometime either well before the funeral, or well after it."

Jae sighed. "I keep forgetting. It seems so odd to bury her when we just saw her. She looked happy. I was worried about that."

Stoan looked at Lina.

"It was not some kind of projection of mine," she snapped. "Remember, you had me locked in that hyperspace chamber."

"So we did," Stoan said. He couldn't press for more. His plans, whatever they'd been, had been thrown for a loop. "Jae. Londo. I want to hear from both of you tomorrow. Now get some sleep." With that, he turned on his heel and left.

Jae and Lon both turned to her after the door had closed completely.

"I came back to borrow some CDs. He didn't knock," she repeated. "Just barged in. Jae, maybe you should start locking your quarters."

"That wouldn't do any good," Lon growled at the closed door. "The man knows exactly when to interrupt, damn him. He's got to be partially telepathic."

"You two didn't...?" Lina looked from one to the other.

"Were you timing us?" Lon gave her his crooked smile as Jae gave a frustrated frown.

"I was getting some music," Lina defended herself. She flashed the CDs at them as proof. "I wasn't keeping track of you."

Lon nodded at her. "You got a new dress. I like it, Kitten. It's not very Sarastoran, thank god."

She broke into a smile; she had pleased Londo. Standing next to Jae, he could still want her. "I assumed you two would want the entire night." She paused. "Did it—"

Jae pushed Londo. "*He* suddenly wanted to talk," he accused the wobbling megapara. "Almost two decades of waiting, and he wants to talk!" Jae scowled at Lina. "You're catching!"

"Sorry," she said, and couldn't help a giggle. "Look, I'll be off to bed now. Maybe a little snack first. I'm still hungry."

"No, Kitten." Londo put his arms around her. "You were what we were talking about. We need to straighten out the final leg of this threesome."

"We can straighten it out tomorrow. Or after Jae gets back. Tonight is for you two."

"*Non, non, non.*" Londo was in one of his team leader moods. "Tonight is for making sure everyone knows where they stand. I don't want you upset for any longer than you have to be."

"I'm not upset," she told him. Did Jae snort behind her?

"Denial."

"I am not–" She stopped and sighed. "Maybe I am, a little. But I can wait, Lon, really I can." She smiled up at him and his face seemed to resonate in her mind. His skin seemed warmer, even more inviting than usual.

"Ooo, Londo, you smell so good." The Nound fragrance on him lingered, as if he'd washed it off hurriedly but not completely. Now mostly clove-like spices remained, but there was an undercurrent of excitement there. She knew what it was now, what its power was, but she couldn't stop the thrill of arousal at touching her husband. She kissed him, kissed him again, wrapping her arms around him and pressing herself to him.

"Shit," Lon finally managed to say. "I forgot how exposure to Nound hits some people. Jae, take a shower."

Jae started to say something, but then left the room.

"Lina. Lina, *chérie,* Nound oil is a very powerful aphrodisiac."

"You bet." She let her hands roam all over him until she found one particular spot to massage.

"Um. Baby, I'd love to continue this, but I think that the whole point here was for us not to be together tonight."

"I want to get you a gallon of that stuff. For your birthday." He eased her hand away from his crotch, so she massaged his firm butt instead. "Five gallons. Let's see. You don't know your birthday, but it's obvious you're a Leo. That's in August, right? August… seventh. 8:05 a.m. I wonder what time zone eastern France is?"

Londo tensed up immediately. "Birthplace?" He snapped out the word in spite of himself.

She squinted her eyes, trying to see a mental map. "Sch… Or maybe it's something sch. On the Rhine…"

"Can you let me see?"

She nodded, and opened her mind to let him view the faintest ghost of a map in her thoughts. One section of it seemed more in focus than the rest. It was France, not really a map but a patch of land that *felt* like France. Northeastern sector. There was Strasbourg, here was the Rhine.

Lon searched in his memory to add to the ephemeral map. "Schwyzen?"

"Schwyzen!" Lina grinned at him suddenly, patting his cheek. "Gold star for geography. That's it exactly."

Lon was a little dazed. "August seventh, Schwyzen, France."

"8:05 a.m., local time."

"Year?"

Lina worked her mouth in thought. "Let's do this the scientific way. Put your arm out."

"What?"

"Just do it. Or we could neck."

He extended his arm straight from the side of his body.

"Don't resist me, but just keep your arm in this position." She put one hand on his opposite shoulder and one on the extended forearm. "Say yes," she commanded.

"Yes."

She pushed down on his arm gently. It didn't budge. "Say no."

"No." She pushed down. The arm didn't budge. She sighed. "I was afraid of that. Those little force fields are interfering in this, even if I touch you. But there are ways around it." She stood next to him and placed her foot so it touched the length of his. "Say, 'I give my body permission to let Lina react for me.'"

"What?"

"Say it. Please."

"I give my body permission to let Lina react for me. *Okay d'ac?*"

"Okay. You said you were either twenty-nine or thirty?"

"Yeah."

"Right. Yes. No. I'm calibrating." She was doing something funny with her fingers, snapping her thumb and index fingers against a circle she made out of the fingers of her other hand. "Twenty-nine. Thirty."

"Now what are you doing?" Jae came into the room behind them.

"Jae, stand here, stand with your foot here." Lina moved out the way.

"What?"

"Humor me."

Jae assumed the position. and Lina pointed at Lon. "Say, 'I give my body permission to let Jae react for me.'"

"I give my body permission to let Jae react for me."

"Jae, say 'My body is now giving information about Londo's body.'"

"Kinky."

"Jaaae!"

"My body is now giving information about Londo's body. What is this about?"

"Hold out your arm," Lina gave him the instructions and put her hands on his shoulder and forearm as she had Londo. "Say yes."

"Yes."

She pushed down and he resisted her.

"No, no, no. Don't resist me. Just keep your arm in this position. Say yes again."

"Yes."

This time when she pushed she seemed pleased.

"Say no."

"No."

She pushed, and his arm dipped.

"Good. Repeat after me: Londo is twenty-nine years…" She suddenly realized that Jae wasn't from Earth, and didn't want to get measurements mixed up. "Londo is twenty-nine Terran years old."

"Londo is twenty-nine Terran years old."

She pushed and the arm stayed in place. "Londo is thirty Terran years old."

"Londo is thirty Terran years old."

She pushed and his arm dipped.

"That's confirmation. You're twenty-nine, Lon. Uh oh, next August's the big three-oh." She grinned at him. "We'll get black balloons and have one of those 'over the hill' parties. Little skeletons on the cake. Black frosting. Maybe a red velvet cake, just for bloody effect. Do you like red velvet?"

"Can I move now?" Jae asked. "Or is now when you swing the dead animal over your head? What the orb's going on?"

Londo turned to Jae, amazement painted over his face. "I was born on August seventh, in Schwyzen, France, European continent, Earz*th*. Twenty-nine years ago." He frowned as he started the mental arithmetic to determine the year.

"Orb. Can you get confirmation of this?"

"8:05 AM," Lina added. "I'll check in the ephemeris when we get back to start your birthchart for you, but you'll need to get a professional astrologer to interpret. I'll call David; he's good."

Lon said, "If any part of that is correct, it'll narrow the field down considerably in the search."

"I beg your pardon," Lina sniffed. "Sir, are you doubting my veracity?"

"Give me a break, wife. You got this all from thin air. What's your hit rate on information like this?"

She considered. "High seventies. Maybe. Mid-eighties or higher if I'm in the groove." She might be feeling some of that Nound oil still. "And sober."

"Not a hundred percent."

"Okay, okay. So we'll just say that *maybe* you were born on August seventh, 8:05 a.m., in Schwyzen, France. And I'll bake you a cake anyway. With black icing."

He leaned in to kiss her, and she could see from the sparkle in his eyes that he knew she was right. "We'll have a huge party," he said. "God, Lina, if it's true, it's like I really exist."

"Of course you do."

"I… I fit, then. I fit into life. That's a strange feeling. You don't understand, Lina. But you do, Jae."

"Yeah. I do." Jae watched them, clasped in each other's arms, Londo gazing at his bride adoringly. "Now you have a birthday, a birthplace. A wife. Maybe in the future a family."

Jae noted how Londo's arms encircled Lina, creating a cage around her. He was getting in a possessive mood again. Was he going to change his mind? It was as if the two of them were leaving him behind.

"We're still here," Londo told him. "Both of us. Lina, Jae needs a family to belong to. I don't want to put any pressure on you–"

"Don't," Jae said. "Let her make her own decisions, like I'll make mine."

"I've managed to make all my decisions for myself until just lately," Lina said. "I haven't forgotten how it's done."

"Talk him to death like you did me." Lon squeezed her as she smiled at him.

"Men."

"That's a sexist comment."

"It is. And I stand by it."

Jae saw how Lina was clutching Londo. Trying to act nonchalant when she so obviously wasn't. "What about not talking? Londo, I want to have sex with your wife."

"There will be no sex," Lina declared.

Londo looked down at Lina with such tenderness. "Our fourth married night together," he whispered. "But maybe that's the way it's supposed to be. Start the marriage off right, with the right people. I've waited for you for so long, Lina. To lose you–"

"You're not losing me. We'll talk a while–"

No you won't, cherie. You know where you'll end up.

Her green eyes burned into his. He could feel her mind going through possibilities. **Maybe a couple kisses, no more. We're just friends. I'll get him to realize that.**

Maybe him riding you. Or vice versa.

No! It's not–

My little Cleopatra, Queen of Denial. I said I couldn't stand the thought of another man making love to you, but this is Jae. He's been my almost-lover for so long. Yesterday we became partners in the most important business this sector *of the galaxy has ever seen. And we're all telepaths now. You need to know what you feel about him. He needs to know the same thing about you. Sex and everything associated with it are the most efficient way to finding that out.*

Lina bared her teeth at him. "Efficiency– there's a time and place for that. Usually talking does just fine."

"D'accord." Londo gave a long sigh. "Use whatever means you two find works best. I want our course to be true from the start, and we need to know where you two stand. Figure it out tonight."

He gave a frustrated grimace, squeezed his eyes shut and slapped the palm of his hand against his forehead. "I should have told Mama Ruth and Papa Mike what time we'd port them tomorrow. Now we don't know when they'll call. Well. Jae, I want her back by… five hundred. That'll give us time to plot the way for the three of us, over breakfast if it takes that long. Then I can work on finishing the eulogy and you and Lina can get some sleep. I doubt if the gRands will port in before early afternoon."

"Five hundred." Jae nodded to him as if they were prepared to synchronize their watches.

Londo squeezed Lina. "Jae and I'll have our time tomorrow night. Be honest with yourself and whatever you do, don't think about what your parents would say. Don't… don't think about what I'd say either."

"Londo–"

"I mean it. Live in the now. Like I taught you."

She paused for a long moment. A very long moment. "Yes, Lon." She gazed at the strong, sure hand she was clutching. The hand of her husband, to whom she'd pledged herself for life.

"We'll have time together once Jae's gone on his mission. *D'accord?*"

Lina looked into Lon's eyes, so lovingly brown. "Absolutely." She opened herself up to him so he could feel her commitment again, her passion for him. He held her hands in his and took a breath.

"Take good care of her, Jae. Okay, Lina. Port me back."

"I love you, Londo," she whispered as she did. She gazed at his after-image.

16

"Puter, lock front door," Jae commanded the air. It beeped back twice. He regarded Lina with a slow, confident up-and-down sweep as she turned to him. "I don't think we'll have any more interruptions." He held out his hand to her and in a daze she took it. One pull and she was in his arms. He leaned down to kiss her.

"Wait."

"Not this time. I'm tired of playing your games and waiting forever for Londo."

"I'm not playing games." She pushed at him, but he didn't budge.

"You two are trying to drive me crazy." He pressed her against himself. His hands told her just how much the situation interested him. He had very skilled hands.

"We're only going to talk," Lina insisted. "Stop that."

"Stop what?" he whispered into her ear before he licked it and then pulled on the lobe with his teeth.

"Ooh, we.. we need to lay down some ground rules. When–" She shut her eyes and tried not to arch as he drew his tongue down the side of her neck. "When are you going to have Londo and when do I get him?"

"When do I get you? When do you finally admit to yourself who and what you want?"

Lina couldn't speak as he drew her hair away from the base of her neck, gifting little kisses on the revealed skin. "Always wear your hair down for me, Angel," he said. "I like it down."

Her fingers had clenched on the neckline of his overtunic and Lina released them with a start. Batting against his chest with her palms, she said, "We are here to talk."

"Sex," he countered. "It's our assignment from team leader."

"Was not."

"Was so."

They frowned at each other.

"Is he going to be team leader for the rest of our lives, Jae? Is that what the center of the dual-thingie does? We don't get any say? I won't sign up for that."

Jae stuck his tongue into his cheek and regarded her. "You don't know a thing about the dual-triune, do you?"

"O ho, a light suddenly dawns."

He grunted in a way that sounded more like a moan.

"So, if I'm the tertiary," Lina asked, poking at his chest to make her point but also to back him away, "does that mean I live somewhere else from him? Londo seems a little uncomfortable with the cats. Separate houses would probably be best in that case, don't you think? Do you think we could afford that? But I want a schedule, none of this waiting around crap. Do I go to him, or does he come to me? I need to know what my boundaries are! Should I get a place near Starhaven? You and he are moving to Starhaven, right?"

Jae looked pouty when he was puzzled. "Why are you suddenly the tertiary?" he asked.

"It just makes sense," Lina replied. "Unless you were planning on fooling around on Londo."

"Fooling around. On Londo."

"I don't like that idea. I don't want him hurt. If you're married, you should be *married*," Lina declared, almost to herself. Jae had released her, so she wandered across the living room with its softly-billowing drapes, a faux breeze through faux windows. Somewhere a faux waterfall added its melody to the ambiance.

"If you're the tertiary," she told him as she faced him, "just how much extra-marital stuff were you thinking of? I know, there are monogamous people, well, mostly-monogamous people and there are– you can't call them polygamous if they're not married? Poly… amorous, that's the word. People who just can't settle down on one person. It's not in their natures and it's right for them, and you seem to be one of those. But to get married and do it– Well, that's wrong. It's breaking a vow. From a Terran point of view, I mean.

"Wait," she added as the thought struck her. "I read Dan Savage. He says it's okay if the spouse agrees. Maybe. I mean, marriage means commitment. What else is it for? Man, I'm so new at all this. Did you get a chance to discuss this with Londo?"

"We were too busy making out and then talking about you," Jae replied wryly. He followed her, scratching his chin. "So what if I want to fool around with you?"

"You wouldn't have to." The brushing-off motion Lina used eliminated the entire concept. "Who wants Lina Muttbutt anyway? Besides Lon, I mean, and his choices are limited."

"Don't say that."

"But would you establish your household here, or on Earth?" Lina continued. "If it's going to be here, does that mean that I still get to go to Starhaven? It didn't look like a road was too near, which is good for the cats. Have you seen the view from there? It's gorgeous."

"Yes. Lon's shown me," Jae said in clipped syllables. He scratched the small of his back as he chewed his lower lip. Then he pointed an imperious finger at her. "Sit down."

Lina blinked but sat on the pillow sofa.

"Let's get a few things straight here. About dual-triune and about us." Jae produced a padd and shoved it at her as he sat beside her. Its screen expanded as she touched it. "Show me what dual-triune is."

Lina picked up the stylus and thought a mere moment before putting a big circle on the screen's top center, labeling it "L." "Londo," she announced.

"It doesn't look like him, but go on."

She drew a dashed line off to the lower left, another circle, not quite as heavily outlined as Londo's, but as large. A "J" went there, "That's you," and Jae grunted. Another, much longer line came off Londo to the lower right, and a small circle without a letter went there. "That's me." she explained.

"You've got two tertiaries here," Jae said.

"No, I don't. There's you and Londo," she pointed at the route, "and me and Londo."

Jae drew a line between her circle and his own. "What about this?" he asked.

"That doesn't look like much of a dual-triune."

"And what would you know about it?" Jae went to work with the stylus, drawing a large circle into which he put the letters A and B, and then a short line from it, not nearer one letter or the other, and wrote "C" after it. "Dual-triune," he said. He added a dotted line from C outward to whatever.

"Oh."

"Sometimes," Jae erased the final dotted line, "the tertiary doesn't want to go outside the marriage." With a few flicks of his stylus, the line to C disappeared, the central circle grew larger, and C went inside, equidistant from A and B. "A full triune," Jae said. He tapped the stylus on the screen and was suddenly quiet.

"So… it's the tertiary's need to have other partners that makes it a dual-triune?"

"Yes. No. It's the relative importance within the relationship as well. The emotional bond isn't as strong between tertiary and primaries."

"That's not right," Lina said slowly. "You love Londo every bit as much as I do. And he loves you."

Lina tried to sort it out. Did that make Lon the tertiary? No, that didn't make sense. "A tertiary's just not going to work," she finally decided. "I know your reputation for two-week affairs, Jae, but you're not going to have the time for them. Londo has a lot of stamina. And determination. He sets his goal and by god, he's going to meet it if it kills him." She gave a little happy sigh, remembering. "And he does it in style. You're going to be too tired to be a Legionnaire, much less the playboy Legionnaire."

"You seem to be weathering everything well."

"I am a healer," she declared, which garnered a laugh from him. Without missing a beat, she asked, "So, how many? How many people will you have to tell that you don't have time for them any more?"

An affair every two or three weeks for forever… Him having his pick of the most beautiful, the most skilled lovers in the sector. Dellen was still pining over him after an affair that must have been long ago. Lina had seen looks that other Legionnaires had given him, longing looks, measuring looks… knowing looks.

Jae stroked her shoulder and didn't say anything.

"I'm sorry," she said. "None of my business. Forget I said anything."

"More than I can remember," Jae said softly. "But it's not the numbers, it's the experience that counts."

"Not the quantity but the quality?"

His laugh was very small. "Right. There've only been a handful who've ever had any kind of impact on me. Everyone else was just something to do. Somebody to make me feel… real. Someone to share a lonely night with. I wanted Londo and they weren't him. Whoever it was, we usually ended up being together but still lonely."

"I can't bear the thought of you being lonely."

"Then what are you going to do about it, Sweet?" he asked, squeezing her shoulder.

She picked at imaginary lint on his tunic. "I don't know." Was this just another game to him? Would he want to play something else next week? With someone else? "All I know for sure is that all of this is going too fast. You can see that."

Jae stretched back on the couch. Lina was enthralled with watching him move. Unconsciously she followed to kneel beside him.

"You're right," he said, "But sometimes you have to make major decisions on the run. The Worlds asked us to travel a new direction, and now we have to fine-tune the rest of our lives to step in harmony with that. We have to do this quickly, Lie-Lie. We have other things to accomplish."

Lina nodded. "But we make our own personal decisions, not the Worlds They don't have any idea of what real, human life is like."

"They pointed us at each other. Maybe they know more than we think they do. Let's find out."

He reached to play with her hair and she brushed his hand away. "Please don't get me wrong," she told him. "I really do like you as friend, Jae. Very much."

"How much?" He rose up and shifted so that he hovered over her.

"Maybe too much," she said. She dislodged some pillows as she tried to slide away. "I've gotten a kick out of doing things upside down all my life. But this…" She shook her head. "This would be a betrayal of Londo. I don't do that."

"He's given you his permission."

"I don't care." She shook her head fiercely. "I am not going to compromise my marriage!"

"Would I compromise it?"

"Not you and Londo. I want Londo to have anything he wants and he wants you. And you love him so much. I don't want you lonely any more, not when you could have Lon."

"So it's just the you and me that would compromise your marriage."

Just his body heat, his warm breath on her, was enough to set a warm flush rising. His golden hair fell across his forehead, but it couldn't hide the bright blue of his marvelous, kind eyes. She couldn't tear her gaze away from his beauty, inside and out.

"Sometimes I find myself thinking of you instead of Londo," she whispered. "What if we… And then I find out I don't love him as much anymore?"

Jae was silent.

Lina jumped up off the couch and slapped herself hard on the head. "And sometimes I'm so damned stupid I can't stand myself. Here I am drowning and now I'm asking the universe to run some more water into the pool."

Jae rose to stand behind her. "The other night I overstepped my boundaries badly, I know, and you were drunk. But for a moment there, you knew it was me and you knew what we were going to do, and you wanted it, too. You weren't worried about compromising anything."

Her mouth worked. "For that moment I… forgot about Londo."

He moved to face her. "So. Without Londo in the picture, you're attracted to me enough to want to get crazy wild under the sheets. But with Londo in the picture you're not. Or so you tell yourself. "

"I… We…" she said. "The other night– we said we were going to forget it." She ducked around him and walked away.

"I'm not willing to be forgotten," he said loudly. She stopped but didn't turn around. "And now you can't forget about me. We're partners for life, Carolina

Starhart. At some point you're going to have to sit and think about the two of us. Me, I have no patience. I'd rather do this the efficient way."

"Efficient!" Lina exclaimed, whirling around.

"Absolutely." He strode over to her. "Bedroom, Lina. Come."

"What, you think I'm one of your little trained Legionnaires? To jump at your command? This from the man who constantly tells me not to trust him? I don't want to be a one-night or two-week stand. It's just infatuation. I'm not going to be a Feithi hag or a celebrity beard. I don't want to pledge myself to something I do not believe will last."

"You want proof?"

"You can't give me that. I don't trust you anymore, Jae."

"I'll prove myself to you." He pulled her to him, crushing her to himself. His voice lowered with passion. "I'll prove anything you want tonight. C'mon, Lina, get rid of this outfit. You can do it faster than I can. Let's get naked. Let's get wild." He took her in a hard, demanding kiss.

Despite herself, Lina welcomed it. But it was too anxious, too unwilling to meet her terms. His tongue skipped several steps of the process, charging far ahead of where she was willing to go.

"Jae!"

He hoisted her up so she straddled him, pinning her against the entry wall. He pushed her capelet out of the way as he worked his way down her shoulder.

"Down, Jae," she said breathlessly. "Talk."

He took a breath. "Sex," he countered, and proceeded down to kiss her breast through the material. His fingers dug into the bare flesh of her butt as he held her.

All of a sudden Jae discovered he was holding nothing but air in his hands. "What…" He looked around to see her standing in the living room with her fists on her hips.

"If you want sex so bad, perhaps we could take five minutes here." She tossed her head. "You can go into the bedroom alone— and do whatever it is you need to do. I'll be out here when you're through. Make sure you wash your hands afterward." She sank into the pile of pillows.

The sound of distant male laughter rang in Jae's mind. He gave her a palms-up gesture of surrender as he crossed the large room to sit down beside her.

"Okay, okay," he said, wondering at the shyness she suddenly exuded. Her cheeks were pink and she couldn't meet his eyes. He brushed a stray lock of hair out of her face. His hands were shaking ever so slightly. Was he nervous? Him? "What do you want to talk about?"

"I want to catch my breath," she said softly. "Dammit, Jae, you told me you were gay. I thought I was safe!"

"I said 'mostly gay.' You know about Dellen at least. That should have given you a hint. And I did tell you not to trust me."

"Why can't I?"

He shook his head at her. "I didn't know myself what was happening until the other afternoon at the bar. Well, maybe before. I wasn't trying to make a play for you. I thought that I was just going to take it easy, feel you out, maybe get you primed–"

She let out a squawk.

"…And then when Lon finally got around to discussing the matter with you…"

Her face morphed through at least a dozen expressions. Finally she blew out a frustrated breath. "We could all sit down and have a calm, logical discussion." The noise she made was not ladylike.

"Why the hell did you two have to get married so quickly?"

"He really said a three-month engagement?"

Jae chuckled. "It's hard to believe that he'd violate one of his own schedules so badly. Londo, get the hell out of my head. No one likes a peeping tom."

****I just wanted to watch an expert at work. So far you haven't done too well, Jae-Jae.****

"I don't want you getting in the habit of reading people when they don't want to be read, Lon. It's impolite."

****Yes, Lina.****

****Don't worry, darling. Get some sleep. I'll see you in a while.****

"Yeah, Lon," Jae agreed. "Keep your damn mind to yourself. Privacy." They both felt his presence leave.

"He really did plan to tell me before the wedding." Then Lina said, "Jae?"

"Hm?"

"How far did we go?"

He burrowed his fingers under his hairline and then made a fist. His tongue worked inside his cheek before he said, "I was crazy that night. It happens sometimes, after a successful mission. You wind up with someone that you never thought you'd ever… I knew all the plans that Lon and I had made. There's this high you get, and the universe turns into some place where everyone's happy and wants to celebrate…"

"I understand that," Lina said slowly. "Did… did we–?"

"Nothing happened. Just a grope, a kiss or two. And the naked part. You knew about that."

"That's it?"

His own blush deepened and he didn't look at her as he lied just a little. "Okay, a really good grope on my part. Maybe a couple dozen kisses. You kissed back."

"Ah." She eased back into the pillow, considering.

"You thought we had all-the-way sex," Jae realized. A half-grin came to his face. "So tell me, how was I?"

She gave a pained laugh. "You're incorrigible. I didn't know, one way or another, and I kept thinking it was Lon, but I knew it had to have been you. But oh god, it doesn't help." Her eyes moved back and forth for a moment. "The dual-triune vows… are they the same as the ones Lon and I took?"

"Yes, I believe so."

"We shouldn't hold you to things you don't want. If you and Londo make some kind of additional vows– Did Feith have that kind of arrangement? A sort of split dual-triune? Lon sharing you and me? Legal?"

"No. Tell me what you feel about me, Lie-Lie. Not what someone has told you that you're supposed to feel."

She gazed at him: Lean and luscious, his hair in a softly-layered golden cloud around that sculpted face. Those blue eyes. That serious mouth that transformed so easily into the shining elf grin. The heart that had been shattered and never allowed to heal…

She didn't know what to say. She made a half-hearted attempt to reach for the bowl of lopas but dropped her hand. "I think maybe we're both too tired to make good choices tonight," she finally murmured.

"Run and hide."

"I'm going." She rose up from the couch.

"Lon told you to stay with me."

"Lon is not my keeper."

"Coward," Jae said. He stood up behind her. Grasping her by the shoulders, he turned her around. "Give me one moment and look at me, Carolina."

Hesitantly, she did. Her eyes betrayed her fright.

"If you're going to go, you have to kiss me goodbye. You owe me that much."

"I don't–"

His long fingers slipped down her back, drawing her to him. "You give me a decent goodbye kiss and I'll let you go forever. You can have Londo and I'll have Londo and that will be that."

Her face flushed and then set in a determined scowl. With her right hand she pulled his head down to her level and pressed her lips to his quickly. "Goodbye," she said triumphantly.

"That was not a goodbye kiss," he replied. "That was an 'I've won this game and ha-ha on you' kiss. It doesn't count. Now give me a goodbye kiss. A final farewell, a cutting away of all the potentials. An eternity kiss."

Lina approached him slowly now. What did he want? This time she wrapped her arms around his neck and he leaned down to accept the soft kiss.

Don't guess what I want, his mind whispered to hers. **Show me what goodbye means to you. This is forever. After this, who knows what will happen to us?**

We'll always be friends.

Will we?

She wanted him as a friend! Her kiss lingered with her resolve.

Forever, he repeated. **Goodbye, little green eyes.**

Oh, never to gaze into his blue eyes again! Desolation welled up within her.

Not ever again, Sweet.

Never to have his arms around her. He'd cared for her so much these past few days, watching for her safety. His arms so tight around her as they flew through the dark caverns beneath Rimhold Rock, the way he'd hovered protectively by her side after Aldierra's Ultimatum, the way he'd barreled after that wolf in the music store…

Gently she kissed his lips, wanting to remember the feel, the texture. Goodbye, Jae. Forever. Maybe in the next life they could…

Not ever again, for all eternity. Tell me goodbye.

They just had this moment.

She couldn't lie to herself any more. She held feelings within her soul for this man. They were still in the bud stage. There would never be a chance for them to mature and bloom.

Goodbye, Jae, goodbye! A kiss for all the woulda's, coulda's and shoulda's. She could only match him kiss for kiss. She was lost now, tumbling into an area that she knew so little about. She clutched him, her lips pressed to his, and all she was aware of was Jae. Just Jae.

At least she had him for this moment. When his tongue demanded complete surrender, she welcomed him and that moment. He was determination, possession, bravado, and she met him with gentleness to encourage his hidden vulnerability. He hesitated, and then their tongues danced slowly together even as their hearts provided a pounding rhythm.

She planted kisses along that soft jawline of his that she loved to gaze at, under the bangs she always wanted to brush out of his eyes. His lips traveled lower and lower on her neck and she thrummed her approval.

"How the blaze does this thing work?" Jae muttered.

He shifted on her. How could he–? They were lying down. The couch had flattened and the two of them were on it and *they were lying down!*

Somehow her skirt had pulled up to her waist. Her capelet was missing. The straps of her dress had been pulled down to her elbows, pinning her upper arms. Jae was bending around her, working at unhooking her bra and her legs were wrapped around him and "Oh!" Lina cried as the bra flew open in back.

Extricating her hands from deep within his shirt and the back of his tights, she unwound a leg and tried to sit up, tried to pull up her top, tried to figure out how they'd gotten in this position.

He propped his head on his elbow and even though he had to catch his breath, he squinted merrily at her. "Helloooo, Lina," he crowed.

Her capelet lay on the floor next to the couch. In a few minutes there would have been a lot more clothing there, Lina knew. "You tricked me!"

He lay back on the now-flat couch with a laugh, watching her out of the corner of his eyes. "I told you never to trust me." That got him a pillow slap on the face for his reward, then another and another. Jae beat the attack back gleefully, but then instead of another hit, Lina held the pillow to her face.

"Ah, I *am* a whore!" The pillow muffled her words. She reached blindly out to grab another pillow to her face and finally threw herself face-down into the pile of pillows that was the couch. "God!"

"Here now, here now!" Jae went after her but every time he got a pillow away from her, she reached for two more. She was burying herself in pillows. "No one's said you were– that word, Lie-Lie Sweet. This is a good thing, not something dark."

She said something into her pillow, shaking her head.

"Tell me," Jae urged. "Tell Jae-Jae."

She said something else, but all Jae could understand was the word "father."

"Your father's not here, Sweet. He has no idea what's going on and even if he did, it's not his right to judge. He's never had the right to call you a… that word."

She said something else, two syllables.

Jae rubbed her back. "Let's break this apart into bites we can handle, right? You're married to Londo. That's a good thing. Nod your head if you think that's a good thing."

She nodded hard into her pillow. Jae patted her on the bottom.

"And you and me," he said. "We're attracted to each other. All of Londo's and my plans can come through now. These Three Worlds, bless their hearts, can be happy that we're all going to work together so closely. And that's a good thing, right?"

Lina shook her head vehemently.

Jae blew out a breath in frustration and frowned. Lina packed another two pillows on top of her head. Jae couldn't have her suffocate in his own rooms, could he? "I like your panties," he said. "Did they come with the outfit, or did you have to–"

She rose up, furiously pulling her skirt as low as she could.

"The lace was a nice touch. Very sexy."

He got a pillow in the face for his efforts.

He caught the next one before she could beat him with it. "Wait! Wait, I've got something to tell you."

She knelt there expectantly.

"I'm not gay. Not even mostly gay."

"Not mostly?" she asked doubtfully.

"I'm bisexual. Just like that crazy husband of yours. So it's all right; I'm allowed to be with women."

"You're allowed to be with whoever you want. Just not me."

He pried the pillow out of her hands. Through her guilt throes, the couch was now a rough terrain of different levels of pillows. Jae added his pillow to the topmost level, snugging it into a pleasing pattern.

"You think I'm Londo," Lina accused him. She reached around to refasten her bra, but it was under her dress and horribly askew. After a short struggle she gave up, and the red straps that had been sticking out from under her dress straps disappeared as she ported it off.

Jae said, "Has anyone ever discussed the difference of the sexes with you?"

"You *know* what I mean. You've been thinking of Lon as inaccessible, so here I come and–"

"No." Jae took her hand and she became very still. "Touch," he said, realizing the implications that had never occurred to him before. "You weren't just a virgin. you'd never even been touched." He let his hand gently brush upward along her arm. "Do you like touching?"

"I like it very much," Lina said, so quietly. "But it's like someone who's been stranded in a desert. When they get to water, they drink every drop they can. They'd even reach for a bottle of poison, so long as it was wet."

She licked her lips. "Touching is a very seductive process to me. I haven't learned how to deal with it normally yet. You've been touching me a lot lately."

"I will never hurt you, Lina," Jae whispered. "I will never poison your heart. The people in your life who have told you that you were supposed to love them– They all betrayed you, they turned you against the real world. They cut you off from it as surely as if they'd used a knife," he realized.

"Jae–"

"I will never betray you, Sweet."

"I can't be hurt again!" She covered her face with her hands. "What if I'm misreading it? What if it isn't just you… it's the ability to be close to anyone else after so long?"

"Let's immerse you in the water. Let's go in there and get crazy like you've never been before. When we both come up for air, maybe you'll be able to tell. Maybe we'll just have a good time– a very good time– and maybe it'll be something even better."

Lina heaved a helpless sigh. He might be right. "Do you always jump into things like this?" she asked.

"Well… yes," he finally said. "It's taking a chance, showing the universe that you're not scared of it."

"So your being here is just a game of chicken between you and God? See who'll give in first?"

"You talk too much." Jae leaned back into his own pillow, away from her.

"And you do, too." Lina poked her finger into his chest. "But when you talk, you jabber. When I talk I'm trying to figure something out."

"I don't jabber." He crossed his arms in front of himself. "And I don't like people telling me I do."

"Even when they're telling you the truth?" Lina climbed up to lie on the next level of pillows above Jae. Looking down on him she thought, what the hell, she'd been wanting to do this for some time. So she began to play with his hair.

It was bristly and strangely soft at the same time, like a thick pelt of luxurious fur. The room's lights picked out wheat highlights among the darker gold. "Well, maybe you don't jabber. But it's close."

He looked up at her at that, but his lower lip still protruded in a pout.

"Did your English lessons give you the definition to *blarney?*"

His eyes wobbled as he searched his memory. "Something about a castle… kissing a stone," he finally said.

She stroked his hair. "It's a gift. You're full of it." He certainly was, and she smiled crookedly at him. "You've got a lot of Gemini energy tucked inside that Irish leprechaun head of yours," she said, making patterns in his hair. It was so thick and comforting-feeling. "Maybe it's Pisces. It's a yakky, watery energy, whatever it is."

He sat a little straighter, a little taller now, stretching as he watched her hand from the sides of his eyes, looking suspicious but allowing it. "You're the one trying to bribe me now."

"Am not. I'm just satisfying my curiosity." She eased herself up to allow for Jae's change of position, and he looked over. Her breasts were at his eye level, spilling out from the low neck of her dress, a little flattened by the pillow beneath them.

"Not trying to bribe me," he said with irony. "And suppose I start to satisfy my curiosity?" The back of his finger lightly traced the curve of her, pulsing beneath his fingertip.

Slowly Lina slid down to sit on her knees on the pillow next to him. Her dress twisted. One of her straps slipped down her shoulder, revealing a soft curve of pale flesh. The hem of the garment pulled up to show the length of her leg and hip, the lace-topped hose. "I think some of your curiosity has already been satisfied. The other night," she said quietly. "Only a good grope, Jae? Is my imagination that vivid?"

Jae's eyes met hers. He could feel her arousal, her hesitancy, her careful shepherding of her emotions. She wanted to understand the entire situation so she could make a decision of how she should allow herself to feel.

"I don't believe in controlling one's emotions." Jae reached for her. He took her mouth hard and she answered him. His hand lowered to press her butt toward him until she was all he could feel. He growled in his passion, and then kneaded the soft flesh of her breast as she gasped. He laved her neck and shoulders with his tongue, nipping to give her little love bites along the way.

"Ooo, god," she breathed into his ear as he settled down to enjoy the warmth and softness and sounds of her. He chuckled at her surprise. She and Lon were children when it came to sex. He had this power over the both of them.

"Ooo, shit," she said. "I am… ohh… not a child!" She squirmed away from his tongue and he raised his head to look at her. He kept his hand where it was.

"Children," he repeated, and swept what remained covering her left breast off. He dove at her nipple, locking her in his arms so she couldn't get away.

And yet the surprise of telepathy, of empathy, hit him as well. He could feel that she didn't know what to do. She wanted to hold his head so he'd keep on, but now he'd made her mad. How funny she was!

"Aaah!" She squirmed some more, pushing him away. Jae eased back, a satisfied smirk on his face as he watched her pull the material up, back over the golden tattoo there.

"You see what you miss when you let logic dictate your life?" he asked her as she irritably rearranged her clothes back to order. "You are a child, Lina O'Kelly. Starhart. Sexually speaking. You and Lon have only been at this a few days. Let me educate you."

"Why?" Lina seized on the opportunity. "I know why Londo, but why me? Because I come packaged with him?"

Jae flopped back into his pillow. "More talk," he said. "Where did you and Londo ever find the time to have sex so much?"

"By talking very quickly," Lina told him. "Now you talk. I listen."

Jae grumbled. "I see what he means about 'talking to death,'" he said, almost under his breath. "Okay. you want me to flatter you. I can do that. Oh beauteous Carolina," he intoned, "She of the bounteous bosoms and greenest of eyes, Singer of–"

"Oh, shut up! I don't want that, and you know it." Her eyes blazed and he smiled slyly back.

"All right. You want the deep and hidden truths. Let's see if I can uncover some."

"Is it so hard for you to be sincere?" Lina asked, but somehow she wasn't accusing him. "Would it be easier if we communicated telepathically?"

He drew back at that. "That's not necessary," he told her quickly. Mind-to-mind talk was too close, too personal.

"Then what?" Her gaze flitted around his face with concern as she stroked his cheek.

"Damn, you're just like them," he said, turning away from her.

"Like who?"

"The people I remember."

"People–"

"On Feith." He was silent for a long moment. "You remind me so much of home. And then there's the way you look at me, like you want to protect me from the universe or something."

"I do." Her voice was very quiet, and he regarded her.

"You're always singing," he said. "So did they. Lon sings sometimes. Maybe that's some of the reason I love him."

"Lots of Terrans sing–"

"But they aren't here. And they aren't off risking everything on a foolhardy scheme to stop an invasion. Or a mega-prison break. Or spending their last credit on a stranger just so he can have some music. You burst into Legion Headquarters while lightning crackled all around you, you practically dead yourself and driving yourself farther that way while you healed Lon. While you brought Londo back from the dead. My Londo. I'll always be in your debt for that."

Lina took his hand and rubbed it, not saying anything.

"You can't begin to imagine what went through my mind when Lon told me he was going to ask you. I thought the world was ending. The only thing that kept me going was Lon's promise that he'd ask you if we could somehow make it a threesome.

"But I couldn't get mad at you." Jae gave a small laugh at that. "And Stoan… He just made things worse. I couldn't believe that he couldn't see the… Londoness of you."

"The what?"

"You're so much like him." He smiled as his lips brushed her fingers. "You two are both such bundles of courage and determination. That is, when you're not screaming at each other. When you two get together I sit back and watch your auras reinforce each other. I've never seen that before." He took her hand in his and leaned against her. "They're both very red, you know."

Lina tried not to blush. Red aura: the color of passion.

Jae continued. "Hell, anyone with half a mind could see that you two are crazy about each other. Stoan can be so immovable sometimes."

"And you–" Lina began to give her guess as to his actions.

"And me," Jae interrupted. "I love Londo. That's all there is to it. I saw you two there, your little complete unit, and I knew I could never find a way to wedge myself in between you." He looked into Lina's eyes. "Until I got to know you," he whispered. "And then I found out I didn't want to come between you; I wanted to join you both. I want to get in on some of that aura interaction. Hell, I figure I've got a bit of courage and determination to add to the mixture."

"I think so," Lina said with a small smile.

"And I want to be on your side when you two finally conquer the universe."

Lina laughed outright at that, and Jae joined in. "The universe is a pretty big place," Jae said. "It might take three to really make sure it's given in."

When Lina's eyes sparkled at him, he realized that she'd never guessed most of his intentions.

"You give me too much credit as a psychic," she said. "That's why I talk so much, I guess, to get me the information I don't get otherwise."

Jae leaned over her and put one hand on her leg. He met her mouth in a soft kiss as he stroked her hip and leg. She raised her hands hesitantly to explore his back and neck, then her fingertips traced the length of his arms. He kissed her harder, letting the tip of his tongue tickle the corners of her mouth, and she opened to him gently. His arms wrapped more firmly around her and he settled her back down on the cushions.

Their lips finally disengaged, leaving them both breathless. He took her face in his hands, gazing at her. "Let's get this straight, Lina. you and I– we are never going to be just friends. Are we?"

"I, I don't think so."

"Then that makes us lovers at the very least," Jae said. "We've got tonight to sort through things. It's just a little sex. Just a little fun."

She laughed miserably. "Men and sex," she said.

"What you're looking for is another miracle. Lights, angels, voices… Someone Out There confirming that what you're feeling is right."

Lina looked helplessly at him. "Are you sure about all this?"

"Not one bit."

She covered her trembling mouth with her fingers.

"Life loves to surprise us. It gives us a signpost and tells us we're going down one road, and then it leads us astray."

"Really far astray," Lina groaned.

"Sometimes we run down that road and then think we're lost. But now and then, if we're really on the right road, waiting around the bend is something that we never dreamed of. Something that's so wonderful we never imagined it before."

"I never imagined you," Lina whispered.

"Sometimes we have to take a chance. Sometimes the miracles come true. And very often we have to make our own miracles." He took those fingers from her mouth and kissed them. "We are the co-creators. We have a say in our lives."

"I don't want anyone to get hurt. For the first time in my life everything is wonderful, and I don't want to mess anything up."

"I promise you I won't get hurt," Jae said. He touched her tears away tenderly. "Lon has given us his blessing. I don't think you'll be hurt by opening up to this new possibility."

His eyes crinkled. "I know– Just for tonight, think of it as only a little fun. Nothing permanent about it." He eased to take her face between his hands again. "I want to have fun with you tonight." He gazed at her, past her eyes, past her brain, into the recesses of her mind. **You want me.**

I… It was so obvious and she couldn't bring herself to face it. She was such a whore.

"When I meet that father of yours," Jae said softly, "I'm going to beat him up."

"Jae!" Her astonishment gave way to a surprised laugh. "Why is it that everyone's saying things like that?"

"Because it's true." Jae heard the echo of Lon's voice cursing her father. "But because he hurt you doesn't mean that anyone else wants to."

She was silent at that, so he asked, "When are Lon and I going to meet him?"

She laughed again and shook her head. "What, and have the two of you *Legionnaires* up on murder charges? Isn't that against club rules? Would Stoan approve?"

Jae chuckled with her. "You have a nice laugh, Lina. It always makes me smile."

"And you have a wonderful smile. An elf smile, like you're always up to no good."

"Let me make you laugh some more, Sweet. Let's have a little fun."

"Just fun?" Sex with no commitment. Could you actually have sex that way? Oh, but Jae was heaven to touch. And kiss.

"We don't have to go in the bedroom for this. It might be more fun out here." He began to pull his shirt out from his belt.

"You're sure you're into girls?"

Like lightning he pulled her so she was sitting on his lap. "I am very much into girls," he said with a grin. "In fact, I'm going to be in a girl in just a few minutes."

Lina licked her lips, feeling a thrill of excitement begin to build inside her. "It's all a game to you."

He gave her his squinty-eyed elf-smile and slid his hand from her shoulder down to her breast. His thumb outlined her nipple under the fabric. "That's good. We'll play a game. We need rules."

She'd forgotten how to breathe, waiting to see what he had in mind. "Definitely rules," she said, unsure if she should be getting away now while the going was good. "You can't get around on Sarastor without them." His golden hair hung down in his face, and all she wanted to do was brush it back, and maybe nibble on his ears for a while. Or maybe on his neck. Or maybe…

His eyes unfocused slightly and he smiled anew. "Rules," he said again. She leaned back as he finished unfastening the front of his tunic, removing his belts. "First goal. Let's see." His eyes roamed down her, and he picked up the hem of her dress to unveil her panties. "Goal is to get these off. And for you, to get mine off."

She straightened her dress as best she could, keeping her hand there to protect her… goalpost. No telling what this cheater might do. "You're wearing more clothes than I am," Lina said, starting to feel less anxious.

She liked having fun with Jae. This wasn't sex; it was a game. No it was a game, and it would be sex. This could indeed be fun. She felt herself revving for the game. She eased herself off him, his shirt open to her gaze. The slight fuzz there was just enough to give the sharply-defined muscles tiny golden highlights. She wondered how sensitive those brown nipples were. And she wondered why down below hadn't reacted to her yet. She certainly knew that she was reacting to him. Was Jae too blasé about sex? Had he had it so much that–

Jae whispered. "You're thinking too much again."

"Fire good." Lina grunted caveman-style.

He chuckled at that. "The rules: There are no rules. Points given for each layer of clothing removed. You win if you reach your goal first. But I doubt you will. You're dealing with a Legionnaire, Sweet."

"Sooo… I think I want to even the odds more." She stood to look around for her capelet and bent to pick it up. Movement behind her, intent– She ducked and rolled onto the carpet as Jae tried to abort his lunge gracefully. He fell into pillows and then sprawled onto the floor. They lay there, a yard apart, just watching each other for a moment.

"Did I mention that the game had begun?" he asked innocently.

"Cheater."

17

"L egionnaire," he gravely corrected her.

Her eyes narrowed and she grinned a challenge at him, then scrambled to her feet. She ran into the kitchenette, laughing, with him chuckling but on her heels. He cornered her, only to have her slip out of his grasp. She timed her moves just right. Often, it was true, he let her get away–but not always. Once Jae thought he had her, to be left only holding her capelet in his hands. She was full of surprises, full of laughter.

As they ran through the rooms of his apartment he unfastened his wristbands. Stopped and pulled off his shirt, stopped again and took off one long boot. He tried the other, hopping so as not to lose his momentum.

When he slowed, she pantomimed that she was going to open the door to the private sanctum he held off-limits to visitors, but before he could stop her she whirled and dashed toward the living room instead. There she paused long enough to turn to him, taunting. Jae didn't hear. All he could think of was the way he could suddenly see so much more of her when she leaned over.

He sat down hard as he lost his balance, his left foot in his hands. She noticed where he was looking, and eased the straps of her dress down so he could see a bit more. Jae let out a frustrated yelp as the boot stuck. The more he pulled at it, the more it refused to move.

Lina's courage seemed to increase with his difficulty as he directed full attention to the boot, now twisted hopelessly on his leg. Jae turned to find her kneeling on the rug next to him.

"Legionnaire!" she chortled as he growled.

She leaned against him as he tried to straighten the boot and line up its fastenings so he could release them. She rubbed the long line of her leg up against his unbooted one, letting her stockinged foot caress him. "Have you ever thought of switching to soled tights?"

"I like my boots," he grumped.

She laughed softly. "So do I. But some forms of clothing are easier to get out of than others." She turned her back to him and slipped the straps of her dress down over her shoulders. Looking back, she saw she held every fiber of his attention. Slowly she pulled the rest of the dress so that it slithered down her body. She eased up to her knees to pull it down and off, her back always toward him.

"Lina," he whispered.

Then she turned to him, holding the dress to herself so it covered her. "Still not out of that boot," she coolly observed.

"All of it," Jae said, lying back on the floor so he gazed up at her. "Drop it, Sweet. Do you want me to beg?"

She shook her head at him. "You are giving gays a bad name." His gaze fastened immovably on her as she loosened her hold on the dress. The material slid slowly down the length of her.

Jae reached for her hip as he rolled over. His other hand pulled her to him. Even as his lips started to close around a pinkly-brown tip, Lina grabbed his upper arms and pushed until he was flat on his back. She rubbed her breasts in his face and over his chest, then sat on him to grind her hips against his.

"Baby," he croaked, but her grasp on him was surprisingly strong. She dangled her nipples over his lips and drew back. Again she teased him, and he snapped his teeth trying to gain a hold.

"You know I'm a Legionnaire," Jae said and grinned his most evil, elfin grin. "I could have you on your back and your feet in the air in a second, but you'd have some bruises. Or I could arrest you. Tie you up. Perform some very excruciating slow torture on you."

"You haven't shown me that you could go slow in anything yet," she said. "And you aren't in any position to do much at all. Maybe I should tell some paravillains about how they can keep you under control. Just trap him in big, hulking, manly-man Legionnaire boots."

Her eyes smoldered under those thick, dark lashes as she settled down to lie next to him, letting her silk-clad foot stroke him again. "Let's see if you can get your boots off at least."

She lay there on her elbows and tossed her head so her hair swept over his bare chest. She ignored him except for that foot of hers and hummed a little tune.

Lina Starhart a tease. Jae would have never guessed, not in a million years. Londo had never stood any chance against this.

"You really think so?" she asked, and shook her head again, glancing back at him with those brilliant green eyes of hers.

That eminently kissable pink mouth curled in a small, mocking smile. Mocking him. He pulled himself up and pretended to ignore her, the nearly-naked goddess next to himself. Jae leaned down to adjust his boot. He had five more pairs in his closet. Lina stopped rubbing him to watch, so relaxed now that he was helpless.

He grumbled about the impossibility of his boot while he mentally ordered it to change, aging in seconds to dust. Lina let out a little gasp beside him, turned over to get up, but he launched himself at her, free at last, and pinned her underneath him, her face to the floor.

He crowed his victory as she shrieked. Pulling her butt up into the air and pushing her panties down, he stopped to kiss and nip her ass, keeping a firm hold. She shook her head in frustration, her hair a storm around herself.

He rubbed her between her legs. "Goal," he laughed at her as her shriek turned into a coo. She was so soft and smooth, so hot. He let his fingers trace her before he moved in to start unfolding her moistness.

"You… ooo… don't have them all the way off… ah.. yet," she gasped.

He gave her a little spank. "Be quiet," he ordered as she gave a surprised yip. "Game goes to the home team. The judges have decided." His hands rubbed where he'd just spanked her and then moved to go back to that mysterious wet place between her legs. Whoa– something was… different on him. She reached back to him, waving something in her hand.

"Goal to the visitor," she laughed. His underwear. But he was still wearing his tights. She'd teleported his underwear! He grabbed at them, releasing her.

She glanced behind herself, checking him out and sparing his protective cup a glance. "You even wear cheater underwear," she observed with a smile that was satisfied at the condition he was most clearly in.

"You're the cheater!" he yelled as she jumped up, pulling her panties back up with a snap, and ran out into the living room. He threw his jockstrap down and dashed after her. "Foul!"

"I don't see any umpire around," she laughed. She ran with those long, stockinged legs of hers, showing that backside that he'd thought he'd captured, and a lot more. For some reason he kept missing her. Seeing her like this was distracting enough, but she kept reading his mind, knowing where he'd try next.

He thought he'd caught her once and reached for her, but she grabbed his wrists and swung him round, releasing him. As she ran off triumphantly, Jae remembered Lon's advice: "First you have to rev her up. You do that and she starts thinking how a woman needs to think, and not with her head." Jae knew that Lina was revved, but he was, too. Revved and getting to the point of crazed.

He cornered her at last in the bedroom, by blocking the doorway. He pointed at her: "No porting. Play fair."

She was out of breath, an action which distracted him, but still she grinned defiance at him. She faked a move to the left, and he didn't fall for it. She moved to the right, and he lunged to intercept, but it was a fake after all and she ducked around him. Jae launched his Legion ring's propulsion system to leap after her as she fled down the hallway. It was tricky to use without the balancing wrist and ankle bands, but he swooped around and then ducked low to grab her and haul her over his shoulder. Her legs kicked futilely as he pulled her panties off, and she spanked him.

"Cheater! Cheater!"

"Oh, baby, keep that up," Jae laughed as he marched back to the bedroom with his prize. "I like spanking games." He dumped her onto his bed. It was bouncy and deep. She sprawled there, catching her breath as she pushed her hair out of her eyes. He stood over her in triumph and let his tights dissolve slowly off him, from his feet up to his waist.

All at once she became serious. Her gaze was smoky as she met his burning one.

"Jae," she whispered, and reached for him.

"Lina."

Something was missing, so Lina kept her mind as guarded as she could while she tried to put a label on it. He held her in his arms, a satisfied smile on his drowsing face.

Dear, dangerous Jae. He'd been a whirlwind of passion, a wildfire of sexual expertise, with a touch that could spark flashes of unbearable desire surging through her. Exciting, that's what it had been– like a roller coaster ride at Carowinds. He'd had her do a headstand on the floor, then directed a balancing act against the bedposts… He was an acrobat, using his entire body to elicit response, to evoke shudders from depths she didn't know she had.

Perhaps whatever the missing part was, was just the difference from loving Lon. Perhaps it was because there was no double-loop, because when she reached out to Jae's mind to touch him there, she found firm barricades.

Had she even done it right? How could you tell without the feedback, without being plugged into the very life of the man you were making love with?

He'd spun her around until they both were breathless. He'd caught the brass ring. But it was all surface. Wasn't it?

Oh hell, maybe the problem was because she was a spoiled little girl, always wanting things done her way. Selfish!

He certainly seemed quite satisfied by the experience: very vocal about it throughout. Was that all that sex was to him? He had so much that he wanted to forget in his life. Was this how he did it? Cover it all up with sex and sweep the past under the rug? Or was this the way he needed to experience sex? To experience life?

And what about her? It was all surface, very glittery and breathtaking to be sure, but… It was several running steps closer than she'd been with Jae. To play without inhibition, to trust him enough to allow him inside her… She realized that she did trust him more now, though not remotely as totally as she did Londo.

She hadn't extinguished her wayward passion. It still pulsed along the core of her being. She gazed at him, at that angelically manly face of his, and she still wanted him. She wanted to know all about him, to have some more of this ultimate physicality with him, to play with him like both of them needed to play.

He felt other-worldly, his skin cooler compared with Lon's hot flesh. The slight fuzziness of chest and arms as opposed Lon's thicker fur. His glorious mane of hair– she stroked it and he nuzzled at her shoulder. She ran her hands down his back, down the part of his leg that curled around her. Solid muscle, flexible, dangerous, and absolutely alive.

He had no center, but the illusion was fine indeed.

And here she was, exploiting him. Shame on her! But still… they had talked and made the decision. They were both adults.

What was missing was the sex of the soul. She and Lon had started out sharing minds, quickly learned the double-loop. Those things they did out of necessity, and now it seemed that that necessity had spoiled her completely.

She stirred in his arms. "Jae," she whispered and he opened his eyes. "Share minds with me. Please?"

He nuzzled at her ear, skrunching her hair. "Your hair smells wonderful. It always does."

"Please, Jae." She squirmed around so she could see him. Such sultry eyes, the curve of his mouth…

"So you want it all at once, just like Londo. Maybe someday."

Lina realized that Jae wasn't ever going to share his self with her. He was going to stay hidden behind his beautiful mask of a face, pretending to live life in the real world while shutting himself off from it forever. She wasn't good enough for him to open up to. She should have realized that.

"Well," she said and rolled away from him. "Well." She eased herself up to a sitting position on the edge of the bed. This was a difficult decision to make, but best it was done now. She could do this. She'd had a backbone once. Time to take possession of it again.

Where had she left her dress? Somewhere. All she could see were her stockings on the floor. Upset, she couldn't search with her mind. Instead she ported on a black lace nightgown that she knew was hanging precisely *there* in Lon's closet.

"I suppose this was for the best after all," she said tightly. "Tell you what. I'll port home– to Earth– and you and Londo can have the rest of the night, is that all right? You can call me when you're awake in the morning."

"What?" Jae said.

Where was the robe that went with this? It should be– ah. Lina stood up and swung it shut with a snap of its sash, steeling herself so when she turned around to Jae she'd be composed. "I said that I was leaving now. I can port you to Londo if you'd like me to. Or I can port him here."

Jae eased up on one elbow, the long muscle groups moving sinuously, hypnotically. "You're leaving?"

"Really, Jae, you're a little slow. Must be the ratchet. I'll make breakfast for you and Lon if you want to try Terran. We all have a lot to do tomorrow. What do you think, three hours Sarastoran? Four? You probably want to get in some sleep afterward."

He was sitting now, not bothering to cover himself with the sheet, a distinct puzzled look on his face. "Londo wouldn't want me to be with him yet. What are you up to, Lie?"

"And do you do everything Londo tells you to? Is he always team leader where the two of you are concerned?" Using the large mirror on the wall, Lina tried to smooth her hair with her hands. "Go to him, Jae. You have my blessing."

"Didn't you like it? Wasn't I good enough for you? You're not going to tell me that Londo can–"

"It was lovely, Jae. It was fun."

"Fun."

"Wasn't that what you wanted it to be? I've always liked going to the State Fair for the thrill rides. I had a wonderful time. And I found out some things, just like we planned."

"No one's ever told me they didn't–"

"And your record still stands. I said it was nice," Lina told him firmly.

"Nice!" Jae hissed. With one movement he pulled Lina back to the bed and crouched over her, his fist around her wrist. "What the *skurn* do you mean, it was just nice? It was passionate, there was… thunder!"

Yes, thunder that still echoed in the corners of this room. "Lust can die after a few weeks," Lina told him. She could feel the electricity crackle anew between the two of them, feel her desire rise like a cresting wave. But she was not an animal to cave in to her desires, not when there were larger issues at stake! "I'm not in the market for a quickie romance with no substance to it. I'd rather we go back to being friends. I'd rather see the real you, not whoever you were here in bed."

His eyes narrowed into slits. "What, you want me to swear allegiance to you and not to Londo? To whisper sweet nothings to you as if they were true?"

"It's truth that I'm after, Jae. Apparently you're not willing to share any. You have Lon already. You can do what you want with him, promise him whatever he'll believe. I won't stand in your way. But you feel you have to go through this play-acting with me, and I won't have it."

"You want me," he growled at her. "You're white-hot, I can feel it." He leaned down so their lips were inches apart, their breaths rebounding on each others' faces. "Lie to me and say you don't feel your lust! You can't control yourself when it overtakes you. You can't control yourself around me– like the other night. You'd even betray your husband to have me!"

Lina went absolutely still. "I will never again betray Londo. Tonight was for discovery. That's what we did. Goodbye, Jae. We'll talk in the morning when you're calm and straighten all this out." Jae was tracing her hard nipple with his thumb, watching her eyes. "Stop it. If you don't mean it, don't start it."

"You want me," he purred to her, a terrible, tight grin on his face. He whispered it in her ear. "You want me bad, barbarian woman."

"I want a lot of things, but that doesn't mean they're good for me." Lina tried to push away, but his breath on her neck incited flames to race along all her nerves. Instead she found her fingers pressing into his skin.

"One more time." Jae's tongue traced the line of her neck, moving up to her jaw and laving her cheek. **This time feel it all the way through,** he told her. "Touch me. Touch me!"

His fingertips brushed her hot flesh as he reached under the robe, pushing her short skirt aside. His mouth fastened on her neck. His long-fingered hands squeezed. His hair swept her face, carrying with it the aroma of the stars. And when his mouth came back to hers she met his with Terran ferocity.

With a shout and a sigh, he fell exhausted across her, and spread her arms out with his. "Oh yeah," he crooned, "that was something you'll never find anywhere else." He blew the strands of sweaty hair from her face, giving her a triumphant, heavy-lidded smirk. "Tell me how great it was."

Her eyes opened to his. They were lustrous, sleepy, fulfilled. "Share minds with me," she said softly. "Just once. Please."

His jaw jutted out as his gaze hardened. "You didn't like it," he accused.

"All I said was–"

"You didn't like it!" In a huff he rolled off her and sat up, his back toward her, his arms crossed. "Get out! Just get out!"

"Oh, Jae." Arms went around him and she pressed her chin against his shoulder. "Don't be angry. It was wonderful. You're one of the two sexiest men I have ever met in my life. You can't help it if you're not ready for what I want. Maybe someday. We'll keep it open, will that be all right?"

She stroked his hair. "Don't be mad. I couldn't bear it if you were angry with me." She kissed his shoulder with a sigh.

"I am angry. At you."

So Lina took him in her arms again and kissed his other shoulder, then brushed his hair back and planted tiny kisses on the back of his neck. "I kiss away the anger," she told him. "Sweet Jaeson, don't be angry."

He let her kiss him and then offered his cheek, which she didn't refuse. She even kissed his eyelids, then very gently on his lips.

"You go to Londo now." She brushed the hair in Jae's face back, smiling softly at him. "Don't you abuse him like you did me. He might not be able to take it. I'm strong, all-American mutt stock." She whispered confidentially, "But he's from France. They don't grow them too strong there. Veddy Old World civilized, you can tell."

Jae chuckled and then he laughed, reaching around to swing Lina across his lap. "You're an uncouth barbarian wench," he declared. "I like uncouth barbarians. Why can't I make you like me?"

"But I do. I do like you so much."

"Then why can't I make you... love me?" The silly expression was still on his face, but now it was a mask.

"What is this to you?" She lay her head on his shoulder, running her hands down his muscled body. "My dearest of friends, Jae Rallene. I do love you and I'll always love you. But I have my standards now. Londo taught me that much, that I should demand what should be mine. Respect."

"I respect you," Jae said softly.

"You don't trust me, and trust is a form of respect," Lina replied. "Come back when you think you can trust me a little, and we'll talk. All right?"

"You don't trust me either. Trust me; I'm a Legionnaire."

"Oh, so I can trust you now?"

He grinned at her and shook his head. "Don't ever trust me, Sweet."

She rolled her eyes. "I trust the Legionnaire enough. The rules say you have to," she said. "But the Legionnaire isn't necessarily Jae Rallene. I don't think I've ever met the man, but if he were to tell me to trust him…" she touched his lips with her finger, letting her gaze travel up the noble features to those wondrous eyes, "that man I'd follow to the ends of the universe. As long as Londo were there, too."

Jae was silent for a beat. "Well," he finally said, "if you ever meet this Jae Rallene, tell him hello from me."

He wasn't going to open himself to her in any fashion. A wave of desolation swept Lina. Not good enough for Jae, was she? Well then, the reverse was true as well and the universe was poorer for it. She slid away as he rose from the bed. Did Lon know the true Jaeson? Probably. If not now, then certainly by morning. Jae wouldn't hide from Londo. Jae needed to reveal himself with someone.

She tugged her nightgown into decency. Somehow it had gotten all wrapped around her middle.

Jae was securing a midnight blue half-robe around himself and reached out to her as he stood up. "Come with me," he ordered.

Whatever for? He was so unreadable when he wanted. Lina took his hand and followed him through the dim apartment.

It was his secret room, the room of no entry. But now Jae put his hand to the side of the sealed door and it slid open:

Forest.

Up through the treetops Lina could see a star-studded sky that would be a holographic illusion, but these trees were real. And fairly large, with trunks perhaps seven inches in diameter. The bark was heavily patterned like a palm tree, with ridges that V'ed upwards. Soft needles let off a spicy fragrance when she bunched them in her hand. Dust coated the ridges and the tips of the needles. This room had never seen a wind or rain.

It was chilly in here. A fog clung to the ground that smelled of rich humus. The ceiling had to be forty feet at least to hold these trees, and there were maybe ten of them, closely-packed. Voices in Lina's head whispered that those others over there were holograms.

"These are real," she said to Jae, who'd been watching her touch his trees.

"Yes," he said. "I grew them from seed. Feith donated native seeds to an interplanetary seed bank hundreds of years ago, and people forgot about it after the Disaster. I found it. I grew the seeds all by myself."

"They're beautiful." In her bare feet, Lina could feel that the two of them were on a path of hard-worn dirt through it all.

"This way," Jae instructed, and led her. A desert-style tent sat comfortably between the trees. At Jae's gesture, soft lamps ignited within. He ducked under the doorflap, striped material in beige and orange, and lifted it for Lina to enter.

The tent was furnished with layered rugs, intricately woven with thick fringes and rich colors, and piles of pillows in similar design. Figurative sculpture sat on low wooden tables. Lina knelt down to admire them: beautiful people captured in stone, in glass, all graceful, their elongated lines somehow erotic and noble at the same time.

Small table screens were placed as if they were picture frames. Jae touched one. A picture came alive within: a forest much like this one, a tent that this had clearly been fashioned to resemble, with a man and two women in front of it. The man wore his spectacular red hair down to the bottom of his shoulder blades. Both women were blondes, one with long hair, and the other with it in a pixie cut to show off her elegant pointed ears.

She was the one talking to the camera that had recorded the scene. The voice was melodic, the syllables exotic. The clothes they wore were almost sheer but not quite, revealing but not at all revealing, tied and webbed to their bodies just enough to hold them in place while the material flowed around them in graceful, light drapes.

"This is my blood mother," Jae explained. "And that's my father and my other mother. They had a dual-triune."

"You look like your father."

"They were very much in love. I knew that even as a child. And I knew that I was loved by them all. My father was teaching me to be a healer like they were. That's what our family did, we traveled all around, sleeping in tents like this," Jae gestured at what they were in, "tending to the life of our world. We lived off the land.

"There were others in our group. Sometimes others would join us for a time. My great grandparents lived with us until a couple years before the end. They were working in another part of the world then. My sister and her husband had just joined us maybe a year before. That was nice. I'd seen my sister a lot when I was growing up, but not enough."

"She was thirty years older than you, you said?"

"Yes. Too young to think about having children yet, for our people. She was in a dual marriage, a beginner marriage. Dual marriages were for the young, the immature– although there were those that were not. I'm not quite sure about those."

"Four-ways? Duals that joined?"

Jae smiled and shook his head. "Not formally, although I'm sure there were informal groupings like that." The picture had gone to a closeup of his three parents and he stroked the frame, freezing the picture.

"They were so beautiful," Lina said, "and they had a beautiful son."

"I told you that I was the last Feithi child born. There was no one younger than I. But it wasn't lonely. People held on to their youthfulness, a child-like way of thinking. I played all the time with the adults and they played back or just with each other. We'd sing to the land sometimes and everything was in harmony." He paused.

"We two would have beautiful children, Lina. They would sing and heal and laugh," Jae said quietly, and Lina didn't reply. He started the movie again from where he had stopped it. "I don't know why I was taught to heal," Jae mused at one point. "Just before the Great Silence, we packed up and moved back to the city. Mama said it was because nothing was sick any more, no disease, no injury. She told me that things would never get sick again."

"Ah, Jae," Lina sighed, "you'd think they would have set aside a generation or two just to enjoy that before they advanced to the next level."

"You'd think. But the Great Silence began almost immediately after that."

"What was that all about?"

He sat quiet for a moment. "There was an ingathering of our people," he told her, "Everyone was called back to Feith, to the cities. We had rooms and I remember lots of friends coming over and talking very late into the night. Every other day or so we'd go to a big amphitheater to listen to people discuss the matter of the AffSys' Machine of Destruction and the spiritual evolution of the sector. Sometimes we'd just stay at home and watch the debates on screen. I didn't realize at the time, but now it seems so clear. They were talking about whether Feith had anything left to contribute to the sector or if they should move on. I thought we'd all pack up and move to a new forest on another world."

"Maybe they did," Lina whispered.

"By the time we let General Padget come to the planet, I was bored sitting and listening to all the talk. I was used to running around. The general had a marvelous antique spaceship so I slipped in past the guards to explore. And then I heard that he was taking off. I thought that we were going to the new world. I'd beat everyone by getting there first. It'd be a great joke. So I stowed away."

The stillness of the forest was palpable. There were no insects here, no night birds. "I came out of hiding just in time to see the beam hit Feith. There it was, such a beautiful, tiny world shining in a dozen shades of green. She was in gibbous phase as we were heading out of the system. One of the moons was a tiny black dot against her. And this yellow light, like sunlight through a break in the clouds... It turned the night side yellow, and then the dayside went yellow, too. And I heard them crying out. Just one long cry, all together–"

Jae beat his own knees with his fists as Lina hugged him tightly. He tried to speak, shook his head and tried to speak again. Finally he got it out. "It was all planned. I don't think the general knew, but someone did, someone did!"

"Yes," Lina said. "It was planned. It wasn't an accident. Does it matter now? Is there anything you can do about it?"

"No." The word escaped his lips like vapor. "The AffSys is not as altruistic as they'd have themselves appear. There is a rot deep within it, a horrible, deathly disease. And I work for the AffSys. Lina, I work for the rot!"

"No you don't, no you don't," Lina soothed, stroking his hair.

His grip increased as he lay his head on her shoulder. "I work for death and fear!"

"You work for the Legion. From what I can see it has a noble mission. You're helping people."

Jae's head shook back and forth on her shoulder. "Some of them… of the Legionnaires, Lina, aren't–"

"Aren't here for noble causes," Lina said. "I know. There are always some. But they aren't the majority, are they? You know who they are, and their actions can be controlled if you watch them. And if you ever get any orders you disagree with, you can refuse them, right?"

"No," Jae groaned, "I can't. It's happened, and I had to do it."

"What were they going to do if you didn't obey? Kick you out?"

"Yes."

"I can't picture them doing that. Kicking someone out of the Legion for upholding their own beliefs. What a load of rubbish! How damnably civilized of them!"

"Sometimes I want to spit on them. They're so low! They're… they're not *us!*"

This was coming from his gut without any filters, Lina knew. How would she think if she knew these people? Ah, but she knew bad people of her own. "Maybe they're afraid. They've never been taught any better," she suggested. "Maybe they've never had anyone show them the way."

"What, you mean me?" Slowly Jae's head raised up, though he looked beyond the tent walls and not at Lina.

"Maybe. Maybe others. Maybe Londo, too. Have you known him to stand up and say 'No, this isn't right'? Maybe he needs to assert himself here as well. Maybe things would begin to change."

"We're just two people."

"And a few days ago you said that you were just one person, Jae. Now you're two, with Londo. And I'll throw my lot in with you, if a non-Legionnaire can. That's three, that's a three hundred percent increase in just a couple of days. Pretty good in my book."

She turned his shoulders so he'd look at her. "So now we're in league with Three Worlds, too. We can't afford to lower our standards for this job. Whatever we do, we've got to have the strength to say that the ends don't justify the means."

Jae pondered it and shook his head slowly. "No, we have to live up to our standards rather than living down to *theirs*."

"But all of *theirs* is not necessarily lower than ours," Lina said. "We have so many people to learn about. Maybe there are lots of them out there, just waiting for an excuse to do the right thing. Maybe the Feithi had it wrong. Maybe others weren't so far below them on the spiritual scale."

Rubbing his hand tiredly through his hair, Jae said, "I don't know anymore."

She shivered in the chilly damp and Jae drew up a soft rug around the two of them. He showed Lina more pictures: of his beautiful sister, her husband; of Jae's ancestors. These were all records that had been saved through the nets at one time or another, usually personal taped letters, not conscious recordings for history.

"Where's the picture of little Jaeson?" Lina asked. "Didn't they send home movies of you to anyone?"

Jae's mouth quirked in a half-grin. "You don't–"

"Oh yes I do."

There was nakie toddler Jae running through the forest, his non-blood mother running after him, both of them laughing. Jae looked to be about three or four, his hair halfway down his back and streaming behind him as he played Keep Away from Mommy.

How sweet to watch the innocent boy. Lina wondered if they'd ever find some childhood pictures of Londo to match this. Londo had had his childhood stripped from him, too. He and Jae belonged together. They were a matched set.

Jae stopped the playback and the picture went gray. "What's wrong?" he asked. He rubbed her back.

"I'm still damned jealous of you and Londo."

"You mean of me and your husband, who loves you very much."

"Oh, I am an ungrateful bitch." Lina covered her eyes with her hands. Face the reality. Jae and Londo would– "Uh oh," she said suddenly.

"What?"

"When Lon and I did the double-loop for the first few times, he didn't have powers." Lina searched Jae's face, trying to see if he grasped the problem. He didn't. "We made mistakes. We tipped the balance more than a few times. By the time Lon's Valiant powers came back, we were experts."

Now his face tightened. "Lina, I really don't want to make mistakes with Valiant. It could be fatal."

"It might not be. Lon's very good at it now." She could feel her cheeks flush. Would he think she was looking for an excuse to come on to him? Was she?

"Look, I know you don't want to share minds with me. But you're going to have to learn how to do the double-loop and practice it. With me, before you get to Lon. I'm sorry. But it's really not sharing minds, it's just sharing touch."

"Just touch." Jae considered her. Finally he nodded. "I've never had sex in here. We will have sex, won't we?" He set about gathering pillows and rugs.

"We don't have to do it in here," Lina said quickly. "This is sacred territory. Wouldn't it be like having sex in a church?"

"Absolutely," Jae declared. "Sacred sex."

"The double-feedback isn't too holy. Mind sharing is."

Jae shrugged. "Don't worry about it." He settled back with her, wrapping the first rug around the two of them again. "Now, how exactly does this thing work?"

She tried to remember how she had first explained it to Londo. Maybe they wouldn't need to have sex for this after all. She put her hands to either side of Jae's neck. "You feel what I feel," she told him. "I'm going to exaggerate what I feel so you can catch it."

She kissed him lightly but at length, letting the skin of their lips brush each other, tingling and warm. Apparently Jae was more interested feeling her up than in feeling emotions, for she didn't get any bounceback from him.

"No," she corrected. "You have to feel what I'm feeling."

He was preserving himself, she realized into the kiss. He was barricading himself from her even at this level. "*Non non non.*" She blew out a frustrated breath. "You just relax. If you can't feel what I'm feeling, then concentrate on what you're feeling."

She kissed his mouth thoroughly then, but he was still tense. A tiny giggle sounded through Lina's mind: Jae, tense during this? Maybe she should give him a little Treatment to show him that perhaps she wasn't as childish as he thought she was.

She pushed him back on his bank of pillows and lay on him, slowly slithering down his body leaving a trail of kisses and touches. She eased the blue wrap off of him and went to work under the rug.

"Feel what I feel," she ordered him, sure that she had his complete attention now. He sucked in his breath. "Deeper," she told him.

"Ah… ah."

"That's a good boy." She smiled at him as the bounce started, the feedback rapport. This was what sex was supposed to feel like, both bodies interacting, nerves connected, passions matching. Judging from the sound effects, Jae agreed, and Lina went in for the kill.

He pummeled his fists on the rugs as he arched, pulling his hair back and twisting under her mouth and hands. He shouted incoherently and cried out three more times before he fell back, totally limp on the pillows. He let out a melodramatic groan.

"*That* was a double-feedback loop," Lina announced with the satisfaction of a job well done.

"No, that was certainly sacred to me," Jae said with his eyes closed. "The holy blow-job." He paused. "And you and Londo do *that?*"

"All the time."

"Oh boy. Oh, I can't feel my feet. Where are my feet?!" He wiggled his toes and held up the rug to watch them. "My feet," he said. "For a moment I thought they were yours. You do this with *Valiant* and when you finish, you aren't dead?"

"Very much alive." Lina grinned.

"Marry me, barbarian woman," Jae sighed happily. "I'm never going to find anyone who can top that."

"You should sample my foot massages," Lina told him. "Londo is very fond of those."

18

"What are you doing?"

With a small shock Lina realized that she was funneling Jae the same healing energy that she was so used to giving Londo. It seemed a natural part of lovemaking. Lon certainly hadn't complained.

"Lon calls it the Viagra touch," Lina said, and explained the brand.

Jae's chin tilted to the right as he tried to figure it out. A slow smile lit his face. His eyes crinkled mischievously. "This is how Londo did it. All those ridiculous boasts of his. Confess, Lie-Lie."

"Well–"

"It's certainly working for me," he grinned at her. "Oh yeah, I like this. I like this a lot. Do it some more, Sweet. We'll go all night long."

So she stroked his aura as he lay next to her, nuzzling her shoulder. "Before that, let's share minds," she urged. "Bonus points."

"No more games," he told her, and she shook her head.

"I'm not saying that anything was wrong, I just want… more."

"I can give you all you need right now, baby."

"Jae." She slapped him lightly. His mouth being on her skin muffled his laugh. "Jae, honey, stop that and listen to me. There. That wall you just threw up. You're distancing yourself."

"Don't know what you're talking about. I'm planning on getting a lot closer. C'mon, one more time."

"Be serious for one minute." She eased him up off herself so he'd listen. "I want to know the real you. Please."

"Or you'll leave? Play your favorite game and run off to deny a while longer?"

Lina brushed his hair out of his eyes. "No," she said. "I'll stay with you."

He was silent as he watched her hands. Finally he asked, "Who do you think I am?"

Lina shifted around on the pillows they lay on as she tried to sort through her impressions. "Sometimes I see you as a soul as old as a star. Or as young as a spring flower blooming for the first time. And sometimes I see a rip in the fabric of the universe and I think that the emptiness is you, and I hear the universe ask me to heal it back to rightness."

Jae turned onto his belly, propped up on his elbows. His eyes focused on a past she couldn't see. "What else?"

Lina reached out to her visions. "I hear a wind howling through a barren wilderness in a voice of despair. It's yours, out of harmony by just a half-step from the angels singing all around you. You don't hear them, but you know they're there. And you can't get in tune with them."

He gazed at her cheek, not her eyes.

"Sometimes I just see a man who honestly doesn't have any idea what he's supposed to be, where he fits, and he's just faking his way through life. He's very good at faking it, he's the best, but he knows the dishonesty and it eats at his soul."

"That sounds like it should remain hidden." Jae said bitterly.

"Teaching is the best way to learn. Maybe that's what *they* meant when *they* said you should teach."

He twined a curlicue of her hair through his fingers. "So simplistic."

"Why complicate things to where you can't unravel them? Share minds with me. The contrast makes things so much clearer. It might help you as well as me."

"No." He set his jaw and frowned his determination. "You'll just have to settle for me as I am. Untrustable."

"All those thick barriers," she sighed. "Someday maybe you'll trust me. You trust Lon; do it with him."

"Not Lon. Never Lon!" He shook his head violently.

She caught his cheek to rub his jaw with her thumb. "Ah. Too ugly a mind to show him. We are too alike in some ways, you and I. Lon won't see any ugliness, I promise you."

"Never Lon," he repeated so softly she could hardly hear him.

"It's all right. Someday you'll do it. Just like I needed to be touched, like Lon needed to be loved forever, you need to share minds with someone so that you know you're not alone in this universe."

"I'm not alone now." A hunter's gleam lit in those mercurial blue eyes now as he held her gaze. He squeezed her thigh. His hands on her were strong but not rough as they explored.

"Ooh. A diversion to get us off-subject. This is only the physical, Jae."

"And it will do nicely, love. You're beginning to sound like Lon. He always wants a little more than what he can get."

He rolled against her like warm chocolate icing on a cake, like the ocean foaming against the shore. He fit into her contours as he explored her with his tongue.

"I don't…" she tried to say. "I feel… I… Oh." And Jae laughed so quietly at her. "Oh." He smelled so very, very faintly of orange, or maybe ginger, but more like musky spices she'd never tasted, of dappled meadows she'd never visited. His touch was a song she almost knew, just out of reach.

"Children," he whispered into her ear with a soft snort and was rewarded with a pillow blow to his shoulder. "Hey!" He wrestled the pillow from her. "We've got to keep you away from these things. At least use a softer one." He offered her a heavily-embroidered pillow and Lina ran her hands across it wonderingly.

"I wouldn't want to hurt it. It's beautiful. Everything in here is so beautiful. I love your forest."

Why did he look at her so? "Would you live someplace like this, Sweet?" he asked. "You spent days on a primitive beach with Lon. Would you be content to live in a forest for the rest of your life?" Jae sat up suddenly and took her hands between the two of his. "Come with me and we'll walk the forests together, just wander around and heal."

"Which forest? Are there any real ones on Sarastor? Or Aldierra?"

"There are a few here– heavily protected and posted against trespassers. Of course, they let a Feithi slip by. They might let a Terran."

"Lon wouldn't like it. Not for forever."

"He'd like the trampling about." Jae sighed. "But no, Lon was meant for bigger things. He's larger than just a forest, bigger than a world. I don't think he'd have made a good Feithi. But you would have."

"Do you love me?" he asked her abruptly.

The tension of his fingers in hers tightened. She knew that great, uncrossable lump in her throat, the paralysis of her vocal cords. And she still whispered, "I think so. When does friendship become full-blown love? How do you know?"

"Maybe when your friend is howling because he's coming inside you?" He tried to make her smile.

"Humph. Men and sex. Sex isn't love. It's a symptom, not the disease."

"Love a disease. I hope the Three Worlds weren't listening. *Skurn,* I hope we haven't shocked them with what we've been doing tonight. Have they been watching us?" He gave her his most scandalized look as he wiggled his eyebrows.

"You're so funny. You and Lon both. He's always making me laugh."

"We're talking Londo Rand or whatever he's calling himself these days? Short, brown eyes, dark hair…"

"Legionnaire. And he's tall, that's the one. The guy with the smile."

Jae set his features in a scowl as he imitated Lon. "The most serious person I know. I may get depressed on occasion, but he runs around in angry black moods all the time. People at the wedding were asking if that were really him and not some impostor."

Lina chuckled, and realized once again that she did not know her husband well. She knew she loved him and would all her life. He was a part of her now. But for the past hours she'd been only thinking about Jae and the way he made her feel. Could she imagine that two people in the universe could love her? Could Jae really love her someday? But she did care so much for him. His presence was secondary only to Londo. His happiness was all-important.

Anything for Jae.

She couldn't tear her eyes from his face as she whispered, "Oh God, what is happening to me?"

Jae brought the palm of her hand to his lips. "Do you think you could love me enough to stay together forever? With or without a marriage? Alongside Londo?"

A real, non-theoretical, marriage? "I don't know if I could take third place forever. I'm not a whore."

"A whore?" He rolled off her with a sudden movement and rose up on knee and arm to stare at her. "You think the tertiary is a whore?"

"But–"

He pulled at his hair and rolled his eyes. "Terrans. You think my mother was a whore?"

"I don't mean it that way, not a prostitute. Not that there's anything wr– well, I haven't quite figured out prostitution yet either," Lina said quickly. "I mean someone who uses others to make themselves feel good. Someone who's dishonest to further their own purposes. Someone who juggles others' emotions and damn the consequences, as long as they get what they want."

Jae studied her in puzzlement.

"Whore," she repeated. "Marriage is about commitment, about sharing the good and the bad. It's about a lot of things I only started to learn in these past couple days. Someone who's part in and part out doesn't hold a real commitment to the people or the concept, don't you think?"

"You have no idea what a dual-triune is." But he slid back down to the rug to lie on his back.

"No," Lina told him. "But if a certain someone would just take some seals off some Net files, maybe somebody else could do some research and find out."

"All right, I'll unlock the records, but just for you and Londo." Jae huffed his cheeks and looked out the corner of his eyes at her. "And if anyone's the tertiary, I'll be it, not you. Lon and I will keep you safely tucked between us. Lon will be at the center along with you because, well, Lon is Lon."

"Anything for Londo." Lina nodded.

Jae turned to her at that and then nodded as well. "Yes. Anything for Londo."

"If…" She hated even considering the possibility. "If something were ever to happen to Lon… It would be just you and me." She gazed into his bottomless blue eyes. "What happens then?"

"Could we do it?" He gazed at the still, striped walls of the tent. "Without Londo. I can't promise, but I think I could. I don't know. It helps that we're friends."

"So being friends is important." She nudged him.

"Yes, *skurnit,* it's important," he growled back.

"Like you and Lon are friends as well as lovers."

"Is that what we are? Best friends, but not best friends. Lovers but not lovers. Frustrated as hell, that's what we've been! We've been stymied in a field of possibilities."

"Not any more. How many people around here know about you and Lon?"

"Aiko… Aiko knew, but she tried not to think about it. It wasn't following the rules. I don't think anyone else knows, not for sure. A few suspect. Kuttr– you met him at the wedding."

"I met everyone at the wedding. Don't remember anybody." Except Aiko.

"He's the martial expert, the Silent Dagger. Let's see… The one Lon threw into the crowd."

"Oh." The one who'd won the loss-of-virginity pool on Londo.

"Well, Kuttr and I are pretty good friends. I think he suspects something."

"Wiley?"

Jae wrinkled his nose as he settled deeper into their nest. "He's a close friend, and I love him as that– but he's got his minds so tightly up his ass that I doubt if he really notices relationships at all. That's why he's still a virgin."

"Really? I didn't get that impression, but then I haven't really thought about it that much."

"Really. Lon says he isn't, too, but I know."

"He told you?"

"Not in so many words." Jae considered the tent's roof. "Virgins are over-rated."

"Ah, the philosopher reappears."

"I mean it. Look at me. Here I am lying next to a beautiful woman, and we've just made wonderful love and we're going to make even better before the night's over, and she's no virgin. Virgins are inept. Give me someone who's got a little skill any time."

"Do you really mean that?"

"I spit on all virgins—"

She slapped him lightly on his shoulder. "Not that blarney you were spouting." Lina rubbed his chest absently. "If you were to find a virgin it would be your supreme pleasure to initiate him or her. I meant…"

"You meant what?"

She paused. "With Londo, well, he's coming at it from a different perspective. I suppose being soulmates sort of blinds you to certain things. They're perfect in your eyes. Maybe that's love. I mean, I can see that he's not perfect, but he is. He just is."

"And your question is—?"

"No. Forget I said anything."

"What?"

"It's sheer vanity. Forget it."

"You have an ego problem."

"I do. It's getting better."

Jae lay there looking at her.

"Did you mean it," she finally asked in a tiny voice, "when you said I was pretty?"

Jae's mouth opened in surprise.

Lina babbled in her embarrassment. "I mean, you don't have to say anything like that to me if you don't want to. I prefer honesty. I understand that men like to lie to get women to go to bed with them, but I figured, we were here already. Maybe… you meant it?"

"Who wouldn't?" He took her face in his hands. "I have been the child here, not to have mentioned that. I can't believe I never said— It was so obvious, I thought you'd always had people making a fuss over you about it. Sweet, you are so beautiful I have to stop and catch my breath sometimes. No, you aren't beautiful. There's a better word: lovely. You are my lovely Lina, and when you smile the whole room lights up. You make others around you smile, too. The worlds sing within you and where you walk, beauty reigns."

She blushed pink. "You do know how to charm the birds out of the trees."

"And I was being honest. That doesn't happen too often. You know that, don't you?"

"I know you're the blarney master," she leaned her head back on his shoulder, sighing. "Thank you, Jae." Jae thought she was pretty. Lon thought she was pretty. That was all she needed, the only people in the universe she needed to think that. Otherwise it wasn't important.

This time Jae made non-alcoholic drinks in his kitchenette. They'd both put on robes, and Lina took her time exploring Jae's living room as he puttered. "How long have you known him?" she asked him. The leaves on all the plants in here had not one iota of dust on them. "How old are you?"

Jae emerged with glasses and handed one to her. It was warm. Lina sniffed and took a sip. Not something she'd choose every day, it tasted like a light chicken stock with a dash of lime. Surprisingly interesting.

"Lon's maybe a year older than I am, Sarastor time," Jae said as he settled on the couch that had regained its structural integrity in their absence. "I was ten when I joined the Legion. I was here for over a year before Hal brought Londo by to check us out. He was around 12 or 13 then– cute as a *leeshing*–" he shook his head to remember– "and he roomed with me for a week while the Legion looked him over. We were the only Legion kids back then."

"So you got to meet Maximus, too."

He patted the couch beside him and Lina sat. Jae passed her a framed picture of the hero that alternated scenes of him in heroic pose, and then walking around a park with both Londo and Jae in tow, stopping to wave at the camera.

"What's he like?" Even she could hear the tremble in her voice.

He grinned at her. "Afraid of meeting your father-in-law, huh?"

She set the picture on the coffee table. "Maybe yours, too," she observed. Her eyes crinkled when she saw his surprise at the situation.

Jae shook his head. "Maybe. He– He scared me to death for the first few months. Well, maybe a year. It wasn't fright as much as awe. I didn't see that much of him. He was often off on a mission somewhere or back on Earth, attending to business. But when he came for a long stay– Did I say that Lon was full-time here? Lon was seeing a bunch of Sarastor shrinks at the time."

"He mentioned that."

"Anyway, when Hal would stay for a while, he'd take the two of us out to dinner, watch a game, go on sightseeing tours… You know, the usual bit with parents when their kid's at boarding school. Which this practically was. I was Lon's best friend, so he let me hang around."

"So you two were roomies through the years?" She reached to twist Maximus' picture on the table to face away from the two of them. Better.

"Oh no, only that first week. A Legionnaire is entitled to their own quarters, no matter how young they are. Lon needed a place of his own. I made his apartment walls impervion so if he needed to, he could bash his head against them. He did that a lot back then. When Hal stayed for a while he lived in Lon's quarters. He helped out the Legion a lot, but not enough to step on Lon's toes. I always admired that about him."

"Ah, so that's where he was," Lina said almost to herself. "I remember when I was a kid hearing people remarking that Maximus was almost never at home any more. I read about that first year he decided to go galactic. He up and left Earth for a whole year to see who in the galaxy needed help. Then he came back and things were almost normal… until Lon appeared."

"He made his reputation in that year," Jae said. "I even remember him visiting Feith back then and helping on some kind of emergency. I was really, really young, but I remember that his costume was the coolest thing going. I remember…" he smiled in wonder, "I just had to have a white cape, just like his. I haven't thought about that in years. And then later on as I was growing up, there were all these news stories about him, and I thought that all Terrans were like him."

"He's not Terran."

"I didn't know that. I met Lon a few years later and that early impression remained, I'm embarrassed to say. I thought that all Terrans had all their powers. Then I found out that Lon was a Terran who had been given the powers, and that

Hal wasn't Terran at all. Orb, was I confused. Lon sat me down with a study padd one day and taught me all he knew about Earth. Which wasn't much."

Now the photos that Jae passed to her were of a younger Londo. There was a set of solo civilian scenes, formal scenes of Lon and Jae together in uniform, and one that was just of them here in Jae's room, sitting together and laughing.

So Lon the Terran didn't know about his own world because he hadn't lived there much. That was a new concept for Lina.

Jae smiled to himself as he remembered. "That's also when we first got serious. We were both so lonely, it was natural for us to gravitate to each other. Incredibly frustrating. But it was as if we both decided, 'The universe has conspired against us so much already, this is just one more thing to put up with.' It was a unifying ritual. Side-by-side masturbation, kissing, sleeping together– we couldn't even do that properly. Once Lon broke my arm just by rolling over on it in his sleep. After that he made sure he stayed awake until I slept, and then he'd get out of bed and sleep on the floor."

"How terrible for you both," Lina said, feeling the loneliness echo within Jae. **I'm here. We're both here now.** She hugged him tightly and he relaxed. "So… What first attracted you to Londo?"

He chuckled at that. "What do you think? There he was, the second-most powerful being in the known universe, running around my rooms bashing his head on my walls. And all I could think was, 'That is the most gorgeous guy I have ever seen!'"

"And he was probably looking back at you and saying, 'That is the most adorable guy in the galaxy!'"

Jae smiled at her. "Is that what you think of me?"

"You look like you might have been adorable when you were a kid. Like I remember Lon being really cute. I had his pictures all over my school notebooks."

"But he's not cute any more?"

"I wouldn't call him cute. I'd call him dark and handsome. I'd call him…" Lina thought. "Wuff. Take him by the scruff of the neck in my teeth and shake him. Wuff."

Jae laughed out loud. "Wuff. I agree."

"But you're not a wuff." She didn't look at him, but smiled slyly.

"Not a wuff?" He huffed out a hurt breath.

"Uh uh. You're an oo. Definitely an oo."

"What's an oo do?"

"That voodoo that you do so well. I look at you and I say, oo, so very nice. And I'm around you and I think, oo, he makes me happy. Very happy to be around this extremely good-looking crazy guy who thinks he's still a kid."

"I do?"

"You'll never forget your exuberance for life. You've kept it through everything so far."

He considered. "You're a yum. Yum yum yum yum–" He rolled over and wrestled with her, planting tiny kisses all over as they rolled around on the couch, then down to the room's lush rug. She giggled at him and he laughed at her. They finally rolled to a stop and caught their breaths.

Lina pushed herself away. "Wait! Waitaminnit. If Maximus was here so much and the Legion had already accepted a– slightly to be sure– lesser-powered, unstable version of him, why didn't the Legion offer membership to the Big Blue Max himself?"

"We did," Jae chuckled, "and the old boy turned us down flat. Said he missed Earth too much and Sarastor was too quiet for his tastes." He opened his mouth in surprise. "I wonder now if he meant there wasn't enough action, or there wasn't any music?"

His mouth quirked from one side of his face to the other before he continued. "Hunh. As soon as the shrinks said it was okay to go onto the next level, Hal packed up Lon and had him reduced to part-time status. They both went back to Earth." His eyes closed in pain. "I thought I was going to die," he said. "I had a bit of a breakdown for a while." Lina stroked his shoulder. "But I got better. And around then Erik joined…"

"You didn't…" Lina breathed. "With Erik?" She giggled.

He grinned. "Uh huh," he said. "He and I experimented during a very convenient bivouac. Lost my official virginity to Erik 'I Can Spread Those Legs in 60 Seconds' Gallad. It was a short fling to him. He's definitely straight."

"I noticed."

"But he had some gay friends that he introduced me to."

"And you got a hobby."

"Oh yeah," he agreed and laughed. He drew some pillows to them. "Too much talk, child. Mouths were made for other things." He taught her then by example, playing with her until they both giggled, then became deadly serious. "Try this," he'd urge, and she caught on quickly.

She touched him differently than anyone had before. Jae experienced the newness of touch through the way her fingers moved on him, the way she kissed his body. He tried to do the same for her, discovering the sense anew.

He pulled the last of her nightgown from her. "Let's try out that double-loop again, see how it goes."

He'd rarely had a woman all-out shriek under his mouth before, but she did now and he knew that it was real because he could feel almost everything she did. He was absolute concentration as he sought her sensations. He tested all over until he felt something react, and then he bore down on that place with his mouth, with his fingers, with his mind.

She cursed and told him he was double-looping too deep, she told him to stop, and then ordered him to keep going. And he was feeling it all from both points of view, feeling himself coming as she came again.

Jae paused every so often to catch his breath. He had to back off as he squeezed himself and tried to shut his mind down a level or two to numb it to what she was feeling. Her shudders took a long time to subside.

"Do you think you're ready?" he asked from between her legs, laughing as well as he could in triumph, breathless as he was. He let her have a few moments and then pulled her legs wider and entered. He felt her take him and thrust quickly, knowing that he was going to come sooner than he wanted.

Skurn, so this was what it was like for a woman. So different, giving herself over to his power. The sensations weren't as absolutely focused as they were for him. So many more places responded but more subtly. No wonder there had to be a long prelude. The sensations weren't as bold, but they seemed to work together like a choir building to its crescendo. A small voice here, a sweet song there, all coming together and straining for climax.

Jae concentrated, trying not to lose it too fast. He shook with his passion, his drive, and her strength came back so she could add to it. She whimpered in little howls. He gasped and cried out wordlessly as he panted. He was going for power and sensation now, not finesse. All his skills were out the window. This was just sex, down and dirty. Him in her. Him possessing her. Him feeling her like he'd never felt anything before.

She came when he came, and he wasn't sure if it were truly her coming or her feeling what he was feeling. It hit like a double explosion, drenching him in sweat as he shouted his release. Falling onto the rug, he gathered her in his arms.

"Shards and splinters, Lina. Shards and splinters and shreds." He kissed her and caressed her, and she nestled against him.

"Oh. I can't move," Lina laughed softly against his sweaty chest.

"That was amazing," Jae sighed.

"Even if you went too deep, devil boy. We'll have to work on that. Oo, you feel so good."

He kissed her forehead, smoothing back her hair.

"I love you, Jae," she murmured. "In heart, mind and body. I didn't think I could love two men this way, but I do. It's just that–" She went silent and lay her head against his chest.

He took three deep breaths, then another three as he steeled himself. "Lina," he finally asked, "how do you share minds?"

She raised up her head and looked into his eyes. "Are you sure?"

"Can we… take it slowly?" he asked.

"You be in control, Jae," she said, nestling her head back onto his chest. "You go in as deeply as you want. You stop when you want to stop." She kissed his shoulder. "You do this to whatever degree you feel comfortable with."

"Okay." He closed his eyes, as if he were starting a double-loop. He could feel her doing something. Her mind was so close, just like in the loop, but now… something opened to him, like a flower blooming. It was as if she were reaching out a hand to him, and he stepped inside her, experiencing her on an entirely non-physical level.

"You do it, too," she whispered.

"I'm afraid." Had he said it out loud?

"Only as much as you want."

He opened a tiny crack on himself and was ashamed of how little he offered her and what her view of him must be.

"That's perfect," she said. He could feel the love that she held for him now, glowing pink and white and golden, trickling into the tiny opening.

"I remember this," Jae whispered. His parents had communicated to him this way, so personal, so loving.

That was for a child, Lina told him. **Come in deeper now. Come to me, my love. Open yourself a little more.**

It felt so good inside her self. He opened himself wider. It was like basking in the sun, cradled in the arms of a lover but ever so much more so. It was an exquisite drowning in love, in life itself.

Jae saw her fears and the insecurities as symbolic things, chains which held her back from doing the things she loved. **Don't be afraid,** he told her. **Take a chance. I'll help you. I'll protect you.** He let his own love stream to her. Music flowed through her like a fountain, and he could hear the angels sing when he looked at her.

She was so frightened of life. Jae exposed more of his mind so she could see that he was riddled with much of the same.

A mountain of guilt about Feith rose up around his core while fear and loneliness raged about it like a storm. Anger at being left behind crashed in fierce lightnings. His inner world gathered dark clouds of hate against a universe that would have done this to him.

I'm here for you, whenever you need me, Jae. Best friends at the very, very least. I'll do my best to protect you, I promise. You were supposed to survive. To grow. You were the volunteer.

Her love surged through him. Inside the darkness, above the storm clouds, Jae was a tremendous glow of white light plugged into the center of the universe itself. He'd stanched the flow for so long. Now there was the possibility of it opening up someday. Until then he was still white and golds, and an infinite aurora of pastel colors cascading through, a perfumed breeze that excited the universe with its passing, that roused it and brought it up to levels it hadn't attained before.

How long did they lie there, the river of love bonding and strengthening them? There seemed to be more in the river the longer they let it flow.

"I know a song that says that love taken is equal to that given," Jae recalled. "That's wrong. We make more."

"We create," Lina agreed. She eased herself up on him, and they kissed softly. Then softly again, but thoroughly, and Jae lost himself in it, wrapping his arms around her, while she wrapped her legs around him. He vowed to himself that he'd never let her go.

Her liquid arms gradually tensed.

"What?"

"I'm sorry. Oh, terrible timing. I'm sorry, I'm sorry. Oh, I have to leave. Now." She rolled off him and fumbled around for her nightgown. "Lon needs me."

"No," Jae said. "Stay with me. He told me we could take all night, that it was all right."

She smoothed back his hair, then caressed his cheek with her knuckle. "Feel him, Jae," she whispered. "Don't touch him. Just sense."

Jae thought of the essence of Lon that he knew so well, and he felt a deep darkness around it. Someone weeping. Loneliness, fear, the spirit becoming heavier and heavier…

"He needs me right now," Lina told Jae. "He is so insecure in so many unexpected ways. After the other night…" She bit her lip in shame. "I lost faith with him. I thought–"

"You thought he didn't love you any more," Jae realized.

"Can he ever trust me again?" Her fingers clutched him. "I betrayed the essence of what we are–" *I was a whore.*

"No, Sweet. You couldn't help it. Lon understands. He knows that he hurt you."

"And now I'm hurting him by being here with you." She pulled her discarded gown over her head.

"He understands, Lie." Jae sat up desperately. "It's okay."

"He understands with his head, but not his heart. Sometimes the two don't hear each other." She turned around to squeeze his fingers. Quickly she stood up and ran out of the room, gathering clothing from around the apartment as she went.

Pulling on his own wrap, Jae followed her. She had slipped into her robe without tying it shut. "So you're running out on me," he accused her.

"I am not." She turned to face him. "This is going to be a huge balancing act until we all figure things out in our heads as well as our hearts. With two people it's almost simple, compared to this. The human heart can be very fragile."

A wash of confusion changed Jae's face. "How did they handle this?" He looked sharply at Lina. "My people; they had so many dual-triunes. They had to have worked out a system that functioned well."

"We have to find out." Lina reached for her red dress and straightened slowly. "I don't want to mess us up. I want whatever we've found tonight to grow."

Jae held her close. "I bared my soul to you in a way I've never done even with Londo."

"I am so honored." Her eyes glowed as she gazed at him. "Blessed."

He shook his head as he tried to express himself. "I want a home that won't be pulled out from under my feet. When I was a child, I was happy. I didn't think there was a chance of being that way again. I want a family. I want people around me who think of me as family. And I want children to be a part of that."

He came out of it to shake her gently into absolute awareness of his needs. "I want someone to pass on whatever it is that defines me as Feithi. I feel a terrible need to keep something of Feith alive in this universe. I think the cosmos is out of balance without it."

Now she was the one who was silent.

"I want you to be the mother of my Feithi children. Only you could do it. Anyone else would skew the balance."

"Child or children?" Lina steeled herself for the answer. "I'm terrified of the idea of being pregnant. Of delivering, of having the responsibility. My mother, my sister– they were both so ill when they were pregnant. Mom had five miscarriages between my sister and me. My sister's had two miscarriages. I lost a grandmother because she died in childbed. And   I'm so screwed up. What kind of screwed-up children would I make?"

He gazed at her and her eyes did not leave his. "At least one child, Lina. They and you will be fine."

"We don't even know if we're going to do a dual-triune. If we don't… no. I'm sorry, Jae, but kids need to have a stable family. It couldn't be me and Lon raising your child and you visiting every now and then. And I think you wouldn't like that."

"I wouldn't, but if it's the only way I can get a child, I'll take it. What about within marriage?"

"If, if we go through with this… I think that it would only be fair," she whispered. "But there's fair and then there's what I want, too. Let me think about it. Please." Her gaze went to the wall and beyond it. "Lon…"

"The problem is–" Jae felt he had to reveal his heart before she left, to cement her to him, "I don't think I have the nerve for a secret dual-triune in AffSys society. I don't think I can get into a deep relationship and never be acknowledged."

Lina said, "Maybe there's something in Feithi literature about this. Someone who's been through it before, who found a way, maybe even someone in the AffSys who did it. We're going to need to study your world's history to find the way around the jealousy and performance comparisons anyway. I can see those as real obstacles."

"So," Jae adjusted his hold on her, beginning to smile, "does that mean I was better than he is?"

"See what I mean?" Lina said. She cupped his face so he'd listen carefully. "What if I said that he was better?" That stopped Jae cold. "I'm not saying that he was. Besides, I think 'better' means something different to women than it does to men. But you see the danger. Please, find us something to study. How did they handle all the interpersonal relationships? What did they do with the jealousies, the inequities that are bound to come up? All I can think of is that two people can find a balance, but three–"

"Three is the number of dynamic energy. Even a two-person marriage has problems."

Ruefully she closed her eyes. "Yeah, I think I can confirm that. Find us a way, Jae. Call me when you find it. No, give us an hour or so. A Terran hour."

She kissed him so he'd remember her in that hour. "Sweet Jae," she whispered in his ear, "I love you so."

"I love you, too." He gathered her for a final kiss and another and another before he took her by her wrists to hold her away from himself. "Go to him now. Just one final thing," he said solemnly.

"What?"

"I swear. I swear that from here on throughout all time– you can trust me. Anything I do, anything I say: trust me."

She drew a startled breath and then threw her arms around him.

Somewhere in the cosmos a tiny, unbalanced rift healed.

19

Lon wasn't in bed. Lina tiptoed past the dark living room to his office. He sat at his desk, but he faced away from it, illuminated only by the glow of his text screen. He was staring at the wall. Emotions roiled within him: fear upon fear, memories of losses, fresh wounds.

Her beloved.

"Londo," she called quietly. She stood in the doorway dressed in the black lace, her hair disheveled and her other clothing in her hand. She was covered with dried sweat and thick musk. He would know how far she had gone if he hadn't sensed them already.

He whirled, leaping up as the chair spun, running to her. Clutching her to him, a tear of relief escaped from his eyes. "Lina, Lina, you're back," he whispered so fiercely, so tenderly, into her hair.

She hugged him hard, trying to beam him all the love she felt. "Of course I am, Londo," she said. "Sarastor told me to follow my heart and I'd take the right path." She took his head in her hands so he'd look at her face. "That path will always lead back to you." She kissed him tenderly, then again, and joy sparked between them, the joy of knowing that they'd found each other and their souls would never part.

Jae couldn't bear to wait a second longer than the hour he'd been allotted. ****I've found something,**** he telepathed to Lina as soon as his timer signaled him.

****Oooo. Five more minutes.**** Afterglow lay languorous in her mind.

****Now is good,**** Lon said. ****Port him over, Lina. Right here.****

With a start, Jae appeared in Lon's bedroom dressed only in his black tights as they rolled apart. The spent passion of sex in the room was so thick it permeated to his bones. Lon threw back the sheet and patted the mattress even as Lina gathered her part of the sheet to wrap around herself.

As Jae sat beside him with padd in hand, Londo asked, "Whatcha got?"

"The start of a great hard-on."

"Besides that." Londo looked at Lina, and the satisfaction that flowed between them was palpable.

Suddenly uncertain, Jae wondered who truly was the better man in bed. He covered it up with business. "I've got a number of scholarly and recreational articles here, some fiction that showed the day-to-day operation of the family unit as well as how they handled sex. And here's a couple old marriage manuals," he said triumphantly. "One for the couple considering dual-triune, the other for the newly-made dual-triune."

"Pay dirt," Londo said as he arranged his pillow so he could sit up.

Lina wriggled next to him to see the screen better. It was in Panlingua, which she couldn't read anywhere near as fast as the other two. She was still new to the language. Besides, her brain didn't want to rev up right now. It, like her entire body, bore a close resemblance to a wet noodle.

So she rolled back to her side of the bed. It had been a long, hard, wonderful day and night. She needed to rest her eyes. "Just give me the digest version when you finish," she managed to murmur. "I'll read it later."

Londo made a noise that sounded like an affirmation as he and Jae studied. Despite her best intentions, Lina dozed, only to crack open her eyes when the bed shifted. Londo and Jae were embracing. Jae was busy on the other side of Lon's neck as Londo discovered Lina awake. He gave her a sheepish smile that she answered with a sly one of her own.

I'll just give you two some privacy, love. She ported to her own little bed on Earth.

She woke covered with cats: purring cats, snoring cats, Obi of course who kept nudging her for petting, Bran who stuck his paw in her eye as a subtle hint that breakfast was overdue. Ember was standing on her hind legs on the pillow, her head inside the ceiling hole Londo had made, to investigate this new landmark. The sun was low in the western sky through the skylight above them, but that didn't tell Lina what time it was on Sarastor.

They had a funeral tonight to prepare for. She still had to figure out a song. At least she'd gotten a little rest. If she felt tired, she had memories that would last a lifetime. She was filled with love for two incredible men and they were in love with her.

After five minutes of healing passes to firm up her wobbly legs, Lina eased out of bed between the cats to grab her ratty old robe and pad downstairs. She sang as she fed them and cleaned up afterward to the sound of her top five picks so far of ancient tribute music.

Damn it, Aiko didn't deserve a generic funeral song, but it was all Lina could give her. Still, the music itself was lovely, inspiring stuff. Aiko would like that part at least.

Time to be getting back and doing more research. Lina didn't think Lon was asleep, but he wasn't *busy.* **Lon?** she called softly.

Um... Lina. Where are you?

Earth. Is the coast clear?

Come on in. You're on Earth? I can still hear you loud and clear.

"That's strange," he told her when she appeared in bed beside him. "I couldn't hear you when you were porting, but I could feel your presence. It wasn't like hyperspace." His face broke into a grin as he hugged her. "But it's one hell of a lot faster. I can't get over that. Good morning, my beautiful wife."

A long, welcoming kiss later, Lina smoothed his hair back as he relaxed into the pillow. "You look like the cat who ate the canary, Honeybear," she teased. "Any particular reason?"

A sense of euphoria wafted from him as he again enfolded her in those thick, strong arms of his.

"So how was losing your virginity the second time?" she asked.

"Baby," Lon said with a broad smile, "it was great. Beyond beyond. I don't know why you women put up such a fuss."

"Excuse me? Apples to oranges."

He was totally contented and relaxed. He felt safe, he felt loved, and Lina marveled at it. If Jae could do this to him then keeping Jae in Lon's life at this higher level was the only choice to make.

Among other reasons.

"Kitten, it's not just Jae," Lon murmured into her throat. "It's you, too. My beautiful, passionate wife. Thank you for teaching him." He began to place tiny kisses all over her shoulders. "Thank you for being so understanding. Sweet Lina, soft Lina." He moved down and his hands discovered that she wasn't wearing panties under her robe. "Hot Lina. Lina who says 'Oh Lon, oh Lon…'"

"Oooo, Londo," Lina breathed, clutching him against her. Here she thought she'd had all the sex she could ever want in the past day. But she wanted Londo again. Oh, how the man could make her feel! She positively pulsed around him.

"What say we take the ride one more time tonight?" Lon whispered against her chest.

Her focus on the world narrowed to just Londo— except for one thing. "We don't have time." The funeral was scheduled for this evening, but so many things had to be completed beforehand.

Lon paused. "Plenty of time for everything. You know Sarastor days are long."

New hands slid on her hips now, lips on the back of her shoulders. "Isn't it rude to start without everyone?" Jae asked. He must have been in the bathroom. Now he slid into bed with them so Lina was in the middle.

Lina heaved herself away, kicking at the bed to propel herself to the headboard. She grabbed the sheet to cover herself and Lon gave a puzzled grunt of protest.

"Hold on," she told them. "Stop."

"What?"

"I don't know if anyone else has noticed it, but there are three of us here."

Jae raised up and looked at them. "One… two… three. How about that?"

Londo gave him a grin before leaning over Lina's legs to deliver Jae a kiss.

Lina gathered more bed linen to herself, creating a thick cocoon. She felt very vulnerable as they considered her, crafty looks on both their plotting Legionnaire faces. "I think," she said in a small but defiant voice, "I've been a… very good sport in taking all the changes of the past few–"

"An excellent sport," Lon said. He snuggled up to her. "We'll get you a trophy."

"Sex is best between two people," Lina said. "Two means intimacy. But three at once–"

"Sometimes you want three," Jae said. "For fun. For excitement. For extra attention."

"'Ah'm not shoah ah'm ready fo' this,'" Londo gave a bad imitation of her. "I've heard this before."

"Oh, Lon! I'm serious. You guys talked about this days ago. No, years. You've had time to– What?" Lina clutched Lon, her eyes unfocused. "What is that?" Again she grabbed the blanket, this time pulling it up to her neck. "Is His Holiness bugging this room again? It's–"

Lon scanned the ceiling and corners for a camera as Lina searched for the answer. A screen appeared over Jae's left wrist with a diagram and quick-scrolling writing.

"It's not electronic," Jae reported, and Lina added, "I see eyes looking at us, but it's not eyes. What is it?"

Londo turned toward the shared wall between them and the apartment next door. "I know those eyes," he said. "Damn it, she's gone too far this time."

"Who?" Jae watched them. They were both looking at the bedroom wall. "Deegel?"

"She's putting on a show tonight," Londo said sourly.

"Deegel?" Lina asked.

"Aka Neuron. My next-door neighbor."

"From the wedding? She's the one with the–?" Lina made boobie gestures at her chest.

"She had 'em done just as soon as she found out that Lon has an eye for well-endowed ladies," Jae said.

"I remember *them*. I guess that means I remember her."

Jae frowned at the blank wall. "I don't–"

*****Like this,**** Lina said, and gently guided his mind, sweeping covering cobwebs of shadows away so he could clearly feel the presence that wanted to spy and tell.

"Don't put your feet on the floor, either of you," Londo ordered. "Don't touch the wall. Her power needs physical connection to work."

"How subtle can you be?" Jae asked Lina. "Can you work just below her conscious perception?"

"I can try."

Londo glided upright across the room, inches above the floor, and grabbed a long robe. "I want to pay her a visit and then file a formal complaint," he growled. "If there's anything left of her to complain about."

"Let us keep her busy while you do that," Jae smiled grimly.

"Lina will have to come along with me for appearance's sake." Lon began to rifle through a drawer of his bedside table.

"I'll start Jae off," Lina said as she ported on a new chemise and the robe Lon had given her. Couldn't wear her ratty stuff in public. She let Jae hang on to her mind as she sought out the spy, the woman propped up against the other side of the wall, sending out feelers like extensions of her own nervous system. How had Lina influenced that guard on Tiawa again?

*****Ah, got it,**** Jae said. *****I see.****

"Wait a sec…" Deegel warned the others in the room. "Yes! They're there now. That Londo has insulators on his bed, I'll bet you anything, but they're not in the bed now."

The black-haired, bosomy woman readjusted the placement of her hands on the wall and concentrated. "Oh yeah. Oh yeah. They're hot. Maybe I think… down on the floor. Ow! Ow! Oh shit, it hurts!" She alternated hands, shaking out the free one before replacing it against the wall.

"Great shards of the orb, how can she stand it? Shit, no. The pain! The pain! But he's not stopping– it's just arousing him. She's hurt; she's injured!"

"Grigach!" Someone else in the room exclaimed, "We can't have him murdering her! Computer–"

"Can't have who murdering whom?" Londo asked as he and Lina stepped through Deegel's bedroom doorway.

"No! No!" Deegel screamed. "He's killing her!"

Londo reached into his robe pocket to pull out a small wrist control with a button protruding from it. Theatrically he snapped the button flush before sliding the flexible band onto his wrist.

Deegel stopped screaming. She panted hard as she recovered from the ordeal. Her hands dropped to lie limply at her sides. "It's stopped."

Londo looked over the small group in the room: Deegel of the industrial-sized boobs, barely covered by a short robe and sprawled on the floor next to the wall that adjoined Londo's bedroom. Ferman and Nichi, clutching the sheets to themselves in the bed. Rondil, alert and sitting in his underwear in the chair on the far side of the bed.

Deegel's eyes refocused as she saw who stood before her, thunder in his face. She tensed and then slumped back as she was, heedless of her dishabille. "Tricked," she decided.

Londo's scowl was deep. "How about that. Absolute privacy a rule in Mega-Legion Headquarters– and who do I find trying to spy on me? Presenting a little tableau to her guests?" He held up the hand with the watch on it. "Do you want me to turn it on again?"

"What in sunfire is that?" Deegel demanded.

"Just a little something I came up with. I didn't think I'd ever have to use it." He turned to the others in the room. "Explanations. I know Deegel's motives. I don't know yours. I don't want to hear stories about how you were investigating mind control, either."

"Leave Nichi out of it," Ferman said. "She didn't want any part of it."

"Nichi?"

The woman's guilt-ridden gaze avoided Londo. "If I hadn't been curious, I wouldn't have stuck around, Valiant. I'm sorry. You can include me in your report."

"You all can turn yourselves in. The commander will deal with you easier if you do."

"And if we don't?"

Londo slowly turned his head to regard Deegel. She lay seductively against the wall, her legs spread in posed casualness.

"Then I'll be happy to report you, Neuron, and bring you up for internal prosecution. Except that you're going to do one thing to prevent that."

"Don't try it," Lina warned Deegel, who had shifted, placing her hands flat on the floor with a subtle movement. The Legionnaire looked sharply at Lina.

Lina swept her free arm twice in a large circle to de-energize Deegel's major meridians, and Deegel sank back against the wall.

"She can't concentrate fully now. That'll last maybe a minute," Lina told Londo softly.

Londo nodded. "The only way I won't prosecute you, Deegel, is if you agree to move. Today. Switch quarters with someone else. I know. With Jae. We're partners now. We should be neighbors, too. And his room's on the outer perimeter. That means you'll have that fewer people to torment."

Deegel shook her head, trying to focus. "I like it here. This location is convenient to me."

"Getting suspended from the Legion will be more inconvenient."

"Suspended?" Deegel allowed a smirk to liven her face as she sinuously stood up, shaking back the silent ebony beads in her short hair. "You're trying to divert them from prosecuting your… wife. They wouldn't dare suspend me. Violation of privacy is not a—"

"Violation of privacy, when combined with a number of other violations that you've attempted in the past, combined with what I'm sure other members will bring up in addition to that—"

"You wouldn't, Londo. I could report a few things myself."

Lina whispered to Londo. As Deegel came around the side of the bed, she would see how Londo hovered just above the floor. Both in their bare feet, Londo supported his wife so she was also above the surface.

Londo's face showed shock and he demanded, "Who have you been telling things to? Are you violating security as well?"

"What did she say?!" Deegel spat. She reached for her overrobe now, something to guard her from Londo's gaze. "She's just a witchdoctor, Londo, an ignorant, savage, mind-controlling—"

"There's a man," Lina said evenly. "He has two-color eyes, an outer ring of purple and an inner color of green. He's wearing plaid: a business suit, maybe, and there's a quill pen following him. That usually means journalist of some kind. He likes you very much, and he's very generous with his compliments. He gives you a lot of publicity, doesn't he? Hm, lots of headlines. He's been in here. I can feel his eagerness as he reads computer readouts, up to… *They're* telling me Level Two. No, now he's reached into Level Four. *They're* showing me a symbol: a Pentagon official stamping a file Top Secret. Isn't Level Four a security clearance, Lon?"

Lon's face was grim. "It is."

Lina shook her head. "*They* say he's not even a Level One."

Deegel's skin had turned dead white. "I… He's just a friend. No security breach. He's just someone I have over every now and then. For my own personal amusements."

"Letting him into our secrets?" Now it was Ferman's face that was set into such grim lines, matching those of the other Legionnaires in the room.

"Blood's ice, people, you're listening to a witchdoctor! A Terran witchdoctor! So she's got some kind of telepathy, and she knows I had a guest up here. She's just jealous of what Londo and I had going, and now she's trying to get back–"

"You and I never had anything going," Lon sneered. "Just in your pitiful imagination. One time you caught me in a weak moment, and I learned my lesson. But I never suspected for a moment that you'd betray–"

"I'm no traitor!"

"Letting an outsider into the system," Nichi said. "A reporter, on top of it all." She turned to Lina with the snappish authority that she must have when in full uniform. "Was there anyone else? Anyone from, say, the Yanist-Glory Empire?"

Lina licked her lips and closed her eyes. Londo released her so she could turn in a circle, asking, asking.

"Stop it," she ordered. Someone had tried to touch her in a creepy, non-physical way. Londo picked her up again so she didn't touch the floor.

She saw ghost images of men sliding immaterially through the apartment. A few looked into the computer records, but she always saw a quill pen hovering in the air next to them. That meant TV, newspaper or magazine reporter, writer. She shook her head. "Just reporters," she said.

"Plural?" Now it was Rondil asking.

"Two… three… maybe four of them going into secured files. Different men, fairly recently, *they're* saying, but how recent is recent? A calendar. Ah… past half year. Three reporters in the past half year, definitely."

"Easy enough to check the security records, see who Deegel brought in with her during that time," Rondil said to Londo. "See what stories they reported afterward."

Lon nodded. "We can cross-check computer access during those visits." he said. "An extremely serious charge, Deegel. I know what I'd do if I were commander."

This place was rank, stinking of jealousy and anger, of self-hatred. Fear. Lina began to move the stagnant energy out, when she felt a misty hand touch her arm. **No.**

"No?" she asked.

"What, love?"

"I was just going to get rid of some bad vibes, and *they* say not to. I don't know why."

"Puter, when is Chimrin due back?"

#*Five days travel time plus length of mission,*# the toneless voice from mid-air said.

"Why don't you leave it until she can get in here?" Lon suggested.

"Chimrin's the telepath, Psyche, right?"

"Right. She'll need to check this out."

"And to think," Nichi told Deegel, "Just last week I was congratulating you on all the great publicity you've been getting." Nichi discreetly pulled on a robe under the sheet, letting the bedding cover her until it was secure. The others were also getting semi-dressed.

Deegel got to her feet. "This is hearsay," she said. "You're taking her word for it."

"I only provide a starting point," Lina said quietly, though she thought it odd that people who would get into this position with Deegel wouldn't defend her character. "I'm sure that no sensible Sarastoran court would ever listen to a Terran witchdoctor."

We have regulations, Londo told her. **Honor to uphold. Deegel's often strayed too close to the line that can't be crossed.**

"We'll take care of it from here, Valiant," Rondil said. "Puter, Legion priority order. Copy immediately to the commander. Effective immediately and until further notice, Deegel Garrim is denied access to information above level one security."

"No! This is preposterous!"

"What it is, is absolutely unacceptable, coming right on the heels of Aiko," Nichi said miserably. "Death and now dishonor. How could you do it?"

"You can't take this seriously!"

"This was done before Aiko," Londo said. "Don't link the two events together."

"He was here yesterday… early this evening," Lina said quietly. "The man in plaid's vibrations are very fresh. He was in here for a while, and then they moved out to the main computer station, I think. *They're* showing me an old-fashioned switchboard with operators frantically plugging in lines. I see two people walking around there, with drinks and in robes, and he sits down and she guides him through it."

"Yesterday?" Londo's eyes narrowed on Deegel. "What, even our dead aren't safe from you?"

"What in ice and blaze is going on?" Stoan's voice rumbled through the room from some unseen speaker. "Rondil? Are you in there?"

"There are a lot of us here, Commander," Rondil said to the air. "We need to investigate possible security violations by Neuron. Starting with a reporter yesterday afternoon that she may have let into Level Four."

Silence for a moment. "Are you drunk? Is this on the level?"

"It's that woman!" Deegel's voice went shrill. "They've been talking to that woman!"

"We have some unusual leads that we need to check," Rondil said. "And I have been involved in some other action that I highly regret. I want to apologize to you, Valiant, and to you, too, Mrs. Valiant. It was a… joke that got out of hand and imposed on your privacy. I'm sorry I was a part of this."

"Me, too," Nichi said.

Ferman spoke up. "Nichi isn't to be blamed. Well, not too much. We three played along in here, and I'm sorry, Lon. You're a good friend, and I don't want to lose that. We were… a little crazy tonight. We've been drinking. What other excuse can I give? It's been rough and we've been drinking, and we thought this might be amusing. And it backfired. On Deegel, especially. If… If this is all true, then let me assure you that none of us had any idea. We stand ready for punitive action."

The commander's voice heaved a sigh. "Ordinarily I'd ask if this couldn't wait until later. I still have three more hours of sleep scheduled. But a possible security breach can't wait."

"Commander."

"Valiant. How the shards many people are there, anyway?" Stoan asked tiredly.

"Lina and I. The three of them, and Neuron. Whichever way your verdict goes, I want Neuron's room relocated immediately. She's tried to violate my privacy too many times. Tonight was the last straw."

"Neuron? Assuming you're innocent of the security charge? What say you?"

Deegel glared daggers at Londo, then at Lina. "Agreed," she snapped as she strode out of the room.

Nichi snuffled and Ferman patted her back. "Londo, I am so sorry," she said.

"Tell me that when you're sober," Lon told her. "I can smell the alcohol on all of you. Sober up before you see the commander."

"You're not coming?"

Lon put his arm around Lina. "I've got better things to do," he said. "If any-one needs me… tell them to wait until morning. Late morning. Lina?" She ported them back to Londo's bedroom.

"Did you get all that, Jae?" Londo asked. He'd maintained light contact with him throughout.

"Yeah, after I finished broadcasting the torture scene to her," Jae said. He let out a low growl. "I should have made it hurt more."

"Torture?" Lina asked. "I thought that was Lon's little miracle. After all, it takes a licking and keeps on ticking."

"It's not a Timex," Londo said as he pulled the ordinary watch off and set it on his dresser. "That's an advertising slogan, Jae."

"Shards, Deegel violating security protocol." Jae shook his head. "I've heard a rumor–" He glanced sharply at Lina.

"Pretend I'm not here," she smiled.

"I don't violate security."

"So let me go get something to drink while you two talk. What security level are you two anyway? How many levels are there?"

"Six," Londo said. "Our level is Unlimited. Most top-ranked Legionnaires are."

"Deegel's a five," Jae said.

"I take it Deegel is about to go down to zero," Lina said with some satisfaction.

"You can't be zero clearance and be a Legionnaire."

Lina considered that as she left the room.

They joined her fifteen minutes later as she lay on the couch listening to a smooth Jessye Belleval album. She sat up as they came in. "Is everything okay?"

"No, but there's nothing we can do about it right now." Jae headed toward the liquor cabinet. "I'm going to make something up," he said and paused. "Maybe some fruit juice instead."

"Me, too." Londo told him.

"I'll get it," Lina volunteered. "Oh. Problem."

Lon raised his eyebrows at her.

"I only know drinking water with the replicator."

"Still?" Jae asked.

"Ask the rep for *du jus de pamplemousse* or *jus d'orange,*" Lon told her.

"So what'll happen to her?" Lina asked when she returned with the grapefruit and orange juice from the food replicator. Why hadn't she thought about using French on it? "Kicked out or suspended?"

"Four times in five months…" Londo shook his head.

"More like a dozen or so, somewhere in that order of magnitude, for the past year," Lina told him as she set the glasses on the coffee table. "I got the impression that just lately she was afraid of getting caught and eased up."

"*Osti de tabarnak de calice.*" Londo sat down beside her and lay his head on her shoulder. She kissed what she could reach.

"We'll find them," Lon declared. "We'll find them all. Those reporters will be locked up for a long time, violating Legion security. God, she didn't even respect Aiko enough to wait a few days!"

"I suspect Aiko was the reason the reporter came around," Jae said as he joined them. "Unless it had something to do with your marriage, Lon, or with this Three Worlds business. That kind of publicity would certainly eclipse anything mere Legionnaire Neuron could come up with. She'd want to spin it her way." He sat next to Lina and touched the table in front of them. The television screen came up.

"Two-toned eyes," Jae mused. "Computer, is there a major news network with a male news reporter with two-toned eyes? Purple outer rings and… green interior? One who's given reports about Legion activities or Legionnaires, Neuron in particular."

"RealNewsToday," the bland computer voice replied.

"Stream it," Jae ordered.

They watched the realtime news channel as it ran through declarations of regret from planetary leaders throughout the Affiliated Systems and beyond as to Aiko's death. Subscreens included an in-depth obituary and her family's reaction. A renowned poet on her world had written an elegy that had gone viral. Several suicides had been blamed on grief for the hero's passing.

Stoan's announcement of Aiko's death to the media four days ago replayed with him looking so tired that Lina actually felt sorry for him. Once, the network projected a still of Lon's face beside Aiko's. They'd chosen smiling poses, placing the pictures so it looked like the two were looking at each other. Of course this report concerned the romantic link there, the rumors and the hopes. Then they went back to highlighting the monumental missions and triumphs of Aiko's career.

Finally the blue-skinned male news anchor, who didn't have two-toned eyes, faced the camera. "Unnamed, high-level sources have linked the death of Orenya to the Unaffiliated and Out-of-Sector World of Aldierra."

"Uh oh." Londo's head raised up at that. "Puter, record this part of the story and relay it to the commander." Two beeps acknowledged him.

The anchor went on. "Rumors persist of an attempted invasion of Sarastor itself by Aldierra, a warlike, overpopulated world insistent on increasing its scope by taking over the capital of the AffSys.

"Sources reveal that the Legion halted the invasion, but that Aldierra attempted to divert the major forces of that organization through sabotage of the giant hyperspace vessel *Travern*. While the majority of the Legion responded to that disaster, Aldierra's invasion fleet hoped to slip by planetary defenses. Luckily the remaining members of the Legion prevented that, but a legendary hero of our age has perished all the same. Officials at Sarastor Planetary Defense refused to comment on the rumors. Stay 'grammed for more on this story as it develops."

A beep toned in midair. "Go ahead," Londo said.

"Got it, Lon," came Stoan's voice.

"Lina says there've been about twelve or so reporters in the past year," Lon said.

"We'll be checking. I've seen security tapes—"

"Should I be listening to this?" Lina whispered.

"Lina's here," Londo told the air.

"All right. She already knows, doesn't she? Security tapes show Deegel receiving a male visitor with two-toned eyes this afternoon after the meeting was over. He wasn't wearing plaid."

"Ah. He is now," Lina said. There on the screen in front of them sat a smiling reporter with two-toned eyes talking about purely celebrity news in a pre-taped segment. The sound was low, but the plaid of his draped suit was loud.

"Grigach." Stoan said. Apparently he was watching, too. As footage of people flashed behind the reporter, one shot of Deegel remained onscreen as he spoke.

"Nichi said she'd been getting great publicity lately," Lon commented.

"Deegel's always gotten great publicity," Stoan rumbled. "I hope this smiley guy is getting a good night's sleep, because I sure am *kicking* not. He's going to get some visitors in a few minutes."

"Not me," Lon said. "We're sleeping in. Good night, Stoan. Starheart out."

He looked over at Jae. The blond Legionnaire was fast asleep on Lina's other shoulder.

"Maybe a couple of hours would do us good," Lon said. "We haven't gotten much rest lately."

"And there's been a lot happening," Lina said softly so only he could hear. "Londo Honeybear, what have you gotten us into?"

"Kitten, it's going to be the most exciting ride of our lives. And it's forever, love."

"Yes, Londo. I'll be sure to stock up on motion sickness pills tomorrow."

He gave a little snort at that and squeezed her arm. Then he turned serious. "Honest to god, Lina, you know everything now. I'll never lie to you, never keep anything from you… except if security demands it."

She nodded. "And I'll always trust you, Lon. I'll always have faith in us."

"You do that. I won't let you down." He looked at Jae there on her shoulder and got up, "Time to put him to bed."

She held out her hand to stop him from lifting Jae. "Here we go, Jae. Don't wake up." She ported them all to the bedroom and Lon pulled the sheets up over them. He glanced at the clock, did some calculations. "Puter, wake-up alarm in an hour and a half," he whispered. Two beeps answered him.

20

Lina watched the two of them well before the alarm would go off. Jae lay between them on his stomach, one arm over Lon's shoulders, the other over Lina's waist. She'd been awake for some time, thinking about the situation in her bed. Thinking about the song she had to come up with before tonight, a song that would be good enough. Thinking about the fact that she would have to sing before an audience the size of… No, don't think about that! Instead she considered these men once more and what they meant to her, what they needed.

Thinking about what she wanted, too.

Lon's eyes opened slowly and he gazed at Jae for a long time lying there beside him before he met Lina's eyes. She gave him a helpless look and shook her head at him. He laughed soundlessly, his eyes crinkling in that way he had.

She started to ease herself out of bed, slipping under Jae's arm when his hand tightened on her. "Not so fast," he murmured.

"If you don't mind," she said, "I'd like to go to the bathroom."

He pulled on the tie– they were all still in their robes– wrapping it around his fist. "You'll come back?"

"I was also thinking of breakfast. In fact, I insist on it."

"We can discuss that when you come back," Lon told her.

"Yes, massa Lon." Lina got out of bed when Jae released her.

"I am not a dictator."

They were lying there stroking each other and talking softly when she returned. Londo patted the bed beside himself. "We should figure all this out right now," he said sternly. "Before breakfast. We've got a big day ahead and we need to get through this."

"The entire thing?" Jae asked.

"Is torture permitted in Legion Headquarters?" Lina asked. "Starving prisoners until they do as they're told?"

"Come, Lina." Lon patted the bed again. "Be a good girl."

Lina sat next to Jae instead. "At Deegel's– Was that the normal way around here of doing things? Orgies every night? Should I have been embarrassed?"

"Absolutely," Jae said as he slid his arm around her to pull her closer.

"The blushing virginal bride intruding upon a den of iniquity," Lon said. "You played your part well. Damn Deegel to hell and back. A traitor and scandal at this time."

"They'd better have found a substitute for her for Honor Guard duty," Jae muttered darkly. "If I saw her parading herself out there I might strangle her."

Lina ran her tongue across her upper lip. "She said she had something she could blackmail you with, Lon."

Lon frowned and shook his head. "Anything she says now won't hold anyone's attention. She'll claim anything she can to save herself."

"What if you came out with it first?" Lina asked.

Londo looked at her sharply. "No."

"Why not?"

Now his frown was directed at her. "You've jumped," he accused.

"I believe someone pushed me last night," she said but nodded all the same. "Now I've landed. I'm committed all the way, ready to pack up and follow you two wherever you go. Why can't we go public? According to Jae, this is perfectly legit."

"But people will say–"

"Who cares what people will say?" Lina slapped her hand on the mattress. "They're *them* and we're *us*. We do what's right for us, not what *they* think we should do. I won't have other people deciding my life for me. I haven't enforced that rule very well up to now, but from now out I will live by it. If we do this legally, we should stand up straight and do it proud."

"And what if we don't do it legally?" Jae asked.

Lina gave him a dark look but he blinked at her innocently.

Londo said, "I've been trying to imagine how people would take to the concept of dual-triune. People here, people on Earth. No, it's got to be kept secret or as a last-minute contingency before a baby."

"The other day Erik explained about prostitute and slave three-way marriages. They're legal."

Jae nodded. "Polygamy is legal on more than a few worlds in the AffSys, and the Systems honor the legalities, but it's more a possessive," and here he looked hard at Londo, "kind of estate, with at least one of the partners being viewed as chattel, either as a slave or as a paid prostitute.

"Feithi dual-triune wasn't that way at all. It was an honorable, *committed,*" and here he returned Lina's dark look to her, "partnership. I think that after the surprise died down, the Legion would react well to finding out if we went dual-triune, as long as we stressed that it was Feithi." His tongue worked inside his cheek. "Maybe."

Lon rubbed his nose and then his chin, deep in thought. "Maybe," he said. "And then some people were pretty scandalized when they realized that Lina and I had signed up for life."

"Swell," Lina drawled. "If we do it, it has to be secret. That's so unfair to the secret tertiary." She covered Jae's hand with hers. "Jae said he might be the tertiary."

"If the tertiary knew what he was getting into in the first place he might be completely willing," Jae said to the wall.

"You said the tertiary was free to take other partners," Lon said. "How free? Would you be going out with people on a regular basis? And, well, how far would you be going with them?"

Lina asked, "Do you agree that Jae would be the tertiary? Or do we flip a coin?"

"No, we do not flip a coin." Rolling his eyes, Lon shook his head at Jae and Jae did the same at him.

"Okay, so what about STDs?" Lina wanted to know. "I read that there's no communicable disease on Sarastor, but on Earth one in five people have an STD."

"*Vraiment?*" Lon sucked in a breath of astonishment.

Lina nodded. "How are we going to know you've been having safe sex?" she demanded of Jae.

"Wait a minute, wait a minute." Jae waved them down. "Just because the tertiary has more leeway, that doesn't mean that there's casual sex involved. The tertiary does make a commitment to the primaries." He scowled at Lina. "You think I'm promiscuous."

"You said your hobby was sex."

"You can enjoy something without being wanton about it."

"Okay, Lina, Jae's not going to be coming home with a new lover every night."

Jae was suddenly quite serious. "You two don't understand yet. You need to find out what the dual-triune was. What marriage is supposed to be." He waved his right hand in circles to take in Legion HQ, all of Sarastor. "It's not like what *these people* do, not at all."

Lon placed his hand on top of Jae's arm. "I think Lina and I had a hard lesson on that two days ago. We weren't ready before. But we know now." He squeezed Jae and Jae nodded.

"We all need time to think about this. I can't just… charge into this like you two did. I," Jae swallowed, "I need time."

"At last something sensible," Lina declared. "We all need time. And we need to find out lots of stuff, cultural and personal and who cleans the toilets and who balances the checkbook. But at some point– soon– we need to figure out this Three Worlds deal," she told them. "I mean, day before yesterday there *was* this big Investiture thingie. Twenty billion people on Aldierra…"

"We'll start on that today," Lon said. He turned over so he could see the clock: 400 hours, before dawn. "I don't know about you, but I'm awake for the day. Anyone want to get started now? We can take naps later. It's going to be a long time before we can hit the sack tonight."

"Breakfast first," Lina said promptly. "I'm starving."

When their orders arrived, Jae looked at Londo's plate and turned up his nose.

"It's catching all right," he announced.

"What is?" Londo dug into his meal of sausage, bacon and eggs. He'd chosen one of his favorite spots, which he'd known would be almost deserted this early. They were all dressed in tee shirts, jeans and jackets, but the staff had still recognized him and honored his request for a booth in the back.

"I've always been a vegetarian by choice. But now I can feel it." Jae pointed at the entree.

Lon looked from Jae to Lina. "Murdered pig vibes," Lina explained. "Enjoy it while you can, Lon. Take some and cook it for the chefs at the Pares Restaurant so they can synthesize it later. You're next."

"What, you think I'm going to become a vegetarian?"

"My bet's on within three weeks," Jae told Lina.

"I'll give him six," Lina said. "He's going to fight this one hard."

"And I say never," Lon declared. "I can see it now: the three of us at the nursing home, and you two choking down your gruel while I enjoy a nice, thick steak."

"There's a picture," Jae said sourly.

Lina poured more maple syrup onto her waffle, since she had exercised so hard this past night and thus could afford the delicious calories. The restaurant windows next to their table looked out onto San Francisco's famous bay. "Starfleet Academy is here, you know, to be founded about a hundred fifty years from now."

Londo closed his eyes in pain. "You've been to Sarastor and all you can talk about is *Star Trek?*"

"What can I say? I'm one sick obsessed fanatic.

"Okay, I'll change the subject. Did you two find something useful in all that literature last night?" Lina asked hopefully.

Londo nibbled in a slightly obscene way on a piece of bacon. "It was pretty general. We got some questions answered, like looking around for the tertiary. We did it correctly. Both spouses agree on a sexual tryout. Of course, they didn't say how many times you could audition the applicant and still remain proper." He bumped against Jae under the table, and Jae laughed.

"I remain open to be bribed through whatever means," he said.

Lina asked, "But was there anything about keeping secrets?"

Jae shook his head. "Not a word. We shouldn't have expected any. The dual-triune was quite legal and in fact the usual mode of marriage. Why should anyone hide that?"

"For the same reason they hide some marriages on Earth," Londo said. "Politics, parental disapproval…"

Jae speared a biscuit with his fork. "I'll keep looking for something along those lines."

"Maybe we'll just have to play it by ear, see how it goes," Londo said. "Adjust things if we need to."

Lina took Jae's biscuit from him, sliced it and buttered it. "Maybe even come out and make it public," she said.

Londo's lips pressed together hard but he didn't say anything.

Lina spooned some jam onto half of Jae's biscuit so he could try it both ways. "Use your hands for things like side breads," she instructed as she returned it to him. "And that is, if we decide to do it," she amended to the dual-triune conversation.

Jae bit into the barbarian concoction, considered, and nodded. "I am getting curious about how Admiral Bracken and his crew are really taking the idea." His cheeks puffed as he played with the thought. Then he said, "I can get better information on the trip. It's three days to Aldierra, even at Level 3."

"One hell of a long way," Londo mused. "It's going to be lonely without you. It always is."

He looked up as a group of loud, laughing young men came into the restaurant. Dressed in leather and neon colors, their costumes were as odd as Sarastoran clothing. Two definite couples made themselves known by the way they wrapped their arms around each other. No one else in the place gave them a second glance.

Londo scowled to himself.

Lina told Jae, "At least I can port you back here when you're done there."

"Thanks, but no," Jae said slowly. "Hyperspace is pretty private. I was going to use the travel time to Earth to think. Make a few decisions."

"Sure," Londo said too quickly, letting Jae have his time. "We'll contact you on Aldierra and you can give Lina a picture so we can go there while you're still in hyperspace and introduce ourselves, too. We can start on our daily rounds, get a schedule roughed in, make more contacts. Before that Lina and I can get started here on Earzth with basics. I have to introduce her to Hal–"

"Oh god," Lina moaned.

"*Non,* I told you to call him Hal," Londo said sternly. "And to the ParaNet as well. I need to meet your family–"

"Heaven help us all," Lina moaned again.

"And set up Starhaven for the three of us." Londo pointed at Jae. "The three of us. Even without the dual-triune, you're going to be spending a lot of time on Earth from now on. You'll stay at Starhaven."

The staff didn't mind that they lingered so long. They cleared off breakfast dishes and set them up with drinks as the two Legionnaires set up a series of holoscreens to float around themselves. As morning progressed, the restaurant began to fill to capacity, but the staff kept their corner clear.

Lon set up their schedules for the day, deleting many items that had been there already. "I need to polish the eulogy. That'll take two hours, maybe more. I don't like what I have, but L-PIC may have made some good suggestions. Flight rehearsal's at, when? Thirteen, and then after fifteen-fifty the night is filled with…" He didn't finish his sentence as he frowned to himself.

Jae adjusted his to-do list, and Lina reminded them that she had to sing a proper funeral song that hadn't even been found yet. Lon added those preparations to the schedules, then finalized them.

Now Lina took official notes on her padd as they tried to figure out what they had been instructed to do. Jae told them about Feith and how its people had lived as caretakers of that world.

"I think Feith should be the blueprint for our final goal."

"Wait," Lina said. "Shouldn't we take different cultures into account? Feith sounds wonderful, but is it really the best for the Three Worlds? I think we should have separate goals for all three that play to their individual cultures. Sarastor is a capital world. I don't think Feith would have been a good capital."

"But Sarastor doesn't really have a culture," Jae said. "It's like a blank slate. We can superimpose Feithi culture on it."

Lina made a rude noise.

"Marge Simpson," Lon approved. "I didn't know you did impressions. And Jae, that's a good impression of God you're doing there. How will the Sarastorans react to becoming Feithi? They don't even know how to be good Sarastorans."

"Somewhere on that planet is some kind of aboriginal culture," Lina told them. "You two have just been holed up in HQ. You haven't found it yet."

Lon popped two raisins into his mouth from a muffin the staff had left. "*D'accord,*" he said. "You find it, you present it to us, and we'll consider it. It can't be worse than what they have now."

"How very liberal of you. But yes, I don't see why we can't mix a liberal dose of Feithi ideas in on all three planets."

Jae spread his hands, framing the four screens of Aldierran information they already had open in the air, "So we set our goals and figure steps on how to get there. *Skurn,* I wish we knew more about Aldierra. Bracken's downloaded some files, but they aren't nearly enough. I'll see that we get lots more as soon as possible, even if I have to steal them. We need everything they've got."

Londo pointed at a screen that showed the globe of Aldierra. The interior of one continent held a large, black sea without an outlet. "I want to know what that is," he said. "That bothers me."

Jae continued, "What we need are big goals, lofty goals. Let's get out there and poll people's opinions."

"*Oui,* sounds good. I like big goals."

"Small goals," Lina countered. "Baby steps to the big ones, so people can check them off, see they're making progress."

Both Jae and Lon made agreeable noises at that, so Lina added, "For the first stage we should aim for the basics. Let's divide this into at least two parts. No, three."

"Which are–?" Lon hiked an eyebrow at her.

"Stage one: seeing Aldierra safely through her deadline with no casualties incurred."

"Of course," Jae said. "We concentrate wholly on Aldierra until then."

"*Oui.*" Lon nodded at the two of them. "Accepted. Stage two?"

"Basic human needs and rights provided for on all the worlds. We use that pyramid chart, that thing, that…"

"Ah… Maslow's hierarchy of needs?" Londo blinked, surprised that he'd remembered the term.

"That's the one." At Jae's inquiring expression, Lina said, "The base level of that chart is things like food, shelter…"

Londo brought up an image of the pyramid on another screen and read off it. "Breathing, food, water, sex, sleep, homeostasis–"

"I'll have to look that up," Lina said.

"–Excretion. Okay. Healthy environment, political stability, basic physical needs provided for. Terrans have been trying to do this for years, *chérie*. What we need are these big goals to get them excited."

Jae checked out the next level. "Security. Health needs. I can see that as well. Big enough goals right there."

"What's the matter with a little spectacle?"

Lina tapped her teaspoon against her husband's arm. "People can't get excited when they're cold and starving and dying. When you don't have enough for yourself, you have this survival imperative going on. People are more than happy to look around themselves when they feel comfortable with what they've got. They'll help others. People naturally want to help. Survival and fear get in the way of that instinct."

"So we get them comfortable and they start to help each other. It makes our job easier." Jae copied the pyramid image to his own personal screen.

"Exactly. That's where stage three comes in, the lofty goals."

"Timeline?" Lon asked.

"I don't know. You guys do some thinking for a change."

Jae threw a stylus at the exact center of a pie chart suspended in a screen. It zipped straight through the immaterial colors and Londo caught it on the other side. "I can see where we can't get around having stage one, and where we probably need stage two in and of itself," Jae said. "But I want to get the people on all Three Worlds excited right away. That's where Lon's big goal comes in."

"Living through all this should be exciting enough for the Aldierrans," Lina put in.

"Granted. But I want all the people we've been assigned to look forward to the completed process, to be excited about the future. I want something that will unite their thinking, make the Three Worlds one big family working together. How do we do that?"

"*Bon ben,* we don't have to come up with everything today." Lon rubbed his sticky fingers into his napkin and picked up a notepadd. "I'll just make a note to come up with some kind of spectacular whatever, and we can all think about it."

He held out his hand to accept the check he'd signaled for, and then began to dig into his pocket for his wallet. "Thanks. Okay. We know that Jae's got to do the preliminary work on Aldierra. We'll join in as soon as they'll let us. Maybe sooner."

Non-essential Legion duties had to be scrapped. L-PIC had to be alerted as to their changed work schedules. Jae suggested that the Legion declare that Sarastor couldn't involve them in any glorified busywork for the next nine months. Such busywork could make up a significant day's routine when a Legionnaire was assigned to Sarastor duty.

"If we can make that pertain to the entire Legion in the next meeting, it'll pass," Jae said.

"Hell, they'll shower us with undying gratitude. It's about time we did something about that." The two Legionnaires chuckled with evil glee. Lon leaned back to imagine the two of them being carried in triumph on the shoulders of their fellow members.

Lina brought up her own thoughts while he was in Fantasy Land. "We're going to need one hell of a big organization for this. It's going to involve lots of people."

"Small teams," Jae countered.

"Individual action," Lon piped in. "We just get up there and set an example and people follow us. Lots of publicity will do it."

Jae shook his head. "No. It's going to take teams tracking down trouble and fixing it."

Lina made the sound of a game show buzzer. "Both wrong answers. Tell the contestants what they've lost, Mr. Announcer." The two of them looked at her blankly.

"Thirty-plus billion people total; twenty billion on Aldierra," she said. "That's just the humans involved. How many animals, how many rivers, how many dumping grounds?

"We've got an entire planet of people that's willing to kill everyone on another world so they can run from their problem, another planet where people are too busy fighting with each other over money and scrabbling for survival and ignoring global climate change to get anything done, and another planet where people just sit around and expect others to run their lives for them. Or at least that's the message I've gotten these past few days.

"These are not people who are going to wake up one day and say, 'Hey, I want to be just like them! I want to do what they're doing and change the world!' And everything becomes peaches and cream cheese."

Lon scowled. "I like working alone."

"You also like to be team leader," Jae poked him. "I like working on teams, too, small teams."

"Plenty of room for teams and individuals in this organization," Lina nodded encouragingly. "But there's going to be more to it than that. Communications– that's got to be our first step, even before sociological surveys. We won't know what needs to be fixed if people can't tell us."

Her husband turned his head to give her a level look. "My answering machine can't handle over ten billion calls." He grunted and sat up, stretching in place. Jae began gathering up their card-sized padds, the screens clicking off one by one. "So we get a lot of operators. How many can cover thirty billion? Maybe the entire population of, of…" Lon tried to think of a country just the right size.

"We'll need to research how organizations do it. Police. Ah, the Legion and ParaNet. Will they let me research them?" Lina asked. "How's my security clearance?"

"We'll need to turn it all into a lean, mean fightin' machine." Lon massaged his head wearily. "This is beginning to sound like work to me, urgh." He nodded as the waiter returned with his card, and signed off on the bill. Hovering to gather the table's detritus, the waiter took a look at Lon's figures and for a moment, seemed about to faint.

"For giving us privacy," Lon assured him. "See if you can spread some of that around. Good food. I wanted to impress my guests."

"Yessir, Valiant. Thank *you!* Thanks! Come back anytime."

Back on Sarastor, Londo checked his messages for word from his father. Still nothing. He settled to working on his eulogy while Jae discussed his Aldierran trip with AffSys officials behind a privacy screen, and Lina searched through her padd for more Feenish funeral songs.

She wanted one that would allow her to plug in Aiko's name, *à la* "Candle in the Wind." It didn't seem enough to honor the heroine. With one selection as bad as the next in this respect, she decided to work with her top five previous selections. They were all magnificent music. Maybe no one would notice that the words were generic or pointed at someone else in Feenish history. After a while Jae slid over to help her puzzle it out.

The murmur from Lon's office as he tried out parts of his speech out loud almost lulled Lina to sleep. She looked up to see Lon rubbing his head tiredly in front of his computer. Jae left Lina's side to settle next to him. Lon told him what he'd been trying to say, and Jae recounted a story of Aiko. Lon nodded and told another.

The two men had been so close to Aiko. They excluded Lina from this small wake but still she was grateful that she didn't know the heroine. She wouldn't have been able to take a friend's death on top of everything else.

Jae got a drink. Londo cleared a spot for it– by sliding everything in the area off onto the floor. Immediately the kol-vanasche oozed out of its storage area to attend to the mess. The crystalline pancake slithered around the area. Parts of it broke off to wrap themselves around the discards, then dragged them up surfaces to form artful arrangements on other pieces of furniture.

Lon dropped two printed books he was through with onto the floor and within ninety seconds they'd been replaced neatly onto the room's bookshelves.

Lina remembered that the Bolt had teased Londo about the condition of his apartment in Montreal. It had never occurred to her that her husband might be a slob. When they went to Earth with no kol-vanaschen in sight, who would he expect to do all the straightening?

Who would clean the toilets? Who would balance the checkbook? They still had so much to talk about. All three of them now. Well, that was not Goal A. First things first.

The work on the eulogy went on. Lon had told Lina how he couldn't dictate his writing. He had to type or write, and feel the words he created coming out of his fingers. Holding his coffee in one hand, Lon tapped with the other as he sipped and then returned to two hands when he set the cup down. Jae murmured a helpful thought and Londo nodded.

Jae took another swallow from his own glass, which definitely didn't contain anything like coffee. Alcohol, this early? He tried to smile at Londo, holding a brave front, but Lina knew that Lon could see as easily as she that the impact of Aiko's death wore heavily on Jae's spirit.

Dissatisfied with what he'd written, Lon took a typing break. He decided to cruise the interstellar internet and look for memorable eulogies of the past, see how others had written about history's notables. Screens scrolled down around him running talking-heads videos and text.

Jae ducked out under the screens. He stood and stretched, then pulled his hands down his face. When he saw Lina watching him, he came to her.

"Come with me, Sweet," he told her.

She spread her arms to show off her music. "I have to figure out–"

He brushed her hair with his hand, his fingers combing through it, before he whispered into her ear, "Taking a break will clear your mind. And mine."

With a simple brush of his fingertips, he stirred every cell, every nerve along her arm. She couldn't think when he did that. His movements hypnotized her, heated her from within.

Even so, she had important work to do. "Can this wait?" she asked.

"Please." There was a frightening urgency in his mind.

"I– Are you sure? It would have to be quick. Londo?"

Londo didn't look around at them, but he'd heard. His shoulders hunched.

"Lon?"

His shoulders twitched before he waved a hand of permission at them over his shoulder.

Jae needed her. The universe was overwhelming him again, and the only control he could exert was in this. It was in no way romantic, but Lina couldn't stop the tumult of matching lust that swept through her like a whirlwind when Jae took her into his arms. Jae was solid, real and warm. He loved her. He wanted her. Lina lost herself in the wonder, the excitement and the intimacy of him.

Afterward it was she who led Jae deeper into her mind. He reached and she let him touch whatever parts of her he needed– but she guided him to what she thought he should choose.

He lay beside her as she stroked his body, soothing him. "It all starts to make sense," he whispered to her.

"Does it?"

"The universe isn't as immutable when I'm with you," he said.

"Is that good?"

"When we're together I think that maybe the future has yet to be written. Maybe it doesn't have to turn out bad." He nestled his head under her chin and wrapped his arms around her.

"You done?"

They both looked up to see Londo in the doorway. How long had he been standing there watching?

Lon strode towards the bed, pulling his shirt out of his pants. "Sorry, Jae," he said. "My bed; my turn. Is that okay?" he asked Lina.

Jae slid out of bed but didn't bother to get dressed. He took a seat on the far side of the room as Lon unfastened the rest of his clothing.

In front of Jae? Lina swallowed. "Lon?" But his face was as tight with tension as she had ever seen it.

"Help me with these." Lon indicated the straps on his boots to her as he finagled the ones at his wrists. "Please."

Men could be so strong on the outside and so fragile and confused within! Lina only hesitated a moment before she threw the sheet off her naked self and knelt beside Londo. The boots didn't pull; they peeled. She reached for Londo's waistband, still kneeling, and pulled his clothing down. He groaned as she took him, then wrapped her hair around his palm and guided her to the rhythm he wanted.

How strange to feel Londo searching for the same control Jae had. Maybe all men tried to make sense of the world through sex. This was not the time to be on top, not the time to ask for herself. Sometimes Londo felt even more lost than Jae.

When he lifted her up to the bed, Lina made sure that Lon knew how much she trusted him, how much man she realized he was. And oh, he was. She allowed him to proceed at his own pace and cried out his name when he concentrated on pleasuring her as well.

Afterwards, too, she let him reach for what he wanted within her mind. He knew her now. He knew where to search. He also knew what she needed from him and gave it: love and lust and respect and safety…

"Yes. Now," he murmured.

Lina didn't know what he meant until she felt Jae slide into bed behind her.

She should protest. She should say something. But she'd just made love to the two men in the entire universe she trusted. The two men who ran the "hot" meter all the way up to its limit and beyond.

The hairs all over her body stood on end in anticipation. Her heart began to pound.

Jae touched her. His mind expanded hers and Londo's so that the dual-feedback became a triple one. As Jae entered her, Londo fondled her body, then began to kiss and lick her, alternating with tiny, exciting bites. He whispered such sweet complements to her, as if she were the supreme empress of love and beauty.

His tongue was… His penis was… His hands– Oh dear, his pinky–

"Easy, Lon," Jae warned, and someone backed off.

"She can take it," Lon said. "You can take it, *chérie,* can't you? You can do it over and over."

They started up again and Lina's senses spun. Sensation congealed to a center and then tightened–

"Hold on, Jae!"

Lina arched and gasped. She mewled like a cat and then squealed.

"Easy. Easy!"

Jae searched for the larger orgasm he sensed lurking just beyond where they were.

"Not yet," Londo cautioned. "Different set of gears here. Three riding in this car, not two." He patted Jae's hip sharply. "Let me drive."

Jae released her. Londo pulled her up to all fours. Jae knelt in front of her while Londo took her from behind.

"Different strategy," he told them. "We stay at a lower level but spread out farther."

Lina dizzily swirled in an ocean of sensation and hot flesh. She trusted Jae and Londo implicitly. This time both their attentions were turned on her and what would please her, which she clearly laid out for them.

But what did they want? This was tricky, coordinating three at once…

"Oh yeah," Jae sighed from above her head.

"Go easy on him, Lie," Londo told her. An intake of breath followed by the slightest of chuckles told him that he appreciated what she was doing for him as well.

Their minds meshed with teamwork. When the whirlpool began to spin deep within Lina, Londo told his team, **Now. Go for it!****

Fireworks and earthquakes! Thunder and tsunamis crashing! Lina catapulted out of her body into the sky, still enmeshed in the minds of her two lovers. She screamed something that was both their names in one. Londo howled like an animal. Jae shouted unintelligibly.

Then they clawed their way up to the pillows, where they sprawled upon each other, spent.

Their skin vibrated softly to their caresses, warm and sweaty under moist lips. Contentment and love rolled off them to wash over the others and return anew. Their minds intertwined softly, the light streaming through them in patterns and colors and song.

This was not the sharing of two minds, where you could compare and contrast. This was three minds balancing, steadying each other. Londo's strength, Lina's connection, Jae's understanding. In the world Londo held them safe. Jae reached to the universe's center. And Lina stood between them as a lifeline and reality that would never allow either to break away or hurt themselves.

They were one.

They lay there tangled in each other's bodies and minds.

"*Mon dieu.*" Londo was the first to open his eyes. "We've got to do that again sometime. Maybe in six months."

Jae kissed his forehead, brushing his hair back from his face. Their lips met as they lay so close, embracing, with another body pressed up behind Jae, her arms around both of them.

Lon raised up to look at her, her head nestled against the back of Jae's hair, and a lazy smile played upon her lips. Her eyes opened and met his.

He gave her a small grin. **Give us a kiss, Kitten.**

She rose up and kissed him quite thoroughly.

"When I ask for a kiss, that's exactly the way I want it," he sighed.

"Yes, Commander," she said. She put her arms around Jae's neck and leaned around to kiss him much the same way.

This felt so right to Lina, not perverted or queer or anything. After all, the universe was love. Love, love, love… With a lot of joy blended in. She'd been off-balance all her life and never known it, but everything was all right now.

No longer Lina Muttbutt at all, but something new: Carolina Starhart.

She wanted to lie here in the arms of her lovers all day and–

"Oh!" she cried and sat up.

"I tell you, she just keeps coming and coming." Lon nudged Jae.

"No, silly. Someone wrote an elegy for Aiko. Remember? It was on the news. Can I get permission to use it? If it's got meter, I can match an old song to paste it into. There's got to be one somewhere. Maybe even one with orchestration. If I'm lucky it'll fit one of my top five." She scrambled to find her robe and dash to the living room.

"And she's off," Londo said. He threw the sheet off himself and swung around to get out of bed. "I need to be up and about. I know where I went wrong.

Maudit niaiseux, it seems obvious now. All I needed was…" He paused only a moment to grab his wrap before running off to the living room and his computer keyboard.

Jae eased up and rubbed his head. "Huh. I can help with the song," he called as he squinted at the clock. He joined the two in the hallway. "I met that Feenish poet not long ago. Don't know why I didn't think of it before. I saw the viral performance yesterday. It's got meter. Music would make it even better. Get your song library, Lina, and I'll set up the communications. We've still got time to do it all justice."

21

Lon's eulogy for Aiko made Lina cry as he practiced it in front of the two of them. Jae could only offer improvements as to his delivery, not the language or sentiment.

And although it was kind of embarrassing singing to just the two of them, after six full run-throughs accompanying orchestration recorded 350 years before, they pronounced her song ready to go.

Jae added, "Nice touch, resurrecting ancient Feenish music. The heritage factor takes away the 'offense' of singing."

Even so, the poet who'd produced the elegy had been upset that her now-famous work was being set to music. Having the Last Feithi on the line helped, and the woman had even adjusted her verse to fit the bridge of the music. By the end of the process, she'd been smiling. "I'd wanted to add in that part," she admitted of some lines that hadn't made the final cut of her finished poem but had fit the music. "I couldn't figure where it should go." She'd approved the repetition that came with having a chorus, especially since those were her best lines.

After Jae left to meet with his team, Lina learned about some of those spare costumes in Londo's closet. A few had odd color schemes, and he chose one of stark black and white. There was no trace of the subtle blue or violet in the charcoal striping of his shirt. It was now shiny white stripes on flat white. A closer-fitted black vest seemed much more formal than the usual.

"Black and white are the colors of mourning here," Londo explained to Lina. "Absolutely no extraneous colors. Sometimes people even use black or white makeup to cover up their skin tones. Others use a personal desaturation filter to eliminate any color on their bodies besides black, white or gray. We don't need to go that far. You get a black and white dress and use muted makeup, you'll be fine."

"Do I have to run the dress by anyone?"

He considered. "Make sure you use tights and sleeves. Otherwise, we'll let PR see it at rehearsal. There'll be time for changes, if needed."

The Comm called for more team ports. Lina went by herself as Lon finished getting ready for his own team meeting.

"Come on, it's not that bad," Eila, aka Stormshock, chided the latest team to port in to Comm. They had arrived paler than they'd left, and two of them were holding hands.

Eila told Lina that fifteen more were scrambling to get back in time for the funeral.

"Please have some stims standing by," Lina warned her. "I'll do as many as I can."

The group jogged off to debriefing as Jae strolled into the room, dressed in black tights and long-sleeved white tunic not his uniform but still in homage to the day. "All done?" he asked. Londo entered behind him.

"One individual to go," Eila said, switching screens.

"Morning, Chimrin," Jae addressed the screen.

The blue-tinged woman dressed in green and golden spandex looked tired. With an out-of-breath heave, she plunked her duffel bag on the ground next to herself as if she'd just gotten there. She smoothed her short, pastel-green hair into a semblance of order.

"Rough mission." Jae made it a statement.

"Bad enough." She gave a wan smile. "But everything's patched up here as best I could do. They hurried the talks through as soon as the news about Aiko came out. I missed the meeting the other day, but I hear we have an interstellar teleporter available." She shook her head at them. "Londo and Jae both smiling. I hope Headquarters is still standing."

Eila clicked two items off her console. "Next time, check in periodically," she told Chimrin confidentially. "I don't care what kind of security cloak they have you under. These guys have been up to no good, Londo especially. You've missed a lot."

Chimrin's gaze moved to Londo appraisingly. "That sounds ominous." Her gaze slid to take in Lina. "You're the teleporter?"

Londo stepped forward. "Chimrin Dinar, meet my wife, Lina Starheart, resident interstellar teleporter."

After a noticeable start, Chimrin looked at Lina curiously but in a friendly way, glancing back and forth at the two of them. Lina could clearly see The Question– do they have sex? How?– in her eyes, but she was too polite to speak it out loud.

"Wife," she repeated. "Londo Rand, married? Ah, nice to meet you, Mrs. Valiant."

"Just Lina. Cab driver to the stars," Lina said. "You're the Legion's telepath, right?"

"I'm a telepath."

"I've been hearing so much about 'wait until Chimrin's back' this and 'wait until Chimrin's back' that. You're kind of far away, aren't you?"

"You can't tell? How will you teleport me if you can't tell where I am?" Chimrin turned to Eila. "You're not joking, are you? I mean, real interstellar transport?"

But Lina answered. "I don't teleport through space. At least I don't think so. Wiley's running some tests to find out how I do it. He was trying to convince me to port as far as I could, but that's hard to do if I don't have a reference point. Would you be willing to stand in for me on this? As long as you're already out there, I mean."

Chimrin looked skeptical. "What do I have to do?"

Lina searched in her mind for the bracelet that she had since taken off, and found it. "Just wear this as I port you. It will send telemetry to Wiley. Is he here now? I think he needs to set it up each time."

Eila did something to her board and a smaller screen came up on the side of the room. Wilder rose from the couch in the lab, rubbing his short violet hair so it stood on end. "What is it?" he demanded irritably. "This was going to be the first good nap I've managed in six days or more."

He saw that Lina was standing in the monitor room, could see Chimrin's face on the screen behind her. "Lina! Admiral Bracken was asking for you. You're going to have to make an appearance for him someday today, funeral or no funeral."

"Who's this Admiral?" Chimrin asked.

Lina said, "We saw him yesterday, and we've already planned to go again tonight. Wiley, we've got Chimrin coming through, and I think she's pretty far out. I'd like to give her your bracelet to wear so you can catch the information."

"Good idea. Chim, you're where? The Searchor System?"

"Yes."

"Oh, excellent. Excellent." Wiley turned to Lina on screen. "That's about five days' journey by hyperspace. Can you reach that far?"

"It feels to me like the same distance as everything else," Lina said.

Wiley rolled his eyes, but in different directions. "Somehow I knew you were going to say that. Give me a moment to set up, and that way I can get data from the bracelet going and coming." He went over to his console and fiddled with it a moment. "Ready," he told them.

Lina ported the bracelet to Chimrin, wherever she was.

"Give it two minutes," Wiley told Chimrin as Lina concentrated.

The bracelet appeared on Chimrin's wrist in under that time and she gave a little start. Lina let out her breath, and concentrated again. "Incoming," she warned the people in the room. On screen, Chimrin disappeared. After a long silence no one in the room broke, she reappeared in the room, duffel bag next to her feet.

Chimrin looked around, blinking. "Wow," she said. "That's a nice timesaver. Spooky, though. But there's no post-hyperspace feedback."

"So that's what it is," Lon told Lina privately. "I always wondered what she meant with that."

Chimrin was still musing. "Maybe I was more concerned with when it was going to end."

Jae chimed in, "It seems about five times as long as it actually takes. You get used to it after a while."

Wiley examined his preliminary data. "And it's just what I suspected, too. It took exactly the same amount of time to bring her in from that distance as it took for all your other singleton interstellar porting." He looked up at Lina. "I'll figure this out. Eventually."

"I know you will." She wrinkled her nose at him.

Wilder pointed at her. "Meet with the admiral. Today."

"Yessir," she said dutifully. She saw the curious glance he gave both her and Londo, clearly asking if they'd gotten over their argument. She put her arm around Lon's waist and nodded at Wiley. He gave her the smallest of nods in return.

"Chim," he said, "I want to run a scan of you, see if distance makes any difference in RNA-activants."

"Brügz, Dellen and Erik got back yesterday," Lina told Wiley.

"I haven't had time to get to them yet, but I will figure this out!" The screen with his face on it blanked.

"What's this about–?" Chimrin asked Londo, and then stared at him, holding up her hand for silence. She looked at Jae, then at Lina. Finally at Eila.

"Well, you're not one," she declared to the copper-haired woman.

"One what?"

"Telepath. I thought for a moment that everyone here had gone telepath on me."

"Just me and Londo," Jae replied cheerily. "Lina's always been one."

"You've missed a few things while you've been gone," Londo said.

"Evidently. Including the story of how Aiko died. Blood's ice; blood's freezing ice, I still can't believe– How did–? Oh, I'll listen to the debriefing so you don't have to go through it again. When?"

"This evening. Ceremony begins at fifteen-fifty, flight rehearsal at thirteen."

"I can get some sleep before that, then. Shards, Aiko." Chimrin shook her head and started to leave.

"Um," Lina started to say, not sure if she should interrupt, but Chimrin turned back to her. "I think that Stoan will want to talk to you as soon as you can make it."

Chimrin's eyebrows went up questioningly, but she nodded and turned again to leave.

"Just a second if you would," Londo said. "I've been meaning to ask you, Chim. Lina, Chimrin's been to the top telepath institutions on Tishan. Did they ever say anything about spirit guides? Guardian angels?"

Chimrin looked at Londo as if he were crazy. "Spirit guides? You mean as in hoodoo? Casting charms? Faerie tales?"

"No," Lina said. "As in that group standing around you right now, shaking their heads at you. How do you train in telepathy without getting into guides and angels?"

Jae watched the interplay curiously.

"This is a little primitive to me," Chimrin said. "But then, you must be from Earth, aren't you? That would explain that."

"But it wouldn't explain Feith," Jae said. "Why can I see them, too? Feithis consulted their guides all the time."

Chimrin almost said something, but decided against it. "You were a child when Feith was destroyed," she finally said. "You brought your child's imagination with you."

"That doesn't explain me actually talking to a deva the other day," Londo said. "We convinced him to make us a thunderstorm as a diversion. And check the records, Chimrin. We got Aiko's… ghost… on record day before yesterday. Everyone saw her."

And yet Lon silently told Lina, **I told you so. No guides. None for her, at least.**

She's got 'em by the score, Lina said. **All the people here that I've met have lots and lots of guides and guardians.**

We need all we can get, Jae said. **Legionnaires are in danger more than most people.**

I don't believe any of this guardian business, Chimrin joined their mental conversation. **But I don't believe that you two have become telepaths, either,** she said to Lon and Jae. **And powerful ones. You need training.**

No we don't, Lon said. **If we feel the need, we'll get it. But we're doing fine.**

"I'll be teaching them how to channel soon," Lina told Chimrin. "And probably Wiley as well; he's interested. You're welcome to join us if you want to see if there's something there that you can connect to. Or you could disprove it for yourself."

"Wilder isn't a telepath, is he? Has he become one, too? Great orb protect us all!"

Lina could understand her consternation. "No. But you don't have to be a telepath to channel. Some of the best channelers aren't, as a matter of fact."

"I'll think about it," Chimrin said and paused. "But first, the four of us need to go somewhere… private." She gave Eila an apologetic look. Eila merely shrugged her indifference.

"Private?" Londo looked at Jae, then at Chimrin. "Okay. Lina?" He pictured in his mind…

They appeared in the living room of Lon's apartment. Lina and Jae sat down. Chimrin paced.

"Shards and splinters, why don't you just hang out a sign?" she exclaimed, practically sniffing the room like a wolf. Her posture fit the rest of her: lean and tight, alert and professional, her decades as a Legionnaire showing.

"A sign?" Londo asked.

Chimrin stopped and pointed at them all. "You three are linked in mind– and body. What kind of a marriage is this?" She planted her fists on her hips. "This room is filled with the three of you. Does Stoan know? I can't imagine he would. Or is this what he wants to see me about?"

Lina started to clean the apartment with energy as Londo spoke, bringing up a disc of white light from Sarastor to filter out and catch impurities in the vibration of the place and then gather them to be disposed.

"Stoan doesn't have any idea. I think. It's none of his business. We won't bring scandal to the Legion."

"You'd better not. I won't mention this to Stoan unless it becomes a problem. What kind of legitimate contract marriage is it that has three people in it?"

"Actually," Jae said, "It's called a dual-triune. But it's not one yet. We haven't figured out all–"

"What is she doing?" Chimrin interrupted, glaring at Lina.

Lina paused. "I'm just cleaning the room. I don't want anybody else to come in here saying that we've hung out a sign."

"What are those bands of light?"

"What, you can see them?" That confused Lina. "Actually see them? They've always been just a visualization exercise to me." She looked at Lon and Jae. "Can you see anything?"

They shook their heads at her. Chimrin raised her hand to just above her head. "The band is here, and it's stopped."

"I didn't want to move it unless I had full concentration. It would just drop everything and then I'd have to do it again. You can really see it?"

"Finish what you're doing. Let me watch."

Lina brought the light up to the ceiling, then swiftly up and up above Legion Headquarters, where the circle of light tied itself up like a bag. She had some angels carry it to toss into Sarastor's sun, where any discordant energy would be converted to whatever was needed.

"What in the orb is it for?" Chimrin wondered.

"How does the room feel to you now?" Lina asked.

Chimrin turned in a circle, getting that wolf look on her face. Her face lit in astonishment. "It's clear, well, clear enough, like someone had used a vibratory wash on it. How did you do that?"

"That's the first thing I ever learned in psychic school," Lina said. "Cleaning up after myself. Could you see the angels I employed?"

"Angels? I didn't see any… angels."

"All right, I'm using Terran symbology. How about spots of living light? Entities? Higher vibrations than what we are?"

"No, nothing like that."

Lina sighed. "Too weird."

Jae said, "Lina, didn't you say that there were some healing techniques that seemed to work for some people, but you couldn't get them to work for you?"

Lina thought and compared. "So you're saying that we're not resonating to each other's techniques. Yeah, that must be it. But not to deal with entities–" She looked at Chimrin. "It seems an incomplete education."

"A scientific education," Chimrin corrected her without any malice that she could detect. "Unhampered by fear and superstition."

"And probably a lot less fun than what I got," Lina said with a small smile. "Entities are interesting people." She sighed. "At least now I know why *they* stopped me last night from cleaning up next door."

"That's right," Jae said. "You'll need to run a scan of Deegel's room, too. Her room's being relocated to my spot sometime today."

"Ah *oui*." Londo squinted at nothing and shook his head. "I forgot already about her. Too much going on."

"Deegel?" Chimrin's head rotated to look toward the side of the room closest to Deegel's apartment. "Why should I–" She paused, puzzled, and then turned to Jae and Londo. "What in the orb has been going on while I haven't been here?"

"She's going to claim that it's all the Legion's fault for not getting her constant input," Jae murmured to Lina, loud enough so Chimrin could hear. "She's a control freak."

"Am not. I see strangers in there."

"And what else?"

Chimrin frowned at the wall and cocked her head. "Vibrations of– She was trying to drum up publicity for herself. There was going to be some huge news story… about you, Londo… and she knew she couldn't top it without something– Oh no." She whirled to face the two Legionnaires. "Security breach!"

"Stoan will want your confirmation," Jae said.

Chimrin sat down hard in a chair. "What," she finally asked, "did a wind from the Timeless Realms blow through Headquarters while I was away?"

Timeless Realms? Lina asked Lon.

They appear on lots of worlds, Lon explained to her, **but only Earth has the Gateway.** "I don't think we'll even mention Three Worlds to Chim at this point," Londo said, crossing his arms as he enjoyed Chimrin's reactions. She'd always been the most reserved Legionnaire.

"No," Jae agreed. "She couldn't take it."

Chimrin remained frowning as she considered the two of them, but she used it as a smokescreen to measure this girl's presence, this girl's power. Mind control immediately came to mind…

"It comes to everyone's mind, apparently," Lina said dryly. "If you want to test me, tell me what to do, but please don't do it on the sly."

Chimrin's eyes slid between the three of them now. The two most powerful men in the Legion. A strange telepath who suddenly appeared; at least, Chimrin couldn't remember Lon or Jae ever mentioning her. Aiko dead. Her mind recoiled from that, not accepting it yet. But Aiko had been… something… to Londo. A lover; who knew how much of one? And Deegel had made no pretensions about how she felt about Londo.

"It appears that I'm not going to get much sleep before the ceremony," Chimrin muttered.

Londo shook his head. "Probably not. Go ahead, think up every conspiracy and mind control theory that you can and run them by Stoan. I want Lina absolutely cleared by the time we leave for Earth."

Chimrin said, "He's going to want her to go to Tishan."

"He's not going to get his wish. We have things to do."

"You should all three go, for training if nothing else. Your thoughts are leaking out. They're uncontrolled." Chimrin looked at Lina. "Yes, that's it. That's better." She glanced to Londo. "See? Even a little learning can help. If you ever got around a group of telepaths–

"Perhaps it's time a team from Tishan paid your world a visit," Chimrin continued. "I don't believe Earth is listed as a source of great telepathic activity. I can't conceive that the Supreme Institute wouldn't have spotted it by now if it were."

"Unless it was considered so incredibly barbaric that they thought the only way we could harm anyone was by bashing their brains in with a bone club," Lina said. "And then singing to them, god help the poor bastards."

Lon and Jae laughed outright at that.

"Give me a rough debriefing," Chimrin instructed Londo. "Five minutes, organized, so I know where Stoan wants to start."

So Lon filled in his Legion mentor, taking pride in the amazement she held for all that had happened. Chimrin did not amaze easily. She held the shadow of fear, too, for him and Jae, the two most powerful Legionnaires. What were they caught up in?

"Enough, enough," she waved him down after ten minutes. "I have enough information to know that I'm not going to get any rest for two days at least. Let me get some stims and I'll check in with Stoan. Jae, let me see you do it."

Jae looked up at that. "Do what?"

She gestured, and Jae reached over to push Londo, who wobbled very prettily for Chimrin.

"Training," she ordered them. "You will sign up for immediate, close-combat exercises."

"Why– oh." Jae's gaze met Londo's. Lina tried to understand.

Chimrin went on. "Londo, you're not invulnerable if you go into action with either of these two around. It's a new universe you find yourself in. And Jae– if you're fighting with Lon at your back, you can no longer assume that he's going to stop all fire just by being there."

"Let us get settled, Chim," Lon told her. "We'll set up our own training schedule."

"And you–" Chimrin turned her gaze to Lina. "Marrying or about to marry two of the, oh, five biggest names this side of Galactic Center. You aren't planning on snagging any more, are you?"

"We can't marry Maximus. That would almost be incest," Jae grinned at her.

Chimrin grunted, only semi-amused. "What, no Ruby Guards waiting in the wings? Training for you, Lina, first thing. Self-defense courses until you drop."

Lina looked helplessly at Jae and then Lon.

"I told you," Lon said to Chimrin, "first we have to get settled. You're not commander any more, so we don't have to follow your orders. Although we will take them under advisement."

"Oh yes, definitely get settled," Chimrin said scathingly. "Just try not to die in the process."

"We have twenty billion people that we need to make sure don't die," Lina said in her defense.

Chimrin nodded but her lower jaw jutted forward. She was not pleased. "Point taken. So see you get settled ASAP and trained right afterward. Shall I have Kuttr standing by?'

"We can train ourselves," Jae huffed. "We aren't amateurs."

"Not amateurs, but blinded by your feelings. You'll be too easy on each other."

Jae was about to challenge that when Londo held up his hand. "We will consider this, Chim. Right now though, our priorities are to learn more about Aldierra and then sort out what we've gotten ourselves into. In a number of areas."

Chimrin looked as if she wanted to retort, but she held her silence. Finally she nodded and looked from Londo to Jae. "You," she said, pointing at Jae, "I've always known about. You," she looked at Londo, "I would never have suspected."

Jae and Lina gave a small laugh. Londo just gave Chimrin one of his crooked smiles.

Chimrin took a deep breath and released it. "You say I should talk to Stoan?"

It was Lon who replied. "He's been looking forward to you returning," he said.

"I'm surprised he didn't send a ceremonial escort to fetch me." Chimrin considered her next move. "I'll be back," she said. "When Stoan's through with me, and when I've had a nap and some stims and caught up on some records. Try not to destroy the universe in the meantime, will you?"

"We can't guarantee anything these days," Lon said with a grin before the door closed behind her.

Five large teams of Legionnaires awaited porting this time. Combat teams not only consisted of five or six Legionnaires, but also a medic and an equipment/gofer regular, plus whatever paraphernalia they dragged around with them. Bringing them all in was tiring. Boroh, now on comm duty, warned her that twelve more groups were desperately trying to finish their missions to return for the funeral. She should prepare for more calls.

When she got back to the room, Lon was gone with a note to her about rehearsal time and location. He was at "formation rehearsal," whatever that was. She ordered a conservative black and white outfit off the Internet and then took a few minutes to watch streaming coverage of Aiko. The crowd of mourners passed by her coffin, which had been moved just before dawn to the Central

AffSys Governing Complex some distance away so that there could be a funeral parade up to Legion HQ tonight. Millions of people were gathering along the wide route to watch the casket on its final journey.

The network switched to a studio for taped interviews with individual Legionnaires. Jae and Londo were interviewed together. The reporter introduced them as good friends as well as close friends of Orenya. Poor Londo sat like a dark, distinguished statue, a cloud of deep grief around him. And Jae, so solemn under his halo of blond: there was not a spark of mischief in him for this event, to honor his friend.

At least Jae would be around for another night so the two of them could comfort each other. After that, it would be up to Lina alone to take care of Londo. She had never had to do anything like this before. It scared her to have the responsibility, to realize that he had this kind of need for her. She was Lon's wife and his friend. Maybe all she had to do was to give him a sympathetic ear, a soft shoulder to cry on. She could do that. Lord knew she'd been crying on his shoulder enough lately.

But what of Jae, who'd be stuck on a semi-hostile ship for how many days, away from his friends and lovers? He said he had his emotions well in hand, but did he? Didn't he deny things almost as much as she did? How could she help him through his journey?

She knew them both in so many wonderful ways now, and all she wanted was to love them, to do anything they wanted as long as it would make them happy.

Her rose-colored glasses were securely in place. She hoped that it would be a long, long time before they came off. What an inexplicable miracle that these two incredible men had chosen her!

That's because you're easy, her father's voice taunted her. *Men go after cheap girls like you. They use them and then throw them away. You'll be lying in the gutter before too long. Don't call on me to help you!*

Jesus, thinking about her father here. *Well, Dad, I'm a long way from that gutter you always told me I'd wind up in. Good riddance to you!*

With a triumphant laugh she dismissed him from her mind. She was cured now. Lon and Jae had done that for her. Instead of hiding two steps back from everyone else, she could touch, love and be loved. *So there, Dad!*

It was only a few hours before rehearsal. Again she turned on her music and practiced tonight's song. How many people would be listening? Her stomach began to contract. Her voice caught on a few notes, and she felt dizzy.

She couldn't fail in this. She ordered her body to cooperate. This was for Aiko, but Lina also represented Londo now, as well as the Three Worlds. Aiko's people needed her to do her honor. She shouldn't think about the thousands–

The communications room interrupted her thoughts. Four teams wanted transport. When she returned she flopped on the couch, winded. Maybe she should grab a nap while she had time.

She was dozing on the couch when the TV beeped an incoming call at her. Thinking it was Lon or Jae checking in, she gestured for it to play.

Lon's grandparents!

Lina bolted to attention. She was still wearing her ratty tee shirt and jeans. And her hair–! She hurriedly finger-combed as they stared curiously at her.

"Oh, hello," she managed. He called them "gRands." How should she address them? "I wasn't expecting– I mean, I'm sorry I'm… such a mess," she finished lamely, giving up on her hair. "I was just about to get ready."

"That's quite all right, hon," Mrs. Rand said to her. "Is Lonnie there? Can we arrange for that teleportation whatsis now?"

"He's at some kind of rehearsal, and I'm the teleportation whatsis," Lina told them. "Could you give me a full view, please? With your luggage showing? Oh no, I haven't gotten the guest room ready yet. How could I have forgotten that? I'm sorry. My mind has just been… going places lately."

"We wouldn't dream of interfering with you newlyweds," Mr. Rand told her. "We've arranged guest quarters. So you're a teleporter? A mega? From Earth?"

"I guess so, sir. I mean, yes, I'm from Earth. And some people are saying I'm a mega."

"Well. Well, what do we do here?"

"Just stand there, that's fine." She warned them about the time lapse and they took hands.

Then they were standing in Lon's apartment.

Lina jumped up and brushed herself off as if she were dirty. She bobbed and covered her mouth with her hand so she wouldn't laugh out loud.

"What is it, dear?" Ruth asked.

"It's just nice to be around normal-sized people," Lina said. "Everyone here is so *tall!*"

They both laughed with her. "I understand," Mr. Rand said. "Lina, wasn't it? It's so good to meet you. Now give us hugs. You're family now."

They were enthusiastic about the hugs. Mr. Rand– no, Papa Mike, he insisted– hugged her too hard. Maybe he thought she was invulnerable like Lon? And maybe they didn't disapprove of the marriage anymore?

"I'm such a mess," Lina babbled. "Have you eaten? Would you like some tea or coffee? Lon has some snacks around here, but I'm not sure what's left. I could take you to the cafeteria."

"Don't worry, hon," Mama Ruth patted her hand. "We know our way around. We'll just make ourselves at home."

"All right." Oh dear, she really was messing this up. "Lon says hey, that he'll be here in a while and that I should relax– oh, you weren't supposed to hear that part."

They did indeed appear to be in their forties, these grandparents of Lon's (they always called him by the forbidden name "Lonnie"), hale and hearty and trying to make her feel comfortable. They seemed very nice.

Mike was in a normal Terran black suit and tie, the white shirt underneath adding the needed second color. Ruth wore a simple black dress (sleeveless! How could she get away with that when Lina knew that she wouldn't be allowed to?), sheer black hose and shoes. Her jewelry was lavish, beautiful strings of white pearls with diamond clusters in platinum settings holding them together.

Everyone knew about the Rands. Papa Mike had been founder and CEO of a big drug store chain until he'd retired about a decade ago, and Mama Ruth was a retired nurse. Lina told them she was a commercial artist. *Don't make waves on the first meeting.*

Help! she cried silently to Londo, but he just laughed at her, assuring her that they were finishing up, though there were a few more interviews afterward.

So Lina babbled. She always babbled when she was tired or nervous. When she slipped away for a few minutes to start some tea brewing– why hadn't she done that this morning so it would be ready for iced tea now?– she hit herself on the head and screamed inwardly to *shut up! shut up!* That seemed to help.

A call from the Comm Room let her excuse herself from the Rands' company. When she came back from that, she didn't feel inclined to open her mouth. There'd been three more teams: hordes of Legionnaires and their support personnel. She sat slumped in the living room, listening to the Rands's polite conversation and nodding occasionally, until Mama Ruth noticed her condition. Then it was Nurse Ruth getting her some water, asking her if she needed to be taken to Legion Medical.

"Thank you, but I'll be fine," Lina assured her. "Maybe I'll just take an aspirin if I can find one."

Mama Ruth instantly produced one from her purse, bless her. But another Comm Room call interrupted almost immediately.

"Six teams," Boroh announced.

"Did anyone ever stock some stims up there?" Lina asked.

With two long-release stims, seven groups of eight and five didn't seem that much of a strain at all, especially when they gave her an extra, minimal stim when she finished. Just about everyone who was trying to be here had come in, though three more small teams might make it. If so, it would be a while before they were ready.

Lina breathed a sigh of relief. She excused herself from the Rands so she could get dressed for rehearsal. Papa Mike settled on the couch with some magazines and the news running behind him as Mama Ruth called around across the sector, hunting for her son so he wouldn't miss the funeral.

Lina had to look semi-elegant for this occasion, civilized even though she was a Terran. She stared at herself in the master en suite's mirror: plain ol' Lina O'Kelly trying to be elegant. Her father would have a field day, wouldn't he?

At least her new makeup kit was easy to use. She told it what the occasion was, nixed the idea of black and white makeup, and it discussed her eyebrows with her. Then she stuck her face in it and closed her eyes. Two minutes later, she was finished. Her skin tingled under the astringent. Thank goodness for Sarastoran technology! Lina had never been one to use much makeup.

The dress she'd chosen looked like sedate winter evening wear for Earth. It was the innermost layer of one of those bulky parachute styles: a slender knee-length slip dress that Lina had added sleeves to.

She accessorized with a white enamel necklace and earrings to match the white belt she'd found, hoping that Lon would approve of her decision. Most of the people modeling these clothes had worn soled tights, so she'd ordered black ones and crossed her fingers that her choices had been correct. At least she wouldn't have to hunt down shoes, so difficult to find here.

Now– what to do with her hair? Maybe a Victorian twist, sedate and formal, so all her hair wouldn't freak out everyone. It had been a long time since she'd done one of those.

Yes, put up your hair like a whore, her father's voice grated in the back of her mind. *Painted woman. Fornicator! You're looking forward to two men in your bed, you harlot!*

Lina winced as that old pain in her leg, the one she'd thought was gone forever, came back.

Why weren't you born a boy? Shut up, you're just trying to get attention! Stop crying or I'll give you something to cry about, you ugly little girl! You stupid, stupid brat!

She touched her fingers to the reflection of her cheek. A red imprint stood out there as if Dad had just slapped her, as if she were twelve again and he was in one of his big rages. This was wrong. Something was wrong here. This shouldn't be happening. These were old things. Two years ago she'd healed that leg completely. It never bothered her any more.

Lina drew the white light to herself with a terrible need, and in response she felt someone gasp. *Felt,* not heard.

Chimrin!

There was no response, but she knew that she was there.

I said that you could scan me with my permission, not without.

Sometimes scans are best done when the observed doesn't know about it. You have parent problems. Father problems.

I could have told you that in person.

Does Londo know?

Of course he does. We've shared minds.

Does Jae know?

Yes.

You've shared minds with him?

Not as deeply as with Londo, but yes.

The sharing of minds is a very high-level technique, very difficult. Who taught you how to do that?

Sharing minds is easy. All it takes is courage and trust.

Chimrin stood in the doorway to the bathroom. Her green, gold and white costume was now black, platinum and white.

"I'm getting ready," Lina said. "This is what's difficult for me, trying to look presentable. Could we wait to do this scanning until afterward?"

"We still have time," Chimrin said. Her face betrayed nothing of what was going on within her mind.

"The Rands are here. What are they going to think?"

Chim shrugged the argument away. "Your father wanted you dead. He abused you physically and mentally."

"…And yours cast you out. I don't think he did, really, but that's the way you think of it."

Chimrin bowed her head in acknowledgement. "Trying to read a Tishan-trained teep. If you were a man I'd say you had balls and a half."

"Sorry, I didn't know there was Tishana etiquette involved." Lina worked on her hair, trying to appear calm. More persecution from the Legion, today of all days. "Did the Rands see you come in?"

"I told Ruth I was completing a simple security check," Chimrin told her. "How did you get past my shields to know about my father?"

"Shields? What are those?"

"My constructed force barriers. How did you get past them to read my mind?"

Lina turned to look the tall woman straight in the face. "I wasn't reading your mind. I was looking at your past. You carry it with you, like everyone does."

"Looking at my–"

Lina rifled through her hair pins, trying to figure a way to hide the ends of her twisted hair while Chimrin regarded her. "I need a barrette of some kind. I take it gold isn't allowed at a funeral?"

"No. White and black, no exceptions. You don't dishonor the dead."

"Bother," Lina muttered as she walked around looking for something she could wrap around a gold barrette that would be white or black. Flowers? No flowers here. The narsaws in the dining room? A close substitute. She hurried past Chimrin and examined them. There were sprays of tiny, rose-like shells filling up the arrangement, all in the purest of whites. How were they fastened in?

"All through?" Mama Ruth asked, coming up to them. "Don't you look nice, Lina! But what about your hair?"

Lina brought her hand back automatically to check the smoothness. That jar of Londo's hair goop absolutely eliminated frizzies. Lina opened her mouth to ask what was wrong, but Ruth interrupted.

"You need a pin to finish it off."

"I was thinking about taking some of these narsaws and using them." Damn it, Chimrin was still scanning her! The presence was a light buzz through her brain.

"Narsaws!" Mama Ruth pooh-poohed the idea with a wave of her hand. "But flowers would be nice. Do you have any here?"

"I think these will do fine, if I can just figure how to attach them to something." What could she use? "Can we take a little trip?" Lina asked the Legionnaire following her.

"Hm. If we're back in time."

Mama Ruth wanted to go, too, curious to learn more about her granddaughter-in-law. Papa Mike was engrossed in the newsnets, so they left him there.

For two minutes they held suspended in utter nothingness, just out of reach of reality. Then they stood in a cool, open-ceilinged room. Large windows lined one wall facing a night forest. Home.

"Please excuse the dust," Lina said as she clicked on the lights and then hurried into the kitchen with a handful of the smallest narsaws. "I haven't been back to clean for weeks now."

Chimrin froze as a small, furred animal approached and yawned, showing a mouthful of sharp teeth.

"Look at the kitty cat!" Ruth exclaimed in a mild voice. The tabby cat regarded her and decided it was more interested in Lina than in the lady with the longish white nails. "Here, kitty, kitty. Aren't you a cute fellow! And isn't this a darling little house, Lina. Passive solar, isn't it?" Ruth followed the cat and Lina into the kitchen.

Chimrin heard Lina say something to it in a strange language. Because Chimrin didn't have her translator with her, she couldn't understand, but she understood the little shriek Lina let out. The cat scampered back into this room and then upstairs. Chimrin rushed to investigate.

"They didn't run." Lina was open-mouthed in her awe. "He got me right on my tights and they didn't run!"

"Should they have?" Chimrin asked.

"I go through hose like water with the cats around here, so I never wear the things." She checked her legs again. "They didn't run!"

"The wonders of modern technology," Mama Ruth remarked with a withheld laugh. "I always stock up on hosiery whenever we visit Sarastor."

Lina snapped her fingers at her. "The wonders of modern technology," she repeated. "That's it!" and wove past the two other women. Ruth examined what turned out to be a cat door inside a box in the utility nook as Lina ran upstairs. They heard drawers being opened hurriedly, over and over.

"Ah ha! I won't have to solder, either!"

Lina hurried back down the stairs with a big plastic jar in her hand. She threw open cabinets in the kitchen until she found a large bowl. At a spray of small lilies in a window, she clipped five flowers off with scissors. These she delicately layered with the granular material from the jar into the bowl. The entire mixture went into the microwave.

Then it was back up the stairs. By the time Chimrin decided she wasn't coming back down, Lina had a smock on over her dress and was rattling a tall metal canister.

"Stay back," she warned Chimrin and pointed the canister at something she held on a handled instrument. Jewelry? Perhaps. It was a very simple, flat golden bangle with a large clasp behind. With a spritz from the can, it turned white. Lina spritzed again and again, very lightly from all angles. Finally she nodded and set the equipment down so that the bangle didn't touch the surface of the rather messy table.

"Let me get the gun heating up," Lina said as Chimrin examined the displays in the room. "Glue gun, not gun-gun."

Ruth joined them up here in the small open studio. She and Chimrin looked around, Chimrin rather mystified and Ruth exclaiming in a kind, grandmotherly way. The artwork here looked strange to Chimrin's eyes. It wasn't exactly photography. Instead it was blurred, which was made worse because it had been output on some kind of bumpy fabric. And these lights were yellowish except for two long ones, their bluish tones reminding her of home.

Chim looked out the large windows trying to see something outside in the darkness as Ruth engaged Lina in conversation about the art: she'd done all this herself? kinds of questions. Good girl. Ruth kept the conversation in Lingua so Chim could keep track. Spiky shadows lurked outside. Trees, so close to this place? Yes, bare trees, and they seemed to be in a nature park, not a solarium.

Lina had finally found whatever kind of gun she was after. It had a long cord, which she attached to a modular plug-in point along the wall. Something dinged downstairs and that big bowl appeared on the table in front of Lina. She stuck her fingertips into the sand.

"Hot, hot, hot!!" Lina blew on her fingers and turned to the two women. "Okay, so we have to wait a few minutes. Paint has to dry, flowers have to cool, and glue has to melt. I guess have time for a quick scan now, Chimrin. Am I allowed to call you that? How do we do this?"

"You do not do anything. Just–"

"No no no, Molly! Stay away!" Even without the translator, Chimrin got the gist as a round orange cat thing jumped onto the work table. Lina gingerly reached for the cat and then decided against it. The cat disappeared to the floor, looking around as if to say, "What happened?" and then up at Lina.

"No no, baby. You'll get hurt. Hot, Molly, hot."

The animal stretched out its mouth and made a scratchy little whine.

"No. Hot. Stay down." The cat stood on its rear legs, stretching out to her.

"No. I'm sorry. Oh, okay, Molly." Lina scratched the animal behind its ears, apparently what it had wanted all along. "Now that's all I can do." She'd switched to Panlingua without realizing it. "I can't pet you any more. Mama's got to be a lady today. Uh huh. Mama's got to be a lady."

Even from this light scratching, Chimrin could see clots of fur floating off of the animal. Lina swatted at it. Apparently it was the source of her main concern.

"What is that, anyway?"

"This is Molly, and she sheds like anything." Lina tried to get some hair off her black dress. "Bother! Watch out for her, Mama Ruth. I think I have a lint roller around here somewhere, but it doesn't work too well."

"I'll just have the kol-vanasche clean the dress when we get back," Ruth soothed. "So this is Molly. And that one?"

A gray and white face peeked around the edge of the library door at them.

"That's Obi."

"And that one?" A black cat there in the corner, staring at Chim.

"Moosie."

Chimrin watched all the creatures suspiciously as Ruth pointed out more and more of the things.

"Does Lonnie know you have all these?" Ruth asked.

"He met them a couple days ago. I warned him about them all before we got married. I made sure he knew that they were a part of the deal."

But he didn't tell you that Jae was part of the deal, did he?

Lina frowned at Chimrin.

"Lonnie's always wanted a pet." A chuckle escaped Ruth. "I hope he's happy now. How many?"

"Seven."

Ruth slapped her belly with glee.

Gingerly Lina dug through the sand for the now-dried blossoms. She trimmed them with an X-acto, spritzing white paint on a piece of cardboard and using the small puddle to load a tiny brush. She applied the paint deftly and precisely, Chimrin noted, covering up the browns and greens on the flowers. Chimrin had never seen anyone do anything like this before.

Lina's glue gun came into play as Lon's grandmother explored the rest of the upstairs. Darn it that she hadn't cleaned! Lina tried to ignore her new relative's curiosity as she held what would be her new barrette with needle-nose pliers, giving an explanation of her actions for Chimrin. She laid down glue into which she carefully placed the blossoms, alternating with the tiny white narsaws.

At one point Chimrin asked, "Can you feel this?"

"Feel what?" Lina asked.

Suddenly she was lying on the cold cement, the basement floor, tossed down to the bottom of the ugly gray stairs, crying for the agony of it all. Her leg throbbed. She couldn't move it without intense pain.

22

She was ten years old.

It was dark and everyone had gone to bed, ignoring her cries. Dad had locked the basement door and turned off the circuit breaker, after closing the heat vents down here. He said she could have power and heat when she got up and stopped acting like a baby.

Lost here in the dark, left with nothing but pain and cold and hunger. Any time she moved her right hip, sharp stabs screamed through her like someone sticking thick needles up her leg. She had wet herself. The smell mixed with that of the blood that lay drying in a puddle by her leg.

All alone. There was no one in this world who gave a damn about her. She lay still. She became cold, just like the floor. *Go away, world, just go away.* She didn't care any more. Just… go away…

Lina! What happened? Lina! Come back!

Lina, Lina! Chim?

I'm here with her. I'm taking care of it. Don't distract me!

"Lina!" Someone was shaking her, jerking her back and forth by the shoulders. "Come out of it!"

Lina scrambled back from Chimrin. She was touching her! Touching her and she didn't want anyone to touch her, ever!

"Snap out of it!"

Something like an electric shock racked through her brain. Lina couldn't catch her breath. Chimrin shook her again and Ruth pushed her away. "Come on, Lina!" Chim ordered.

"What happened?" Ruth asked in brusque, businesslike tones. "What did you do with her? Lina honey, tell me where it hurts. Oh. I see."

Lina fought the grip. Get her fingers off– Lina blinked. Oh. Oh. Londo's grandmother. She tried not to flinch as the woman touched her. She gritted her teeth against the onslaught of touch.

"Don't worry, hon. I'll get some ice." Ruth hurried downstairs and called, "Where's your first aid kit?" but the question didn't register to Lina's mind.

"Grigach," Chimrin hissed. "I didn't know. I'm sorry. Does it hurt bad? Can you port us back? I want Gorgeon to look at this."

Hurt? The fractured leg had been years and years ago. Lina looked away from Chimrin's anxious face and down to her leg. It seemed so big, not a ten-year-old's leg at all.

The tights had melted from where the glue gun had fallen on her. The silky material of the dress sizzled and smoked as it shrunk back in a big pucker. A great slash of angry red skin blistered just above her knee.

Lina's lip began to tremble and her eyes welled up with tears.

Oh, Londo!

Honey baby, are you okay? What's happened? Can you port back?

Oh, Londo, I'm so sorry! She was such a lousy wife! She didn't deserve Lon, much less Jae. They must be so ashamed of her. She was trash. She was scum.

"Do you have anything here that–" Chimrin stopped. It wasn't the pain that bothered Lina, it was the –

"L-Lon won't like it if I'm a spendthrift," Lina struggled to say. The cold basement floor– she could still feel it on her back, the white terror of icy cement and darkness. Londo was the way out. She couldn't give him a chance to get rid of her!

"Is… is there any way I can transfer my own money so I can get another dress? I might have some black hose here, I don't know. But I'll need to find some shoes, too. I don't have nice shoes."

"I'm sorry," Chim repeated. "I didn't know things were like– I thought maybe your father was–"

"Was… like yours." Lina's hands shook in Chimrin's. She fought off the white curtain of panic. She could touch now. How did she do that? Remember!

"Misconstrued through a child's eyes," Chimrin said softly. "You hate him, don't you?"

"I love my father." Lina looked at the mess of her leg and ordered herself not to cry. Goals were the only thing that could save her when she got upset. Keep her cold, hard priorities straight, and she could get through this.

She began to breathe light in, pain out. Pain was good. If she could feel such a scald, it meant the nerves hadn't been burned. Back at Tiawa she hadn't been able to feel most of her burns. It had taken a miracle to fix that.

She set her jaw against the sizzle and looked around for the glue gun. There it was, beginning to melt the linoleum. She picked it up carefully. Should have used the smaller gun anyway. Stupid. Messed everything up because she was stupid! She eased herself up off the floor and placed the gun back on its stand.

"Let's get something for that leg," Chimrin urged. "We shouldn't let that go."

"In a minute," Lina replied. "First things f-first. Goal A." She finished gluing the final blossom to the barrette, controlling her breathing as if she were man-handling a wild horse. Her hands shook almost uncontrollably. "G-give me a little warning before you pull another stunt like that. Please."

Chimrin fumed at her stubbornness. "You have to have something around here," she burst out, exasperated. "Poultices, leeches–"

"Here we go," Ruth stomped upstairs with a damp washcloth wrapped around ice. She glared at Chimrin. "Back off." With a nurse's gentle touch, she applied it to Lina's leg.

"Oh. Oh." It hurt. Christ, she was such a bother to everyone!

"Where's your first aid kit, hon?" Ruth asked, her palm on Lina's forehead. "Let's get you to lie down a while. Do you understand me? Where's the first aid kit?"

"First… aid?" Someone was talking about something that wasn't a goal. Lina didn't know why they'd do that. She unplugged the glue gun and tried to blink order back to the world of shifting colors and pain.

"What the hell did you do to her?" Ruth snapped at Chim.

Before Chimrin could answer, Lina hauled herself up and limped heavily into the library, past the sliding double mirror that was the door into the storage closet made into a bedroom. Inside was the little dresser she'd made from a kit. She ransacked her lingerie drawer. Goal B. Hose... hose... There. She checked. Right color, but they had a run already. She tossed them over her shoulder to bounce against Chimrin and drop onto the floor. She searched again.

By the time Ruth had joined her and pushed her into bed where she could hold the ice against her, Lina had found black hose without any flaws. She leaned around Ruth and down off the mattress, sorting through her shoes next to the bed. She held one pair up for Ruth's approval.

"Will these do? I can take a black marker and cover up this spot here–" Oh god, Lon and Jae were both dressed their best. She had to be, too. There were going to be important people there. It was a state occasion, a tribute to somebody as big as... as big as Valiant or Maximus. And she was going to be presented as Londo's wife.

She shook her head. "No disrespect. Mama's got to be a lady today."

What would Lon do? Lon would be confident, absolutely sure of himself. Spare no effort to show honor to a fallen friend. And Jae... Jae might be afraid, but he'd cover it up so well that no one would ever notice. He'd even manage to flaunt something at them to show how fearless he was.

"We need to get that burn taken care of." Chimrin put on a no-nonsense tone. "Screw the clothes and let's see to that first. Port us back. Now."

She can't port in that condition! Jae shouted at her.

"How much is a credit?" Lina looked up at Chimrin. "I've got some money coming to me from work. I have to pay bills and make the mortgage payment, but I should have a little left over for clothes. How much are dresses? How do I transfer interstellar funds?"

Chimrin knelt down on the floor beside Lina in the bed. "You're not thinking straight. You're still in shock."

Baby, you lie down for a while. You listen to Mama Ruth.

I've got her, Lon. You and Jae stay out of this.

Oh, Londo, I don't want to embarrass you ever. Or you, Jae.

Shut up, Lina. Londo, she's just… Never mind. We'll be back on Sarastor in no time. The quicker you mind your own business, the quicker we'll be back.

"Credits," Lina said. "How much have I spent so far? Londo's money, and now I've ruined something. I have to get a replacement from my own money."

"Uh huh."

"I think we should call 911," Ruth told Chim gravely. "It's not the burn I'm worried so much about, it's the state of her mind. We need to get her to a hospital."

"I'll take care of her mind," Chim said tightly. "They always told me I shouldn't become a psychiatrist, but I can do this much. Your new granddaughter is just a little… ill. Like Londo."

Ruth sat back, still holding the iced washcloth against Lina's leg. "How so?"

"They've both had traumatic childhoods. Londo got help for his. Lina hasn't. That, plus I think she may have been on stims today. *Skurnit,* I should have checked on that possibility before doing anything."

"I bought four nightgowns with Lon's money," Lina told them. "No, five. The last one was to punish him."

"Punish him?" they both asked despite themselves.

"And, and three dresses, with tights and hose. And a jacket. A tee shirt. Shoes. They aren't black, they just won't do…"

Lina looked at Ruth wildly, reaching for her but not making it. "The stores are closed now. I have to get something to wear! I might have a hundred dollars left in checking. All my big credit cards were blown up. They say most marriages fall apart because of money problems. I don't want to hurt my marriage!"

"Don't worry about that now," Ruth insisted. "Lie back and rest."

Londo. Jae. Tell her to rest. Order her to rest.

With a sigh, Lina lay back on the pillow. She made motions toward Ruth and said, "Thank you. I'm sorry to mess up. I'm so sorry. All my fault. Stupid. Stupid Muttbutt."

Ruth stuffed some pillows under Lina's feet, drawing a blanket up over her. "That's a good girl," she crooned. "You've got a good head about money, that's good. But just remember all that money you got at the wedding. You remember?"

"Money?"

"Yes, everyone gave you lots and lots of money. And there's one wedding gift you haven't opened up yet. You remember it, don't you? It has a big bow on it."

"It's red. Red bow."

"That's right," Ruth said in the same sing-song voice. Lina's eyes closed. "If you open it, I bet you'll find another dress just like this one, all pretty and ready to go, and some nice tights with it."

"All… pretty."

Chim held up her hand to Ruth and Ruth fell silent. Lina's breaths came deep and regular. Chim's concentration was fierce.

Silence reigned in the tiny space with the roof sloping so low over the bed. Over Lina's pillow the pebbled ceiling showed a deep, ragged indent needing repair. A pitter of rain started on the skylight inches away but didn't soak through the hole.

Ruth grabbed one of the cats who had decided they wanted to join Mama in bed. She fumed as Chim's fingers rested Lina's forehead. Chimrin had obviously done something to provoke this episode. What had she said, a security check? A telepathic one. Mind police. She liked Chim very much. She had trusted her grandson to her oversight for many years, but often forgot that she was Tishana-taught.

But Lina had seemed so normal, so common-sensical. And now to find that she had mental problems like Londo? Maybe Chim had meant that in present tense. Lon's problems weren't that bad any more. Maybe Lina's weren't either.

But Lonnie–! That little scamp! Didn't Lina have any idea what he earned? Why else would Lina be so worried about money? Lonnie could be so close-mouthed sometimes. She'd have a private conversation with the young lout when she got back. Money matters could indeed wreck marriages. She'd seen more than a few come to bad ends because of it. Londo had to learn to trust.

A tired groan announced that Lina was gradually coming around. Chim leaned back, sighing in relief. "I think that did it," she announced.

"You sleep a few minutes," Ruth told Lina.

"Have I fed the cats today? They feel hungry."

"I'm feeding them right now. You sleep, girl." After she made sure that Chimrin held the washcloth in place, Ruth went downstairs to attend to the task.

With nothing to do now but wait and hold the cold cloth, Chimrin looked around the larger room outside the bedchamber. Pictures filled in spaces between bookcases in the tiny library, photographs that looked like proper photographs, although they were two-dimensional. One was larger than the rest.

She could feel that Wiley had been here, could feel him scanning this: two older adults, maybe in their mid-hundreds. Graying hair and smiles. A younger woman with them, at that ageless time between eighteen and seventy-five. She felt very young, though. Hard toward the eighteen mark then. She resembled Lina around the eyes and mouth perhaps, the same that the older woman did. But the man…

He had laugh lines around his eyes, and his mouth was turned in a pleasant smile. But there was hatred on his side of the photograph and hatred directed toward the photo from this, the viewing side. The man had serious mental problems he tried to keep hidden, but he had one outlet that he couldn't control: his hatred toward Lina.

The older woman was hiding from the world as well as the man. She was living to live and nothing more. No ambition here, just tired survival.

"What time is it?"

Chimrin turned to help Lina sit up in her hidey-hole of a bedroom. "It's time to be getting back as soon as you're feeling up to it."

Lina groaned as she squinted at the light in the library. "Oh no, I have to sing in a little while." She rubbed her throat and then rearranged the washcloth on her leg to a cooler side. "It hurts it hurts. Yes, Londo, I'm all right. Jae, we're heading back in a few minutes." She stood up, supporting herself against the wall and Chimrin, and then looked down to see the remains of her dress and tights. "Oh god," she moaned.

"Time enough to get replacements from the Nets," Chimrin said crisply. "I don't think the seluvon can fix this extensive damage."

Lina looked away and bit her lip.

"I must insist that you let me pay for it," Chimrin said. "I haven't been that heavy-handed in years. It was all my fault."

"Thanks a lot," Lina hissed. "Here I thought everything had been healed, that I was finally normal. Now you come around and make me remember how… fucked up I really am. Thank you so much. Wonderful timing. Simply fabulous."

"You are in need of professional psychological help. I know Lon and Jae think they've completed doctorate study in psychiatry, but don't let them snow you. Does Londo–"

"Of course he knows. And Jae, and probably Wiley and probably the whole… fardling Legion by now! There are probably bets on the Legion boards on when I'm going to go completely bonkers."

"I doubt if more than five Legionnaires know, including Lon and Jae," Chimrin soothed. "And I suppose anyone who married Lon and was even slightly considering marrying that lunatic Jaeson Rallene would have to be considered certifiable."

Lina hissed at her leg, turning the sound into a series of repeated soft but heartfelt curses, and then folded the iced washcloth to a new position. "Maybe," she admitted over her trembling. "Do you think Legion Medical can fix this without much problem? I don't think I can sing with my leg like this." She grimaced and then panted rhythmically.

"I want you signed up for psychiatric counseling right after you start self-defense classes."

Lina didn't say anything, but she stopped panting. Instead she blew out a deep breath, long and slow. A sudden clench interrupted it, but she tried again.

"I mean it."

"Thank you for offering to pay for the dress," Lina hedged. "But maybe Lon can afford for me to get a new one. If he can't, I've got a paycheck coming in a couple weeks. That might handle everything. And if it doesn't…"

Lina looked around and Chimrin knew she was thinking about selling the house. How much would a custom dress like this cost?

"Listen," Chimrin ordered. "Lon doesn't like to tell anybody anything. I don't have any idea about exchange rates, but I can tell you that he makes enough to cover the price of this house every time he sneezes."

"And how often does Valiant sneeze?" Lina asked as again she folded the washcloth with a whimper, willing the cold within it to penetrate her burn.

"We've created enough of a scene here. I need to make sure I've disconnected everything. I don't want the house to burn down while I'm gone."

Lina checked the barrette to make sure it was finished, and even Chim had to admit that it was kind of cute, if you liked flowers in your hair.

"I didn't know cats made such a great noise when they ate!" Ruth exclaimed as she joined them. "How are you feeling, hon?"

As soon as they appeared back in his apartment, Londo scooped Lina into his arms and set off flying toward Legion Medical. The Rands hurried behind him. Jae brought up the rear when Chim grabbed him by the shoulders.

"Let me go!" he hissed at her.

"In a minute." Chimrin didn't know how to put this, so she decided to say it straight out. "Don't go to Tishan."

"What?"

"They'll tell you that you have to, but don't. If you find you absolutely must, see me first. I know people there. You go there by yourself or with just those two crazed Terrans, and the Tishana will eat you alive. Look what I did by accident, by finding the wrong button by chance. All three of you have serious emotional problems, and the people on Tishan who'd want to get their hands on you quickest would be the first to use those problems to their advantage."

Jae nodded.

"And speaking of advantage–"

Jae's jaw jutted out. "I jumped her," he told her. "I was on duty, her confinement officer. She was drunk coming down from stims, and I jumped her."

"That's a *skurny* serious offense, Legionnaire."

"Are you going to report me? For any of this?"

Chim pressed her lips together and jerked her head towards the lift door. "Go," she said. Jae flew off.

Jae wore the funereal version of his costume as he watched them from across the room. The white sections stayed white, but some of the blue had gone white, some had gone black. His white cape was black now to balance, as was all the faux leather, but nothing could cover the startling blue of his eyes.

Lina thought he looked stark and unnatural. Maybe that was what all the black and white was about, the seeming unnaturalness of death.

She, Lon and the Rands were together. This was silly. Jae hadn't been allowed to be by her side in Medical because he wasn't family.

Lina wore a new dress same as the original, and her leg didn't give a twinge. Not even a bruise remained. Sarastoran medicine was practically magic. She'd even managed to port one more team in without a hitch.

Lon made a show of motioning to Jae, and he ambled over to join them.

The entire ceremonial chamber was pointedly black and white. Located on Headquarters' almost-public ground level, it was the size of a convention hall. Draperies flowed onto the floor in rivulets of material. Row upon row of cushioned chairs were set up in tiers to handle the hundreds of Legionnaires and dignitaries who would be arriving soon.

Onstage was a raised dais where the coffin would rest, surrounded by sprays of black and white narsaws and more draperies. A larger-than-life-size holopicture of Aiko provided a backdrop, the only splash of real color in the room

Dozens of people bustled, checking their small, hand-held monitors instead of watching where they were going. Stagehands? Perhaps. Others dressed in the ubiquitous black and white milled about aimlessly. Every minute produced a near-collision or worse.

Jae pointed out the President of the AffSys, the Potentate of Sarastor, and the Bi-lates of Feen, Aiko's homeworld. Her parents, her younger sister, her ex-husband.

"Orb, I wish we could have gotten hold of Hal," he muttered.

Lina asked, "Did he know Aiko well?"

"Oh yes, they had great respect for one another. Well, wherever he is, by now he's got to know about the funeral. Maybe he'll be watching it. He'll feel better to know Lon's here representing him in a way."

"There's still time for him to check in," Papa Mike said.

"Admiral Bracken isn't here," Lon noted quietly. "Good."

Less than a half-hour until rehearsal for the hall's activities. Lina kept ordering her nerves to straighten up. Lon spoke to Stoan, who was in charge of the ceremonies. Stoan was making last-minute adjustments to the schedule.

"Who ever heard of music at a funeral?" the Legion commander wanted to know for the umpteenth time.

"Who ever heard of a funeral without music?" Lon retorted. "On Earth it just isn't done."

"This isn't Earth."

"No, but Aiko herself requested a song. You were there. You heard."

It was clear that Stoan hadn't figured out yet if the ghost of Aiko was real or a trick of Lina's. "If it's proper. Not one of those songs *she* was singing at that bar."

"It's perfectly proper for a funeral. It's beautiful, adapted from an ancient Feenish work. This may shock people today, but a week from now, or maybe a month, they'll understand its worth."

"I'll probably be censured for doing it… but she did request it. Permission granted." Stoan restored the slot.

"And play another short piece at the very beginning. Not a song, just instrumental."

"A funeral dance?!"

"*Non.* A tribute."

"I don't remember that in her request."

"It wasn't. Jae, Lina and I decided about it, as a Three Worlds matter. It's to honor her and her role in the Investiture."

"This funeral is a Legion matter, not Three Worlds. This is going out to a lot more planets that just those three."

"*D'accord,* then take it as a request from Aiko's closest friend. Play the music, Stoan, please."

Again he sighed. "All right, all right. You're catching me at a weak moment." He turned Lon's data crystal over so it projected a label. "*Fanfare for the Common Man,*" he read. "Common? Aiko?"

"It's an uncommon fanfare, befitting a hero."

With a silence barrier around the two of them, Stoan listened to the music. His gaze kept straying to Lina.

"He's staring at me," Lina muttered to Jae. "At you, too." **Your quarters aren't bugged, are they?** she asked him.

Quarters have absolute privacy. He could have seen us outside last night, though. He had a break in duties about then; I checked. He might have seen us in the park. Damn, I knew I shouldn't have done anything outside Headquarters. There're too many eyes and ears out there. I thought we were alone.

Maybe this will get Londo to go public?

Don't push him, Sweet. Now we know to be even more circumspect. If we don't do anything else, it'll wear off. Stoan will forget about it.

I hope you're right.

It was with that suspicious glare that Stoan called for rehearsals for the interior ceremony. First was a walk-through, then a full rehearsal, except for the eulogies which would only be heard at the actual ceremonies. Londo of course had his, and Stoan had one as Legion commander. There were others as well.

The President of the AffSys would also deliver one, and Lina regarded her curiously. Her being female showed that the AffSys was at least partially civilized, and she might be used as a teaching tool for the Aldierrans. She wasn't quite what Lina would classify as normal human, with skin of a decidedly bluish hue and large cat eyes, no eyebrows but a good forehead ridge. Still, she was a pleasant- and wise-looking woman, a leader instead of a puppet actor for a political party. She seemed pained at having to say goodbye to such a great hero, cut down in the prime of her life.

It took a while to explain to the sound people that there was to be a song, and for them to comprehend that the music had to run in the background while Lina sang. Eventually they worked out their cues with her.

They fitted her with an unnoticeable earplug so she could hear the music properly, and she sang as people around her leaned to each other to comment. When she finished, she saw Stoan shaking his head as he stood beside Lon and Jae, but Lon said something to him and Jae added to it. Stoan sighed and looked away. He'd do it but he didn't like it.

"That was lovely, dear," Mama Ruth told her before the Rands and Jae were ushered away for last-minute interviews.

Lina's stomach wasn't comforted, though. The whispers she could now hear clearly didn't help: "Terran. Witchdoctor." People made a wide path for her, not wanting to be contaminated by her presence. At least no one here was talking about mind control, but there were few Legionnaires present.

The introvert inside her was relieved she didn't have to socialize with so many strangers. Still, she had a duty, both by Legion standards and society. When Lon returned, she belonged by her husband's side.

Lina's pleasure was to watch Londo among the important people of this interstellar confederation. He walked with a confidence and majesty that she hadn't had the chance to savor before this. He had grown up among the most important people in the galaxy, and he moved in their circles as if he'd been born there. He was a crown prince roaming in disguise among the commoners.

While people bowed reverently to Jae, they stood in awe of Londo.

How had he ever come to be hers? Lina reminded herself that she would never, ever do anything to embarrass him. No matter how nervous she got, how overcome with shyness, she would disguise it for his sake and pretend to be the gracious princess who belonged at his side.

Even if she had to lie about her relationship with Jae.

But could she lie if they committed to a legal marriage?

Adding a warning about secrecy until an official announcement, Londo introduced her as his wife to the President of the AffSys, who gave them both a curious Look (*Married? Do they have sex?*), but masked it professionally. She asked about the song and Lon explained that Aiko herself had requested it. The woman nodded, satisfied. It was clear that she had been informed about the mysterious happenings surrounding the Three Worlds Investiture.

For the Potentate of Sarastor all three of them presented themselves as the Chosen of the Three Worlds. Lon and Jae already knew the man. He surprised Lina by thanking her for her work in dismantling the Aldierran invasion. He told them to make an appointment the soonest possible for further discussion.

Time was running short now. Those who hadn't already, changed into special clothing for the broadcast ceremony. Lina's was a white choir robe she'd ordered. She completed it with the black ministerial stole Jae had worn at their wedding, the one with the symbols of the Order of Uriel and the Three Worlds on it. A stagehand used a desaturating filter to disguise the gold accents to white.

Lon came over while she was in makeup. This time an actual woman did it because broadcast requirements were different than Lina's automated system could handle. Apparently the woman didn't approve of singers or maybe Terrans so she worked on Lina without saying a word. Lina supposed you could only shock people so much before they turned negative. How would a dual-triune go over, she wondered?

"Just sing it exactly as you did, *chérie*." Lon leaned over her, looking at her in the mirror. "That was perfect. They say the expected audience of this is—"

"No. Don't even give me a r-rough estimate," Lina ordered. "Are you okay, Lon?"

"Not really. *Non*." Lon looked uncertain. Not nervous, but emotion-wracked.

"Lon, listen." Lina swung around in her chair so she could see him face-to-face. "You saw her after she went over to the other side. Was she in pain?"

"*Non*."

"Was she unhappy? Sad in any way?"

He considered. "*Non*. She was joyful. She said she was home."

"That's what a lot of people I've talked to, Near Death Survivors, have said. They say that the other side is so wonderful that you can't even imagine it. They say that they'll never be afraid of death again, because that's where they'd prefer to be. That's where she is now."

He caught her hand in his. "I keep telling myself to treat having had her in my life as a blessing, not to obsess that she's died." He pressed his lips together.

"That doesn't mean you can't grieve for as long as it takes. Don't think for a moment that that's wrong. But keep reminding yourself of what she said to you."

"Yes." Determination washed across his features. "The universe is better for her having been here."

Such a wonderfully brave front he put up. Lina squeezed that hand. "So go out there and tell them that, darling."

At a signal from Stoan, the Legionnaires still in the building left as a group. Screens scrolled down from the ceiling, allowing a view of the long nighttime procession along the main boulevard of Lirravon. It was easy to imagine that more than a million civilians lined the route, as had been reported, throwing sparkling glitter at the coffin as it floated slowly past the mass of humanity. The glitter flashed into sparks, joining thousands of other sparks, and slowly died.

People along the sidelines openly sobbed and comforted each other. Some merely watched in silence as dignitaries rode behind the coffin on floating discs.

Spotlights raked the sky. A cloud of flying humans descended to a hundred feet above the parade. They swooped in patterns, weaving in and out of each other's flightpaths with incredible precision. Delicate trails of light followed their boots and accentuated their movement. It seemed as if a huge flock of birds were making their way across the sky, changing their leaders and their paths in amazing, precise order; geometric beauty.

And they always kept an empty spot within their ranks.

There were over a thousand of them: not only the Legionnaires, but their auxiliaries and reserves from across the sector. As they neared Legion Headquarters their trails became brighter and did not fade. Abruptly the combined streams of light coalesced to spell *Orenya*.

The procession pulled into the plaza at the base of the man-made mountain that was Mega-Legion Headquarters. Eight Legionnaires broke aerial ranks: Lon and Jae, Eila and Andri, and another woman and three men Lina didn't recognize. They swooped down to take their places next to the coffin and lift it from its transport.

A section of the wall of Legion HQ groaned and cracked open, spilling street-light into the hall. The eight Legionnaires escorted the coffin inside and placed it on its dais. Stoan draped a black and white flag onto it as the rest of the Legionnaires and the officials who had been in the parade filed silently in. Legion family members followed behind them.

The side of Legion HQ slid heavily back into position.

The lights dimmed. A single spotlight shone on the coffin and the holopicture behind it. *Fanfare for the Common Man* sounded, its brass, timpani and gongs echoing in the recording as well as in this chamber. As the music faded, another spotlight came up, and Stoan addressed an unseen televised audience of who knew how many, as well as the gathered Legionnaires and dignitaries. Then the AffSys President spoke.

Lon's turn came. He spoke of his friendship with Aiko, told stories that revealed how human she was, how humorous and warm. He recounted the tales of heroism that had never received much attention, but when added to those that had, created the life of a hero of legendary proportions.

He told people that they shouldn't look at Aiko as a hero whose feats they could never hope to emulate, but rather as a role model, so that the smaller steps they could take would be in her footsteps. Eventually those steps would create a path through their own lives that would make them heroes, too.

He mentioned Aiko's favorite charities, her favorite causes, and asked people that if they wanted to do something in remembrance that they should do something for the causes that were important to her. Lina's eyes misted over as she listened to the love that her husband had for this woman, to the inspiration he was providing anyone who could hear him.

I'll take care of him, Aiko, she promised again.

Now a relative of Aiko's had a turn in the spotlight. Then there was a holographic biography of Aiko's life, showing her from a child growing up on a distant planet, to a young woman being inducted into the Legion, blooming into a hero of galactic proportions.

Desperately Lina tried to ignore her stomach, her nerves. She breathed rhythmically and straightened her chakras. In her inner eye, she reached upward to loftier realms, outward to the universe itself. *Help me here,* she begged her Worlds. *Help me do her justice.*

She recalled the vision she'd received as a gift at the Investiture: of her fitting into the cosmos. It meant that all the cosmos was connected to her as well.

And then it was Lina's turn. She stepped into the spotlight, imagining that it was only the gang at the Romaki Club waiting for a song. She could do this.

The music started and the words flowed easily to her mind so she could concentrate on getting the emotion of the music across as she sang. Lina felt worlds gather around her to join in: Worlds that had been aided by Aiko. The world where she was born. Sarastor, where she had served with the Mega-Legion. Other presences who wanted to honor Aiko, or who were happy to give of themselves to aid Lina. They all helped lift her voice:

We witnessed when you fought Nig Mire,
You gave no quarter, hard and fierce,
But fought on, their armors pierced.
Defender and warrior, blazing with fire.

Orenya ours,
You bloomed in our darkest days.
Orenya ours,
You broke our winter's storms with joy.
We pledge to you as you, to us,
Orenya ours! Orenya ours!

As the song and ancient orchestra progressed, living energies streamed through Lina, resounding within her. She raised her arms for the final triumphant verse and chorus to release them all. The hall vibrated with their presence.

From the plains of Breklet to the moons of Wry,
Our hearts rejoice at every deed,
We follow the light wherever you lead.
Let the stars now write across the sky:
Orenya ours!
Orenya ours!
Orenya for the ages!

The spotlight on Lina faded and she moved in the darkness to stand with Londo. He held her tightly.

"Beautiful. Just beautiful," he whispered into her hair. "It was perfect."

The casket floated up and the wall opened again. Slowly the casket moved into the plaza. As soon as it had cleared Legion Headquarters, it suddenly shot

skyward, disappearing into the starless night sky, heading toward a sun four parsecs away where the body of Aiko would return to stardust.

23

After a formal dinner seated with Wiley, Chim and the three of them, Papa Mike announced that he was homesick and didn't want to stay on Sarastor. He gave his wife a troubled look. Mama Ruth seemed ill, for her eyes were red and swollen from the funeral, and she had barely picked at her meal. She made Lina swear that she had recovered fully from the afternoon, and that she and Lon would stop by soon after they both got back to Earth.

"Make that after the honeymoon." Papa Mike gave Lina a much gentler hug than he had before. "You two get busy. I want to play with my great-grandchildren while I'm still able to run faster than they can."

Lina ported the gRands home to Earth. Lon stood looking at the empty space they'd taken up. "I'm homesick, too," he said. "I want to go somewhere where I can veg out and sort through everything's that happened."

"Things are still on the move," Jae told him. "We have a stop to make before you can do that."

They found the Aldierrans busy readying their fleet to return to their home world. Admiral Bracken assured them that likely nothing of import would be decided while the fleet sped through hyperspace, for the Doomsday situation was still stuck in talks on Aldierra. Significant people within the government refused to believe in the Ultimatum.

"Even if they don't believe, they must know that things cannot stay the same," Jae said. "This is the chance to make major changes and enjoy the backing of the people."

Admiral Bracken agreed, but he didn't rule the planet and he was a long way from home.

At least they left with study padds filled with information about the world. Lon whistled when he examined the data, and said each padd held at least a zettabyte, which he then had to explain to Lina was about three orders of magnitude larger than a terabyte. Which was hugely big, Lina knew. Even so, it took Jae only moments to copy the files to the Legion's database with a flag for Wiley's attention. While online, he double-checked the arrangements for his departure the next day.

Lina could sense Lon's great unease with Jae's situation of being the only Legionnaire in a perilous, enclosed situation. He squeezed Jae's shoulder.

"You'll be opening up relations with an entire world. If anyone can understand a new culture, it's you. Just keep–"

"I will," Jae promised.

The Legionnaires and family members who still roamed the hallways of Headquarters regarded them strangely. Not only were there whispers of "witch-doctor," "mind controller," and "she sang in public," but raised eyebrows as the newlyweds returned with Jae to his room– newly relocated– so late at night.

"This is ridiculous," Lina muttered after the door had shut behind them. "If we're going to do this, we should go public. We don't have anything to be ashamed of. I mean, not if we make it legal. We are still considering that, aren't we?"

"You've certainly done a one-eighty, *chérie*."

"I just came to my senses. Like I'm hoping you will."

Jae set drinks for everyone on the coffee table. "So who's scheduled for what tonight and when?" he asked. "I'm not tired in the least right now. Lina? Lon?"

Appraisingly Londo rubbed his left shoulder as he gave Jae a leer. "You're going to be gone for days, bug-bug."

"That thought had occurred to me."

"I think–"

The door buzzer sounded. They all thought it at the same time: *Stoan*.

The buzzer went off again and again rapidly.

Jae sat down in a chair with a whump. He made an intercom motion with his hand and asked in a voice remarkably calm. "What is it, Commander?"

Stoan's voice sounded in the air. "Jae, I want to see you and Lon now, before you leave tomorrow."

"Must you?" Londo asked. "We were discussing some important matters. We just got through with the Aldierran delegation."

"I'm not going to insist, but I'm not going to beg either, Starheart."

Lon raised his eyebrow at Jae. Stoan had called him "Starheart." Damn, he liked that name. "Come in," Lon said, and Jae made a face at him.

Stoan stepped inside. His scrutinizing gaze moved from person to person. "It was a great speech," he told Lon. "Very moving."

"Thanks. Yours was *kicking* good as well. Aiko would have liked it. By the way, Jae and Lina said you've been giving them the evil eye all day."

"Evil eye?"

Jae leaned back in his chair, which snuggled around him. "We assume you saw us in the park last night," he said. "The kiss."

Stoan took a defiant stance. "As long as you brought it up, let's talk about that. Let's talk about appearances and protocol and the presence of the media *en masse* in the immediate neighborhood."

Londo waved his hand as if everything were of no import. "From what I understand, the media was at least two miles away."

"Near enough there could have been a camera drone."

"There was no drone." Lina scowled at the pervert commander. "I check for them now."

Stoan regarded her. "All right," he said, "there was no drone. I didn't even have time to summon my own."

"So here's what happened, Stoan," Londo said. "They've both told me about that before I even asked. We'd been having some… difficult discussions about the Three Worlds project. Oh hell, even Wiley saw that we were having some fights. Lina was upset and went out. Without a guard, which she won't do again." He gave Lina an Evil Eye of his own. "Jae went out to talk to her about it and make sure she was okay. If I'd been awake, I would have gone with him."

"It wasn't just talk."

"Okay, they gave each other a little make-up peck. Look, Stoan, we're going to be working closely on this project. Lina's a very demonstrative person. You're not used to Terran culture. This is normal behavior. Girls kiss when they're happy or grateful. It doesn't mean anything."

Stoan did not look convinced at Lon's lie. "And is it normal for her to… conduct herself the way she has at that bar every night? Has she told you about that?"

Lon gave a quick grin. "I want to go there, the three of us. Maybe we'll all sing for them. Ask around to the Terrans there. They'll tell you what're acceptable Terran norms. How they appreciated her coming in and singing for them. Singing is an *art form,* get that through your head."

"Sarastor is a silent world," Lina said.

"And Terrans seem to want to sing all the time," Stoan said sarcastically.

Londo draped his arm around Lina's shoulder. "That's right, Stoan. We do. Maybe you should pay Terra a visit sometime and check it out yourself. There's always music, no matter where you go."

"A frightening thought. All right, Lon. We'll let it pass this time."

"Let what pass?" Lina demanded. Lon gave her a warning look. "Hell. Okay. Peace."

"Hem." Stoan clearly did not want to give up on his campaign against Lina. "I want no more kissing episodes."

"We'll only make out in private," Jae joked, but the commander obviously didn't see the humor, so he said, "Yessir."

"Did I finally get cleared today?" Lina asked.

Anger twisted Lon's face. "Chim's mistake sent Lina to Legion medical for a half hour. I've known Chim for a long time, and I can't remember her ever–"

"Chimrin and the Tishana authorities made investigations that have only preliminarily cleared her," Stoan said.

"What?"

Stoan glared at Lina. "It will take a lot of testing to determine whether new mind control methods are being used."

"Oh, swell. What's next, thumbscrews?"

"Lina." With a motion of his hand, Lon told her, *I'll handle this.* "If you're going to be stretching the boundaries of evidence, not even knowing what kind of new technologies the Empire is using, I think you should classify Lina as innocent until proven guilty."

"Is that all?" Lina huffed.

"Lina. It's only fair, Stoan."

Jae added, "And there's precedent. Wiley was looking into it."

"We paid that lawyer how much, Lon?"

Stoan frowned at his own thoughts. He reached down to claim one of the untouched drinks from the coffee table. "Perhaps." He altered his stance to a more open one and addressed Londo. "I'll expect you to change your work schedule before you leave for Earth."

"*Pourquoi?* To what?"

"Instead of periodic visits, I see you having instant access throughout AffSys territory for major emergencies. That is correct, isn't it?" Stoan turned pointedly to Lina.

"What, he's going to be called away even more than he has? I've barely had any time with him."

"You're a teleporter. It used to take Londo a day just to get here, a day to return. His scheduled visits have not occurred as often as we'd like."

Jae interrupted, "He has duties with the ParaNet, now with the Three Worlds. We have plans."

"And precedent is that off-world part-timers do keep to periodic schedules," Lon reminded Stoan.

"But there's never been a case of a Legion member having access to an instantaneous interstellar teleporter before. Londo, you have a duty to the AffSys."

Lon rose to pace in silent thought and found himself behind the couch and Lina. He rubbed her neck as she sat curling up on herself.

"I have a duty to the Mega-Legion," he told Stoan. "I have a duty to the Network, and now to the Three Worlds, especially for the next nine months or so. But you've forgotten: I have more even than that now. A duty to my wife. I need to re-examine my priorities. Give me a few weeks to figure things out. Right now it looks that it's my Network duties that will have to suffer, but I'm not sure. Lina?"

She raised her head from her knees that she'd gathered up to herself. "It's kind of odd that he'll allow a possible mind controller to do all this. I'm getting mixed messages. But okay, if something major comes up, of course I'll be happy to port you back and forth to wherever. As long as someone can picture where the destination is, I can handle it. I'll port whoever needs to go. Just keep in mind that I have a problem with hyperspace."

She thought a moment and gave Stoan an even gaze. "Londo is Protector of Sarastor now. That means that he'll be spending an awful lot more time here than he has. I've been here a few days, seen a lot of minor emergencies come up that the Legion has been called to handle on the planet. Is there any way he can combine those with his Three World work, get the duty credit for it, whatever he needs to satisfy you?"

Londo cocked his head at Stoan as Jae replaced the drink Stoan had taken. "Some of my Three Worlds work will fall under Legion guidelines, Stoan. It should prevent many future emergencies. That should count in our favor as well. Make Jae and me special Legion liaisons for Sarastor matters, something like that."

"I'll consider it. But major emergencies–"

"Maybe I don't even need to be put on any kind of periodic schedule at all. We've been talking about what we'll do after we secure Aldierra's safety. Each of us will make daily or every-other-day visits to each of the Three Worlds. I'll be able to accomplish more in less time. That combined with being called on emergencies should more than make up full-time status requirements."

Jae spoke up. "And I'll be needing leave time more often. I'll have Three Worlds duties as well, completely separate from Legion or AffSys matters. I have the same access as Lon to Lina for emergencies. Brügz has been working with my team as he's training Erik. I think Brügz would be willing to take on occasional leader duties with us, as needed. Maybe we should bring Erik up to lieutenancy now. He's almost ready. A few more missions and he'll settle in."

Stoan took a swig of his purloined drink and then rubbed the side of his mouth with the his thumb, looking from Legionnaire to Legionnaire with his cold metallic blue eyes. "All right, we'll keep an experimental schedule for what, the next two months or so? Then we'll reassess."

"Agreed."

"Agreed."

"The Legion will officially announce the marriage late tomorrow. And the name change."

About time, Lina said.

Lon squeezed her shoulder. "Thanks. What kind of reaction will there be?"

"This on top of the funeral– bad timing."

"The best of timing," Jae said softly. "Aiko would approve."

They spoke of Legion PIC and interviews, of releasing the tapes of the Investiture to the general public.

"I want to get some Tishana opinions about the ceremony and publicize them," Jae said.

"Not through the Legion, no." Stoan said.

"Through the Three Worlds, independent of the Legion."

Stoan shrugged and Londo nodded. "I'll get in contact with them, Jae," Lon said. "We'll coordinate through Legion Security and L-PIC so we don't tread on anyone's toes– or at least do so quickly enough that there's no lasting damage. And we don't let out any word of Three Worlds until Jae's back."

Jae nodded. "Good. Speaking of security, how's Deegel's case? That'll be bad publicity."

"Investigation still going on," Stoan said, eying Lina. Obviously he didn't trust her hearing secure material. Just as obviously, he didn't like that she'd been the one who'd discovered the problem. "We'll decide on a trial date, if we need one, once we've rounded everyone up and sorted out the facts to our satisfaction. Tomorrow morning, Lon, I want you in L-PIC. Tell me how many interviews they need to schedule."

"We're going home tomorrow right after Jae leaves. Lina's tired, and I could use some recharge time. No interviews. Not yet."

"I'm sorry, Lon, but you have to."

Lon ran a hand through the top of his hair. "It's been a crazy two weeks. Not even that. Stoan, I don't even have a house ready for us yet." He gave Lina an apologetic look. "Maybe it's in a little rougher shape than I led you to believe." Then back to Stoan: "Give us a couple weeks, maybe less. We've got to go through this whole rigmarole on Earth, too."

Stoan nodded his head slowly. "One interview scheduled through PIC. If they balk, tell them I ordered it. They'll have my head for this."

"Sorry."

"Maybe I'll have Andri inform them."

That brought a faint smile to Londo's face. "Then she'll have my head," he said.

"That's the idea."

Lina bit her lower lip. She had hoped she could stay in the background, secure within a private marriage known only to a few people, just like Maximus' Else. Else must be a very wise woman.

Of course, everyone at the Terran Zone and Romaki Club knew about her and the marriage now. And all those people who'd attended the funeral that Lon and Jae had introduced her to. It wouldn't be fair if people knew about her and not about Jae. By the time they fully announced, maybe they would have figured out this relationship. Maybe Lon would have revealed all.

Lon rubbed her shoulders. "At the very least you're Speaker for the Three Worlds, Lina. There's no way you are going to escape being a news item."

"I don't want to be famous." She put her head back on her knees.

"Hey, you'll like it."

"No she won't, Londo," Jae said. "Some of us don't like it at all."

"*D'accord, d'accord.*" Londo jumped the couch to slide in next to Lina. "How's this: you'll get used to it. Fame's got its perks, Kitten. You'll be surprised at how fast people will run to help if you're famous. Didn't we agree that Three Worlds are going to need as much help as we can get?"

She gave him a wan smile. "If you say so, Lon."

"I do."

Lina sighed. "Thus it shall be written. Thus it shall be done."

"I am not a dictator!"

At last Stoan left. Jae theatrically flicked a drop of imaginary sweat from his forehead. "That went better than I thought," he said.

Londo scrolled through the nets on the coffee table. "Let's get some Tishana opinions tonight on the Investiture," he said. "If anyone can keep it a secret, they will. It's going to take them a while to sort through it."

"Time enough for me to catch up with you two on Earth, and for you two to scan through my info," Jae said. "I'm going to come back with as much practical news as I can. People are going to ask what the blaze Aldierra is."

Lon rubbed his nose as he eased back on the couch. "You're right. Maybe hold off for a week? three days? after you get back. Until then, we just issue a general 'something's up and we'll announce it soon' message?"

"Yeah."

Londo resumed his scrolling. "It'll probably take a week just for the Tishana's heads to stop spinning about all this. Maybe the head of the After-Death branch of the multiversity there should see the record. I didn't even know they still had a school for that until that goatee guy let it slip on Twoday. We should try to get more information out of him. He seemed pretty slipshod with his security information."

"Good idea. You do that." Lina's voice came from the back hallway and Londo turned. She stepped out into the light. Her dark auburn hair curled around her bared shoulders. She was dressed in a full-length gown of white lace and satin. Though she tried to assume an air of confidence, she held the plunging neckline closed with a clenched hand. "Jae and I will be busy for a while."

"That's right," Jae said after he could get his voice to work. "I mean, unless you already have a schedule, Lon-Lon."

"I don't think he does," Lina said, her expression defying Londo to contradict her. "But I do. We go in shifts, and Jae can sleep all the three days to Aldierra if he needs to."

"Excellent battle strategy," Jae declared. He hopped out of his chair and made a beeline to Lina, wrapping her in his arms. "We can play 'captured spy' until Londo comes in."

Londo tried to frown at Lina but failed. "So it shall be written…"

She lifted her chin at him. "So it shall be done." She couldn't keep up the face. She wiggled her eyebrows at him before turning her attention to the most delectable Jae.

Lina squirmed over Jae so she could snuggle between the two of them under the sheet. She was so heavenly exhausted. Shifts were definitely the way to go, though it had become apparent that the shifts would center around almost-inexhaustible Londo. But this last part had been amazing, too.

"Can I get security clearance for the roof of this joint? I want to go up there right now and shout to the whole world that I love Jae and Londo. I want everyone to know!"

"You'd get cold up there dressed like that." Lon smiled and took advantage of the situation.

Lina declared, "My love will keep me warm."

"I'll be up there with you, Sweet," Jae told her. "I want to tell everyone as well. Londo, we go public with this."

"Oh yes, Lon. It's the only way."

"*Non.* Absolutely not. Never."

His vehemence almost broke the spell, but the fear inside him was plain for them to read.

"Do you mean 'never' as in 'never'," Lina asked, "or 'never' as in 'not until I change my mind'?"

Lon huffed– but he thought about it. "I don't know."

"So never for the near future at the least," Lina deduced.

Jae's jaw worked in that way it did when he was upset. "There are things that need to be researched," he said. "We need to do some quiet, subtle surveying within the Legion at the least."

"Scope out how other people would react," Lina said. "We can do that. I can. I can be real subtle when I need to."

"I don't know–"

"Lon, while you don't know, we can start investigating as a contingency," Jae said. "And there's another thing I wanted to broach with you two. I don't think we should be considering a dual-triune at all."

"What?" Lina sat straight up even as she grabbed the sheet to cover herself. "Then why are we here? Why go through all this? Jae, I'm in love with you. If you wanted to back out, you should have–"

Jae put his hand over her mouth. "Triune," he said. "Full, complete triune." He released her. "As a possibility," he added.

"Oh." Her mouth opened slightly as it sank in. "That's the all-equal one, everyone within the big circle. It's legal?"

He gazed into her eyes. "Absolutely. All three members with full commitment to each other. No tertiary."

A beautiful smile blossomed on Lina's face. "Oh. That's nice. Londo, that's so nice, don't you think? Jae, are you sure? A triune? Could we really?"

"Triune," Londo said slowly.

Jae studied him. "It was the highest form of marriage. Honorable. Celebrated. Public. And at this point it's just a suggestion. A possibility."

Lon gave Jae a steady look. "Does that mean you're willing to totally commit?"

"I think so. Maybe."

Lina asked, "Could you do it, Lon? Be an equal?"

"You think I'm an egomaniac," he accused her.

"I think you have a little problem with possession and being in charge. You're working on it, I know. There'll be problems enough with all of this, 'Was I better than he was?' crap."

Both men looked hard at each other and then laughed.

"So settle it now and we won't bring it up again," Jae said.

Lina crossed her arms over her chest. "Performance is nice, but it isn't everything. I won't answer that question so don't bother asking it. Ever." She could feel the question rise in both their thoughts, and felt them read it in each other. They laughed again.

"Something else to work on," Lon said.

"Okay," Jae agreed.

"We can decide this later," Lon said. "Let me and Lina have a while together, Jae, just as a couple, and get used to this marriage idea. A few days while you're gone."

Jae rolled over onto his back and gazed at the ceiling. "Or a few weeks, Lon?"

"We can report back with the problems that need to be addressed, assuming we run into any, before we take another step. I'm just saying that we need–"

"Will a few days or weeks make you think of her even more as just yours alone? And vice versa?" Jae asked. "I've been relying on this dream for years. So have you. And now you want to cut me off?"

"I will never be your possession, Londo," Lina said softly. "Not now and not a few weeks from now. I am your wife forever. There's a big difference."

Londo pulled his hair with both hands and then fell back onto the round pillows. He stretched his arms to heaven. "Let us *assume,*" he orated, "just assume that I can get over this, whatever, possessiveness you think I can't handle. Let us assume that you, Lina, can make a decision without talking it to death, just make a gut-level decision for once."

"I think I've been able to do that in the past," she said from between clenched teeth.

"But you keep taking these things and stopping and throwing things into reverse and then full speed ahead and I can't catch up. You work on that. And you, Jae–" Londo eased up to examine the man in bed with him. "Let us assume that you can rein in your wild and wandering ways to consider becoming domestically inclined to the fullest extent of the law."

"Assume that everyone in the Legion and the AffSys suddenly become ultra-liberal overnight and forget about slave and prostitute marriages," Jae added.

"No. Everything else as it is. We'll deal with it when and if we have to. Just assume these things. Vote on triune, equal triune."

"I need time," Jae said.

"Oh no! Lina's catching!"

"Londo." Lina flashed him a warning took. "Ease up."

"Was not pushing. Don't baby him, Lie."

"There is a time and a place for making quick decisions," Lina told him firmly. "This is not it. This is the rest of our lives. We all have things to think about. Londo– what if something were to happen to you?"

Londo stopped at that. "You've been talking to an insurance salesman," he finally said to her.

"I think we could handle it," Jae said.

"Gee, thanks."

"Lon sweet, we've just been trying to think this thing through, like realistic people," Jae said. "Even you have to admit that you're in your Vivid Imagination Land most of the time. What's bothering me after the other day, is this Three Worlds situation. People can put up with many things that Legionnaires do. We have the reputation of the entire organization and its long history to shelter us. The peculiar celebrity that comes with being a Legionnaire ameliorates many things.

"But this. People are going to think Three Worlds, and they're going to think of us, not anyone or anything else. We not only work for the Three Worlds now, we *are* the Three Worlds, the personification of them."

"*Ch'tedi,* the Worlds don't mind. They're the ones who brought us all together."

"Fine, Lon, just fine." Jae joined Lina to sit upright against the headboard, his arms crossed. "We'll just tell everyone, 'The Worlds wanted it this way,' and let them argue with that." He snapped his fingers haughtily.

"I won't stand for any scandal," Lina told them. "The Legion doesn't allow it, I promised Londo, and I'll promise you this, too, Jae: I will try never to do anything, ever, to bring you embarrassment. The Three Worlds are going to have a hard enough time operating without having to fight a scandal. I say we bring this out public and proud, our heads held high. Then let people think what they'll think."

"We are not going public," Londo declared.

Silence hung over the bed long enough that Lina noticed the change in the wall screens. Dawn was breaking outside Legion Headquarters. There wasn't much time left with Jae.

"You've opened all the Feithi nets for us?" Lina asked Jae.

He nodded, but his jaw protruded in that way he had when upset. "Just for you two," he said.

"Wiley would probably appreciate it as well."

"Yes. He would. I'll open them for him, too." A flicker of amusement lit his blue eyes. "I just won't tell him. We'll see how long it takes for him to realize it."

Lon remained silent. Lina nudged him.

"I'll set up some cultural search programs for handling this kind of thing," he finally said just as the morning alarm went off.

Jae disengaged himself. "We're leaving in two and a half hours," he said. "I've got to finish up some paperwork here, talk to my team, Wiley, Stoan and Andri, upload some files…"

Lina hugged him tightly. "Five more minutes," she begged him.

He kissed her and then shifted to get out of bed. "Nope. I'm shaving things close as it is."

She fell back into the pillows. Londo reached across her to grasp Jae's upper arm. "You be careful," he ordered Jae. "Aldierra is a warlike world. There'll be factions that don't want peace talks. Whenever a Legionnaire walks into a roomful of people fighting each other, everyone aims at the Legionnaire. You know that."

"I'll give a yell if I run into anything I can't handle," Jae said as he pulled on a robe. He grabbed some items from his closet, and some more from a dresser. Before he entered the en suite, he looked at the two of them in bed and held out his hand. A camera drone zipped down for him to palm, its filming complete.

"Jae!" Lina cried. This time she pulled the sheet up to her chin.

"It's just a personal film," Jae said before he closed the door behind himself.

Lina surged back against the pillows, thinking. Lon didn't say anything.

"No," she said.

He turned to her and opened his mouth, but she interrupted.

"You have had a story in mind for years of how your marriage was going to be."

"*Met—*"

"And you made Jae believe in that story. He made it his."

Lon shifted so he lay on his side. Coaxingly he rubbed her arm. "Then you came along," he told her.

"Someone changed the plot." Now she stared him right in the eye. "But it wasn't all my fault. You came around and gave me my own picture of what marriage should be– a false one."

"I said I was sorry."

"I know you are. But this is what happened. Somewhere along the line I started building my own ideas about marriage." Lina picked up one of the funny round pillows Jae had and wrapped her arms around it. "You taught me that it wasn't wrong of me to want things. To want people and love and passion and forever."

He turned to lay on his belly and propped himself up on his elbows. "You want Jae?"

"I want a marriage that I can believe in. I want the whole fairy tale, Londo, and that means both you and Jae and a white picket fence– well, maybe not that. I hate painting fences, and white picks up dirt so easily. But something like that. I want pies cooling in the window and friends dropping over on Sunday after-noon to chat and the cats sleeping in the sun."

He caught her hand and twined his fingers through hers. "So how is any of this keeping you from that?"

"I can't invite those friends over if I can't show off Jae to them as well as you. We can't have that bright picket fence drawing anyone's attention if we hide the truth behind it."

"Scandal," Lon replied.

"Is that your opinion or everyone else's?" Lina asked. "Is the idea of joining with the man and woman you love in a legally recognized union really so scan-dalous to you, Lon? Or are you just afraid of what others would think of it? What others would think of *you*?"

He kissed her fingers but didn't respond when he released her hand.

Londo stared at the headboard. Lina ran her fingers through his soft hair. "We all have some misgivings about this," she said. "You and people drawing away from you because of it. Me and babies."

"Babies?" Lon turned to her. "You promised me–"

She nodded. "Two. But Jae wants baby or babies as well. I– I just don't know. I promised you in the heat of passion. I'll keep my promise somehow. But more than two–"

Lon reached to race the line of her cheek. "You'll be a wonderful mother. You can do this."

For that she gave him a wan smile. "You always have faith in me."

"In us, too."

They clasped hands in promise.

Lina said, "Maybe there's a starting point for us all. Or a compromise. We don't have to jump, but maybe take a tiny step to get things started."

"Can you do tiny steps, Kitten?" Londo tilted his chin to scrutinize her.

"Can you?"

"Let me tell you a new story. A story about three people who loved each other very much."

"I do love your stories," Lina said. "Will it have a happy ending?"

"You can help me create it," Lon told her.

When Jae returned from the bathroom, costume on and duffle slung over his shoulder, they were waiting for him in their robes.

Londo said. "We need a few minutes here, just to keep you thinking of us." He took Jae's hand between his own.

Then he got down on one knee.

"This is a formal proposal of marriage, Jae. I've loved you as long as I've known you. I've always wanted you. Now that I can have you I want you even more.

"We're going to be partners for the rest of our lives. I think it would be good for us to be partners in marriage, too. It'd be fun. And healthy for us. We'd have a built-in support group, a telepathic support group, and you've already seen the advantages in that."

He clutched Jae's hand to his chest as Jae watched him, his lips opening and closing as if he might say something but decided against it so Lon could continue.

"I love you with all my heart. You know me like nobody else does, even Lina, and Lina loves you, too. Marry me; marry us, and I promise you you'll never regret it. We will be a real family." He bowed his head to kiss Jae's knuckles and then released him.

Lon rose and stepped back to let Lina come forward.

Jae swallowed. "The Speaker speaks," he said, but his mouth trembled.

Lina reached out, coming up on her tiptoes. She threw her arms around Jae and beamed him all the love she felt for him. She gave him a goodbye kiss that promised a lifetime of hellos.

"Please marry us. Me. Us," she whispered. "Full triune. We'll find a way. We'll celebrate it always. I don't want to spend the rest of my life without you."

Jae caught his breath as she broke away.

"So much for prepared speeches," Londo tried to laugh.

The blond Feithi stood there and looked back and forth at the two of them. "Public?" he asked Londo.

Lon screwed his mouth around, pressing it in a circle. "We need to discuss that some more," he finally said.

Jae turned his attention to Lina. "Children?"

"More than one?" she asked as she pressed her hands against her stomach.

"Maybe."

"I don't know. If we don't go public–" she shook her head. "I don't know how we could do that. Are you sure you want more than one? Could you combine one with Lon's?"

"How about you, Jae?" Londo asked. "Can you make a commitment just to us? Would you move to Earth?"

"Would you change your name to 'Starhart'?" Lina asked.

Jae looked down at the floor and scratched his head before meeting their gaze. "I don't know," he sighed. "I just don't know what to tell you. All I know is that I love you. Both."

"That's a start."

"Take your time. Be sure," Lina said softly. "We don't need your answer right this minute. This is the rest of your life. No divorce, no separations longer than two seasons."

"Two seasons?" Jae asked with a questioning smile.

Lina nodded. "If it's like the dual-triune. I looked it up the other day. Maybe you need to do some research, too. If there's some point that you absolutely can't live with or without, come up with some options, no matter how crazy they are."

Londo said, "We'll consider them. We'll use them to springboard more ideas."

"All right."

Jae took one of their hands in each of his and brought them all together. "I will be thinking about this every moment I'm gone. I should be on Earth in nine or ten days. I'll give you my answer then."

"And maybe we'll have some new options for you to consider, too," Lina said. "Don't say anything until you hear them."

He smiled at her. "I won't. I've got to go now."

It was Londo's turn to grab a camera drone out of the air. "Here," he said, and Jae held up a padd to upload the recording. "So you don't forget us."

"As if that could ever happen."

Londo stood in full uniform and Lina in her demure black dress as they joined Jae and Admiral Bracken and his staff before they left. They stood in the grand hotel suite that had seen the first post-war negotiations. Stoan was there already to reiterate the Legion's commitment to cementing the AffSys-Aldierra alliance. Wiley, a major player in the negotiations, stood by Stoan's side.

Lina reminded them that if they needed any of the Three Worlds, she could have them at Aldierra within two minutes as long as she could get a picture of where they were needed. Communications during hyperspace mode was out of the question, of course.

The admiral thanked them all, paying Stoan deep respect. Stoan obviously approved of the admiral's attitude towards him, and Lina recalled what Londo had told her about Stoan's possibly misinterpreting her attitude as lack of respect. It did not help things when Bracken practically groveled before her, taking her hand and holding it to his left cheek and calling her "Speaker" in the most reverent of voices.

"Call me Lina, Admiral," she said and smiled. "That's my name."

"It's difficult to do that, Speaker– I mean– Lina," he said, acutely uncomfortable. "You have changed the course of our entire planet. The fate of my people lies in what you tell Aldierra herself."

"I'm just an interpreter," Lina said kindly. "I have no doubt that Aldierra will be very pleased with whatever plans your people come up with. It's the Aldierrans themselves who will change their world, not me."

"If you say so, Speaker," the admiral said, not even aware that he hadn't called her by name.

Lon and Jae did a final data sync between notepadds.

"Y'all have a safe trip," Lina told them, and it sounded like a command.

She ported the departing personnel and Jae up to the Aldierran ships, leaving the three Legionnaires and herself in the empty hotel room. The Aldierran officers who remained on Sarastor were already ensconced in their own offices elsewhere.

"He's going to hate me in a few months," Lina predicted of the admiral. Londo nodded agreement.

"What for?" Wiley asked.

Lina said, "God help me, I'm going to start a revolution on that world."

Stoan's eyes narrowed. "You'll start a war?"

Lina turned to him. "A cultural revolution. Lincoln freed the slaves; we'll free the women of Aldierra."

She gave a small laugh and turned to Londo. "It's a good thing that we're not on *Star Trek*. We'll have violated the Prime Directive: non-interference with the normal development of a culture."

"In this instance," Londo said, "it's a case of change or die. The gender problem is just the beginning. I'm getting the feeling we'll be turning the entire planet head over heels before we're half-through."

"Jim Kirk would agree with us," Lina said. "Londo, I've got to get you in front of a TV."

"I'll do it. Not today. Too many things to do today. Let's do our duty with Legion PIC for a few minutes and get out of here. It's time we started making our own home."

She beamed at him and took his strong, safe arm. "Yes, love. Bye, Wiley. Get some phony ID ready and we'll take you to the Library of Congress next time."

"I'll do that," Wiley said with a smile. "The book cart is in my lab, anytime you want to take it back to Earth. I'm finished with all of them. Your books are on top of the stack."

"You read that one book in detail."

Wiley chuckled at that. Lina had filched a "how to attract women" manual for him.

"Waitaminnit, Wile," Lon said, a mischievous grin starting on his face. He snapped his fingers at Lina and she handed him her note padd.

"Arf," she said.

"Hush, wife. You'll get a kick out of this, Wiley." Lon punched up the Three Worlds data and handed the padd to the genius.

Wiley took a half-moment to realize that he was looking at a schedule of planetary equinoxes and solstices, and then gave a start.

"Oh, yeah!" Lon laughed out loud at the seldom-seen reaction. "That's what I was hoping for."

"Do you have any idea how… inconceivable this is? Three worlds with the same solstice date? Your Three Worlds?" He handed the padd to Stoan so he could see the coordination of solstices, a year away.

Lon shrugged. "We don't know what it means. It's not exactly a star in the east, but it'll do as a start."

Lina gave him a bop on the shoulder. "Don't get too big for your britches, Londo Falcon!"

"I thought you liked 'em tight," Londo murmured to her. She huffed a little and then wound her arms around him in surrender. "That's my girl."

Wiley checked to see if the nets had provided correct information to come to this conclusion.

"It's astrology on a comic, cosmic level," Lina told him grandly.

He looked up at her at that. "So what does it portend?"

"Hell if I know. Beginnings, maybe. Maybe rebirth."

"We'll find out," Lon said. "What's the fun in knowing before something happens?"

Lina poked her finger at the base of his neck. "You can be prepared if you have some idea. Stock an extra pocket knife or cell phone in that vest of yours."

"Uh huh. And if I'd done that, where would we be now?"

She looked up at him and their smiles matched. He held out his hand for Wiley to return the padd.

"Please," Lina prompted with a whisper in Londo's ear.

"Please give me my goddam note padd," Londo said.

Wiley handed it reluctantly to Londo, who was about to put it in his vest pocket when Lina took it from him and ported it away. "Mine, mine, mine," she said softly. "Jae gave that to me. You have one of your own."

"I thought we were going to compromise."

By that time Wiley had dug out his own, much more complicated padd. Screens rolled out in midair all around him displaying planetary orbits and scrolling calendars. Stoan joined him in examining them. "Lina," Wiley said offhandedly, using a spare mind, "if you truly do have mind control of him, perhaps you'd better do something about his manners."

"I'll get to work on it right away," Lina replied dryly.

"*Non non non!*" Lon gave Lina a gentle shake. "We have more important things to do." He admired his beautiful bride as she gazed so contentedly at him. Where had he been just two weeks ago?

I was only half-alive, a quarter alive, and didn't know it, Lina told him. **I was hiding from life.**

And life kept itself separate from me.

Her eyes glowed with love.

I am a contented man, Lon said. **I finally know that this is what it's all about. Connecting. Sharing. Working together to make the universe a better place. And sex.**

Lina laughed out loud at that. **And sex, Londo.**

Lots and lots of sex, babychérieKitten. We'll save so much money, never having to buy you shoes. He tossed her in the air just to hear her shriek.

"Londo! You're the craziest man I've ever met!"

"By far? By light-years?"

She leaned against him breathlessly and shook her head. **You forget, I know Jae now.**

"Ah. Not by much, then." He grunted and then picked her up in one arm as if she were luggage.

"Looonn!"

"Time to get our marriage started, wife. Let's see. Legion PIC, press statement, then meet with my lawyers for just a few minutes, just to make sure all legalities have been met. And then home. Home!" he said it like a command, snapping his fingers twice. "See you, Stoan, Wiley. *On y va!*"

As Lon yodeled an exit fanfare, they disappeared.

art by Colleen Doran. Copyright the artist.

Don't miss the next chapter in the Three Worlds saga…

Worlds Apart

Three Worlds vol. 4

by Carol A. Strickland

Who reported this?" Emperor Yanist-Glory slammed his right fist onto the desk. "I want to know if this is true or just some bastard trying to make points with his command!"

As one, the group surrounding the desk took a step back. It was rare that the emperor lost control when he was angry, but once he did, heads could literally roll.

General Riant licked his lips and tried to look like he hadn't just been pulled from a sound sleep to come here to the palace's study. Though the emperor was in his bathrobe, his famous imperial hair standing on end like springs all over his head, his staff had hurried in full formal dress to his call. No one had dared report in holographic form.

Riant had dressed too quickly. One of his medals had slipped to the inside of his uniform and now scratched against his bare chest. He squared his shoulders. "This agent has furnished excellent information before."

"But twice has been completely wrong," Chancellor Bain said as he looked up from his padd screen.

Riant's upper lip automatically curled at the chancellor. "Only twice after years of solid reports. An outstanding record."

Emperor Yanist-Glory paced behind his desk, his eyes focused on the marble floor beyond his slippered feet.

Into the silence, Secretary Acksum spoke. "I–" He coughed to settle his voice to a lower register. "I hesitated to report…" He gulped as the emperor paused and looked at him. "Two other sightings. These from Deseed, not Jorter."

"When?" the emperor barked.

"Three days ago. From a single agent but spaced three hours apart. This man has only recently come into our employ, so we were waiting for confirmation from another source. We didn't get one."

"Until now." The emperor's voice was a low growl, but one kept to himself rather than directed at them.

"It is another star system entirely, your Glory."

"The next one over." The emperor didn't need to remind them. A meter-wide spherical map of the galactic sector floated over one end of his desk, showing the vastness of the Yanist-Glory Empire. Along the fuzzy edges outside the Empire sat the systems they spoke of.

There lay the great grain fields of Schwann, then the almost temperate, mineral-laden riches of Deseed. Light-years beyond them came the rich variety of both vegetative and technical resources on Jorter.

"Schwann," someone whispered.

The emperor fastened his gaze upon the speaker, a woman of middle age.

"It was last week," she said in a voice more solid. "Discounted. With all our mind control activity we sometimes find that an unprogrammed telepathic group hallucination will take hold over an area. It's a form of feedback. This was an illusion. Or a subconscious wish for, ah, freedom."

Yanist-Glory considered that. Finally he asked, "Which one was sighted there? Or was it both?"

The woman quickly replied, "Both men. But as I said, unreal. You know how it is, your Glory. We often get phantom reports of the Rands from the outer worlds."

"Deseed?"

Acksum said, "The informant there reported Maximus. He said there was a cape."

"Yes, that would be Hal Rand. Maximus," the emperor murmured. "And the Jorter report?"

"Our informant wasn't sure, just that it was a human who flew almost faster than he could see and then disappeared as if he'd gone into hyperspace without using a ship."

"Maximus or Valiant then, either one of the Rands."

The emperor used his fingertips to walk from star system to star system across his insubstantial map: Schwann, Deseed, Jorter… and beyond that, Earth, home of the Rands. Few seemed to recognize the uncut gem that was Earth and its secrets. The ignorance of Terrans was a joke out here among the stars. Let the other galactic sectors think so; let them forget the planet existed. That way they wouldn't put up a fuss when Earth became part of the Empire.

Primitive, self-sufficient Earth, with not even interstellar transportation facilities. Even so, it held the fabled Gateway to the Timeless Realms– probably the reason so many parahumans and their even more powerful counterparts, the megas, had sprung from that world. What unimaginable secrets lay beyond that Gateway, waiting to be plundered?

If he could just get past those Rands.

"Research and development," Yanist-Glory demanded.

Chancellor Bain didn't have to look at his padd for the results. "The last six quarters have focused on improving our mind control techniques. Per your command," he reminded his emperor.

Yanist-Glory frowned. "Yes." He paced again in a straight line and then changed into a circle that took up much of the room. "We need the mind control for this push."

Bain nodded. "After that we can return to finding a way to slow down both Valiant and Maximus."

"They cannot impede my plans," the emperor warned the group.

"They won't," Riant quickly said. "Once we have power points within the populations controlled and the rest cowed, the Rands won't dare interfere. They're notoriously soft-hearted when it comes to innocents."

"What about the parents? Maximus' parents?"

"Extremely well-guarded. We've tried and failed many times already. As you know."

"Hmf. Friends?"

"The same, though we still have hopes," Riant said. "As always, we watch them."

"And Maximus' wife?" After a beat, the emperor laughed at his own question. "No, I've heard the rumors about her. It must be difficult for a man to have that much power, receive that much galactic adoration, and have to settle for the likes of… whatever she is."

"Yes, your Glory."

Yanist-Glory clenched his fist around a projected star system in his celestial map. It did not implode under his touch but rather ignored his august presence. He almost snarled at its impertinence.

"If only the Rands had a weakness."

You can pick the format and store you want to buy from here:
http://www.carolastrickland.com/fiction/worlds.html

ABOUT THE AUTHOR

When you think of strong women and strange worlds, think Carol A. Strickland.

Although born in a small town in Illinois noted for its Nineteenth Century demonic possession cases, Carol claims that all those voices inside her head are a result of having stories to tell and books to write. Even so, her strange devotion to and study of Wonder Woman would seem to indicate an abby-normal brain.

A one-time comics letterhack and outspoken member of various comics message boards, Carol has found herself the basis for two comic book villains (at times her opinions have not been taken well by the books' creators) (both villains were soundly thrashed) (and both, for some perverse reason, were male) and had one superhero wear her costume design. (Light Lass!)

Carol has also become an award-winning painter. Along with her writing, she exercises this skill in her secondary hours (both of them) as she waits for the lottery to free her 9-to-5 time to more fulfilling pursuits.

All product names, logos, and brands are property of their respective owners. All company, product, and service names used in this book are for identification purposes only. Use of these names, logos, and brands does not imply endorsement.